TIM WAGGONER

THE FOREVER HOUSE

This is a **FLAME TREE PRESS** book

Text copyright © 2020 Tim Waggoner

FLAME TREE PRESS
6 Melbray Mews, London, SW6 3NS, UK
flametreepress.com

Distribution and warehouse:
Baker & Taylor Publisher Services (BTPS)
30 Amberwood Parkway, Ashland, OH 44805
btpubservices.com

Thanks to the Flame Tree Press team, including:
Taylor Bentley, Frances Bodiam, Federica Ciaravella, Don D'Auria,
Chris Herbert, Josie Karani, Molly Rosevear, Will Rough, Mike Spender,
Cat Taylor, Maria Tissot, Nick Wells, Gillian Whitaker.

The cover is created by Flame Tree Studio with
thanks to Nik Keevil and Shutterstock.com.
The font families used are Avenir and Bembo.

Flame Tree Press is an imprint of Flame Tree Publishing Ltd
flametreepublishing.com

A copy of the CIP data for this book is available from the British Library
and the Library of Congress.

HB ISBN: 978-1-78758-320-7
PB ISBN: 978-1-78758-318-4
ebook ISBN: 978-1-78758-321-4

Printed in the UK at Clays, Suffolk

TIM WAGGONER

THE FOREVER HOUSE

FLAME TREE PRESS
London & New York

CHAPTER ONE

Their vehicle makes no noise as it slides along the streets of Rockridge, Ohio, at 3:32 a.m. on a Thursday. Rockridge may be a relatively small town, but it has its fair share of generic fast-food joints, tacky chain restaurants, and cramped strip malls. Its schools, if not great, are still fairly decent, and the populace gets fired up on Friday nights in fall when the high school football team plays. They lose more than they win, but that's okay. They'll get 'em next time. There are a dozen Christian churches in town, along with one Jewish temple and one mosque. Some of the residents like having a temple and mosque in their town because it makes them feel worldly and cosmopolitan. Other residents are less happy, but they keep their feelings to themselves. Mostly.

None of these things matter to the Eldred, though. They judge a place by far different standards.

Their vehicle is blacker than night, than shadow, than the inside of the deepest cave or the lowest level of the darkest sea. It has no recognizable make and model. It's a conglomerate, a hodgepodge, an amalgam of many different cars. It most closely resembles a four-door sedan crossed with a Model T, with bits of other vehicles – fire truck, ambulance, hearse – tossed in for good measure. It's an ugly, freakish-looking thing, but that's all right with the Eldred. They believe a car – like a house – should reflect its owners' personality, and their vehicle does this perfectly. Of course, it's not *really* a vehicle, although it's currently performing the same function. It's not constructed from metal or plastic, and it has no engine under its hood, no tank for gas, no brakes for stopping, no wheel for steering. It has what look like tires, but a closer examination would show these 'tires' don't roll across asphalt. Instead, the bottoms are covered with thousands of tiny filaments that work in concert to propel the vehicle forward. The reason there's no steering wheel is that Car – as the Eldred so imaginatively call their vehicle – always knows where it's going. And this night it knows what they are searching for. The same thing as always.

Food.

The windows – as equally black as the rest of the car – are half-lowered, allowing the Eldred to scent the air as they pass soundlessly through the town. Rockridge is hardly NYC, and few people are awake this time of night, and of those who are, even fewer look out their windows as Car goes by. Those who do happen to look outside see only a shadow moving among shadows on this moonless night. They're the lucky ones. Those who sleep as Car passes by dream of a vast dark cloud rolling in, so large that its shadow eventually covers the entire town. The Eldred are aware of these dreams – how could they not be, as their presence creates them? – and they find the dark cloud to be a good metaphor for their arrival. They laugh, a sound like the frantic yipping of starving dogs. This is also apt, for they *are* starving, perpetually so. Inside each of the Eldred is an infinite emptiness, a void that, no matter what they do, can never be filled. That doesn't stop them from trying, though.

Father Hunger sits on the driver's side of the front seat, where the steering wheel would be in an actual car, his long-fingered hands on his bony knees. These fingers have more joints than they should, and they constantly fidget, as if possessing a restless life of their own. He faces forward, eyes moving back and forth in their deep hollows, as if he's searching for something outside, even though the windshield, like the rest of Car, is solid black.

"Smell anything yet?" Father Hunger's voice is winter wind moving across a frozen lake, and the temperature inside Car drops several degrees.

The Werewife sits next to him in the front seat.

"Not yet, dear." Her voice is a scab being pulled slowly away from the skin, wound reopening, blood welling forth. She turns and looks at the teenage boy and girl in the back seat. "Children?"

The Low Prince and the Nonsister shake their heads.

"Maybe this isn't a suitable town," the Nonsister says, her voice a drowning child's last wet breath.

Her brother shoots her a glare. "Don't be stupid." His voice is a finely honed blade sliding slowly into tender flesh. "*All* towns are suitable. It's simply a matter of catching the right scent." He looks to the front seat. "Isn't that right, Father?"

Before Father Hunger can answer, a banging comes from Car's trunk – or rather, the orifice that serves in place of a trunk – along with what sounds like the screams of a disemboweled cat.

The Low Prince turns to his sister once more.

"See? Grandother agrees with me."

"That's not what she said." Father Hunger's thin, cracked lips curl away from his mouth, revealing jagged yellow teeth set in sore, bleeding gums. "She said, 'Slow down, you idiots.'"

A scent drifts in through the open windows. It's not the smell of what the Eldred seek, what they *need*, but it is the smell of something they can use.

A metal object rests on the front seat between Father Hunger and the Werewife. Father Hunger pats the top of this object lovingly, his multi-segmented fingers twitching with excitement.

"It'll be good to have you back, old friend."

And once more, the Eldred laugh.

★   ★   ★

Shoes pounding on sidewalk, air moving in and out of lungs, heart pulsing, muscle and bone working together in perfect harmony, his entire body moving with strength and ease, night air cool on his flesh.

Three-thirty in the morning wasn't a normal time to go for a jog, but Kevin Cummings wasn't a normal person. He worked as a freelance artist – doing illustration and website design, mostly – and he kept his own hours. He'd learned long ago that he was at his most creative very early in the morning, from four a.m. to nine a.m., and he'd ordered his life accordingly. He went to bed around seven or eight p.m., got up at three, ate a light breakfast, and went out for a run. He came home at four or so, had a quick shower, brewed some coffee, sat down at his computer and went to work. He'd knock off around nine, spend an hour or two answering emails from customers, and afterward he would have lunch at eleven. After that, he did whatever he felt like until dinnertime – which for him was around four – and then he'd hit the sack and do it all over again. The lifestyle suited him, but it played hell with his social life.

During the week, he rarely saw friends or went on dates, and on the weekends, he had difficulty staying awake past seven, so he couldn't go out and do anything. What social life he had was primarily confined to Saturday and Sunday afternoons. When most people were working during the week, he ran errands, did his shopping, went to matinee showings of movies – almost always alone. Sometimes he felt like a ghost, an unseen entity that walked the world without being a part of it. He wasn't sure what he could do to change this. He was forty-two and while he wasn't old yet, he wasn't young anymore, either. Increasingly, he had the sense that if he didn't find a way to bring better balance to his life, he'd remain a living ghost until he died, and this prospect both saddened and frightened him.

He loved running at this time of night. The streets were quiet and empty, the whole world hushed and still. It felt as if he were the only person left on Earth, that everyone else had for some mysterious and inexplicable reason vanished, leaving him to inherit the planet. As his body worked, his mind drifted, thoughts wandering like butterflies in a field of flowers, flitting here and there as the mood struck them. He came up with his best ideas on his night runs, which was the most valuable part of them. The health benefits he derived were appreciated but of lesser importance.

He wore only a T-shirt, shorts, socks, and running shoes, but despite the time of year, it was a bit chilly tonight – more like fall than early summer – and the air hitting the light sheen of sweat he'd worked up made him feel even colder. He wished he'd worn sweats, maybe a jacket, too. He increased his pace, hoping the extra speed would warm him up some.

He lived in an apartment building on the edge of Rockridge's business district, but he liked to run in the neighborhoods nearby. Row after row of houses, most ranch, some two-story, small, neatly kept yards, cars parked in driveways and along the curb. There was almost never any traffic here this late – or this early, depending on how you measured time – and it enhanced the feeling of peaceful solitude that he sought. There were no streetlights in these neighborhoods. Porch lights were on more often than not, and they provided enough for him to see where he was going. Plus, he felt safer running here than he would in other areas of town. No drug dealers or prostitutes hanging around on street corners, no muggers hiding in alleys, no homeless people approaching you and begging – sometimes aggressively – for money. Who was going to bother him here? The worst he had to worry about was a dog in someone's backyard barking at him as he went by.

But even though he knew he was safe, had come here especially because it *was* safe, he sometimes played a mental game as he ran, pretending that someone was chasing him. He'd heard of people using phone apps that helped them imagine they were running from a horde of ravenous zombies. If their speed dropped too low, the zombies caught up and ate them, at least virtually. It was a fun, if silly, way to motivate yourself when running, and he played his own mental version of the game. He imagined there was a shadowy figure running behind him – twenty feet back, thirty at most. The figure held a hunting knife in his right hand, and despite the figure seeming to be cloaked in shadow, the knife gleamed silver in the moonlight, almost as if the metal gave off its own illumination. Kevin didn't give his imaginary pursuer a reason to be chasing him. It was scarier that way. Besides, if the scenario had been real, he wouldn't know why the person wanted to kill him, and maybe there'd be no reason at all, save that the shadow man simply felt like making someone bleed.

When Kevin played this game, he had only one rule: no looking back, not even a quick glance. That way he'd keep his speed up, never knowing how close the shadow man might be. If his pace slackened, even for a moment, he might feel a cold blade stab him right between the shoulder blades.

He tried playing the game now, tried to picture the shadow man running behind him, feet moving lightly on the sidewalk, knife gripped tight in his hand. He tried hard, put the whole force of his imagination into it, but it didn't work. He knew there was no shadow man, no knife, no danger. Maybe he'd played this game too many times, and it had become routine for him. Or maybe he'd come to accept how childish and ridiculous it was.

The skin on the back of his neck went cold, as if a blast of wintery wind struck him. He wasn't sure what prompted him to break his rule and glance over his shoulder. He heard no sound, sensed no movement. But he turned to look anyway and saw something large and black racing toward him. For an instant, he thought the shadow man had somehow escaped his mind and manifested in the real world. But the shape was all wrong. And when a pair of baleful red orbs flared to life, he understood that he was looking at a car, one with extremely strange headlights. Except it couldn't be a car. It made no noise. No engine sound, no whisper of tires on asphalt. So what the hell *was* it?

And then the dark thing slammed into him and he knew exactly what it was: his death.

The impact sent him flying, and his last thought was that it was a shame he was going to die. He would've loved a chance to paint the dark vehicle with its fiery-red headlights. It was *bad-ass*. Then he hit the ground, his neck snapped, and he was gone.

★   ★   ★

Car comes to a stop several yards from where the jogger has landed. The man lies on someone's front lawn, arms and legs bent at unnatural angles. The Eldred can smell death settling on him, and they inhale deeply, savoring the sweet odor.

An orifice opens on the side of Car where the driver's door would be on a real vehicle, and Father Hunger emerges. He carries the metal object tucked beneath an arm as he walks across the grass toward where the dead jogger lies. He kneels and places the object – which resembles a crude, almost cartoonish, robotic head – on the ground next to the corpse. Father Hunger then takes a moment to assess the damage the body has sustained. It's more broken than he would like, but he thinks their old friend will be able to make use of it.

He fastens the multijointed bony fingers of one hand around the dead man's neck and grips one of his shoulders with the other. Then he pulls in opposite directions. In his natural form, Father Hunger looks like a skeleton covered with a thin veneer of flesh, with no muscle at all. But he's able to separate the head from the body with ease, flesh and bone parting as if the jogger is a well-cooked chicken, the meat falling easily off the bone. The moist tearing sound as skin and muscle parts is music to Father Hunger's ears and the smell of released blood is the finest of perfumes.

Father Hunger grips the jogger's head by the hair as he stands. He fixes his gaze on the metal head and waits.

Nothing happens for a moment, then green lights begin to glow in the head's empty sockets. Spider-like legs emerge from the bottom and lift the head several inches off the ground. The head then scuttles toward the jogger's body, maneuvers itself until it stands next to the ragged, bloody stump where the man's head was connected to his neck. The legs stretch toward the stump, sink into the flesh, and when they have a solid grip, they pull the mechanical head onto the jogger's body. There's a clicking and whirring as the head connects to the dead man's nervous system, and the body spasms several times, arms and legs flailing, as the head tests its new nerves and muscles. Then the body falls still, and the green light in the metal eye sockets dims and goes out.

Father Hunger frowns. Has the body been *too* damaged?

But then the eyelights blaze to life once more, stronger this time, and Machine Head sits up.

Father Hunger smiles, desiccated lips drawing back from dry yellow teeth, their skin cracking. He crouches next to Machine Head and puts a featherlight hand on his shoulder.

"Welcome back," he says.

The robotic head swivels to look at Father Hunger then inclines once in a nod of acknowledgement. Machine Head is a creature of few words.

They both stand, and Father Hunger – still holding on to the jogger's head – remains close to Machine Head in case he needs some support as they walk to Car. There's always a transition period when Machine Head takes a new body, and the jogger was extensively damaged when Car struck him. Machine Head wobbles a bit as he walks – especially on the left leg, which appears to be damaged – but he manages well enough. The front of his T-shirt is covered with blood, and Father Hunger wonders if they should get him a new shirt, but he decides against it. The look suits his old friend.

Father Hunger doesn't care about leaving any evidence behind. What can the authorities do to his kind? But if he left the head, it would be discovered come daylight, and that would create potential complications. The Eldred believe in keepings things as simple as possible. They like to feed without interruption. Blood drips from the ragged open wound on the bottom of the jogger's neck, but Father Hunger isn't concerned with that. Anyone seeing the blood in the yard or on the sidewalk or street will most likely put it down to the activity of some nocturnal animal. A predator catching prey, perhaps, or an animal struck by a car, badly wounded, but still able to move well enough to crawl away. No one will guess the blood was human. People want to feel safe where they live, and they will tell themselves any number of lies to create the illusion of safety. It's one of the qualities Father Hunger likes most about humans – their endless capacity for self-delusion.

Once Father Hunger and Machine Head are settled inside Car – the servant seated between Father Hunger and the Werewife – Car squeezes its orifice-door shut. Father Hunger reaches past Machine Head and offers the jogger's head to the Werewife. He's hungry, of course. He's *always* hungry. But he doesn't want a piece of the head. He prefers to save his appetite for the actual feeding.

"Something to tide you over until we can get a real meal," he says.

The Eldred derive little nourishment from flesh, blood, and bone, but the jogger's head will put something in their bellies.

"Thank you, dear."

The Werewife opens a mouth filled with sharp teeth, and in a single swift motion, she lunges forward and bites off the dead man's nose.

"We want some!" the Nonsister says.

"Give me the tongue!" the Low Prince demands.

A muffled shout comes from the trunk.

"Grandother wants the ears," the Nonsister says.

The Werewife grinds skin and cartilage between her teeth. She swallows and then glances back at the children.

"Make sure to save the ears for your Grandother."

She hands her children the noseless head, and the two fall upon it eagerly, snarling and snuffling like animals as they eat. Father Hunger and the Werewife exchange looks.

The Werewife draws the back of her hand across her lips to wipe away a smear of blood. "Kids," she says.

Father Hunger laughs.

Car begins moving once more, sliding silently down the street, its eyes now closed. It doesn't need to illuminate the road in order to find its way.

"Now let's see if we can find the scent," the Werewife says.

The Eldred fall quiet as they breathe deeply, resuming their search for the right scent, the right *place*. They have no doubt they'll find their Stalking Ground. They always do.

Car drives on.

CHAPTER TWO

Lauryn Delong drove her Kia Sorento down narrow suburban roads at close to fifty miles an hour, twice the posted speed limit. She prayed that someone's pet – a dog or cat, or god forbid, someone's *child* – wouldn't dash out into the street in front of her. The worry didn't make her slow down, though. She didn't even consider it.

Fifteen minutes late wasn't so bad, was it? The Eldreds would wait. They *had* to. She'd shown the Raines house to three different families over the last sixth months, and all of them had lost interest the moment they learned what had happened there, and it hadn't mattered how cheap the place was going for. Who wanted to live in a house where four murders and a suicide had taken place? Not that she could blame them. She could barely stand to set foot in there herself, let alone take buyers through it. She feared the Eldreds were her last chance to unload the goddamned place, and if they got tired of waiting for her and left, she'd never find anyone to buy it. Hell, she might have to look for a new job.

Last year, her mother had a stroke that necessitated moving her into an assisted-living facility. Lauryn's father had died years ago of a massive heart attack at forty-six, and while she had two siblings – an older brother and a younger sister – neither of them lived in Ohio. That left Lauryn with the duty of tending to their mother. She visited as often as she could, three, sometimes four times a week, and once she was there, leaving was a nightmare. Not that she wanted to stay, fuck no. The place smelled of astringent cleaning chemicals that couldn't fully mask the sour tang of old people slowly, inexorably dying. But every time she tried to leave, her mother would throw a fit, becoming an eighty-four-year-old toddler with baggy skin and stick-thin arms and legs who kicked and screamed and called her daughter *bitch* and *whore* and *cunt*, usually preceded by the word *ungrateful*. It always took several tries before Lauryn could leave, and even then, she only managed to do it because her mother's tantrums exhausted her until she nodded off and fell asleep. Today had actually been a fairly good day – only one tantrum – which was why Lauryn was only fifteen minutes late instead of thirty or forty-five.

Why had she told her boss that she could sell the Raines house? Other real estate agents had tried over the years, and all of them had failed. She'd been so desperate to rise in the company that she'd opened her big mouth before she'd thought through what she was promising. But her mother's care cost a fucking arm and a leg, and she needed as much money as she could get. Her ex-husband wasn't about to help. He'd left her two years ago for a girl half his age, and Lauryn's only child with him was a sophomore in college. Tiffany was racking up a mountain of debt already thanks to her student loans. There was no way she could help pay for her grandmother's care.

Lauryn turned onto Brookside Court – a fancy name for a cul-de-sac – and when she saw the driveway of the Raines house was empty, she was relieved. But then she had a bad thought: What if the Eldreds had changed their minds? What if her last chance to sell the house had just been flushed down the crapper?

She hadn't been out to the Raines house for a while, and she was irritated to see the state of the lawn. The grass needed cutting, and dandelions grew everywhere. Last summer she'd planted flowers along the front of the house, perennials that she'd hoped would return come next spring. Curb appeal was a huge part of selling a house – arguably the most important thing, since the outer appearance of a house was what buyers saw first. Some of the flowers had come back, but not as many as she'd hoped, and those which had returned looked half-dead. Add to this the fact that the lone tree in the front yard, an elm, was pretty much all the way dead – no leaves on its branches, wood dry and gray. It listed to the left, toward the house, and Lauryn feared that a strong wind would knock it over. If that happened, the tree would strike the house's roof, right over the garage. She'd tried to get her boss to pay someone to cut down and remove the tree, but he'd refused.

We've already sunk too much of the company's money into that damn place, Tony had said. *If you want the tree cut down so bad, you do it. I'll even lend you an ax.*

Lauryn sighed. It was bad enough trying to sell a goddamned murder house. The least her boss could do was help her out by making sure the place looked decent.

She pulled into the driveway, parked, and got out of her car. She stood next to it, smiling, waiting to see a car turn onto Brookside.

Waiting....Waiting....She'd almost convinced herself that the Eldreds were going to stand her up when they turned onto Brookside Court and drove their black Cadillac – which she thought looked too much like a hearse – into the driveway of the Raines house and parked behind her Sorento.

She hadn't met any of them before this, not in person, anyway. Mr. Eldred had called the office this morning, specifically requesting to be shown the Raines place. To say she'd been surprised to learn that someone was interested in the Raines house was an understatement. She should've asked if he was aware of the house's history, but she hadn't. She didn't want to blow what might be her last chance to sell the goddamned thing. Just in case, she'd asked Mr. Eldred if he and his family would be interested in looking at several comparable houses – ones that hadn't been the site of a bloody slaughter. He'd surprised her once again when he'd said he and his family were interested *only* in the Raines house. She'd wondered then if the Eldreds were already aware of the house's history and were the kind of people who got a sick thrill at being inside a place where murders had occurred. Maybe they were dark tourists, people who traveled around visiting places where horrific events had occurred. Maybe they weren't interested in buying the place at all. Maybe they were only pretending to be buyers so they could get inside the house. Whatever their purpose was, she remembered something that her boss had told her back when she'd first started working as a real estate agent. *If people don't look, they don't buy. Always get them inside and keep them there as long as you can.*

As the Eldreds got out of their car, Lauryn was reassured – but also slightly disappointed – to see they were perfectly normal, almost eerily average in fact. Medium height, uninteresting mouse-brown hair – except the grandmother, whose hair was dishwater-gray – all possessing features so unremarkable their faces might as well have been blank. Their clothing was generic as well. Polo shirt, blouses,

T-shirts. Jeans, sneakers, flip-flops. The Eldreds reminded Lauryn of the families displayed inside of picture frames when you bought them at the store, images placed there to give you an idea of how your own pictures would look when you put them inside. Absolutely and utterly forgettable, as if they didn't really exist at all.

She put on her best I'm-the-gal-who's-going-to-sell-you-your-dreamhouse smile as she stepped forward to greet the Eldreds. She made sure to project energy and enthusiasm into her voice as she spoke.

"Hi, I'm Lauryn. It's so good to meet you in person."

She stuck out her hand as she approached Mr. Eldred. She knew this seemed sexist on the surface, but her policy in these situations was to first greet whoever she had the initial contact with. After that, she would watch the interplay between Mr. and Mrs. to determine which one was most likely to drive the decision-making process in the family. Then that's who she'd focus the bulk of her attention on.

But Mr. Eldred didn't reach out to take her hand. He didn't even look at her, and neither did the other members of the family – wife, kids, grandmother. Instead, they were all looking at the house, eyes wide, nostrils flaring, as if they were eager to take in every detail of the place.

Creepy, she thought.

She lowered her hand, not wanting to make her new client feel awkward.

"May I have your names?" she asked.

The girl frowned. "Why would you want them? You have one of your own."

The mother smiled at her daughter. "She's asking us what our names *are*." She turned to Lauryn. "I'm Lacresha. My husband is Arnoldo, our children are Vanita and Damarcus, and my mother is Cleora."

Lauryn thought the woman was putting her on, but when she said nothing more, Lauryn decided she wasn't.

"What—" she searched for the right word, "—*colorful* names."

The girl frowned again, and Lauryn wondered if she wanted to say something about how none of their names had colors attached to them. But she glanced at her mother and remained silent. *Strange child*, Lauryn thought. *Maybe she's on the spectrum somewhere.*

"It's a beautiful day, isn't it?" Lauryn asked.

First step in sales: Find something you and the client can agree on, no matter how seemingly insignificant. This way, you begin as allies instead of adversaries.

Mr. Eldred didn't seem to hear her, but his wife turned to her and smiled.

There was something about the woman's features that disturbed Lauryn, but she couldn't say precisely what that was. On one hand, Lacresha was a plain-looking woman, so utterly forgettable that she was practically invisible. But her flesh had a mushy quality, and Lauryn felt that if she reached out and pressed a finger to the woman's cheek, there would be no resistance, and her finger would keep on going until her entire hand was lost inside the woman's head. The thought made her queasy, and she felt a bead of sweat roll down her spine.

She told herself that there was nothing wrong with the woman, that her strange imagining was nothing more than the result of work stress combined with the emotional burden of trying to care for her mother. The rational part of her mind was eager for an explanation – *any* explanation – and it grabbed hold of this one and held on to it tight. The deeper part of her mind, the part that dreamed, that sometimes sensed when something bad was going to happen, the part that hadn't changed significantly since her far-distant ancestors had been small apes just starting to walk upright.... That part knew a predator when it saw one, and it screamed for Lauryn to get the fuck out of there. But her rational mind overrode her instincts, and she remained where she was, struggling to keep a pleasant, relaxed smile on her face.

An unpleasant musky odor wafted off the Eldreds. It reminded her of the stink of an animal enclosure at the zoo, rank and wild. The smell of beasts locked away in cramped quarters too long, itching to be free, to run, to bite, to kill.

She shuddered. Where on Earth had that thought come from?

You're working too hard, girl, she thought.

She became aware of an awkward silence then. She had no idea how long it had gone on, but now all of the Eldreds were looking at her, all of them smiling, but their gazes were empty, devoid of apparent thought or feeling. They reminded her of insect eyes – alien and unreadable. But of course, they were normal eyes. Human eyes. They just *seemed* odd.

To break the silence, Lauryn – still facing Mrs. Eldred – said, "You look lovely today." It was a lie, of course, but one Lauryn had used with success in the past.

The woman's smile didn't change. It remained fixed on her face, as if it had been painted on.

"Thank you. We always look different in sunlight."

Lauryn, not sure how to take this, laughed uncomfortably. She glanced past Mrs. Eldred and saw the shadowy outline of someone sitting in the front seat of their Caddy. The windshield wasn't tinted, but Lauryn still had trouble making out the – man's? woman's? – features.

"Are we waiting for one more to join us?" Lauryn asked.

Mr. Eldred looked over his shoulder at the Cadillac for a moment before turning back to Lauryn.

"No," he said.

"Our friend is tired," Mrs. Eldred explained. "And looking at houses doesn't interest him."

For an instant, Lauryn thought that their 'friend's' eyes glowed a soft green, but the light soon faded.

"What the hell was *that*?"

She'd blurted out the thought before she could stop herself.

Up to this point, the son and daughter – both of whom were young teenagers – had been silent. But now the boy said, "Machine Head is still adjusting to the Mergence. He'll be fully operational soon."

The girl snickered, as if her brother had just made a joke. The boy didn't react to his sister's laughter and continued to stare impassively at Lauryn. The real estate agent had no idea how to respond to this, so she decided to ignore it.

"Let's go take a look inside, shall we?"

Without waiting for a response, she walked up the driveway, onto the short concrete walk, up three steps, and onto the porch. She didn't check to see if the Eldreds followed her. She didn't hear them move, didn't sense them crowding onto the porch behind her, but she knew that's exactly what was happening. During her time as a real estate agent she'd had her share of eccentric clients, ones who struck her as a little off in one way or another, although never to this degree. She suddenly felt small and vulnerable. Her hands trembled as she worked the combination to the lock box affixed to the doorknob. Her hands shook so badly that she had to enter the combination three times before the box opened. She removed the house key and inserted it into the lock – an action which took her four tries – but she managed it, and when she turned the key, she was rewarded with a satisfying *snick*. She removed the key, slipped it into her pants pocket, and pushed the door open. The house hadn't been shown for weeks, and it had remained closed the entire time. The air that escaped was stale and smelled of mold and mildew, and something else, something Lauryn couldn't immediately name. *It's like something died in there,* she thought, and almost laughed. Of course, something *had* died in there. *Four* somethings, as a matter of fact. She chided herself for the morbid thought. She needed to maintain a professional attitude if she was to have any hope of unloading this fucking two-story albatross.

She turned to the Eldreds, who, as she'd sensed, stood directly behind her on the porch. She intended to say something about how the place would be fine after a good airing out. But they'd closed their eyes and were inhaling deeply through their noses. Several of them made *mmmmm* sounds of pleasure, as if someone inside the house was in the process of cooking a gourmet dinner.

She almost bailed then. Almost turned to the Eldreds, muttered some excuse why she couldn't show them the house after all, and then hurried back to her car, got in, fired up the engine, backed out of the driveway – not caring if she hit the Eldreds' black Caddy with its mysterious occupant on the way – floored the gas pedal, and roared off, never looking back. But she thought of the bills for her mother's care, and she pushed the door all the way open and stepped aside so the Eldreds could enter. It was important that buyers saw the interior first, without the real estate agent in the way. They needed to picture themselves living there, and the agent's presence would interfere with that vision.

Lauryn turned to the Eldreds and noticed the teenage boy –

Demarcus – looking at the house next door. He smiled and waved.

"Do you know someone who lives there?" she asked.

The boy shook his head. "Not yet. But I will. We *all* will."

The rest of the family smiled at his comment, and Lauryn felt a chill run down her back. Their mouths might've formed smiles, but they didn't seem natural, more like they were imperfect imitations of smiles. And their eyes remained cold, flat, and empty.

She gestured toward the door with a shaking hand. "After you."

As the family filed past her, she once more became aware of the zoo smell, and she held her breath. Once the last one, the grandmother, was inside, Lauryn entered and turned to close the door behind her. She was tempted to leave it open, although she wasn't sure why. Maybe she wanted a means of escape? She'd meant the thought as a nervous joke, but it wasn't funny. Not in the least. She closed the door – not without reluctance – and then turned to face the house's interior.

They were in a short vestibule, a coat closet on their right. Normally, Lauryn would've opened the closet to show the Eldreds how much storage space there was. But they were going to get the no-frills tour from her today. In and out as fast as she could manage it. The less time she spent in the presence of these people, the better.

The Raineses' relatives had wanted nothing to do with the house after the murders, so the bank took possession of it and hired Lauryn's company to manage the sale. To get the house ready, the bank hired a cleaning service to deal with the bloodstains – and there'd been a *lot* of them. The bank then arranged for the Raineses' furniture and possessions to be removed. What could be sold at auction was sold, and the rest was donated to a shelter for homeless families. The bank then hired painters to paint all the rooms in what people in the realty business called 'relocation beige'.

Lauryn was on the fence when it came to showing an empty house. On the one hand, it made it easier for buyers to imagine how they might furnish and decorate their new home. But on the other, an empty house was just a bunch of rooms. It wasn't warm, wasn't homey. Lauryn thought some buyers reacted negatively to empty houses because of this, even if only subconsciously. Today, though, she was glad that the Raines house was empty. The less the Raines family felt like a presence, the less chance the Eldreds would picture the awful things that happened here. Assuming they knew about the murders, of course. And even though she should make sure they were informed about the house's history – it was Ohio law, after all – she intended to keep her goddamned mouth shut and deal with the consequences later.

She moved past the Eldreds and led them into the front room. It had a picture window that faced the street, no curtains, but it was covered by blinds. Lauryn's company had installed them to keep the morbidly curious from walking up to the House of Blood, as it had come to be called, and peering in the window to see what, if anything, remained inside. Lauryn stepped over to the window and raised the blinds to let some light in. Buyers didn't make offers on dark, gloomy houses. They liked bright, spacious rooms. She turned to the Eldreds, professional smile firmly in place.

"So what do you—"

Her next words died in her throat. From where she stood, she could see into the vestibule, and what she saw was a young girl – six years old, maybe seven – wearing a yellow T-shirt with a cartoon character on it and a pair of blue panties. The girl was running. At least, her body was positioned as if she were running, but her movements were slow, as if the air around her was a semisolid mass retarding her movements. The girl didn't look into the room toward Lauryn and the Eldreds, and the Eldreds didn't see the girl since their backs were to the vestibule. This left Lauryn the sole observer to the terrible scene that was about to play out before her disbelieving eyes.

The girl – short blond hair, chubby cheeks – had an expression of absolute terror on her face. Tears flowed from her eyes, and her mouth was open wide, as if she was screaming. There was no sound, though. No voice, no sound of the girl's footfalls, either. The girl made it only one more step before a woman came into view – naked, skin splashed with blood, large kitchen knife clutched in her right hand. She was tall, lean, fit, small-breasted, with defined muscles and a faint abdominal scar from a C-section. She had long brown hair, which streamed out behind her, remaining in place as if it had been sculpted that way. The woman's expression was one of absolute rage – eyes wide, teeth bared.

Lauryn instantly knew what she was seeing. Or rather *who*. The woman was Cherie Raines, and the girl was her oldest child, Elisa. Somehow, Lauryn was witnessing a slow-motion replay of the final murder Cherie had committed in the slaughter of her family. And then, without warning, the scene continued at regular speed, but still without sound. Cherie lunged forward and brought the knife down with a vicious swipe. The blade struck Elisa's left shoulder, and the girl fell forward. She hit the vestibule's tiled floor face-first, and her mother jumped on top of her. Cherie plunged the blade into her daughter, yanked it free, then stabbed her again, over and over, moving so fast that her knife hand was almost a blur. The child's mouth was open, and she screamed silently in pain and fear, her cries punctuated with pleas. Lauryn could read the girl's lips: *Mommy, no! Mommy, please stop!* Lauryn was grateful for the lack of sound. She thought she'd lose her mind if she had to listen to the child's death cries, had to hear the *chuk-chuk-chuk* of the knife violating her young flesh.

And then, as suddenly as it had come, the vision of Cherie Raines murdering her child ended. Mother and daughter disappeared, and the section of floor where the stabbing had occurred was clean, not so much as a single drop of blood on the tile.

Lauryn hadn't drawn a single breath the entire time she'd watched Cherie kill Elisa, but now her lungs burned and she gulped air.

"Is something wrong?" Mrs. Eldred asked.

For the briefest of instants, Lauryn thought the woman's eyes looked like those of a predatory animal, gleaming bright with hunger. But then they were an ordinary brown once more.

"I...." Lauryn searched for words, but none came. She stared at the spot where Elisa had died, thought of Cherie ramming the knife into her daughter again and again. She knew from the newspaper articles at the time of the murders that Cherie had indeed killed her daughter in that very spot before heading outside to end her own life. Lauryn had been in this house at least a dozen times before, and never had she experienced a...she supposed *hallucination* was the correct term. She knew she was stressed right now, but not so much that she would see things that weren't there. Something like this was an indication of a full-scale mental and emotional breakdown, maybe even a harbinger of far worse madness to come.

Stop it, she told herself. *You're stressed by the responsibility of dealing with a demented mother, so you hallucinate a mother killing her daughter. It's Psych 101. Disturbing, yes, and a definite sign you need some therapy and possibly a prescription for valium. But that's all.*

"Are you unwell?" the grandmother asked.

The question was innocent enough, but there seemed to be a mocking edge to the old woman's words, and her grandson and granddaughter laughed softly, strange breathy sounds. *Huh-huh-huh-huh-huh....*

"I'm fine," Lauryn answered, more curtly than she should've. She knew she should smile, thank the woman for her concern, but she couldn't muster the energy. Without another word, she led the Eldreds through the rest of the ground floor. Dining room, family room, kitchen, garage. The Eldreds made no comments, didn't discuss the pros and cons of the house, their likes and dislikes, as she led them around. In fact, they seemed to barely notice the rooms. They kept their gazes trained on her, as if she was far more interesting than any aspect of the house. She was already nervous after experiencing the hallucination of Cherie Raines killing her daughter, and the Eldreds' scrutiny only heightened her anxiety. She no longer cared if the Eldreds bought the place. She just wanted to get this showing over with as fast as possible so she could get out of here and head to the nearest bar for a good stiff drink.

When she'd shown the Eldreds everything the ground floor had to offer, including the backyard, there was nothing left to do but go upstairs. She almost called off the showing then, pleaded illness or a forgotten prior appointment, almost gave any damn excuse just so long as it would get her out of there. But before she could speak, Mrs. Eldred took hold of her arm.

"You're doing quite well, Lauryn," the woman said. She turned to her family. "Isn't she?"

Smiles and nods from everyone, their heads moving up and down with the bobbing motion of marionettes. Lauryn found it difficult to make out their faces clearly. The instant her vision began to focus on a feature – an eye, a mouth, a nose – the image blurred and she felt a pinprick of pain behind her eyes. She'd once read about a condition called face blindness where people literally couldn't see faces. At the time, she'd hadn't been able to imagine what the world would look like to someone afflicted with this condition. Now she wondered if she was developing it herself. She told herself it was just another sign of how stressed and exhausted she was, nothing more. She couldn't quite bring herself to believe it, though.

She turned away from the Eldreds and their strange features, which refused to remain in focus very long.

"You're going to take us upstairs, aren't you?" Mr. Eldred asked.

Lauryn wanted to say no, wanted to tell this creepy bastard and his weird-ass family to go to hell. But the man's words sounded like a threat, and Lauryn could almost hear an *Or else* tacked on to the man's question.

She gave Mr. Eldred a weak smile.

"Of course."

Mrs. Eldred still had hold of her elbow, and the woman's grip increased in pressure until Lauryn thought the joint might break. Mrs. Eldred steered her toward the stairs, and once they were there, she released her grip and took a half step back. Mr. Eldred gave a half bow and gestured to the stairs as if to say *After you*. The kids gave their *huh-huh-huh* laughter, and this time the grandmother laughed, too, the sound a grating rasp of rusty metal sliding across ancient bone.

Lauryn turned away from the Eldreds, placed her hand on the railing, put her foot on the first step, and began ascending the stairs.

Please don't let it happen again, Lauryn thought.

But it did.

When she was halfway up the stairs, she saw a child – another girl, this one in footy pajamas covered with cartoon circus animals – come running around the corner and start down the stairs toward her, her mother following. As before, there was no sound, and also as before, the two moved in slow motion. Once more, Lauryn watched as Cherie Raines killed one of her children, this one the middle child – Courtney, age four. The girl had straight brown hair that hung past her shoulders, and with the hand that wasn't clutching the blood-stained knife, Cherie grabbed hold of her daughter's hair and yanked roughly backward. The girl's feet flew out from under her, and she fell backward, landing hard on the stairs. Cherie held the girl down with her free hand and returned to normal speed as she began stabbing. Lauryn wanted to close her eyes and shut out the horrible sight, wanted it more than she'd ever wanted anything in her life. But her eyes remained open, and she did not look away from the grisly scene. It was as if some force was compelling her to witness the atrocities that Cherie Raines had visited upon her family. The scene took long moments to play out, but when Courtney's body was a ravaged, blood-soaked mess, the images faded, leaving Lauryn looking at empty space on the stairs that was unmarked by blood.

This time, none of the Eldreds asked if she was doing okay, and they said nothing about her pausing on the stairs for several moments. She would've turned and run out of the house if the Eldreds hadn't filled the stairs behind her, blocking her escape.

Two more to go, Lauryn thought.

She began moving once more, her footfalls leaden, as if she were a prisoner marching to her own execution. She didn't know why this was happening to her, but one thing was clear. She was witnessing the deaths of the Raines family in reverse order. So rather than disrupt the pattern, she went to the room where the next murder, which in reality had been the second, had taken place. She bypassed the room that Courtney and Elisa had shared – there would be nothing to see there – and went to the room across the hall. This one was next to the master bedroom, and it had belonged to the youngest member of the family: Jacob, the two-year-old.

Lauryn opened the door and stepped inside. Normally, she would've let the buyers enter first, but there was nothing normal about this showing. The Eldreds filed in, and Lauryn watched as Cherie entered as well, moving in slow motion, of course, and walked to her son's bed. She was still naked, flesh dotted with blood splatter, but less than before. Jacob slept in a youth bed, one with wooden railings to keep him from rolling off the mattress and onto the floor while he slept. This murder was far less violent than the other two. When Cherie reached her son's bedside, she knelt, drew back Jacob's blanket, and slowly, almost lovingly, pressed the tip of the knife against his chest. The boy didn't wake, didn't so much as stir as his mother angled the blade and slipped it between his ribs and into his heart. There was a tenderness to this act that struck Lauryn as sweet in a twisted way.

The boy woke then, mouth wide, and she knew he screamed,

although like the other members of his family, no sound escaped his throat. Lauryn guessed that his scream was what woke his sisters, both of whom had tried to flee before they ended up like him, and both of whom had failed. The boy's eyes glazed over and he fell limp.

Tears ran down Lauryn's face as the vision ended and the room became empty once more, but she was barely aware she was crying. She moved past the Eldreds, stepped into the hall, opened the door to the master bedroom, and entered, not caring whether the Eldreds followed.

Here she saw a king-sized bed, a man sleeping on his side, wrapped in blankets like a cocoon. This was Dale Raines, the first family member to die by Cherie's hand. Cherie stood next to the bed, staring down at her husband, face blank. She wore a light blue nightie, and she held the knife – the blade spotless – at her side. After a moment, Cherie, moving in slow motion, placed the knife on the nightstand and slipped out of her nightie, as if she'd decided she didn't want to get any bloodstains on it. She hung it over one of the wooden bedposts, picked up the knife once more, leaned over her husband, and sliced his throat open. Lauryn expected the scene to return to normal speed then, but this time it didn't. With excruciating slowness, blood fountained from Dale's wound and onto the headboard, the blankets, and, of course, onto Cherie's bare skin.

Lauryn was struck by how beautiful the blood looked as it moved through the air in slow motion. It had an almost balletic elegance to it that she found fascinating. She thought she could stand here and watch the blood spray like this for hours. Maybe forever. This time when the vision ended, leaving her looking at an empty room, she felt an almost crushing sadness.

Mrs. Eldred spoke then, her voice a whisper next to Lauryn's ear.

"The house will make a perfect Stalking Ground. We'll take it."

Lauryn continued staring at the space where the bed had been, wishing she could see Dale's murder again so she could watch his blood dance in the air one more time.

"That's nice," she said.

She then turned and left the room. She said nothing more to the Eldreds, nor did she look at them. She walked down the hallway, went down the stairs where Courtney had died, walked into the vestibule where Elisa had breathed her last. She opened the front door and stepped onto the porch.

She saw Cherie Raines standing naked in the yard, her back to the house. This was the final act of the deadly drama of the Raines family. Lauryn watched as the woman – moving at normal speed – carved a deep line into the underside of her left forearm and then switched hands and did the same to her other arm. She then let the knife slip away from her blood-slick fingers to fall to the ground. She knelt next to it, arms held out at her sides, blood running from her arms in crimson curtains, making it look as if she had red wings.

All too soon, Cherie's arms fell to her sides, and she collapsed to the lawn, dead. She'd left no note behind to explain her actions, and whatever motive she had for killing her loved ones would forever remain a mystery. Lauryn liked that, thought it was rather poetic in its way. Cherie vanished then, and Lauryn knew she would never see the woman – and all the beautiful blood she'd spilled – again. The thought was heartbreaking.

The Eldreds had followed her down and onto the porch, but Lauryn was only partially aware of them. She headed to her Sorento, got in, turned on the vehicle, and carefully backed down the driveway, maneuvering around the Eldreds' black Cadillac. She glanced at the car as she passed, and through the driver's side window she saw someone with green eyes and silver-gray features look at her. The creature raised a hand in farewell.

When she reached the street, she put her car in gear and began driving. She saw the Eldreds, still standing together on the porch, also raise their hands in farewell. She faced forward once more and pressed the accelerator to the floor.

★   ★   ★

She wasn't sure how long she drove before she became aware of how fast she was going. When she did, she eased off the accelerator. She was surprised a cop hadn't pulled her over for speeding. She'd been lucky. She took in her surroundings and saw she was on the north edge of town, a run-down area with abandoned buildings with boarded-up windows and an old train depot that hadn't seen use in more than four decades. Trains still used the tracks though, carrying freight instead of passengers. Who traveled by train anymore? As she drew near the tracks, the train signals began flashing red and a wooden crossarm lowered to block the way. She stopped, glanced left, saw nothing, glanced right, and saw the gleaming dot of a train's headlight in the distance.

She'd left her purse on the passenger seat of her car when she'd shown the Raines house to the Eldreds. She reached into it, fished out her phone, and dialed the office. Tony answered.

"Good news!" she said. "I've sold the Raines place. No, I'm not shitting you. To a family named Eldred. You'll find their contact information written on a legal pad sitting on my desk. Why? I'm telling you this so you can get in touch with them and finish the sale. I'm not going to be available."

She disconnected and tossed the phone onto the passenger seat. It began vibrating almost immediately. She knew Tony was calling her back, but she didn't care.

She watched the train approach, its headlight growing larger, until it looked almost like a miniature sun.

We look different in the sunlight.

When the train had almost reached the crossing, Lauryn took her foot off the brake, jammed it down on the gas, and the Sorento leaped forward. As the car broke through the crossarm, she wished someone was filming this. It would look spectacular, especially in slow motion.

★   ★   ★

The Eldred walk to Car and get in, relieved to be out of the sun. Sunlight causes them no harm, but they aren't comfortable in the light of day. Things are what they are in the light, leaving little room for interpretation, for *imagination*. But in the dark, things are less defined, more malleable, and the Eldred are happiest when reality is fluid.

Father Hunger and the Werewife are in the front seat, Machine Head between them. Their friend's new body is already starting to stink, but neither of them care. They find the stench of rot pleasant, actually. The children are in the backseat, but this time the Grandother has squeezed in between them. She likes riding in the trunk, alone in the dark and the stifling heat, but there are times when she prefers to be with the rest of the family, and right after they've found a new Stalking Ground is one of them.

"The woman's emotions made a pleasant appetizer," Father Hunger says.

"Not much to them," the Grandother grumps. "Simple shock and confusion. Barely more than a nibble. All they did was make me hungrier."

"And her mind broke so easily," the Low Prince says. "It was barely any fun at all."

"Yeah!" The Nonsister *hates* agreeing with her brother, but in this case, she thinks he's right.

"Don't worry," the Werewife says. "Can't you smell it? Feelings of sadness and despair, inadequacy and betrayal, love gone sour and sweet-sweet hate? This cul-de-sac is an orchard of rotten fruit, long overdue for a harvest."

The Eldred inhale deeply, and they are reassured. The Werewife is right, as usual.

"Time to summon the movers, dear," the Werewife says to her husband.

Father Hunger opens his mouth. There's a wet gurgling sound in his throat, as if he is going to throw up. But instead of vomit, a multilegged winged insect crawls up from deep inside him and perches on his tongue. Without being asked, Car lowers the driver's side window. Father Hunger reaches up and the emissary bug hops onto his index finger. He extends his arm through the open window, and the insect takes to the air. It flies off and is quickly lost to sight.

Father Hunger brings his arm back inside and Car closes the window.

The movers work swiftly and will arrive this day or the next. Normally, the Eldred would wait to move in until their purchase of the house was complete legally, but it has been too long since they fed properly, and they will inhabit the house as soon as possible. The Eldred have lived a very long time, and they are quite wealthy.

They are confident they can smooth over any difficulties caused by their moving in so soon. Money has a wonderful way of making problems vanish.

CHAPTER THREE

The next day, in the early evening, Neal Wilkerson was mowing his front lawn when a large black truck pulled into the cul-de-sac. He normally made it a point to mind his own business, but the truck was so damn odd that he turned off the mower, wiped sweat from his brow with the back of his hand, and watched the vehicle. The first weird thing about it was the color. It was the blackest black he'd ever seen. He remembered reading an article about scientists who'd created a material called vantablack, which had a surface so non-reflective that it absorbed nearly one hundred percent of the light that hit it. He wouldn't have been surprised to discover this truck was even darker. It was so black it looked almost two-dimensional, and it was impossible to make out any of the vehicle's features. It was as if someone had taken a giant sheet of black construction paper and cut out the outline of a truck.

The second weird thing about the vehicle was the sound of its engine. Instead of the rumbling-chuffing sound he associated with diesel engines, this truck made a thrumming drone that reminded him of a nest of angry hornets. The sound wasn't particularly loud, but it still grated on the ears, and it gave him an instant headache. Mild, but annoying.

The third weird thing was the vehicle's smell. Instead of the harsh tang of exhaust, a scent like sour milk trailed behind the truck – sour milk that had been put on to boil and left on the stove too long. His stomach lurched, saliva filled his mouth, and he felt his jaw muscles tighten. He did his best to ignore these sensations. Bad enough he had to mow his goddamned lawn after a day of trying to teach physics to soon-to-be graduating seniors who couldn't pay attention to anything for more than a few seconds at a time. He did *not* want to puke here where the neighbors could see. Wouldn't that be the shit icing on top of the crap cake of a day he'd had?

"Did you notice the For Sale sign's not in the Raineses' yard anymore?"

Neal's attention had been so focused on the strange truck that he hadn't noticed Cora Hawkins walk over from her house, her five-year-old daughter Vivienne next to her, holding her hand. The girl always gripped her mother's hand so tight that her tiny knuckles whitened. It was as if the girl was afraid her mother would let go of her and was determined to make sure that never happened. Both Cora and Vivienne were looking at the truck, too. *The Black Truck,* Neal thought, and although he'd dubbed it such to poke fun at himself for finding the vehicle so ominous, he couldn't deny that the name, with its sinister overtones, was a good fit.

The three of them watched as the truck backed into the Raineses' driveway as far as it could, which meant the cab stuck out into the street. The engine turned off and the truck sat there. They waited for someone to get out, but no one did. After several minutes passed without either of the cab's doors opening, Cora said, "That's strange."

"Sure is," Neal said.

The Parsonses' house was across the cul-de-sac from Neal's, directly next to the Raines place, on the west side, while Cora's house bordered the Raineses' on the east. No one came out of the Parsonses' house to get a look at the truck, but Neal knew someone was home. Someone always was. A moment later, the curtains over the front window parted a crack, just enough to allow someone to peek out. Neal couldn't see whether it was Lola or her son, Spencer. He supposed it could be either or both of them. If someone was finally moving into the Raines place, it would be the biggest event in Brookside Court since…well, since the murders themselves.

On the other side of the Parsonses was the house of Isaac Ruiz. *Professor* Ruiz, as he regularly reminded Neal, who, while also an educator, had only a master's degree compared to Isaac's doctorate. Neal didn't know what Isaac's teaching schedule at the university was, but his daughter Alex's blue Honda Accord was parked in front of the house. She took classes at her father's school, primarily because she got discounted tuition as the family member of a professor. Neal didn't know how much of a discount she got, but it couldn't be enough to make it worth living with Isaac. Hell, the university could *pay* her to go there while she lived with her father, and Neal still thought it would be a shitty deal.

If Alex was home, she either wasn't aware of the truck or didn't give a damn about it. He figured she didn't know it was here. It was too strange to simply ignore.

Neal was in his late thirties, over six feet, thin, with curly red hair. He had a sprinkling of freckles on his cheeks and nose, but not too many, thank god. When he was little, his female relatives had gushed about how cute his freckles were, while the kids at school had made fun of him for them, calling him Polka-Dot Boy, and worse. It wasn't that hot out today – low seventies – but he'd worn a T-shirt and shorts anyway. He had a tendency to sweat a lot when he did physical labor, regardless of the temperature.

Cora was an attractive Asian woman, ten years younger than Neal, with large breasts that, thanks to her penchant for wearing low-cut tops, were hard to ignore. She also liked to go braless when she was at home. She was completely unself-conscious about her body, and Neal suspected she'd be comfortable talking to him while she was stark naked. She'd never come across as a flirt or a tease. She simply was who she was: a woman completely at home in her own skin. Neal was a married man and had no desire to cheat on his wife, but he wasn't a dead man, and he always felt a little awkward around Cora.

Vivienne – short black hair like her mother's, done up in pigtails, wearing a T-shirt and shorts of her own, feet bare – pointed at Neal's crotch.

"I can see your weenie!" she cried with delight.

Cora looked where her daughter pointed and laughed. There was nothing mean-spirited in her laugh, but Neal still felt embarrassed. He looked down to see that Vivienne was right. The shorts he was wearing were too tight, and he didn't have underwear beneath them – he hated the feeling of sweaty underwear next to his skin – and the fabric of the shorts clearly outlined his penis, which currently listed to the left.

"Sorry," Neal mumbled, and quickly tried to adjust his shorts, but all he managed to do was make his dick flop over to the right, eliciting peals of happy laughter from Vivienne.

"It's dancing!" she said.

"Don't worry about it," Cora said, her smile a little naughty. "The girl's got to learn sometime."

A Honda CRV turned into the cul-de-sac, and both Neal and Cora watched as it pulled into Neal's driveway. Vivienne, bored with Neal's penis by now and uninterested in the Honda, turned her attention to the black truck. Neal was glad Vivienne had lost interest in the contents of his shorts, but something about the girl looking at the truck bothered him. It seemed wrong for someone so young and innocent to be looking at such an – the word that popped into his mind was *obscenity*, but he wasn't sure why. The truck was weird as hell, sure, but obscene? Yeah, he decided. Somehow it was.

Kandice turned off the CRV's engine and got out of the car, carrying a pair of white plastic shopping bags that were full to bursting. She glanced over her shoulder at the black truck, then came toward them, a bright smile on her face. Neal watched her eyes carefully. Were they focused on Cora? Maybe.

"What's going on over there?" Kandice tilted her head in the direction of the Raines house.

"Apparently it's moving day," Cora said.

Cora's smile was as bright as Kandice's. Neal tried not to read anything into it, but it wasn't easy. Kandice was an athletic African-American woman who liked to wear her hair cut close to the scalp. She wore sneakers, purple tights, and a T-shirt that said Rockridge Rec on the front. She moved with an easy, confident grace, as she always did. It was one of the things that had first attracted Neal to her. She was like Cora that way. Both women were completely comfortable with who they were. He couldn't decide if this was a good thing or a bad thing.

Kandice had no trouble lugging the shopping bags, but Neal went over to her anyway and took one from her. He would've taken both, but he didn't want to imply that he thought she was too weak to carry even one bag.

"Thanks, hon." She gave him a quick kiss on the cheek, then walked over to stand next to Cora and Vivienne. All three of them gazed at the black truck.

The shopping bag Neal had taken was heavier than he'd expected, and he set it down on the porch before joining the women. He stood close to Kandice, but not *too* close. And he didn't reach out to take her hand. He didn't want to seem as if he were being possessive, physically claiming her as his – although that was exactly what he wanted to do.

Kandice taught exercise classes at the rec center during the day, and her body was more toned than Cora's. Cora had more pronounced curves, though, and appeared more classically feminine, at least to Neal's way of thinking. Before he could stop himself, he imagined Cora standing on tiptoes to kiss Kandice – who was several inches taller – and he imagined Kandice wrapping her arms around the other woman and pulling her close, pressing Cora's large breasts tight against her smaller ones.

Neal felt himself growing hard, and he forced the images away. The last thing he wanted to do was get an erection and have Vivienne notice.

Mommy, Mommy, look! His wiener is getting bigger!

Maybe Cora was comfortable with her daughter being aware of other people as sexual beings – at least in terms of their anatomy – but the idea of the little girl looking at his erect penis tenting his shorts sickened him. Vivienne was just a kid, for chrissakes. He was also angry at himself for having the fantasy of Kandice and Cora kissing, and he was even angrier at his body for responding to the images in his mind. He was also jealous of Cora, with her large tits hanging free beneath her shirt, and her tight shorts, which showed a little ass and gave her a hint of camel toe. He knew Cora dressed like this whenever the weather was warm – or even warm*ish*, like today – but he couldn't help wondering if Cora had dressed like this on purpose. She knew when Kandice got home from work. Maybe the black truck had simply given her an excuse to come over a couple minutes early. That way it wouldn't look like she *wanted* to see Kandice, that it was mere coincidence that she was standing in the yard when Kandice pulled into the driveway.

Neal gritted his teeth. *Stop it,* he told himself. *Obsessing like this isn't healthy.*

"I think it's a ghost truck," Vivienne said.

"That's a good name for it," Kandice said. "It's kind of spooky, isn't it?"

Cora folded her arms beneath her breasts. This had the effect of lifting them up and out a bit, making them even more prominent.

"Gives me the creeps," she said.

Neal shared their feelings, but he was a physics teacher – a scientist – and he felt it was his job to be logical about this.

"You two feel that way not because of the truck so much as the fact that it's parked in front of the Raines house."

Vivienne looked up at him. "What's wrong with the house?"

"Uh…." Neal quickly looked at Cora. Maybe she thought it was okay for her young daughter to be aware of penises, but he doubted she'd be comfortable with her knowing the truth about the infamous 'House of Blood'.

Cora frowned at Neal, and he gave a slight shrug of his shoulders. *Sorry,* he mouthed silently.

Cora put a hand on her daughter's shoulder.

"That house was empty for a long time," Cora said. "So long we were beginning to think no one would ever move in."

"Do you think it's haunted too?" Vivienne looked at the house, eyes wide, excited by the idea. "Are there ghosts in there right now? Are they walking around and saying 'Boo!' and trying to be scary?"

Now it was Kandice's turn to give Neal a disapproving look. Vivienne was the only young child living on Brookside Court, and the adults – by unspoken agreement – were careful not to give so much as a hint that anything bad had ever happened in the Raines house. Vivienne lived next door to it. Hell, her bedroom window *faced* the house. How could she be comfortable if she had any idea of the awful things that had occurred so close to her own home, the one place in the world where she should always feel safe? It was hard enough for the adults to deal with sometimes. They had no illusions about the Raines house. That's why they'd all moved here after all – because the houses had been so damn cheap. After the murders, the other families living in the cul-de-sac put their homes up for sale and moved to a different part of town. One family, the Bisharas, who used to live where Isaac and his daughter Alex now did, had left town entirely rather than deal with reporters constantly trying to interview them. The media's interest in *The Brookside Massacre* – as one of the true-crime books about the murders was titled – eventually waned, but it had still taken more than a year for the houses surrounding the Raines place to sell. Isaac was first, then Cora and her husband Martin, and then Neal and Kandice. The only ones who'd stayed after the murders were the Parsonses. Neal didn't know why they'd remained. He rarely spoke to Lola or Spencer, as they kept mostly to themselves. He certainly didn't know them well enough to ask them such a personal question as why they'd decided to keep living next to the House of Blood. He had the impression that neither of them worked. Lola was old enough to draw social security, and Spencer was so socially awkward that Neal couldn't imagine him working anywhere.

"It'll be good to have someone living there," Kandice said.

That depends on why they bought the house, Neal thought. Maybe whoever it was had done so because they couldn't pass up such a great deal. After all, if the other houses on Brookside Court had been cheap, the bank would probably have been happy to practically give away the goddamn place. Maybe the buyers were logical people who didn't believe that a physical structure could somehow be tainted by the bad things that once happened there. Or maybe they thought they could redeem the place by living there and creating a new legacy to, if not wipe away the old, at least diminish it somewhat.

"I better go," Cora said. "Martin will be home soon, and I need to whip up some dinner for him. See you two later." She looked down at Vivienne. "Say goodbye to Mr. and Mrs. Wilkerson."

"Bye," Vivienne said, voice distant, gaze still fixed on the truck.

Cora rolled her eyes as if to say, *Kids. What can you do?* And then she started back to her house, pulling Vivienne along with her. Normally, Neal would've watched her ass sway as she departed, but instead he watched his wife's face to see if *she* was watching Cora's ass.

Kandice turned to him, arched an eyebrow.

"Really?" she asked.

Neal didn't say anything, just kept looking at her.

"Do you want me to say it? Fine. She's hot. Happy now?"

She started toward their front door, and after a moment, Neal followed.

⋆　⋆　⋆

On the other side of the cul-de-sac from Neal and Kandice's house, Spencer Parsons was peeking through the living room curtains. He'd heard the weird engine noise of the black truck as it pulled onto Brookside Court, and the odd sound was what had drawn him to the window. What kept him there, however, was seeing his neighbors across the street standing in their yard, talking. About the truck, most likely. They kept looking in its direction. He didn't care about the truck right then, though, had almost forgotten it even existed. There was only one thing he was interested in right now, and that was Vivienne Hawkins. She was such a beautiful child. Biracial children always seemed especially beautiful to him, almost unearthly in a way. As if they were angels made flesh. But all children were beautiful to him. Adults were clumsy, awkward things compared to them, so much so that sometimes it was hard to believe they were of the same species. Children were innocent, pure, bursting with life and energy, skin smooth and flawless. They were *unspoiled*, and they were made even more beautiful by the realization that they could never remain that way. They were like snowflakes, lovely to look at, but temporary. Time would take their innocence and grace, their simple joy at being alive, and replace them with creatures that were taller, heavier, hairier, with careworn faces that reflected a multitude of sorrows.

He was a prime example. As a child, he'd been a skinny little thing, so hyperactive that it was torture to sit still for more than a few moments at a time. Now, at forty-two, he was fat and balding, and hadn't worked a regular job in almost a decade. He hardly ever left the house, and he spent most of his days wearing only T-shirts and boxer shorts. Adulthood had ruined him, the same as it did every child.

Don't bullshit yourself, boy. You were ruined long before you got your first pube, and you know it.

Spencer closed his eyes and concentrated on taking deep, even breaths. He counted them, one, two, three.... When he reached twenty, he opened his eyes. He waited, afraid he would hear the voice again – his *father's* voice – but dear old Dad kept quiet, and Spencer sighed in relief. He knew the voice wasn't literally his father's, that they were his own thoughts, which he heard in his father's voice. At least, that's what Dr. Reiger – *Call me Beth* – had told him. But sometimes the voice seemed too real to be his imagination.

He gazed across the street at Vivienne again. She looked so lovely in the early evening light. Angelic. He imagined trailing his fingers down her neck, her chest, her belly, skin like warm, warm glass.... He felt the first stirrings of an erection, and he knew he should step away from the curtains and let them fall back into place, hiding Vivienne from his sight.

The best way to avoid temptation is to avoid it.

Beth had told him this, and Spencer had found it to be good advice. It was why he didn't go out much, and when he did, he went during the weekdays when most children were in school. He stayed home on the weekends unless he absolutely had to go out, and he spent summers – when children were on break from school – sequestered in the house, with only his mother for company. This self-imposed isolation didn't stop him from thinking about children, of course, but staying away from them physically had made things easier on him. Safer too, for him and for them.

Just a few more minutes, he told himself. *What could it hurt?*

He forced himself to let go of the curtains and take three steps back. The curtains were no longer in his reach now, and he'd have to step forward to open them again. He almost did it, but he made himself turn away from the window and start walking toward the kitchen.

From deeper in the house, he heard the sound of a television. His mother was in her room, binging a trashy cops-and-robbers TV series while she worked on one of her elaborate connect-the-dots books. He'd once asked her how she could stand to watch that crap after what had happened next door.

Bad things happen anywhere, all the time, she'd said. *That's just part of life.* She'd paused, then added, *You should know that.*

He did. But that didn't make living next to the Raines house any easier.

He needed to keep himself busy, keep his mind occupied so he wouldn't think about Vivienne. About how soft her hair would feel as he brushed his fingers lightly across her head, about how her hair would smell, probably like some sort of scented shampoo, strawberry, maybe, or lilac. His dick grew harder, and he reached down and gave it a swift smack. It hurt, but the pain was good. It helped him focus. It was getting close to dinnertime. He'd make something for his mom and him to eat. Once in the kitchen, he searched the freezer and cupboards, looking for something he could prepare for dinner. Pickings were slim, though. Mom had groceries delivered twice a month, and the next delivery wasn't scheduled for several days. He decided on box mac and cheese with small plastic containers of unsweetened applesauce for dessert. He had the noodles on the stove and boiling when he heard his mother's door opening. A moment later, she came shuffling into the kitchen.

She walked over to the stove and eyed the contents in the boiling pot.

"Macaroni again?"

"I'm afraid so."

She hrumpfed, walked over to the counter where he'd left the applesauce containers, and snatched one up. She got a spoon from the silverware drawer, pulled the tinfoil cover off the applesauce, and tossed it onto the counter. She had a bad habit of not throwing things away, and it irritated him because it was always left to him to clean up her mess. She leaned back against the counter and started eating her applesauce.

"That was supposed to be for dessert," he said.

Mom didn't reply. She just kept eating.

Lola Parsons was in her late sixties, but she looked ten years older. She'd smoked ever since she'd been a teenager, and despite having had two heart attacks and a triple bypass, she still smoked, although she'd cut down to four cigarettes a day – one at breakfast, lunch, dinner, and bedtime. Spencer wished she'd quit altogether, but he didn't nag her about it. He knew what it was like to have a compulsion that was difficult to control.

She was a thin, small woman, almost child-sized, he thought, but her appearance was deceptive. She was a lot stronger than she looked, and a hell of a lot tougher, too. He knew this from experience. She'd never laid a hand on him, not even to spank him when he was a kid and did something wrong. But he'd seen what she was capable of when roused to anger. Oh yes, he had.

Her hair was silver-gray – she refused to color it – and she was always cold, even during the height of summer. Because of this, she wore long-sleeved shirts year round, and usually a sweater or sweatshirt on top of them. But paradoxically, she always went around barefoot. *My feet sweat*, she'd once explained to him. Today she had on jeans and a dark blue sweatshirt that said *Rockridge Fire Department* on the front in white letters. He had no idea where she'd gotten it. As far as he knew, their family had no connection to the fire department.

Spencer talked as he drained the macaroni over the sink, then added butter, milk, the contents of the cheese packet, and started mixing the ingredients.

"There's a moving truck next door. It's black."

"Who cares what color it is? It'll be nice having someone else living next to us again."

He thought about pointing out that the Ruizes already lived on the other side of their property, but he kept quiet. Mom hated Dr. Ruiz, and she had as little to do with him as possible. Spencer didn't blame her. The man could be a real ass sometimes. His daughter was nice, at least from what Spencer could tell based on the minimal contact he'd had with her. But Mom liked to pretend the Ruizes didn't exist.

When the macaroni noodles were slathered in cheese sauce, Spencer got two bowls from the cupboard and divided the macaroni between them. He got a spoon for his, and a fork for Mom's – for some reason she refused to eat macaroni with a spoon – and he held out her bowl to her. She'd finished her applesauce and was now licking the inside of the container as clean as she could. Only when she was finished and had put the empty container on the counter – where it would remain until Spencer put it with the recycling – did she take the bowl of macaroni from his hand. She started eating, shoving the food into her mouth as if she was starving. Spencer began eating too, but more slowly. Neither of them made a move toward the dining table. They often ate meals like this, standing in the kitchen, sometimes talking, sometimes silent. Spencer supposed a lot of people might've found this odd, but it seemed practical to him. This way, you were close to the sink and the trash when you were finished.

"Did you see them?"

Mom asked this with a studied casualness that didn't fool Spencer. He knew what she was really asking: Did they have children?

"No one's come out of the truck yet. At least, I didn't see anybody."

He *had* seen the buyers come to the house the other day. Mom had been taking a nap then, and she didn't like being woken for anything short of a life-threatening emergency, so he'd watched them by himself. They did have children, but both were too old for his tastes. There'd been something odd about the family. They'd given off a creepy vibe, as if they were aliens visiting Earth for the first time and weren't sure what the local customs were. And there'd been that weird moment when he'd gotten the sense that they were aware of him watching them. One of them had even smiled and waved at him. He'd moved away from the window after that and hadn't returned to look through it again until the next day. He hadn't told Mom about seeing the new family, though. He wasn't sure why. At first, he thought he didn't want her to worry about kids moving in next door. She wouldn't understand that they were too old for him. She understood his...*proclivity* and why he was the way he was. But she didn't want to hear specific details, and he sure as shit didn't want to talk to her about them. What son felt comfortable discussing his sexuality with his mother?

But in truth, the real reason he hadn't said anything to her was because of that smile and wave. He still sometimes saw it when he closed his eyes, as if the moment had been seared into his brain.

"I had a dream last night that a family had moved into the house," Mom said.

Spencer couldn't stop himself from rolling his eyes. He hated listening to Mom talk about her dreams, but she always did. She believed dreams carried insights and predictions. Spencer listened to her recount them every time, though. That's what good sons did.

Mom put her half-eaten macaroni on the counter before speaking.

"I dreamed that we were both inside the Raines house. There were some other people there too, but they were blurry and I couldn't tell who they were. The house was much bigger than it seemed on the outside. We walked through room after room. Hundreds of them. Before long we became lost and couldn't find our way out. Then for some reason, we became separated. I looked all over for you, kept calling out your name, but I couldn't find you. I just kept walking through rooms, searching, searching...."

Lola Parsons was not normally an emotionally demonstrative person, but a tear ran down her left cheek now. Spencer put his macaroni down, went to her, and enfolded her in his large, fleshy arms. He wasn't comfortable touching or being touched, not after.... But he was the only other person here, and his mother needed comforting. And after what she'd done for him – what she'd *risked* for him – a hug was the least he could give her.

Mom pressed her small body tight against his.

"Don't ever leave me," she said. "Not like that."

He stroked her silver-gray hair with thick sausage fingers.

"I won't," he said. "*Ever.*"

CHAPTER FOUR

Isaac Ruiz saw the black truck the instant he turned his Toyota Highlander into the cul-de-sac. He was still fuming about what had happened at the sociology department meeting that afternoon, and he was still partly buzzed from the drinks he'd had during a bitch session with colleagues at a bar near campus afterward. Because of this, while he was aware of the truck, nothing about it struck him as unusual. In order to boost the department's student success rate, the sociology faculty – at least the majority of them – had voted on changing the departmental grading scale for the upcoming fall semester so that, instead of 95-100 being an A, now 90-100 was. Isaac had been livid at the proposal. It was just another example of higher education being corrupted by using a customer-service model. If students weren't capable of getting As and Bs on their own, the department would simply lower its standards to help the poor dears get the grades they wanted, instead of doing what the department should actually be doing, which was *teaching* the students.

Isaac was in his mid-fifties, and he'd been teaching full time at Koogler College for twenty-one years. When he'd first started there as an assistant professor, the college had been known for its academic excellence and rigor. But over the years, as tuition costs rose and grades lowered, the college made some 'adjustments' to keep enrollment up. To Isaac's mind, none of these changes truly benefitted students. Quite the opposite, in fact. And now Koogler wasn't much different in terms of how challenging its curriculum was than an average high school. And today's new 'adjustment' had infuriated him.

"Why don't we make our classes pass/fail?" he'd said. "Better yet, let's pass everyone, regardless of whether or not they show up or turn in any work. That would *really* raise our student success rate."

A couple of his allies in the department had backed him up, but the rest of the faculty, including the chair, had voted to make the change, and so it was done.

The students Isaac taught these days were silent and listless, with no curiosity or self-motivation. They never did the assigned reading from the textbook, and when they wrote papers, they were too short and riddled with grammar problems and logic flaws. This was not how he'd imagined his career playing out when he'd studied for his doctorate. Only nine more years until he could retire with full benefits. He could not fucking wait. He hoped he'd manage to hold on to his sanity until then, but there were no guarantees.

As he approached his house, he was irritated to see Alexandra's Accord parked out front at the curb. He'd repeatedly urged her to park in the garage – there was plenty of room for both her car and his Highlander. But she always refused to do it. He wondered if this was some passive-aggressive way to tell him that although she lived under his roof to save money while attending classes, this house wasn't home to her, and she would always view herself as a visitor rather than a resident.

Two can play at this game.

Instead of pulling his Highlander into the garage, he parked in the driveway. He doubted Alex would get the subtle comment he was making with this action – that as long as she lived in his house, she couldn't cut him out of her life – but he found it satisfying nevertheless.

He got out of his vehicle, leaving the satchel bag filled with papers behind on the passenger seat. He knew he should grade them tonight, but after the department meeting, the last thing he wanted to do was read drivel written by barely literate millennials. He closed the Highlander's door and locked it with his key remote, and that's when it hit him – a sense of *wrongness*. Maybe it was because he was exposed to the open air now, or maybe deciding to leave the papers behind made him forget about work for an instant, long enough for the Black Truck to make its presence known.

At first, he didn't know what was bothering him, just that *something* was. He frowned, and he swept his gaze around the cul-de-sac. He saw that Neal Wilkerson had started mowing his yard – about damn time too – but the task was only half-done. The man had a sloppy, undisciplined mind. No wonder he taught high school, and he was probably underqualified for *that* job. That only a few moments ago he'd been thinking of his job as basically teaching at a high-school level didn't occur to him. Self-examination wasn't one of his strong suits. His attention turned to the Hawkinses' house then. Martin kept his lawn neatly trimmed, but they didn't use a lawn service, so there were usually dandelions and white clover mixed in with the grass, the latter of which always had an unhealthy yellowish hue. Isaac had little use for Martin, his bimbo of a wife, and their not particularly intelligent child. Martin was a blue-collar Joe Sixpack who believed in guns, god, and the natural superiority of straight white men. Martin was a cretin, and worse, a bore.

The Parsonses next door were only marginally better. They were virtually agoraphobes and the few times Isaac had spoken to either of them, they hadn't struck him as especially smart. Plus, Spencer Parsons gave off a suspicious vibe, as if the man was hiding something. But the mother and son kept to themselves mostly, and Isaac appreciated this. As far as he was concerned, the best neighbors were the ones who minded their own business and left you the hell alone.

Now that he'd checked on the other houses on Brookside Court, only one remained: the Raines house. If you asked Isaac about the place, about what it was like to live so close to the House of Blood, he would've told you that a house was simply a structure – a physical arrangement of wood, concrete, duct work, electrical wires, plumbing, plaster, roof shingles, glass windows, and insulation. What happened inside that structure, whether good or ill, had no effect on the house itself, that a house couldn't be tainted by whatever evil might've taken place inside it. A house was just a house, nothing more.

And yet....

The Black Truck finally registered on his awareness.

He stared at it, trying to reconcile its strange appearance – it looked like it had been formed from solid shadow – with his sense of what was possible and what wasn't. He knew of no material that could absorb light so completely. The military might have something like it, but not some cheap-ass Ohio moving company. The obvious conclusion was that he was looking at something that didn't exist. That, or he was hallucinating. Since either possibility was disturbing, he put the Black Truck as far from his conscious mind as possible, turned away from the Raines house, and – muttering about the imbeciles he worked with – headed for the front door of his own home, wondering what to do for dinner.

★   ★   ★

Neal and Kandice sat at their dining table eating grilled chicken pecan salads. Neal had a glass of water to drink, while Kandice had a glass of Diet Coke. Neal had tried for years to get her to kick the soda habit – even diet cola was bad for you – but he'd never been able to convince her.

A girl's got to have some vices, she'd once told him.

It had seemed like such an innocent comment at the time.

"You need to shower," Kandice said. "Not to put too fine a point on it, but you stink."

"How about I finish mowing after dinner and *then* take a shower?"

He knew Kandice showered at the rec center every day before coming home. He wondered what the women's showers were like there. Were there private stalls or was it an open communal shower, where everyone could see everyone else naked? Did Kandice wrap a towel around herself as she came and went from the shower, or did she walk there and back naked? Did she notice the other women showering and the women changing into and out of street clothes? Of course she did. She wasn't blind.

Kandice snapped her fingers in front of his face and he jumped.

"Sorry," he said. "Got lost in thought."

"Mmm-hmm. And I can guess what you were thinking about."

"I was wondering what our new neighbors will be like," he lied. "What kind of family knowingly buys a house where a bunch of murders took place?"

He hoped that he could distract her with this subject, but he'd never been any good at fooling her. She could smell bullshit a mile away – especially his.

"You were thinking about the same thing you've been thinking… no, *obsessing* about for the last couple months – me."

This was not a conversation Neal wanted to have, and he tried to think of some way to avoid it.

"I told you, it's going to take me some time to adjust. But I'll get there."

Two months ago, they'd been sitting on the couch, Kandice snuggled up against him, his arm wrapped around her. They'd been watching a movie, a drama about a woman struggling to come out as bisexual to her family and friends, some of whom were cool with it, some decidedly less so. At one point, Neal had mused aloud, "Can you imagine how hard it would be to tell someone you were bisexual when you couldn't be certain how they'd react?"

Kandice pulled away from him and gave him the strangest look, as if he'd said something so outrageous she was having trouble believing it.

"*I'm* bisexual," she said.

At first he thought she was making a joke, and he started to smile, was thinking of a witty comeback, but then he saw how serious her expression was, and he felt his stomach drop. She wasn't joking. He looked at her for several seconds, desperately trying to come up with an appropriate response. But the best he could come up with was "Uh...what?"

Her brow furrowed, a sure sign that she was starting to get mad.

"I told you when we first started dating. Remember?"

"No," he admitted. "It's not the kind of a thing a person forgets."

"Are you saying I *didn't* tell you?"

He picked up the remote from the coffee table and turned off the TV. He did this more as a stalling tactic than because he wanted there to be no distractions as they talked.

"I don't recall a specific conversation about it," he said.

He was fighting to sound unbothered by her revelation, relaxed, casual even, but inside he was on the verge of panic. Kandice and he had been together for ten years, and they'd gotten married seven years ago. All that time, he'd believed he knew her, believed their relationship was built on a solid foundation. But now he felt that foundation crumbling beneath him. How could he have not known something so fundamental about his wife's identity? Had he ever really known her at all? What other aspects of their relationship did he hold mistaken beliefs about? Was anything true, was anything *real*?

A memory returned to him then, of a night during the first year when they'd been dating. They'd made love in his apartment and were lying in bed, holding each other and talking about whatever came to mind, when Kandice told him a story.

"When I was a sophomore in high school, I had a fourth period Spanish II class. Every day, at the same time, this girl would walk by in the hall. The teacher kept her classroom door open, so I always got a good look at her. I never learned her name or why she walked by our class at the same exact time every day. Maybe she was a student aide to one of the teachers, and she had to run errands for him or her. Whatever the reason, I was happy to see her each day. I found her fascinating to watch."

Neal hadn't commented on her story when she finished, and she hadn't elaborated further. At the time, he hadn't thought there'd been anything particularly revelatory about the story, but now....

He told Kandice about his memory.

"And that didn't clue you in that I'm bisexual?"

"No. I mean, I understood that you felt some sort of attraction for the girl in the hallway, but I put it down to normal adolescent curiosity. I figured sexuality is a continuum, and people explore different aspects of themselves as sexual beings at different times in their lives. I thought you were just sharing a story about one of these moments with me. I didn't think you were making a statement about a core part of your identity. And it's not like you ever said anything about it again, not once in ten years. Why didn't you ever talk about it?"

"You never brought it up, so I assumed you weren't comfortable talking about it. And I was perfectly happy with you, so it wasn't like my being bisexual was going to have any real bearing on our relationship."

Kandice was an extremely intelligent person, smarter than Neal was by a long shot. She could've chosen any major in college and excelled at it, but she eventually graduated with a degree in art history. She'd always been into exercise, though, and eventually she began teaching fitness classes. She'd done so more for fun – and to keep herself fit – than anything, but she found she really enjoyed it. She said her mind was so busy all the time that it was nice to focus on her body for a while. She found it meditative. Plus, she liked helping people live healthier lives. But the problem with being so damn smart was that sometimes she thought she'd communicated something clearly when in reality she'd left out some important details. It was like half the conversation took place in the real world, while the other half happened in her head.

They'd spoken much more that night, and in the end Neal told her that he'd be okay, that all that mattered was that she loved him and was dedicated to their marriage. He wasn't homophobic, considered himself an ally to the LGBTQ community, had a stepbrother who was gay and who he loved dearly. He was certain he'd adjust in time. But two months later, he was still struggling to come to terms with Kandice's sexuality and how it factored into their relationship.

Kandice speared a chunk of chicken with her fork, brought it to her mouth, chewed, and swallowed.

"I think we should see a marriage counselor," she said.

The words couldn't have shocked him more if Kandice had slapped his face as she spoke them. He couldn't respond, could only sit there and look at her. Since he didn't speak, she continued.

"This has obviously become an issue for us."

"For me, you mean," he muttered.

"For *us*. I have no doubt that we'll eventually work this out. I love you. I just think we could use some professional guidance."

Neal had only a few friends who'd gone through divorces but in each case, the first sign that their marriages were in serious trouble was when their spouse suggested they seek counseling.

"We don't need to see someone." He reached across the table to take her hands. "Like you said, we'll get through this. It'll just take some time, that's all."

He felt Kandice's hands curl into fists beneath his, but she didn't pull away from his touch.

"When was the last time we made love?" she asked.

The question took him by surprise. "I don't know."

"Exactly. It's been so long that you can't remember. I do, though. It's been five weeks."

"That can't possibly be right."

"I marked it on the wall calendar. I put a little s next to the date. S for sex."

"We've gone through dry spells before," he said.

"When one of us has been really sick for a long time, sure. But never anything like this." She paused, then in a softer voice added, "Do you think there's something wrong with me?"

"Wrong? I don't— Wait, you mean because you're *bisexual*? God, no!"

Neal thought of himself as woke, at least as woke as a white man born and raised in the privilege of middle-class America could be. He didn't judge others by their gender or expression of gender, their race, religion, sexuality, or culture. He'd married a black woman, hadn't he? People were people, and they were all equally worthy of being treated with dignity and respect.

But if he was as woke as he believed, why was he having so much trouble adjusting to the fact that his wife was bisexual? He felt guilty, as if he'd somehow betrayed Kandice's love by being unable to unconditionally accept her for who she was. *All* of who she was. But he couldn't help how he felt, and his small-mindedness shamed him.

He stood and pulled Kandice to her feet. He brought her close and gave her a long, passionate kiss. When they pulled apart, he said, "Why don't we go to the bedroom so you can put an S next to today's date?"

"What about the lawn?" she asked with a teasing smile.

"It'll still be there tomorrow."

"Okay, but you have to shower first."

"Only if you promise to join me," he said.

"Deal."

Hand in hand, they left the dining room and headed down the hall toward the bedroom. Neal smiled, but inwardly he was nervous as hell. He was heterosexual, Kandice was bisexual. They didn't match, not in the way he'd thought they had, not anymore. His knowledge of her true sexuality had opened a gulf between them. At least it had on his part. He didn't fully understand the nature of this gulf, but he could *feel* it. The trouble was, he had no idea how to cross that gulf so they could be emotionally close again. He doubted one early-evening session of lovemaking would fix the problem. But maybe it would be one tiny step in the right direction. An image came into his mind, then, unbidden. He envisioned Kandice and Cora in bed, naked, fondling each other's breasts as they kissed. He tried to banish the image, but it remained.

And god help him, it was making him as hard as a rock.

He wondered if Kandice was imagining the same scenario, or one like it, and if so, if it was making her wet. His erection began to subside immediately, and he began to feel that maybe having sex right now wasn't a good idea. Too late now, though. He'd have to do his best to get through it and hope Kandice didn't realize how conflicted he was.

Maybe we do need to see a counselor, he thought.

★   ★   ★

"Fuck, fuck, fuck, fuck, *fuck!*"

Martin Hawkins slammed his right palm on the steering wheel of his Ford F-150 pickup – with bumper stickers that said *Don't Tread on Me, Build the Wall,* and *Fuck Socialism* – as he shouted the last *fuck.*

Goddamn Charlie Knudson! The motherfucker was a cheating bastard, Martin knew it! He just hadn't been able to prove it yet. After a long, hot, sweaty day on the road crew – during which Martin had mostly directed traffic around their current work site – he'd wanted nothing more than to get home, grab a cold one from the fridge, sit on the couch, and put up his aching feet. But Charlie – who'd driven the asphalt paver all day – had an alternative suggestion.

Come on over to my place. We'll have a few and play some poker. I've invited some of my other friends. Ones who are real good at losing, if you catch my drift.

Martin hadn't asked if they'd be gambling. It was a given, and he hadn't called to let Cora know he'd be home a few hours late. He believed a man – especially after working his ass off all day to support his family – didn't have to ask permission to have a little fun. Okay, so maybe he hadn't worked all *that* hard. Directing traffic wasn't exactly back-breaking labor. The real reason he hadn't called Cora was because he knew how upset she'd get if she found out he was gambling – again. Despite what Cora thought, he didn't have a problem with gambling, wasn't addicted to it or anything. But he could get *too* excited about it sometimes, and he'd keep betting when he should probably bow out of the game and minimize his losses. And – while he'd never admit this to anyone – he usually lost more than he won.

But tonight had been different. Charlie Knudson had been the big winner, taking almost every hand. Martin didn't mind losing if the game was fair – a lie; he *hated* losing – but Charlie had obviously done something to rig the cards in his favor. No one won so many hands in a row without cheating. It was mathematically impossible, simple as that. Martin had lost close to three hundred dollars this evening. He hadn't had that much cash on him, so he'd had to run out to an ATM, with fucking Charlie Knudson riding shotgun. *Just to keep you company,* Charlie had said.

You mean just to make sure I didn't drive off without paying, Martin thought. Although in truth, that's exactly what he'd been planning to do.

That withdrawal had cleaned out their checking account, and their savings account had been empty for months. He had a twenty in his wallet, and that was it. They had twenty fucking dollars to live on until his next paycheck, and he wouldn't get paid again for almost two weeks. And all because goddamn Charlie Knudson had somehow cheated his ass off. The man had stolen Martin's money the same as if he'd robbed Martin at gunpoint. Martin had to do something about it. No fucking way could he let this stand. The question was, what *could* he do? He was racking his brain, trying to figure out some way of getting his money back from that thieving bastard, when a black Cadillac pulled up beside him.

He was on McAdams Street, not far from home. There were four lanes – two going south, two going north – and he was in the left lane heading south. The Caddy pulled up on his right, engine so quiet that at first Martin wasn't aware of the vehicle. But something drew his attention toward it. Maybe he saw a flash of movement in his peripheral vision. Or maybe it was the color of the car, a black deeper and darker than any he'd ever seen before. Or maybe it was simply a sense that something wasn't right, like the feeling in the air when a big storm is rapidly approaching, a charged atmosphere of energy building, ready to be unleashed at any moment. Whatever the reason, Martin turned his head and looked at the black Cadillac. He thought the car had tinted windows, but after a few seconds, he realized that the windows, like the rest of the vehicle, were solid black. It looked as if they'd been painted over. No, more than that, like they weren't windows at all, that the doors were solid units with no openings whatsoever. But then, as if to prove his impression had been mistaken, the back passenger window slid downward. Except, that wasn't quite what it did. It didn't slide so much as an opening seemed to *emerge* from the black substance, like a bubble rising out of thick, hot tar. When it was all the way open, Martin saw a girl. At least, he thought it was a girl. He had trouble making out her features. They kept coming into and out of focus, as if his eyes couldn't manage to see her properly. Or as if they didn't *want* to see her.

She smiled, blew him a kiss, called out something, waved, and then the window closed, and the Cadillac accelerated and moved off.

Martin felt a chill travel up and down his spine. There had been something in the girl's gaze, a...the only word he could come up with was *hunger*. And although his pickup windows were closed, he thought he'd been able to make out what she'd said to him. It sounded like *See you soon.*

Martin forgot about Charlie Knudson, forgot about how pissed Cora would be when she found out he'd been gambling again – *and* how much he'd lost. He kept thinking about the car...and that strange girl.

When he reached Brookside Court, he wasn't surprised to see the black Cadillac parked in front of the Raines house. It was almost as if he'd expected it to be there. He also wasn't surprised by the large black truck in the driveway. It appeared to be made from the same kind of shadowy substance as the Caddy, so it only made sense that it was here.

See you soon.

Had the girl known they were going to be neighbors? And if she had, *how* did she know? It wasn't as if she and her family had stopped by his house to introduce themselves.

He slowed as he approached his driveway, hoping to catch a glimpse of the girl again, but no one exited the Caddy. Maybe they'd already gotten out and gone inside to check on the movers' progress. But he had the feeling that they were still inside the car, watching him intently, somehow able to see through the pitch-black substance of their vehicle. It was a ridiculous thought, of course. Why the hell would they do such a thing? But he couldn't shake the impression that they were still in the car, watching, waiting. Waiting for what, he didn't know. Just waiting.

He pulled into his driveway, thumbed the remote to open the garage door, then drove inside. He parked, cut the engine, and pressed the remote once more to close the garage door. On impulse, he looked over his shoulder, and he saw, standing at the foot of his driveway, six shadowy figures, little more than dark smudges in the air. And one of those smudges raised a hand and waved slowly. And then the descending garage door blocked his vision as it closed. He faced forward, put his hands on the steering wheel, and gripped it so tight it felt like his knuckles might break through the skin.

You had too much to drink at Charlie's, and you're so goddamn mad at the sonofabitch that you're not thinking straight. You're seeing things that aren't there – or at least not seeing them the way they really are.

He felt a little better, but he remained in his pickup, staring at the garage wall and holding on to the steering wheel, for a very long time.

★　　★　　★

Sunset is in progress, and the Eldred are in transition between their day forms and their night forms. Car, too. This occurs every dusk and dawn, regardless of whether they are outside or inside. They don't need to be directly exposed to the rising or setting sun for this process to occur. Their bodies always know what time it is and respond accordingly. In some ways, the transition is like taking off work clothes after a long day and slipping into comfortable, lounge-around-the-house clothes. In other ways, it's not like that at all.

After Father Hunger waves and Martin's garage door closes, the Eldred drift back toward their house – their Stalking Ground – moving as silently as shadows, for at the moment, that's mostly what they are. Machine Head clomps alongside them, moving in herky-jerky spastic motions, thanks to the injuries his new body had sustained before he claimed it. The Eldred don't mind. They find it amusing. Machine Head is always good for a laugh or two.

The movers won't begin their work until full dark, but that's all right. The Eldred are eager to enter their new home and begin establishing their separate Domains. They will need some time to prepare them before the movers can begin their work, so the sooner they get started, the better.

When they reach the front door, the Eldred slide between the door and the jamb. Machine Head's form is fixed, however, and he cannot follow them this way. The real estate agent took the house key with her earlier that day. She'd been so traumatized by the visions that the house – with the Eldreds' help – had shown her, that she'd forgotten to put the key back in the lock box hanging on the front doorknob. The Eldred could open the door for him, but practical details like this often escape them, and they have more important matters to tend to. Machine Head steps to the door, glowing green eyes fixed on the empty lock box, relays clicking inside his metal skull as he works to determine the best way for him to gain entrance while causing the least amount of damage. Machine Head doesn't think in human terms, but if he did, the conclusion he comes to could be roughly translated as *Fuck it*.

He grips the knob and presses the full weight of his body against the door. He boosts his host's adrenal gland production and twists the knob, while at the same time pushing the door with his body. He is rewarded with a cracking sound as the wood breaks, and the door swings easily inward. He feels no sense of triumph, not even mild satisfaction, at his victory. Machine Head possesses only the most rudimentary emotions, and he rarely allows himself to experience them. Emotions muddy his thoughts, making it more difficult for him to accomplish his tasks. He sees no benefit in them. He steps into the house, and he can already sense the Eldred are at work. He can feel the house's interior expanding around him, even as the exterior remains the same size.

All is at it should be, and Machine Head feels a sense of rightness. It's a poor substitute for contentment, but it's all he's got. He takes up a position next to the front door where he will wait for dark, and when the movers emerge from their truck to start their work, he will assist them.

"*One lives to serve*," he says, voice a monotone, the words sounding as if they're spoken into a tin can. His eyelights dim, he goes motionless, and waits, as the house's interior continues expanding around him.

CHAPTER FIVE

Kandice sat cross-legged on her front porch, smoking a cigarette. She and Neal usually left the porchlight on at night, but she'd turned it off before coming outside. She didn't want any of the neighbors to see her. If any of them were up and happened to look out their windows, the most they would see was the glowing red dot of her burning cigarette. She'd given up smoking soon after she and Neal began dating. He had mild asthma, and cigarette smoke irritated his lungs and could set off an attack. What Neal didn't know was that she kept a pack hidden away in the house in case she really *needed* a smoke, and tonight she definitely needed one.

She wasn't sure what time it was. She hadn't checked before getting out of bed, taking a cigarette from her stash – which she kept hidden in a plastic storage bag in a kitchen cupboard behind a bag of wheat flour – and a book of matches from the junk drawer. It could be anywhere from one to four in the morning, and what the hell did it matter?

She usually slept in pajamas, but even though the ones she had on now were made of thick, cottony material, she'd still grabbed a sweater from the coat closet on her way out. She got cold easily, and she liked the comfort of wearing an extra layer. She needed that comfort tonight as much as she needed nicotine.

She and Neal had attempted to make love earlier, but it had been a disaster from the start, and it had only gotten worse as they continued. She'd wanted to stop, but Neal insisted they go on, and she'd reluctantly agreed. That had been a mistake – a *huge* one. Neal hadn't been able to get an erection right away, which wasn't normal for him. At least, it hadn't been. It had become more common the last couple months, ever since his *realization*, as he called it, that she was bi. Neal said he could take care of her first, and that would turn him on so much that he was sure to get hard. She was doubtful, but she'd let him try. He'd used his tongue, his fingers, and finally her favorite vibrator. It all felt good, of course, but she didn't come close to climaxing, and eventually she started to get sore inside, and she asked him to stop.

He felt upset then, so she gently pushed him back onto the bed and went to work on him with her mouth. He always came when she gave him head, but this time his dick remained soft, no matter what she did. Finally, she stopped and lay down next to him, and they held each other for a while without speaking. Neal had his hands on her, but so lightly that she barely felt it. It was like he didn't really want to touch her, and was only doing so because he thought that was what she wanted. He seemed emotionally distant, too, and while normally she might've tried to encourage him to talk about what was wrong, lately all they seemed to do was talk about what was wrong in their marriage. And of course, what was wrong was always *her*. Or more precisely, her sexuality. She didn't have the mental energy to go over the same ground again. Unfortunately, Neal started talking on his own, and she dutifully lay there and listened to him say the same shit he'd told her a dozen times before.

He hadn't understood that when she'd told him the story about being attracted to that girl in high school that she was making a profound statement about her sexual identity. If only she'd been clearer, more direct. Now that he *did* know, he was trying his best to adjust, he really was. He didn't think anything was wrong with her, he really didn't, and he wanted to be fully accepting and supportive of who she was. He knew this shouldn't change anything between them. Even if she was bisexual, she'd been so the entire time they'd been together, and it hadn't had a negative impact on their relationship, so why should it now? She loved him, he loved her, that should be the end of it. Except he worried that there was an important part of her sexual identity that she hadn't fully explored. She wished she'd never told him that, aside from a couple brief make-out sessions with her dorm roommate during her freshman year in college, she'd never kissed a woman, let alone had sex with one. He could give her a heterosexual experience, but he could never give her a homosexual one. He could never be a woman. What if she went the rest of her life without ever making love with a woman? Would she feel that she'd missed out on a vital part of being alive? Would she regret her choices, regret marrying him? If he loved her – and he did, so, so *much* – shouldn't he want her to be sexually fulfilled in every way she needed? Maybe they should consider having an open relationship for a while, maybe even bring in a third partner so she and Neal could still be together *and* she could experience sex with a woman. He wasn't sure he could do either of these things, but he was willing to try if that's what she really wanted.

She'd let him spill it all out again, his confusion, his insecurities, his misunderstanding of what it was like – at least for her – to be bisexual. She'd learned over the last two months that no matter what she said to him on the subject, it didn't sink in. He was too wrapped up in his own feelings to listen to hers, let alone understand them.

She hadn't come out to many people in her life, and each time she'd tried, it hadn't worked out well. Her lesbian friends thought she was a lesbian in denial, too afraid to commit to being one of them. Her straight friends thought it was a phase she was going through, a time of experimentation, that she'd eventually settle down with a man. Or they thought she wanted to engage in MFF sex because if she was bi, that meant she always wanted to have a partner of each sex, right?

She'd tried telling them – and Neal – that for her, being bisexual meant that she was capable of finding either gender attractive, and that she was open to having a romantic relationship with either a man or a woman. It didn't mean that she wanted to alternate between male and female sex partners, nor did it mean that she needed to fuck a man and a woman at the same time. Sure, that might be fun, but she liked having a relationship with one person at a time, enjoyed the deep intimacy that for her only came from a long-term relationship with one individual. In short, she was monogamous, and the person she'd fallen in love with happened to be male. For her, that was the end of the matter. She intended to stay with Neal, and if that meant she never had sex with a woman, so what? She felt completely fulfilled by Neal in every way, including sexually. She hoped they never got divorced or – god forbid – he predeceased her, but if either of those things happened, maybe she'd find love with someone else eventually, and that person might be either a man or woman. It all depended on the *person,* not which set of genitals they had.

But Neal couldn't understand this. He said he did, and she knew he really wanted to, was *desperate* to, but emotionally he wasn't there yet, and she feared he might never be. And if that happened, if he couldn't find a way to adjust, their marriage would be in serious trouble.

Sometimes she wished she'd never said anything to him about her being bisexual. Obviously, she'd done a piss-poor job of telling him when they were dating. She'd been so afraid of how he would respond that she'd been too subtle, and when he'd acted like it was no big deal, she'd been so relieved that she hadn't wanted to discuss the matter further. And as years passed and he never spoke about it, she figured that he was okay with it as long as she didn't bring it up. Like avoiding mentioning an old boyfriend, something like that. And she'd been content to leave it at that, although she'd felt a little sad that Neal didn't want to know that part of her. Whenever they watched a movie, she could mention that she found any of the male actors hot, and he'd reciprocate by telling her which women he liked. But she didn't feel comfortable telling him which women she found sexy. She'd never really been part of the LGBTQ community, never marched in a Pride parade, and she thought she'd like being involved, if for no other reason than so she could meet other bisexuals, people who could understand her in ways straight and gay people couldn't. But she feared that if she brought this up to Neal, he'd start worrying that she wanted to explore her identity *sexually* as well as socially and politically. So she'd said nothing.

Despite Neal's emotional difficulties with his *realization* of her sexuality, she felt a weight lifted from her that she hadn't realized she'd been carrying. At least now she didn't have to hide part of herself from someone she loved more than anyone else. That was a relief. She just hoped it didn't ultimately tear their marriage apart.

"Got a light?"

Kandice jumped and turned in the direction of the voice. When she saw it was Cora standing on the lawn, cigarette in hand, she couldn't help laughing.

"You bitch! You scared me to death!"

Cora grinned as she came over and sat next to Kandice.

"I know it was a shitty thing to do, but I couldn't resist. I wasn't kidding about that light, though."

Kandice had brought the book of matches outside with her, and she handed it to Cora. Cora thanked her, lit her cigarette, blew out the match, tossed it into the grass, then set the matches on the porch between them. She took a long drag of her cigarette and blew out the smoke slowly.

"You're up late," Kandice said.

Cora smiled. "Look who's talking."

When the match had been burning, Kandice had seen that Cora wore a red windbreaker, unzipped, and copper-colored pajamas underneath. The nipples of her large breasts were erect in the cool night and strained against the fabric of her PJ top. Kandice was glad when Cora extinguished the match. She wasn't uncomfortable being around another woman whose nipples she could more-or-less see. Boobs were beautiful, after all. But she'd never told Cora that she was bisexual, and she didn't like the idea of Cora sitting next to her with her stiff nipples without knowing about Kandice's sexuality. Knowing Cora, she probably wouldn't give a damn, but she wasn't one hundred percent sure. And she doubted Martin would be thrilled to learn his wife was hanging out with their bisexual neighbor. The man was a complete jackass, one of those people who automatically distrusted or disliked anyone who wasn't like him. She would never understand what Cora saw in him. Maybe he was different with her. Or maybe he had a big dick. He could have a fourteen-inch cock thick as a tree trunk, and it wouldn't be enough to make up for his personality as far as Kandice was concerned.

"Anything wrong?" Kandice asked.

Cora didn't answer immediately. She sat quietly for a bit, smoking. Finally, she exhaled smoke with a long sigh.

"Martin came home late tonight. He missed dinner. Didn't call or anything."

Uh-oh, Kandice thought.

The women spoke softly so they wouldn't wake anyone, or draw the attention of anyone who, like them, wasn't sleeping.

"I grilled him when he got home, but he said he stopped off at a bar after work to hoist a few with some friends and lost track of time.

It was bullshit, though. I can always tell when he lies to me. I think he was probably playing cards again."

Kandice blew out a stream of smoke.

"Fuck."

Martin had what Cora called a gambling 'problem'. Kandice thought that the man was a full-blown addict.

"When I called him on it, he got mad, said I didn't trust him, that I probably thought he was fucking around on me, but he loved me too much to ever do something like that." She let out a bitter laugh. "At this point, I almost wish he *was* screwing some other chick. At least then we wouldn't be in danger of losing our goddamn house."

"Seriously?"

Kandice's cigarette was finished. She stubbed it out on the porch's concrete, and although it was her policy to have only one cigarette, even in an emergency, she removed another from the pack and lit it.

"Yeah," Cora said, sounding weary. "He keeps pissing our money away, and we don't have enough for bills. We're already behind one mortgage payment. If we miss a second one...." She let the sentence trail off. "I couldn't sleep. I came out onto the porch to get some air, and I saw the glow of your cigarette. I figured insomniacs love company, right?"

Kandice didn't know what to say. She was so angry at Martin. How could he do this to Cora and Vivienne? Intellectually, she knew gambling addiction was just as serious a problem as any other kind of addiction, but emotionally she couldn't help feeling Martin was being a selfish, irresponsible prick. But she knew saying these things wouldn't help Cora feel any better, so she kept them to herself.

"Do you need money? Neal and I have some put aside in savings, and we can—"

Cora waved away Kandice's words with the hand that held her cigarette.

"Thanks, but even if I wanted to take you up on it, Martin would just use the money to gamble some more. He can't stop himself."

Kandice searched for something to say to cheer Cora up, but she couldn't think of anything. Cora, perhaps sensing the awkwardness Kandice felt, changed the subject.

"So what do you think of our new neighbors?"

"There's not much to think yet, is there? All we've seen so far is a moving truck and a Cadillac. No sign of whoever drives them."

"Which is weird."

"Very."

The women were quiet for several moments as they watched the Raines house – Kandice thought she'd always think of it that way, the *Raines House* – and continued smoking. Brookside Court had no streetlights. Few of the suburban neighborhoods in Rockridge did. The Raines house was only a featureless dark shape, almost indistinguishable from the night around it. As for the truck and car, they were so black to start with that they might as well have been invisible now.

Then there came a sound, a sort of whirring hum, like electronics coming to life. But underneath this sound was a lower tone that made Kandice think of a rumbling growl of a large animal, something with matted fur and far too many teeth. Pale blue-white light appeared, just a sliver at first, but then it expanded. It took her a moment to realize what was happening. The back of the moving van was opening, and the light they were seeing came from the storage area's interior.

Kandice exchanged a look with Cora and saw the same mixture of emotions on the other woman's face as she felt. Surprise, confusion, excitement, and fear. Who the hell waited until the middle of the night to start unloading their stuff? And that light.... There was something about it that didn't seem normal. It had a strange, diffuse glow, more like bioluminescence than artificial light. What was she thinking, that the truck was *alive* somehow? That was crazy. But then a lot of crazy things seemed possible, even likely, in the empty still hours between midnight and dawn.

The garage doors of the Raines house opened. There was no light inside, but the illumination from the truck spilled into the garage, revealing a group of shadowy forms. One was a man in a T-shirt and shorts who appeared to be wearing a silver helmet of some kind. *Safety first,* Kandice thought. The others were shorter but bulkier, and they all wore dark gray coveralls. *Must be the movers,* she decided. She couldn't make out the features on their faces, and she was sure it was a trick of the light, but it seemed as if the movers had an extra set of arms apiece. She blinked, and then they each had only two, blinked again, they had four, blinked again, two. She rubbed her eyes with her free hand, and when she looked again the movers had only two arms apiece. *Just because you only see two arms,* she thought, *doesn't mean they don't have more.* It was a bizarre notion, but one she couldn't shake.

There were six movers, and they stood alongside the man wearing the helmet – three on one side, three on the other – waiting. For what, Kandice wasn't certain. For him to give them a command? Maybe.

The man in the helmet – which kind of looked more like a mask when she squinted her eyes – raised his right arm and pointed to the truck. The movers hurried forward, as if eager to get to work. A moment after they disappeared into the truck's storage space, the helmeted man followed. Several moments later they began coming out, each of them carrying something. Some carried boxes, large ones, stacked on top of each other. Kandice couldn't see how anyone could hold so much weight at once. *Maybe the boxes don't contain anything heavy,* she thought. Others carried objects such as wrought-iron trellises, rolls of what looked like green felt, dining chairs – so many of them! – bird cages covered by white cloth, and…were those slot machines? Weird.

The last person to emerge from the truck was the helmeted man. Balanced on his left hand he carried a flat of small plants that resembled miniature trees. In his right, he carried a pale white sphere that glowed gently with its own light. Ahead of him, the movers – who still sometimes seemed to have four arms apiece, and sometimes only two – marched into the garage one by one, presumably heading into the house. The helmeted man followed, but he paused on the garage's threshold and slowly his head turned toward Kandice and Cora. The women froze, and Kandice wished she hadn't given in to the temptation and lit a second cigarette. The burning red tip – not only hers, but Cora's as well – had given them away. She remembered reading somewhere that during wartime, soldiers who smoked in the dark made themselves perfect targets for snipers. She felt exposed, vulnerable, *seen.* And did the helmeted (masked) man's eyes flash green for a second? It had to be her imagination, but that's what it looked like.

The helmeted man continued looking in their direction for several long moments before at last turning away and walking into the garage. When he was swallowed by the darkness inside, Kandice let out a shaky sigh. She flicked her cigarette into the grass, eager to rid herself of it, as if it were a venomous creature that might bite her any second. Cora followed suit. Kandice would have to remember to retrieve the cigarettes in the morning before Neal saw them.

"What the *fuck* was that?" Cora asked.

Kandice could only shake her head.

They sat in silence for several more moments before Cora spoke again.

"I better go. I should…should check on Vivienne, make sure she's okay. Her bedroom…."

She didn't finish the thought, but she didn't need to. Kandice knew that Vivienne's room was located on the west end of Cora and Martin's house – the end which faced the Raines place.

"I'll talk to you later, okay?"

Cora's smile was weak, uncertain, as if she was afraid to go back to her house but didn't want to admit it. Kandice put her hand on Cora's shoulder and gave what she hoped was a reassuring squeeze. Then Cora stood and hurried across the lawn back to her house. She kept her gaze focused on the Raines place the entire way. Once Cora was safely inside her home – and likely checking every door and window to make sure they were all closed and locked – Kandice stood. She'd never been comfortable moving to Brookside Court, hadn't wanted to live so close to the infamous House of Blood, no matter how cheap the homes around it were. But Neal had talked her into it, and now she wished more than ever that she hadn't given in. One good thing, though. At least she and Neal didn't live directly next door to the Raines house – and whatever was going on there tonight. She felt sorry for Cora and Vivienne, even for Martin, but she wouldn't trade places with them. No fucking way.

She gathered her emergency pack of cigarettes and book of matches, and she hurried inside. And as she closed the door, Machine Head and the four-armed movers walked out of the garage and toward the truck, ready to get the next load.

*   *   *

Alex Ruiz couldn't sleep. She lay in her bed, covers bunched up and twisted from her tossing and turning. She stared up at her bedroom ceiling, seeing nothing but darkness there. *An apt metaphor,* as her father might say.

Finals week was coming up, and she felt overwhelmed. When she'd enrolled for spring semester, she'd originally only wanted to take three classes so she could concentrate more fully on each one and not spread herself so thin. She also worked in the university library fifteen hours a week. She liked it, so much so that she was considering changing her major from liberal arts to library science. But despite her initial determination not to overwork herself, her father had convinced her to take six classes so she would remain on track to graduate in four years. She didn't care how long it took her to graduate, but as far as her father was concerned, anyone who took longer than four years to get an undergraduate degree was simply being lazy. She wished she hadn't listened to him, but she needed him to fill out and sign the form that allowed her to get discounted tuition as a family member of a professor. And while he hadn't overtly threatened to withhold his signature if she didn't take six classes, he got his meaning across. He always did, one way or another.

She didn't make enough money working at the library to live on her own – unfortunately – but her meager salary paid for her meals on campus and for gas to drive back and forth from her dad's house. She was paying for her tuition through a combination of scholarships and loans – mostly the latter – and she was barely squeaking by. It would be nice if her father and mother chipped in to help her out. She was their only child after all. It wasn't as if they had to worry about putting anyone else through school. But as far as her father was concerned, her tuition discount – along with letting her live with him rent free – was his contribution to her education costs. And as for her mother...she was usually too busy traveling with whatever man she was currently dating to find time to talk to her daughter, let alone give any money to her.

She had to do well in her classes these last couple weeks. No, she had to absolutely *crush* them. Right now, her grades were decent, but not spectacular. She still had time to bring them up, but there was also plenty of time for them to go straight into the toilet, too. It all depended on how she did on the final papers and exams. But right now, she felt so stressed and burned out that no matter how hard she studied, she couldn't seem to retain any information. She'd gotten home early this afternoon, well before her father, and aside from taking a quick break for dinner, all she'd done was school work. She hadn't knocked off until almost one in the morning, and she'd only stopped then because she couldn't keep her eyes open any longer. So what happened the instant her head hit the fucking pillow? She became wide awake, unable to stop worrying about school. Now it was – she checked her phone – 2:13 a.m., and she was no closer to falling asleep than she had been when she lay down.

Screw it.

She got up, phone still in hand, and walked over to her desk. She wore an XXL men's T-shirt which hung past her shorts down to mid-thigh. She loved sleeping in big shirts like this. They felt so cozy, like she was wearing her own personal little blanket.

She sat on the desk chair, opened her laptop, and woke the computer. If she couldn't sleep, she might as well try to get some more work done. She logged on to her student page on the university's website and selected the class she was most worried about: Sociology 102. She wasn't taking it with her dad. That would've been an absolute nightmare. But it was the one class out of the six she was currently taking that he'd give her the most shit about if she didn't ace it. She decided to review the last couple chapters they'd gone over in the online textbook, but after reading for several minutes, it was clear that while her brain might be awake, it was too exhausted to make sense out of written words.

She closed her laptop, got up, and left her room. Her father's bedroom was directly across the hall from hers, but she didn't worry about waking him. He slept deeply, and he snored. She figured if his own snoring didn't wake him, nothing else would either. She went down the hall, into the kitchen, got a caffeine-free soda from the fridge, opened it, and took a long drink. The cold soda made her teeth ache pleasantly, and she felt the coolness spread through her chest as she swallowed. These sensations helped ground her in the here and now, pulled her mind away from looking inward and devouring itself. She'd visited one of the university's mental health counselors a month ago, and she'd told her that whenever she found herself in the grip of anxiety, the best way to counter it was by physical stimulation.

I don't mean sex, the counselor had said, laughing. *Although that works, too. I mean going outside, taking a walk, feeling the sun on your skin, the wind in your hair. Walk barefoot through grass, go outside without an umbrella when it's raining.... Anxiety is always about fear of the future. Physical sensations remind us to stay in the present. They calm us, center us.*

Alex took another long drink of her soda, put the bottle on the counter, then headed for the patio door. It was located in the dining room, probably so people could have an outside view while they ate. Considering that the backyard had nothing but grass in it and was enclosed by a rusty chain-link fence, the view was less than spectacular. Her father usually kept the blinds closed when they ate, assuming that both of them sat down for a meal together. More often they ate at different times, and in different places. Sometimes, she thought it was like they lived in the same house but inhabited separate dimensions, one never knowing that the other was there. On one level, she preferred it this way. Her father was *not* the easiest person to get along with. But she also found it sad. Shouldn't a father and daughter enjoy spending at least a little time together now and then?

She opened the blinds, drew them back, unlocked the patio door, slid it open, and stepped out into the night, phone slipped into the right pocket of her shorts. Once outside, she closed the door behind her.

The night air was cool, and she shivered. She didn't want to insulate herself from the physical sensations of being outside, even uncomfortable ones. She wanted to experience them. She walked to the edge of the patio and sat down, her butt on cold concrete, her feet in dewy grass. She made herself breathe slow and easy, and before long she felt herself beginning to relax.

That's when she heard the noise. It came from her right, a kind of cracking sound that she didn't recognize. It was like the sound wood might make if it was being stretched, but that was impossible. You couldn't stretch wood, could you? You could bend it, break it, saw it in half, but *stretch*? No way.

She drew her legs up to her chest and pulled her T-shirt over them. The Parsonses next door didn't have a fence, and the noise made her think Spencer might be outside, doing Christ knew what in his backyard. Spencer had never done anything specifically to make her think he was a creeper. She hardly ever saw him or his mother. But the few times she'd spoken to the man, she'd felt her skin crawl. She didn't know why he made her feel this way, but she decided to trust her instincts about him. She didn't like the idea of her legs being exposed, didn't like the thought of Spencer looking at her bare flesh. There was no moon out tonight, and the outside patio light was off, as was the Parsonses', so it wasn't like he could really see her even if he was in his backyard looking in her direction.

Not that she was much to look at. She didn't think she was hideous or anything, but she was far from gorgeous. She had a body shape that could best be described as 'sturdy', and her face was plain. Makeup helped, but she felt phony wearing it, so she almost never did. Her blond hair looked like dirty straw, and she got split ends so badly that she kept her hair cut short. When she'd been in middle school, she'd once made the mistake of asking her father if he thought she was pretty.

Standards of beauty can vary widely from culture to culture, therefore 'pretty' is a meaningless concept. In what situation or context are we talking about?

She hadn't understood his answer completely, but she had understood that *he* didn't think she was pretty. Otherwise, he'd have answered yes. But you didn't have to be beautiful to draw a creeper's attention. Just being female was enough. Every woman knew that.

She swept her gaze across the Parsonses' backyard, searching for Spencer's silhouette, but she saw nothing. She was relieved that he wasn't out, but that noise had been caused by someone – or something – else. And that realization was far from comforting.

On the other side of the Parsonses' house was the Raines place. Her father had moved to Brookside Court after the murders had taken place there, which was why he'd gotten his place so cheap. He didn't seem bothered in the slightest that five people had died in horrible ways there. He was nothing if not pragmatic, and he wasn't the most empathetic person. She doubted he felt anything at all for the Raines family. She, on the other hand, couldn't forget about what had happened to them. She kept trying to imagine what could've made Cherie Raines kill her husband and children. What could possibly drive a person to commit such terrible acts?

Sometimes – although she'd never admit this to anyone – she wondered what it would be like to kill her father. Would she feel guilt or sorrow? Or would she feel relieved, feel *free*?

The weird stretching-wood sound came again, and she realized it originated past the Parsonses' backyard. It was coming from the Raines place. Curious, she stood and walked across the yard, grass cool and damp beneath her feet. She reached the fence that separated her father's property from the Parsonses', and she gazed across at the Raineses' backyard. She'd walked all the way to the back corner of the fence. Because the houses on Brookside Court were located on a cul-de-sac, they were arranged in a semicircle, and in order to get an unobstructed view of the Raineses' yard, she needed to stand back here, otherwise the Parsonses' house would be in the way. The Raineses' backyard was enclosed within a wooden privacy fence, so she didn't know what she expected to see. She'd felt compelled to come here, though. Maybe she was curious about their new neighbors. Her father had told her over dinner that someone had bought the Raines house and were beginning to move in. She wondered what kind of family would knowingly move into a house that had such a violent, bloody history. People who were as pragmatic as her father? Or freaks who got off on the idea of living in the House of Blood?

Not only wasn't there a moon tonight, but the sky was overcast, so there wasn't any starlight either. All she could make out were the silhouettes of several large trees in the Raineses' backyard. Nothing that might account for the weird sound that—

Her thoughts slammed to a halt as realization set in. There *were* no trees in the Raineses' backyard. Not a one.

She strained to make out more details of the objects, but she couldn't pick out anything else. No branches, no leaves. But the outlines of the objects sure as hell *looked* like trees.

The stretching sound came again, and as Alex watched, a new silhouette rose up to join the others. When it reached its full height, the noise stopped.

She felt lightheaded, dizzy, and she pushed her fingers through the holes in the chain-link fence and grabbed hold of the thin metal to steady herself. She now understood what the strange sound was: the sound of a tree rapidly growing. In the light of day, she would've laughed at the idea, but the world was different at night. Everything seemed slightly off-kilter, a little unreal, and the darkness invited one's mind to imagine anything could be hidden within it, anything at all. So the idea that the Raineses' backyard was now filled with trees that had grown unnaturally fast didn't seem all that absurd to her.

She wanted to tell herself that she was dreaming, that she'd actually fallen asleep in her bed and only thought she'd gotten up and come outside. But as much as she wanted to believe this, she knew she was wide awake. She was really here, and this was really happening. The sensations – breeze on her face, grass under her feet, her fingers on fence metal – were too sharp, too...too *there*. She frantically searched for a natural explanation, something, anything that would allow her to turn her back on what she didn't want to see and walk away, believing the world was the same fucked-up but sane and rational place it always was.

Stress, she thought. *You're hallucinating because you're so goddamn stressed out.*

She considered this for a moment, and then smiled faintly. It would do.

She let go of the fence, turned, and began walking toward her father's house. When she was halfway to the patio, she became aware of a pale light glowing behind her. It wasn't very strong at first, but the light grew brighter with each step she took.

Don't look, don't look, don't look....

She stopped, turned, looked—

—and saw a white sphere slowly rising into the sky above the Raineses' backyard. At first she thought it was a balloon of some kind, one with an interior light, kind of like a sky lantern, which was essentially a small hot-air balloon made of paper. But as the sphere ascended, it appeared to grow larger, and its light intensified. Alex could now clearly see the trees in the Raineses' backyard – tall, strong, lush with foliage. Trees that hadn't been there before tonight. Then she realized what the sphere was. The new neighbors had put a forest in their backyard and now they were placing a moon, a *full* moon, in its sky.

She tried to laugh, but it came out as a choked sob. She turned and ran the rest of the way to the house, her bare feet nearly sliding out from under her on the way. She did not look back again as she went. There was no forest, no moon. They were illusions caused by stress, nothing more. She began whispering the word, repeating it beneath her breath, as if it were some kind of charm that would protect her.

"Stress, stress, stress, stress, stress, stress, stress, stress...."

She continued repeating the word until she was inside the house, back in her room, and lying in her bed. And she would keep repeating it until sunrise.

★　　★　　★

The Eldreds' moon – the surface of which was pocked with a different pattern of craters than the actual moon – found its place and stopped ascending. Moments later, a shower of tiny sparkling lights rose upward to join it, for what's a moon without a backdrop of stars?

CHAPTER SIX

Lola Parsons stood outside her son's bedroom door. It was closed and – she gently tested the knob – locked. This was no impediment to her entry, though. All the house's interior doors had a small hole next to the outer knob. If a door was locked, all one had to do was insert a small tool – a miniature screwdriver, the end of an Allen wrench, even a bent paperclip would do – and voilà! The door was unlocked. And because Spencer was a child and Lola might need to get to him if he was inside his room, sick or injured, she kept a small Phillips screwdriver on top of the door's lintel. She looked upward – she wasn't a tall woman by any means – and saw the screwdriver there, right where it should be. Kenneth had probably forgotten all about it, else why would he leave it there now?

Because he's not in the room with Spencer, that's why.

She wanted to believe this was true, god how she wanted to! But as if she were two people.... no, two attorneys, defense and prosecution...she responded to her thought with a question.

If that's true, then where is Kenneth? He's not in your bedroom, and you've looked all over the house – including the basement and garage. He's nowhere inside. And the car's still here. Don't try to tell me he went for a walk, not this late at night. There's only one place left for him to be.

Spencer's room.

She'd suspected for a while now, but she'd never allowed herself to seriously entertain the thought. She'd denied it, suppressed it, tried to metaphorically grind it into the ground until it was dust and could never return to nag at her again. But of course it did, and each time it came back, it was stronger, louder, more insistent, until finally it could no longer be silenced, even temporarily. The nights she'd woken up in bed alone. The times when Kenneth and Spencer would disappear for some 'guy time', as Kenneth called it. The way Spencer shrank from his father's touch, couldn't meet his gaze. The screams when Spencer woke from terrible nightmares, which he claimed never to remember.

She continued looking at the screwdriver.

If she reached up and grabbed it, inserted the pointed end into the lock release, opened the door, and stepped inside, her suspicion would become reality. But if she turned around, went back to her bedroom, climbed beneath the covers, squeezed her eyes shut tight and pretended to sleep, then it wouldn't be real. She could go on with her life just the way it was, believing she had a normal husband who loved her, a happy son whom she doted on, and an altogether pleasant existence in a pleasant little town. And she could go on believing those things until the day came to put her in the ground. And after that? She didn't care. She figured she'd find out eventually, one way or the other. Either way, the troubles and trials of this world would be behind her.

Who was she fucking kidding? She couldn't stand by while her son was hurting, regardless of what it might cost her.

With a trembling hand, she reached up for the screwdriver. She had to stand on tiptoes to reach it, and even then she could only brush it with her fingertips. She had to flick her fingers until she managed to roll the screwdriver to the edge of the lintel. It fell and she snatched it out of the air with her other hand before it could hit the carpeted floor. She'd always had good reflexes.

She gripped the screwdriver, her hand less shaky now, and carefully inserted it – *the long hard thing* – into the lock release – *the tiny hole*.

She felt dizzy, nauseated, and a sharp icepick of pain stabbed into her left eye. She ignored these sensations and pressed the screwdriver forward until she felt as much as heard a soft *snick*. She withdrew the screwdriver swiftly, grasped the knob, turned it, and shoved the door open. She did these things fast, before her courage deserted her.

The only illumination in the room came from Spencer's owl nightlight plugged into an outlet near the floor. But it was enough to show Spencer crouched on his bed, naked, spine curved downward, head pressed into the covers. Behind him – equally naked, feet planted firmly on the floor, hands grasping his son's hips – was Kenneth. Kenneth's bony ass was pumping forward and back, forward and back, moving so fast it was practically a blur.

Something wasn't right, though.

Okay, nothing about the scene that confronted Lola was *right*, not even fucking close. But there was one thing in particular that stood out, that didn't make sense, that couldn't be possible. Her Spencer was eight years old. But the Spencer kneeling on the bed being butt-fucked by his father was a full-grown man. Almost middle-aged too, from the look of him – rolls of flab quivering with each of his father's thrusts. He appeared to be older than both she and Kenneth. How could that be?

What does it matter?

The prosecutor's voice again.

Your husband is balls deep in your son's ass, and you want to quibble over a little thing like Spencer's proper age?

Good point, she thought.

She raised the screwdriver high, screamed, and ran toward Kenneth. He turned his head to look at her, surprised at first, but his features quickly contorted with fury. And the bastard didn't stop thrusting, didn't even goddamn *pause*.

In real life, Lola had reached Kenneth and began plunging the Phillips head into his back over and over, moving fast, the makeshift weapon going *chuk-chuk-chuk-chuk-chuk* as it pierced flesh and penetrated muscle. There'd been blood, lots of it. And it was only later, when she was helping Spencer clean up, that she saw the jizz leak out of her little boy's ass and knew that Kenneth had come while she'd been stabbing him.

But now the world shifted, blurred, unmade itself. For a dizzying moment, Lola had no idea where she was, could barely recall *who* she was. But then the world remade itself and she found herself in the kitchen, standing before the open basement door. Kenneth was there with her, still naked, blood running from the dozen small wounds on his back, flowing down the backs of his legs and onto the tiled floor. Lola still held the screwdriver, but Kenneth had hold of both of her wrists and was keeping her arms raised upward. She fought to pull free from his grip, but he was stronger than she was, and she couldn't break free.

She tried to remember how she got here. Hadn't Kenneth pulled away from Spencer and backhanded her across the face, sending her reeling backward? Hadn't she run from the room and he came after her, finally catching up to her in the kitchen? That's what was supposed to happen. She mentally shrugged. Whatever. She was here now. All she had to do was let the next several seconds play themselves out.

Kenneth had never been an especially attractive man. He was so skinny you could see the outline of his bones, and he'd once described his face as looking like the southbound end of a northbound dog. He wasn't wrong. And he had a small penis, one that was barely larger than a pinkie finger when he was hard. It was so small that she sometimes wondered how he'd managed to get her pregnant with it. She'd loved him just the same, though, and while she knew he didn't exactly have a movie-star face, neither did she, and she found him attractive enough, in his own way. But now his face was twisted into a mask of anger, and it was the ugliest thing she had ever seen. Worst of all, she saw no shame in his eyes, no regret, no sorrow for what he'd done to their son, to her, to their marriage. All she saw was a man pissed off that someone had dared to interrupt him in the middle of a fuck.

He kept pushing her arms, and the pressure forced her backward, causing her and Kenneth to rotate in a small circle on the floor, almost as if they were engaged in some sort of insane dance. She didn't know what he was trying to accomplish, and when she would think back to this moment in the years to come – which she would do many, many times – she'd always come to the same conclusion. He was so damn mad that he wasn't thinking straight. He had no goal, was just holding up her arms and pushing her in a circle for no reason other than he needed something to do with his rage.

She would never have a clear memory of what happened next. As near as she could figure it, one of Kenneth's bare feet had come down on a patch of his blood and slipped out from under him. He tilted to the side as he fell backward and struck his head on the edge of the open basement door. The shock of the impact caused his hands to spring open, freeing her, which was fortunate; otherwise he would've pulled her down the stairs with him. She would remember him tumbling down the stairs, would remember the smack of his flesh against the wood steps, the crack of bones breaking, the *oof* as breath was forced from his body. But most of all, she would remember the final sound as he struck the basement's concrete floor: a dull thud followed by a crack so loud and sharp it sounded like a whip.

She looked down at him, curled up at the foot of the stairs like a child, a halo of blood spreading outward from his head, his neck bent at a sickening angle.

Afterward – once she'd tended to her poor Spencer – she would call the police. The officers who came to investigate checked to make sure Kenneth was dead, which he very much was. They then listened to Lola's story, looking from her to Spencer and back again the entire time she spoke. When she was finished, the officers – one man, one woman – exchanged a quick glance then a pair of brief nods.

Sounds like an accident to me, ma'am, one said.

A terrible accident, the other agreed.

She didn't understand at first, but when the EMTs who arrived to cart away Kenneth's body also remarked on what a tragic accident this was – after a consultation with the officers – she began to understand. She cleaned up the blood that Kenneth had tracked from Spencer's room to the kitchen, and no one came to investigate further. She buried Kenneth without anyone asking her a single question to indicate they thought she might've played a hand – even a tangential one – in her husband's death. She was left to take care of her child, to try to help him heal, and she was grateful.

But this wasn't real life, and Kenneth did not remain still and silent on the basement's concrete floor.

First, a hand twitched, then his head turned, flopping bonelessly. He drew in a shuddering, gasping breath and then – slowly, laboriously – he pushed himself onto the stairs and began crawling upward toward Lola. The right side of his head had a dent in it from the collision with the concrete floor, and blood from the wound flowed along the side of his head, down his cheek, across his chin, and onto his lips. His nose was a pulped ruin, his upper lip swollen and split, and the collision with the concrete floor had knocked out several of his front teeth. He smiled, his remaining teeth slick with crimson. His eyes were wide, wild, murderous.

Blood dribbled from the corner of his mouth as he spoke. "You may have killed me, you old, disgusting cow, and you may've gotten away with it."

He continued crawling upward as he spoke, and Lola stood at the top of the stairs and watched, frozen into immobility by the horror of it all.

"But you were too late to save Spencer. The damage had already been done. He's Daddy's boy, and he always will be. It's only a matter of time before he finds himself a nice young chicken to pluck. Maybe that little girl across the street, the half-Asian one."

His head lolled on his broken neck, swinging back and forth, as if he were an old rag doll whose stuffing had been squashed down into his chest from being played with so many times over the years. He was two-thirds of the way up the stairs now. Soon he'd be within reaching distance. She imagined him grabbing her leg around the ankle, pulling her off her feet, dragging her down into the basement with him, and then putting those blood-smeared teeth of his to work.

Kenneth continued speaking as he advanced slowly toward her.

"Spencer watches her, you know. Peeks between the front window curtains every chance he gets, hoping to catch a glimpse of her. And when he finally does see her, do you know what he does? He heads straight to the bathroom, locks the door, and jerks off. He cries when he comes. Every single time." Kenneth's mouth stretched into a hideous grin. "It's really quite funny."

He was almost to her now. He reached upward, tried to grab her leg, but all he managed to do was brush the tips of his fingers against her feet. That touch, slight though it was, was enough to break her paralysis and spur her into action. She moved onto the first step, took hold of the railing to steady herself, then kicked out with her right foot – hard. She connected with Kenneth's grinning mockery of a face, and his head snapped back. He fell, rolling down the steps once more. This time when he struck the concrete floor – landing in a pool of his own blood – he did not rise.

She heard his voice one last time, though, a single sentence, whispered in her mind. *See you soon.* Then silence.

Heart pounding, breath coming in fast, ragged gasps, she took a couple steps down, wanting to get a closer look, wanting to make sure that this time he was going to stay dead. When she stopped, when she leaned forward straining to get a better look, she realized that the man lying in a twisted broken heap on the basement floor wasn't Kenneth after all. It was Spencer.

She screamed, her voice continuing on without pause, echoing through eternity.

★ ★ ★

Lola came to consciousness sitting upright in her bed. She had no memory of sitting up, and she wondered if she'd screamed in the real world as well as in her dream. She hoped not. She didn't want to wake Spencer and alarm him. When several moments passed without him rushing into her room to ask if she was all right, she knew that – scream or no scream – Spencer still slept. Good.

She sat in the dark, breathing slowly, waiting for her body to calm down. This was hardly the first time she'd dreamed about Kenneth's 'accident', but it had been the worst, hands down. And then at the end, when it was Spencer lying dead at the bottom of the stairs instead of his father.... That sight had shaken her to the core. That had never happened before. She wasn't big on psychoanalyzing dreams, but she didn't dismiss psychology outright. After Kenneth was gone, she'd taken Spencer to see a child psychologist, one who specialized in helping abused children. That doctor had given her son a great deal of help, and for that she was grateful. But that didn't mean she thought every dream was an important message sent from one's subconscious mind. But in this case, she feared it was.

The message was clear and unmistakable. If Spencer began following in his father's footsteps, if he began...*hurting* children, she'd have to turn him over to the police. That, or she'd have to arrange a little 'accident' for him. She didn't want to do it, didn't want to even contemplate it. But she was his mother. She'd carried him inside her body for nine months then brought him into this world. She was responsible for all he would become and all he would do. It was her responsibility to make sure he caused no harm to anyone, that he didn't pass on the darkness his father had infected him with.

She knew he felt an attraction toward children of either gender, but he'd never acted on those feelings. Therapy had given him the tools he needed to manage his aberrant desires, and he rarely left the house, staying where she could monitor him closely. Spencer was determined not to do to another child what had been done to him. She believed he was completely committed to this goal, that he would rather take his own life than abuse a child himself.

And yet....

Human sexual desire was a powerful thing, and it could only be denied for so long. Was it inevitable that Spencer would sexually abuse a child? She prayed it wasn't, but she didn't know. Kenneth had owned a .45 caliber pistol, and she'd kept it after his death. Sometimes she thought about taking the gun out of the closet where she stored it, loading it, sneaking into Spencer's room one night while he was sleeping, pressing the muzzle gently against his temple, and pulling the trigger. When he was dead, she'd turn the gun on herself. She kept the weapon polished and oiled, so it would be in working condition if she ever decided she needed to use it. She didn't know if she had the courage to use the gun, and she'd hoped she'd never have to find out.

She thought of what Kenneth had said at the end of her dream. It had felt as if he'd been speaking directly to her, in the present, as if his voice had been real, even if nothing else was. *See you soon.* She didn't know what that meant, and she didn't want to.

Knowing that she wouldn't get any more sleep tonight, that she wouldn't allow herself to sleep so she wouldn't dream again, she got out of bed, left her room, and started toward the kitchen, intending to make herself some coffee.

Rise and fucking shine, she thought as she shuffled down the hallway. She'd get her coffee, sit in the living room, and turn the TV on. She'd keep the volume low, watch the Shopping Channel, and try not to think about her dream – and especially try not to think about what Kenneth had promised.

★   ★   ★

The Eldreds supervise the movers and Machine Head as they bring in the contents for each of their Domains. The work goes swiftly, for they have done this many times before in many different places. Although the boundaries of the house do not change – its outer walls, its roof, the fence enclosing the backyard – inside, the house expands and keeps expanding, growing ever larger and more intricate. Worlds are being born in there, worlds within worlds. Soon the Stalking Ground will be ready. And when it is, the invitations will go out.

It's going to be *such* fun.

CHAPTER SEVEN

Friday – two days after the new neighbors had moved into the Raines place – Neal stepped outside to take a full garbage bag to the receptacle located at the side of the house. It was raining, but only lightly, so he didn't bother with a jacket or umbrella. He didn't plan on being outside more than a minute or two, and today he wore a polo shirt, jeans, and sneakers. It wasn't as if he had on a brand-new suit he wanted to keep nice. Kandice had already left for the rec center, and he was running late. Today was an in-service day at his school, so the students were off, but the faculty had to show up for a day filled with boring, time-wasting meetings and training sessions designed to teach them how to do stuff they already knew. But he didn't have to be at the school until 9:00 a.m., two-and-a-half hours later than his usual arrival time, and they'd probably get out an hour or so before the normal dismissal time of 3:00 p.m. When you looked at it like that, it was almost a holiday. In fact, he'd dawdled so much this morning while getting ready – having an extra cup of coffee, watching *Headline News* on his phone – that now he was in danger of being late to the first training session. He wouldn't have bothered with the trash, but something in it smelled and it smelled *terrible*. He wasn't sure what Kandice had thrown away last night – maybe some uneaten leftovers stored in the fridge too long – but whatever it was had created a stink so powerful it made his gorge rise.

Since their disastrous attempt at lovemaking last night, Kandice and he hadn't spoken much this morning. He hoped this mutual feeling of awkwardness would pass soon. They'd been together long enough to have gone through rough patches before, and eventually the problems were resolved, one way or another. Either they'd talk them out or the passage of time would make the problems seem unimportant, even laughable. He had a feeling this time was different, though, and he wasn't sure why. He'd do anything he could to fix things between them – if he only understood what had happened, was *still* happening, in their relationship.

He was a physics teacher: a logical, rational man. Someone who believed in solving problems step by step, following the proper procedure, until the correct answer was arrived at. Science was all about understanding and working with natural systems, and if he could teach AP physics to bored and horny teenagers, he should be able to come to terms with his feelings about his wife's sexuality. Maybe the problem was that he was too rigid of a thinker. Too *binary*. His profession dealt with right or wrong answers, this or that, one or the other. He could understand *or* just fine. It was *and* that he was struggling with – and what Kandice's *and* meant for their marriage. He'd tried to tell himself to think more in terms of quantum mechanics, where particles could be more than one thing, do more than one thing, depending on the situation. It helped a little, but science and logic were only so useful where human emotion was concerned.

He wished he was teaching his classes today. Working with students kept his mind occupied, leaving him little time to brood about his relationship with Kandice. But he supposed he was going to have to tough it out. He wasn't looking forward to the weekend. He'd have tests and homework to grade – he always did – but the thought of being around Kandice all weekend, both of them uncomfortable with the other and uncertain what to do about it, sounded like a nightmare. Maybe he could think of some excuse to get him out of the house for a protracted period of time. He'd have to see what he could come up with. It would have to be good, though.

It struck him that he was thinking of doing the same thing a cheating spouse would do – invent a false reason to get away from his partner, although in this case, not to have extra-marital sex but to avoid dealing with an emotional issue within the marriage. Not good.

As he stepped off the porch, he bowed his head to keep the rain from hitting his face – he hated getting water in his eyes – and walked around to the side of the house. They kept their trash and recycling receptacles here, the former big and green, the latter smaller and blue. He reached for the trash receptacle's lid, intending to open it, but he stopped. A piece of white paper had been taped to the lid, a message written on it in ink. The letters were an elegant, old-fashioned cursive, but the rain was causing them to run. They were still mostly legible, though. He held a hand over the paper in an ineffective attempt to protect it from the rain, and he read.

MEET YOUR NEW NEIGHBORS!

The Eldreds cordially invite you and your family to attend a cookout at our house – you know the one! – this Saturday starting at 6 p.m. We're very much looking forward to meeting you! You don't need to bring anything except your fabulous selves and the contents of your hearts and minds. RSVP not required. We already know you'll come.

This last sentence was followed by a drawing of a smiley face and five signatures. The names were strange ones that Neal wasn't familiar with, and they had been so damaged by rain that he couldn't be certain he was reading them correctly.

What the fuck?

He opened the receptacle's lid, intending to put the trash inside, but as he did so, a terrible stench rose from within. As bad as the trash he'd gathered from the kitchen had smelled, this odor was a hundred times worse. It hit with almost physical force, making his eyes water and his nasal passages sting. His stomach did a flip, and for a moment it was fifty-fifty whether he'd throw up his breakfast. It was a near thing, but he managed to keep his stomach contents where they belonged. He quickly tossed the trash bag into the receptacle and slammed the lid shut.

The stink lingered in the air, as if not even rain could dissipate it. He almost fled, but the paper taped to the receptacle's lid called to him, as if saying, *Don't you want to take me?* He pulled the note free from the lid, his first impulse to wad up the paper and toss it into the recycling. The tone of the message was off – which made him think the Eldreds were eccentric, if not outright nuts. And who the hell delivered an invitation by taping it to a neighbor's garbage receptacle? It made no sense.

But he didn't throw away the message. He wasn't sure why. Maybe it was so he'd have some proof when he told Kandice about it later. He knew she'd want to see it for herself. One line of the message came back to him.

We already know you'll come.

Was he keeping the invitation because of that line? He didn't know. He just knew he couldn't discard it. He held up the note, being careful to not tear the wet paper, and read the message once more. It was just as weird the second time.

"Looks like you got one, too."

Neal looked up to see Martin walking across the lawn toward him. The man wore a ballcap – presumably to keep the rain off his head – a ratty Cleveland Browns T-shirt, sneakers, and faded jeans that were too baggy on him. Neal had no idea how Martin managed to keep the pants from sliding past his bony hips and dropping to the ground. The ballcap had a phrase displayed on the front: *Fuck Your Feelings*.

Charming.

Neal forced a smile. He didn't like Martin, and he knew the dislike was mutual. But that was no reason not to be civil – or at least make the attempt.

"I take it you received an invitation, too."

Martin stopped when he reached Neal and pulled a folded square of paper from his back pocket. He unfolded it and held it out for Neal's inspection. It was the exact same message, only this one wasn't water damaged and Neal could read the signatures. *Arnoldo, Lacresha, Demarcus, Vanita, and Cleora.*

"Those are some weird-ass names, huh?" Martin said. "Don't sound American at all."

Martin said this last part with a smile, and Neal didn't know if he'd shared an actual opinion of his or if he was merely trying to get a rise out of him. They'd had arguments about immigrants' impact on the country before. Normally, Neal might've risen to the bait, but not today.

"Let's go onto my porch and get out of this rain," Neal said.

The two men did as Neal suggested, and when they were under shelter, Neal said, "I'm surprised you're home."

"It's supposed to rain all day, so the road crew's not going out. It sucks. Staying home means I don't get paid. I don't get summers off like you do. I need to keep working year round."

This was another topic of contention between them. Martin thought public school teachers got too much 'vacation time' each year. Neal had tried on numerous occasions to explain to him that teachers were hired to work nine months each year. They weren't on vacation the other three. They were unemployed – which was why a lot of teachers took summer jobs. A teacher's nine-month salary only went so far. But Neal didn't respond to this barb, either.

"What's Cora think about the invitation?"

"She hasn't seen it yet. Since I don't have to work, I stayed home with Vivienne so Cora could go with her mom and sister to get mani-pedis. Cora likes to do stuff with her mom and sis a lot. I think it's some kind of Chinese family thing, you know?"

Neal had no idea if Martin had made a racial slur, a cultural observation, or some strange combination of the two.

Martin continued.

"I was in our bedroom, gathering up some laundry to wash, and I saw you peel your invite off your trash can through the window. That's why I came over. Vivienne's watching a cartoon. I doubt she even knows I went outside." He smiled and shook his head. "That kid. When she watches cartoons, it's like the whole world ceases to exist."

"Where did you find your invitation?" Neal asked.

"Ours was sitting on our back porch. Whoever delivered it folded it and put a big rock on it. Kept it safe from the rain." He nodded to the wet paper Neal held gingerly by one corner. "Unlike yours." He frowned. "There was one weird thing about it, though."

"Weirder than someone sneaking into your yard at night to leave an invitation to a cookout?"

"Maybe. Next to the rock was a dead pigeon."

Neal thought at first that Martin was making some kind of bizarre joke, but the man's expression was serious.

"It could've been a coincidence," Neal said. "The bird could've flown into a window at the back of your house, broke its neck, and when it bounced off the glass, landed near the invitation."

"I thought about that," Martin said. "But there's the last line of the invitation."

He handed his paper to Neal who took it in his free hand and read it again. Originally, he'd thought the message's contents were exactly the same as the one he'd received, and for the most part they were. But Martin's had an extra line above the signatures.

It's okay to come by before six! We like early birds!

"Huh." Neal handed the invitation back to Martin. "Still probably a coincidence."

"Yeah," Martin said, but he didn't sound convinced. "We'll end up going. You know how friendly Cora is. And nosy. She's been dying to find out more about our new neighbors. This way, she'll have an excuse to meet them. Plus, with everyone else there, she won't be alone. Strength in numbers, right?"

Neal was surprised that Martin assumed the rest of Brookside Court's residents would attend the cookout. The new neighbors were odd, to say the least, and they *had* bought the Raines place. Who wanted to have a cookout at the fucking House of Blood?

"You and Kandice *are* going to go, right?"

Martin sounded nervous, and Neal didn't have the heart to tell him they most likely wouldn't go.

"Sure. We'll be there."

It was strange, but the moment the words were out of his mouth, they felt right, as if his subconscious mind had already decided to go and the rest of him was only finding out about it now.

Martin looked relieved.

"That's good to hear." He gave Neal a mischievous smile. "And if we get into an argument about something political during the cookout, I promise to let you think you won."

His smile widened into a grin, he folded his invitation and returned it to his back pocket, and then he started back toward his house, half jogging because of the rain.

Neal watched him go, thinking about the dead pigeon on the man's back porch. He'd become intrigued by the Eldreds' invitation and he'd forgotten all about the horrible stink that had wafted from the trash receptacle when he'd opened it. It was crazy, he knew it was, but he wondered if the odor had come from something someone had put in there. Something dead or rotten, far worse than a deceased pigeon. There was only one way to find out. All he would have to do was return to the receptacle, open the lid, take out the bag he'd put in, and look inside. And if he did that, what would he find? A dead raccoon that had been disemboweled, its guts piled beneath it, body cavity filled with wriggling maggots? Or something even worse?

Just go look. Whatever it is, it can't hurt you.

He knew this was true, but he didn't step off the porch. He remained where he was, and he looked across the street at the Parsonses' and Ruizes's houses. Had they received invitations, too? And if so, had they also gotten a grotesque bonus gift like Martin? And – maybe, probably – like him? He then turned his attention to the Raines – no, the *Eldreds'* house. The moving van was gone, and the black Cadillac was now parked in the driveway. Overall, the house looked the same as it had the day he and Kandice had moved to Brookside Court. The lawn needed mowing, and the tree in the front yard should've been cut down years ago, but the house looked in good shape. The driveway's concrete was smooth, with no obvious fissures. The gutters didn't droop, the decorative shutters were all straight and firmly fixed to the house, and no roof tiles were missing. The paint on both the front door and garage door looked as if it had been applied yesterday, the colors strong, no cracking or flaking. There was a chimney on the side of the house, well-built, sturdy, every brick present and accounted for.

And yet...

Neal couldn't have said precisely what was different about the house, but there was no denying that something was. The Eldreds' Cadillac was part of it. Whenever Neal looked at it, he had the feeling that the vehicle was somehow watching him, measuring, judging, and ultimately finding him wanting. He hadn't seen any of the Eldreds themselves, but he sometimes felt them over there, moving inside the house, quietly, secretively, like insects that shunned the light. And the longer he looked at the house, the more its edges seemed fuzzy and blurred, as if it was slightly out of focus, not quite all the way there.

With an effort, as if the house didn't want him to take his attention from it, Neal turned and went back into his own home. He needed to get to the school. Suddenly, sitting through boring training meetings, listening to the presenters droning on about nothing even remotely interesting sounded *fantastic*. He left the invitation on the kitchen counter to dry, and then he did his best to put it out of his mind as he headed for the garage. He got in his Subaru Outback, and when he backed out of his driveway and drove off, he made certain to avoid looking at the Eldreds' house as he drove away.

He could feel it looking at him, though.

*   *   *

It's the night before, and the Eldred leave their new home and glide through the darkness, silent and swift, delivering the invitations to the Gathering. As they enter their new neighbors' yards, approach their houses, they scent the air and their minds reach out to touch the psychic residue of the humans. This is the closest they've been to them, their first chance to begin the knowing of them, their first *taste* as it were, and they quiver with excitement and anticipation.

They leave the invitations – handwritten with mundane ink and equally mundane printer paper – in different locations. They also leave a Forewarning at each home. The locations chosen for the invitations speak to the Eldreds' sense of dark whimsy, but the Forewarnings are far more serious. There are no rules that bind or restrain the Eldred, but they have their customs, their ways of doing things, developed and refined over millennia. They long ago learned that some humans are more perceptive than others, more sensitive to violations of reality, more resistant to glamours. These humans – the Aware – are more difficult to hunt. Not impossible, of course. Nothing is impossible for the Eldred. But they are old and prefer not to work any harder than is necessary to feed. Humans who are Aware will recognize a Forewarning for what it is, and they will stay away from the Gathering. Most humans, if they're Aware at all, are only partially so, but the Eldred don't believe in taking needless chances.

The Forewarnings serve a second purpose. There are other powers in this world beside the Eldred, and many more in the worlds that overlap this one: The Multitude, Maintenance, the Harmony Society, the Cabal, the Harvesters…. The Eldred are careful when selecting a Stalking Ground to avoid any territory that has been previously claimed by one of these powers. But there is always the possibility – however remote – that they have failed to detect such a power, and the Forewarnings serve as a calling card of sorts. They let the powers that might be present know the Eldred are here and what they intend to do. And if these powers have any objections, they will let the Eldred know, often in no uncertain and very dramatic terms. In that case, the Eldred will attempt to reach an arrangement with these powers, perhaps offer to share the bounty of their hunt. If an agreement cannot be reached, they will destroy the powers if they can, and if they cannot, they will pack up and leave without feeding.

At the Hawkinses' house, the invitation is left on the back porch, along with a pigeon that flew too close to a Taint, an infected pocket of reality, and whose internal organs became liquefied as a result.

They leave the Parsonses' invitation tucked into their mailbox, along with the desiccated husk of a stingblade, an insect that does not exist in this reality. The Ruizes' invitation is left in their garage, under the windshield wiper of Isaac Ruiz's Highlander. Beneath the vehicle, the Eldred leave a viscous puddle whose color changes every twenty-two minutes. All of its colors are on a spectrum that is difficult for the human eye to see unaided, although one who is Aware can perceive them. This substance is blood taken from a durg, a beetle-like creature the size of a cow, which the Nonsister is especially fond of.

They leave the invitation for the Wilkersons taped to the lid of their trash receptacle. Inside, buried beneath the trash bags already there, the Eldred leave the hand of a chatterer, a creature resembling a small monkey whose organs are outside its body. Chatterers possess a psychic aura so foul that it remains strong even after death. Ordinary humans experience this aura as an unpleasant smell, but to one of the Aware, this smell is intensified a hundredfold, and they will become violently ill.

When all the invitations and Forewarnings have been delivered, the Eldred return to their home to wait. They are confident everyone will attend this latest Gathering, but they never know for sure, and this uncertainty is part of what makes feeding so exhilarating. The anticipation, the will-they-or-won't-they, the waiting to see if any of the humans are Aware or, if like most of humanity, they are blind, deaf, and dumb to anything but the most basic veneer of reality. This is a big part of the fun for the Eldred.

Plus, it helps to work up an appetite.

CHAPTER EIGHT

"I can't believe you really want to do this," Isaac said. "You're trying to punish me, aren't you? Get back at me for my part in the divorce."

Alex gave no outer reaction – doing so was a good way to further irritate her father – but inside she smiled ruefully and shook her head. Her father was usually crabby at the best of times, but he became especially prickly when he was anxious. Not that he'd ever *admit* to feeling nervous. Over the years, he'd cultivated a persona of a man who was always in control, regardless of the situation. She figured his students and colleagues bought into it, but she was his daughter, and she knew Isaac Ruiz was a deeply insecure – almost fearful – man, and he covered this up by acting like an asshole much of the time.

"It'll be good to get to know the new neighbors," she said. "It's hard enough moving into a new area, let alone into a house that has a bad history. It's important to make them feel welcome."

They walked along the sidewalk, moving past the Parsonses' house. Alex felt a cold flutter in her stomach. Would Spencer make a rare public appearance to attend the cookout? She hoped he wouldn't. The dude squicked her out big-time.

The Eldreds' invitation hadn't specified how their guests should dress, but it was in the low eighties today, so Alex wore a T-shirt, shorts, and flip-flops. Her father – who always looked the part of a college professor, even when relaxing at home – wore a light brown suit jacket over a dark brown button-up shirt, khaki slacks, and brown dress shoes. Sweat was already beginning to bead on his forehead, and she knew he would be uncomfortable, at least until the sun went down.

The invitation had also said that guests didn't need to bring anything, but according to her father, *People always say that, but they don't really mean it.* He was carrying a bottle of wine by the neck, an expensive red that he'd been saving for a special occasion. *A housewarming gift,* he'd said. Alex knew her father didn't give a shit about such social customs. The wine's sole purpose was to impress the Eldreds with how sophisticated and generous he was.

When her father had first discovered the invitation, he'd rushed back into the house and waved the paper in her face while he ranted, alternating between threatening to call the police and have the Eldreds arrested for trespassing, and proclaiming that he intended to march over to their house, pound on the front door, and give whoever answered it a black eye. It had taken her over an hour of talking to him nonstop to calm him down, and after that it had taken another hour to get him to agree to go to the cookout. *Maybe.*

"Admit it," she said. "You're curious."

"I'm *pissed* is what I am. What kind of people sneak into someone's garage to leave an invitation on the windshield of their car?"

"Creative people. Fun people. People who don't take life so seriously all the time." She gave him a sideways glance. "If you'd remembered to lock the garage's side door, they wouldn't have been able to leave it there."

He glared at her, and for a moment she thought he was going to start swearing, but he remained silent. His face reddened from the effort, though. If he didn't learn how to control his temper more effectively, he would end up having a stroke one of these days.

Across the street, Neal and Kandice walked out of their front door and onto the sidewalk. They both looked over at Alex and her father, smiled, and waved. Kandice's smile seemed more genuine than Neal's, but Alex didn't blame him. Her father could be a jackass to anyone he didn't consider his intellectual equal – which was pretty much everyone on the planet – and he especially disliked high-school teachers. Not only didn't they have the academic qualifications of a fully tenured college professor, he blamed them for the lack of preparedness first-year college students displayed in his Intro to Sociology classes. *They can barely read and write, and they sure as shit can't think. And it's the teachers' fault, from pre-school all the way up to high school.*

Her father brought up this topic, sooner or later, whenever he and Neal were in the same place. She'd made him promise to restrain himself tonight, but she knew there was less than a fifty percent chance of that happening. Alex liked Neal, and she hated it when her father went out of his way to pick on him.

Neal and Kandice were both dressed casually – Kandice in a black tank top and jeans shorts, Neal in a red polo shirt, tan khaki shorts, ankle socks, and sneakers. Alex and Isaac reached the Eldreds' driveway at the same time as Kandice and Neal. The four stopped to greet each other.

"Nice weather for a cookout," Kandice said.

It was true. It had rained on and off the last couple days, but right now the sky was clear and the sun was shining. It was a little muggy, but as long as you weren't foolish enough to wear a suit jacket – like her father – it was a perfect evening for everyone to meet their new neighbors.

"Sure is," she said.

Her father and Neal scowled at each other, but neither said anything, and Alex took this as a hopeful sign. If the two men couldn't get along, maybe they'd at least steer clear of one another tonight. The last thing Alex wanted was for them to get into one of their arguments and spoil the cookout. What kind of impression would that make on the Eldreds?

Alex always felt a little awkward around Kandice. The woman was beautiful in a naturally effortless way, and being around her always made Alex feel self-conscious about her own appearance. She knew her feelings of awkwardness came from her own insecurities, and she did her best to deal with them. One way she did this was by tackling them head on.

"You look lovely tonight, Kandice," she said.

Kandice's smile lit up her face.

"Why thank you! You look lovely as well."

She knew Kandice was merely being polite, but the compliment made her blush anyway.

Neal's scowl deepened, only now he wasn't looking at her father. He was looking at *her*. She had the sense that she'd done something to upset him, but she had no idea what. Kandice sensed it too, for she reached out to take Neal's hand. She gave it a squeeze and a little shake to get his attention. Neal looked at her, a bit startled, and then his expression eased and he smiled in a way that made Alex think he was apologizing. She couldn't say what for, but she felt the tension that had been building between them dissipate, and she was glad.

Her father appeared to be completely oblivious to what had just happened, but she wasn't surprised. He wasn't the most emotionally aware person.

"Shall we?" He nodded to the driveway, but he made no move toward it, nor did any of the others.

This was the closest Alex had ever been to the infamous House of Blood, the closest that her father had been, and the same was likely true for Kandice and Neal. And now that the four of them were here, none of them was comfortable with going any closer. Despite how Alex had acted when she'd worked to convince her father to come with her tonight, she felt nervous about being at the Raines house. No, more than that. She was afraid.

Alex had researched the Raines house soon after her father moved to Brookside Court. She'd grown up in Rockridge, so she'd been aware of the basic story – woman goes crazy, kills entire family then herself – since it happened, but she wasn't familiar with any specifics. At the time, she'd been considering living with her father to save money while she was in college, but she hadn't been sure she could stand to live so close to the House of Blood. She'd hoped doing some research would serve to de-mythologize the house somewhat, make it seem less like an evil presence infecting the neighborhood and more like what it really was: a place where something bad had happened once.

From her research Alex knew that Cherie Raines had come outside after slaying every member of her family. She'd been naked and covered with blood, and she slit her forearms with the knife she'd used to kill her husband and children. She'd bled out on the lawn – *this* lawn. Alex didn't know the exact spot where Cherie Raines had died, but she knew they stood within mere feet of it. She didn't believe in things like psychic energy, didn't believe that a tragedy like the Raines murders left some kind of imprint on a house, like a wound that would never heal. But just because she didn't believe in mysticism didn't mean she felt comfortable stepping onto the Raines – the *Eldreds'* – property.

After making the decision to move in with her father, she'd

done her best not to think about what had happened to the Raines family, especially to the three children. Most of the time she was successful, but every now and then her mind would return to the articles that she'd read about the murders and before she realized it, she was picturing the events as they might've played out. She fought to keep from doing that now, but it was proving more difficult than she'd anticipated – especially after the weird experience she'd had the other night, when she'd thought she'd seen trees and even a goddamn moon in the Eldreds' backyard. She'd hoped that by attending the Eldreds' cookout, she'd not only reassure herself that her – vision? hallucination? – hadn't been real, she'd be doing her part to, if not literally cleanse the house of any evil that might linger here, as least symbolically do so. But she couldn't stop herself from imagining Cherie Raines raising the knife above her head and bringing it down to violate her children's tender young flesh, couldn't keep herself from imagining the sounds the knife made as it entered and left the children's bodies: *chuk-chuk-chuk-chuk*.

She jumped and gave a small cry of surprise when she felt a hand clasp hers. She turned to see Kandice looking at her, a sympathetic smile on her face, understanding in her eyes.

"It's okay," Kandice said. "I feel it, too."

Alex smiled with gratitude and gave Kandice's hand a squeeze.

"Ready?" Kandice asked.

Alex wasn't sure she'd ever be ready for this, but she nodded and, still holding hands, the two women started walking up the driveway. Alex's father and Neal trailed behind them, and Alex could feel Neal's gaze on her. It was almost like he was jealous or something. She didn't understand, and right then she didn't care. She was too relieved to have Kandice's support as she approached the House of Blood.

★   ★   ★

The four of them found a message taped to the front door, written in ink in the same handwriting as the invitations.

We're in the backyard. Come around the side of the house and enter through the fence gate. We can't wait to meet you!

Neal found the last line of the note to be odd. If the Eldreds were so damn eager to make the acquaintance of their new neighbors, why hadn't they delivered the invitations to their cookout in person? Secondly, they would've wanted to introduce themselves and break the ice so that the cookout would feel less awkward for everyone. But they hadn't. Then again, different people did things different ways. Who was he to judge? Besides, he was too busy dealing with his own emotions to worry about the Eldreds' style of social etiquette.

He understood why Kandice had taken Alex's hand and why she continued to hold it as the four of them stepped off the front porch and began walking around the side of the house. Alex had been overwhelmed by being so close to the House of Blood, and Kandice – considerate, loving person that she was – stepped forward and took the girl's hand to bolster her courage. A gesture that was laudable and perfectly innocent. Yet he still found himself burning with jealousy at seeing his wife holding hands with another woman. And a significantly younger one at that. *It means nothing,* he told himself. She'd do the same thing if she was heterosexual. He knew this, yet his jealousy continued to burn, unabated. And mixed with the jealousy was another emotion. He was getting turned on. Seeing Kandice with Alex made him think of the three of them in bed together. Kandice would get the best of both worlds, and he would get to fuck and be fucked by Alex as well. He felt at once excited by this idea and repulsed by it. He was close to twice Alex's age, and what sounded good in fantasy was often not-so-great in reality. He'd never participated in a threesome before, but he imagined it was less exciting than it sounded. There was probably quite a bit of awkwardness as the three participants tried to find different configurations that worked for them. Almost like a math problem, he thought, a matter of geometry as much as desire.

Stop it, stop it, stop it!

He forced himself to look away from Kandice and Alex, and focused his attention on the wooden privacy fence that enclosed the Eldreds' backyard. From the street, it looked like an ordinary wood fence, boards seven feet high, each coming to a point at the top, as if the fence had been designed to impale intruders. There was something off about the wood itself, though. Despite the rain they'd had the last few days, it was bone dry. It looked more like sandstone than wood, and there were numerous places where the surface was pitted, as if the fence was in the early stages of crumbling to dust. He turned to Kandice, intending to draw her attention to the fence and ask what she thought of it.

But Kandice was walking ahead of him, with Alex, and he found himself looking at Isaac instead. Isaac wasn't looking at him, though. He was looking at the ground.

Curious, Neal looked downward. At first, he didn't understand what had drawn Isaac's attention. But then he saw it: the grass. It was overlong and riddled with patches of white clover. Unsightly, perhaps, but nothing strange. But wherever they stepped, the grass didn't spring back up once they lifted their feet off it. It remained flat, and it looked mushy, as if crushed into green paste. He noticed other flattened places like this ahead of them, and he realized they'd likely been caused by whoever had arrived before them.

Isaac caught Neal's attention, and the older man raised an eyebrow, as if to say, *You see it too, right?* Neal nodded, then shrugged. Translation: *Yes, I do, but I don't have any idea what's causing it.* Probably some kind of weird plant disease that he'd never heard of before. Whatever it was, he hoped it wouldn't spread to Martin and Cora's lawn, and from there to his and Kandice's.

He thought he heard faint sounds as they walked; tiny, muffled *eeps* that made him think of the cries small rodents might make, only quieter. So quiet, he wasn't sure that he wasn't imagining them. Probably just the damp grass squishing beneath the rubber soles of his sneakers, he thought.

The fence's gate faced Martin and Cora's house, less than a dozen yards from Vivienne's bedroom window. This observation disturbed Neal, but he wasn't sure why. Another handwritten note was taped to the gate. This one read *This is where the fun's at!!!,* complete with a trio of exclamation marks.

Isaac *hrumpfed.*

"I highly doubt it."

Alex glanced back over her shoulder and gave him a warning look. The message was clear: *Behave.* This was one of the few times Neal actually agreed with Isaac. He had a rule of thumb: the more exclamation marks after a statement, the more likely it was to be bullshit.

Neal smelled something cooking on a grill, and despite his wariness about coming here, his mouth watered. He'd had a big lunch – Kandice and he had stopped at Bigger-Better-Burger on their way home from the IKEA in Westchester – and he hadn't expected to be very hungry tonight. But the smell of cooking meat triggered a nearly overpowering hunger, as if he hadn't eaten all day. Hell, all *week*. He looked to the others, saw them licking their lips, inhaling deeply through their nostrils, savoring the scent like animals would. Then he realized he was doing the same thing. Or rather, his body was. It seemed to be responding automatically, without his conscious awareness.

The wood, the grass, the meat-smell, and of course those goddamn signs...Neal felt all these things were, if not exactly warnings, then indicators. Of what, he didn't know. But he sensed it wasn't good, was in fact as far away from good as it was possible to get. He started to reach out to Kandice, intending to touch her, get her attention, tell her they should forget about the fucking cookout and go home. Better yet, they should hop in one of their vehicles and get the fuck out of town. Once they'd put Rockridge in their rearview, they could pick a direction at random and continue driving. It wouldn't matter where they ended up, just so long as it wasn't *here*.

His gaze fixed on Kandice's and Alex's hands, fingers intertwined, both grasping so tightly the skin of their knuckles was white.

He let his arm fall to his side. He'd almost let his imagination get the better of him. He was above all else a rational man, and he wasn't going to allow his anxiety about visiting the House of Blood – for surely that's what these strange observations were, symptoms of anxiety – to control him.

Besides, it wasn't as if he had any kind of special insight. Look how long he'd been married to Kandice without realizing she was bisexual. He was about as clueless as they came.

The four of them had been standing outside the gate for several moments, each quiet and alone with his or her thoughts, as if they'd silently agreed to put off going inside as long as possible.

Fuck it.

Neal stepped past the others, opened the gate, and stood by, waiting for the others to go first.

They still hesitated, especially Alex. Her eyes were wide and wild, like a forest animal that had scented fire. But Kandice led her gently forward, and she went along without resistance.

"Might as well get this over with," Isaac grumbled. He walked past Neal without looking at him.

A quick thought flitted through Neal's mind. Had he offered to let the others go first so he could go last? Maybe, but if so, what did it matter? It was too late to back out now. He stepped into the yard and pulled the gate shut behind him.

★   ★   ★

Cora held a red plastic cup that was half full of some kind of sticky-sweet punch. It had the bright green color of antifreeze, and she thought it probably had a similar flavor, too. And the liquid was dotted with tiny specks. She wasn't sure, could only sneak occasional glances at her cup, but she thought the spots had legs, and she could swear the things were swimming through the green goop. She'd already told Vivienne not to drink the punch, but when she'd told Martin about the dots, he'd just said she was full of shit, emptied his cup, and went back to the punch bowl to get a refill. *Asshole.* Sometimes she thought she understood why Cherie Raines had killed her husband.

The Raines backyard was nothing special. The lawn needed to be treated by a professional lawn-care company. It was especially overgrown next to the fence, the tall grass choked by large, ugly weeds. The grass itself turned to green paste beneath their feet, and Cora regretted wearing flip-flops. The green mush – oily and cold – got between her toes, and it felt extremely gross, like they were walking on the rotting corpse of some large green beast.

There was a wooden deck upon which a gas grill rested. Arnoldo Eldred stood at the grill, cooking meat. What kind it was, Cora couldn't say. She'd gone over to chat with the man for a few minutes, and she'd glanced at the grill several times. The meat kind of looked like chicken breast – it had that same pink gummy texture – but it was far larger than any chicken breast she'd ever seen, and it was irregularly shaped. Plus, it had some kind of growths on it. When she'd asked Arnoldo what they were, he grinned and said, "Venom sacs." She'd thought he'd been joking, so she laughed politely and after a few more moments, she walked back into the yard.

There were a pair of weathered picnic tables – wood gray, boards warped – and upon those were the food and drink the Eldreds had put out. Nothing fancy. Cheese and crackers, a vegetable tray, and a bowl of what might've been hummus but which smelled like stagnant water. The antifreeze punch was in a clay bowl on one of the tables, a stack of red plastic cups beside it. There were markings on the clay, some kind of letters that had been engraved into its surface, but Cora didn't recognize the language. For some reason, if she looked at the letters too long, her vision began to blur and her stomach went queasy, so she did her best to avoid looking at the bowl at all. She wondered if it was some kind of antique. It didn't necessarily look old, but it sure as hell *felt* old.

Martin was on the deck now, talking with Arnoldo. Well, more like talking *at* him. One of the things Martin liked to do when he met someone was to gauge where they were politically. Instead of asking them what their opinions of various political issues were, though, Martin would begin lecturing them about his. She didn't always agree with her husband's viewpoints, but she admired how strongly he held them, and how he was willing to talk to anyone about them rather than keep them to himself and avoid causing any conflict. This did mean that he could go on at length about politics the same way other people went on about sports or movies, and that could get old real fast. So far, Arnoldo displayed no sign that he was growing tired of listening to Martin's monologue. Maybe her husband had found a kindred soul.

Vivienne wandered around the yard, head down. She'd told Cora she was going to look for four-leaf clovers. As high as the grass was, Cora didn't think Vivienne would have much luck, but she was glad her daughter had found something to occupy herself. Too bad there were no children her age on Brookside Court for her to play with. Vivienne was an only child, and she was used to playing alone. This made Cora feel guilty, as if she and Martin should provide Vivienne a sibling, if for no other reason than when her parents were gone – which hopefully wouldn't be for years and years – she'd still have family in the world. Cora and Martin had talked about having another child, but neither was ready to commit to it yet. Martin was afraid they wouldn't be able to afford another kid, while Cora was worried that Martin would never learn to deal with his gambling addiction. She didn't want to bring another child into a family that might fall apart sooner rather than later. And if she ended up a single mother, her life would be difficult enough with one child. She didn't know how she'd manage with two.

She wished the Eldreds had put out some alcohol. She could use a stiff drink right now. Hell, she could use three or four.

Three of the Eldreds – the grandmother and the two teenagers – sat at the picnic table with the food. She tried to remember their names. The grandmother was Cleora. That one was easy, since it rhymed with her name. The boy was...Demarcus, and the girl was...was.... *When you were introduced to her, you thought how her name made her sound vain.* Vanita! The teens sat next to each other on one side of the table, while the grandmother sat on the other side. They didn't speak to one another, didn't look at one another. Instead they watched their new neighbors, their gazes flicking from one person to the next with rapid, jerky motions that made Cora think of the way insects moved. Whenever they looked at her, she met their gazes, but they didn't look away. All they did was smile at her until they moved on to look at someone else. It was goddamn creepy.

Lacresha Eldred stood near the deck, talking with a man who Cora hadn't been introduced to yet. Despite the heat, he wore a long-sleeved navy-blue turtleneck and jeans. He had some of kind of disability – one of his legs was bent at an odd angle – but he was able to get around without the aid of a cane, moving with a spastic, lurching gait that made Cora wince whenever she saw it. His face had remained expressionless the entire time Cora had been here, and even though there was a light breeze, his hair remained perfectly in place at all times. *He must use a ton of styling gel,* Cora thought.

Lacresha and the man weren't having a conversation so much as Lacresha was talking and he was listening. Cora couldn't remember seeing his mouth move once since she'd arrived. It was almost as if his face was a mask of some kind or he was a mannequin somehow brought to life. *A mannequin with a busted leg,* she thought.

The Eldreds, for some odd reason, were dressed alike. White polo shirts, black shorts, black shoes, no socks. It was almost as if the outfit was a family uniform of some sort. It reminded Cora of how a large extended family wore the same clothes for a reunion, T-shirts that had the family surname emblazoned on the front and back, so they could be easily identified by other members of their clan. Whenever she'd seen a family dressed like that – at an amusement park or at a picnic area near a lake – she'd always found it to be kind of weird. But at least dressing alike served a purpose for these people. What purpose did the Eldreds' 'uniform' serve, other than to make them seem even stranger than they already did?

The Eldreds had brought out a number of chairs for their guests, but instead of arranging these chairs into a group near the picnic tables to make it easier for everyone to talk, the chairs were spread across the lawn, seemingly without thought. The chairs weren't part of a set. They were all different – a folding card-table chair, a wooden rocking chair, an upholstered office chair with wheels on its base, and such. They'd even brought out a simple three-legged stool that had one leg shorter than the others. So much so that it rested unevenly on the ground. Cora didn't see how anyone could possibly sit on the damn thing.

Spencer and Lola had moved two chairs – one a folding canvas chair used for camping, the other a white plastic one with a round back and arm rests – together. They sat, sometimes talking quietly, sometimes looking around warily, as if they were having second thoughts about being here.

Me too, Cora thought.

The heat was really getting to Spencer. So much sweat dripped off him he looked like he was literally melting. He kept wiping his forehead with his fingers, but it didn't help much. His cheeks were flushed, and Cora wondered if he was going to faint or something.

She'd noticed that Spencer kept watching Vivienne while trying to look as if he wasn't watching her. He'd cast his gaze around the yard, and when he got to Vivienne, he'd linger on her, only for a few seconds, but long enough for it to be noticeable, before moving on. Sometimes he'd look up at the sky, and when he brought his head down, he'd be facing in Vivienne's direction. Sometimes he'd look down at the grass, and then do the same thing when he raised his head. She supposed she might be being overprotective – Martin accused her of it all the time – but her instincts said she wasn't. She was further convinced she was right because Lola kept checking on her son, and if she caught him looking at Vivienne, she'd swat him on the arm or pinch the skin on the back of his hand. Whenever she did these things, Spencer would quickly look away from Vivienne with a guilty expression, but he didn't meet his mother's eyes.

Plus, Spencer hadn't looked at her once since she'd arrived, and she looked good this evening. Her shorts were high and tight, and her T-shirt – which had a cartoon image of a sunglasses-wearing bikini-clad girl chicken lying on a beach chair beneath a blazing sun with the words *Hot Chick* above it – was a size too small for her. It emphasized her breasts quite nicely, she thought. Not that Spencer seemed to care. Maybe he was gay or asexual, or maybe she simply wasn't his type. Although in her experience, when it came to heterosexual men, any relatively attractive woman seemed to be their type.

But just because Spencer wasn't ogling her didn't mean he was a pedophile. Maybe he just liked kids. He wasn't married and she didn't think he ever had been. Maybe seeing Vivienne made him long for the children he didn't – and probably wouldn't – ever have. Besides, if he was a registered sex offender, didn't he have to notify everyone in the neighborhood of that fact? She thought she remembered hearing something like that once.

He'd only be registered if he got caught molesting a child. That doesn't mean he hasn't done it – or wants to. There's a first time for everything, right?

Besides, if Spencer watching Vivienne was so innocent, why did his mother so clearly disapprove of him doing it?

Cora decided it would be better if Vivienne stayed by her side for the rest of the cookout. They might even leave early if she could think of some excuse – *and* if she could get Martin to go along with it. She'd worry about that later. First, she wanted her daughter near her, wanted to put a protective hand on her shoulder and press her body against her leg, to feel Vivienne's physical presence and know she was safe.

She started toward Vivienne – who was still blissfully searching for four-leaf clovers – when Lacresha Eldred stepped in front of her.

Cora was so startled she almost screamed. She hadn't seen the woman walk away from the man with the mannequin face. It was almost as if Lacresha had been standing next to him one moment, and then the next she stood in front of her, without having to travel the distance between.

"Are you enjoying yourself, my dear?"

Lacresha's features – like the rest of her family's – were plain and unremarkable: black hair, pale skin. But her *voice*! If satin could speak, it would've sounded like this. Smooth and sensual, something you wanted to wrap around your naked body, close your eyes, and revel in the sensation of against your skin. The sudden heat Cora felt had nothing to do with the outside temperature.

"Yes, I am. Thank you."

Cora didn't know exactly what she was thanking the woman for, but it seemed like the right thing to say.

"You're very kind."

Lacresha took one of Cora's hands and gave it a gentle squeeze. The instant the woman's cool, dry flesh came into contact with hers, Cora's nerves lit up, as if a strong jolt of electricity shot through her. It hurt, but it also felt good. So good that when Lacresha let go of her hand and the sensation died away, she immediately missed it.

Lacresha glanced toward Vivienne. The girl had evidently given up on finding four-leaf clovers and she was now picking white clover. Lacresha faced Cora once more.

"You must be very proud of your daughter. She seems very special."

Cora appreciated the woman's words. What parent doesn't like to hear good things about their children? But she didn't see that Vivienne was doing anything particularly special right now.

Cora smiled. "Thanks. My husband and I think she is."

Lacresha then glanced toward Spencer. Cora looked too, and she saw the man was once again looking at Vivienne. Or rather, at Vivienne's tiny butt, since she was bent over and facing away from where Spencer sat with his mother. Lola noticed where her son was looking, and this time she pinched the back of his hand so hard that he yelped.

"Evidently, someone else thinks your daughter is special, too." There was something about Lacresha's smile when she said this, a hint of lascivious amusement, that made Cora angry. Before she could say anything to the woman, though, the fence gate opened and Isaac, Alex, Kandice, and Neal walked into the yard.

"Please excuse me," Lacresha said. "I must greet the new arrivals."

Lacresha headed toward the gate, moving with silent grace. Cora watched her go, and although she didn't notice it, Lacresha left no footprints on the grass as she went.

CHAPTER NINE

"—because if you actually do some research, you'll find that the planet's temperature has *always* varied. What's happening now is not something new. It's *normal*."

Martin punctuated his point by taking a drink of punch. He didn't know what the Eldreds had put in the stuff, but it had a tangy zing that he really liked, even if it did burn his throat a little and leave a weird aftertaste. Cora was suspicious of the punch and had tried to convince him not to drink it, but he'd paid her no mind. She was always worried about one thing or another.

Like your gambling, he thought.

Fuck that woman. He took another swig of punch.

He decided he liked Arnoldo Eldred. The man wasn't a big talker, but he was one hell of a listener. And he was interested in what Martin had to say. A lot of people weren't – like Neal, for one – but that was because they were too lazy to think for themselves. They swallowed the lies fed to them by the lame-stream media. He wasn't sure where Arnoldo fell yet, whether he was another one of the mindless horde or if he was someone who understood what was *really* going on in the world. But he took the man's listening as a hopeful sign – *and* he took it as encouragement to continue.

"It's all a part of the great liberal conspiracy – the shadow government. You know what that is, right?"

Up to this point, Arnoldo had merely nodded now and again as he worked on grilling...whatever it was. Martin could tell it was some kind of meat, but beyond that, he didn't have a fucking clue. It could be wildebeest for all he knew. Arnoldo used a pair of tongs to turn over the meat. It sizzled and smoke rose into the air. This maneuver accomplished, he turned to Martin.

"I've never heard of this shadow government before, but I like the sound of it. My family enjoys anything related to darkness, whether it's physical, psychological, or metaphysical." He leaned forward and lowered his voice, as if about to deliver an important – but sensitive – piece of information. "The best is a combination of all three, don't you think?"

Martin wondered if he'd been mistaken about the guy, if he was just another over-educated liberal who looked down on working people like himself. But he detected no mockery in the man's voice, no derision.

"I do," he said, even though he had no idea what Arnoldo was referring to. Evidently, he'd said the right thing, because Arnoldo smiled. Well, *smile* might be too generous of a description. The man's lips pulled away to reveal crooked yellow teeth set into cracked, bleeding gums. Martin thought he saw something small and multilegged in a gap between an incisor and bicuspid, but he blinked, and it was gone – if it was ever there in the first place.

Martin was reluctant to return to the topic of the shadow government after that, so he decided to move on to safer territory. He nodded toward the grill.

"Sure smells good," he said. "I'm getting really hungry."

And he was, ravenously so, although the cooking meat gave off an oily smell that turned his stomach a bit.

Arnoldo smiled again. "I don't know what it's like to *get* hungry. I'm *always* hungry."

Martin didn't know what this meant, either, but he gave a chuckle and said, "I hear you."

Still smiling, Arnoldo turned his attention back to the grill. "I enjoy preparing meals," he said. "It's my...*specialty*, I suppose you could say."

Martin noticed Cora talking with Arnoldo's wife. He tried to remember the woman's name. It was something strange, like Arnoldo's, but it wouldn't come to him.

"I see my wife's over there talking to yours. I don't know what she's saying, but she can be kind of nosy. If she says anything – if she asks any *questions* – that make your wife uncomfortable, I'd like to apologize in advance."

Arnoldo looked to him once more. The man smiled his crooked-tooth smile, but there was something in his eyes that made Martin want to take several steps backward – the coldness of a windswept arctic plain in the darkest part of the night.

"And what might your wife be interested in discovering?"

Arnoldo's voice was calm, warm even, but beneath the words Martin could sense steel. He didn't understand why, but he knew he had to be careful in his reply.

"She's fascinated with what happened to the Raines family. You know, the people who used to own the house? You know about them, right?"

Arnoldo nodded. "Go on."

Martin didn't take his gaze from Arnoldo's face, but in his peripheral vision, he thought he saw the tongs that the man was holding now had sharp points on the ends. Martin swallowed. His mouth was suddenly dry, and his throat hurt from all the punch he'd had. What the fuck was in that stuff? Kerosene?

"We moved in after all that was over. Cora and me. We got the house pretty cheap. Cora likes watching true crime shows on television, usually about murders. She gets into that kind of thing. I don't understand it myself. Seems kind of morbid. But hey, whatever makes her happy, you know?"

Arnoldo continued looking at him for a moment, eyes unblinking, smile frozen. And then, just like that, he relaxed and returned his attention to the grill. The tongs now looked normal again.

"I'm sure Lacresha will take no offense if Cora asks about the murders. There's only so much we can tell, though. After all, we did not commit them."

Martin waited for Arnoldo to laugh at his own joke, or at least grin to let Martin know he *was* joking. But all he did was flip over the hunk of mystery meat again.

"How long do you think it will be before the meat is sufficiently charred?" Arnoldo asked.

The question put Martin off balance, and it took him a moment to shift gears. He looked down at the whatever-it-was.... Pork, maybe? He considered.

"That's a damn big piece of meat. I don't know. Maybe another five minutes each side?"

"Would you like to make a wager on that?"

"Wager? You mean a bet?"

Arnoldo nodded. "Just so."

Martin cast a quick glance toward Cora. She was still busy talking with Lacresha. Besides, she was too far away to overhear what Arnoldo had said, especially with the sound of sizzling meat covering their voices. He turned back to Arnoldo.

"You a gambling man?"

Arnoldo grinned. "Always. What is the point of living if one isn't willing to take chances now and again? We're all going to be food for the Gyre in the end, so we might as well amuse ourselves while we can, eh?"

Martin had no idea what the *Gyre* was, but he understood the basic sentiment. Even though this was such a small thing to bet on, he knew he shouldn't take Arnoldo up on his offer. If Cora got wind of it, she would be royally pissed, and while he wasn't afraid of his wife – a man had to be the ruler of his own roost – he didn't want to air their dirty laundry in front of the others, and especially not in front of the Eldreds. So far, it looked like he and Arnoldo were sympatico on political issues, and it would be nice to have a neighbor who saw the world the same way he did – even if the guy was kind of a weirdo. He had no idea where Spencer and his mom fell politically since they kept to themselves so much, but both Neal and Isaac were liberals. Isaac was the more moderate of the two, but a liberal was a liberal as far as Martin was concerned. That didn't necessarily make them bad people, but it did mean they weren't as smart as they thought. Otherwise, they wouldn't *be* liberal.

So if he wanted Arnoldo to like him, he should take the bet, right? It wouldn't be like he was *really* gambling. He would just be being a good guest and not offending his host.

"I'll take that action," Martin said. As soon as he spoke these words, he felt a familiar and welcome thrill zing through him, as if every cell in his body had been charged with fresh energy. He felt *alive*.

"Excellent! Here are the terms. If the meat takes a total of ten more minutes to cook – five minutes on each side – you win. If it takes less time or more time, I win."

"Sounds good. What are the stakes?"

"If you win, I shall grant you a Pass. If I win, you receive nothing."

Martin frowned. "A pass? What to?"

"It's not *to* anything. It will allow you to avoid something of your choosing. Perhaps even undo it, if you use the pass swiftly enough and with the proper goal in mind. But it's only good for *one* use, and you can only use it for *one* thing." He smiled. "No getting greedy."

Martin had no idea what the fuck the man was talking about. Some kind of New Age meditation crap? Maybe he and Arnoldo weren't quite as sympatico as he'd hoped. Still, given the terms Arnoldo had set, he had nothing to lose by going along with the bet.

"Okay, you're on."

"Good. Does your phone have a timer? Set it for ten minutes, please."

Martin did so, and the two men fell silent. They focused their entire attention on the meat, watching it with the intensity of men who have serious money riding on the outcome instead of some abstract 'pass'.

Martin held his phone so they could both watch the timer. When it reached five minutes, Arnoldo flipped over the meat. Martin grinned when he saw it looked done on that side. Arnoldo showed no reaction, and the men continued their vigil. Another minute passed. Two. Three, four, five....

Arnoldo flipped the meat once more. Now this side looked done.

Martin waited to see if Arnoldo planned to make some excuse to wiggle out of the bet. He knew a lot of guys like that, guys who never had any intention of paying up when they lost. Not that he wanted Arnoldo's 'pass', whatever the hell it was. It was the principle of the thing. He'd won and Arnoldo lost. The man should make it official.

And he did.

Arnoldo grinned, not looking disappointed in the slightest. He offered his free hand for Martin to shake.

"Victory is yours! You now have a Pass. Use it wisely."

Martin shook the man's hand, still not having the slightest idea what he'd won, but pleased that he'd won nevertheless. It was the winning that counted, not the thing that symbolized your victory. And right now, at this moment, Martin Hawkins was a winner.

"Now let us consume food," Arnoldo said.

Martin couldn't help laughing at the man's phrasing.
"Yes, let's!"

*   *   *

Spencer rubbed the back of his hand. That last pinch had really hurt.
And he had prominent veins on the back of his hand. What if she'd
damaged one of them? Would it cause a stroke? If it did, maybe that
wouldn't be such a bad thing, especially if it was a really big one, the
kind that killed you instantly, like flipping off a light. If he was gone,
there'd be no chance of him ever hurting a child, and when he was
dead, he'd never have to feel the *pull*, the *need*. He wouldn't have
to keep fighting himself all the time. He would be free. It would be
such a relief.

Speaking of relief, he'd *kill* to be inside somewhere that had air-
conditioning. It was goddamn *hot*. He felt like he was standing naked
in front of a blast furnace. Most of it was due to the actual temperature,
but that wasn't the only reason he felt hot.

He returned his gaze to Vivienne, watching her out of the corner
of his eye, hoping his mother wouldn't notice.

She was such a beautiful child. She was dark-haired like her
mother, her features a blend of Asian and Caucasian. She moved in
the unself-conscious way children had, comfortable in a body that
wasn't completely coordinated yet. She was obviously capable of
entertaining herself, and she possessed a focus that set her apart from
others her age. She conducted her search for clovers – four-leaf ones,
he suspected – patiently and methodically, and Spencer wondered
how this focus would manifest itself when she was older. Would
she go into a technical field, perhaps become an engineer? Or into
healthcare, becoming a surgeon? Or might she go a different route,
becoming a dedicated musician or perhaps a skilled practitioner of
some other art? That was one of the wonderful things about children.
They were all potential, and they could go in a multitude of directions
as they grew, becoming anything at all. He found it so exciting to be
close to all that potential, but he wanted – *needed* – to be closer still.
Close enough to touch....

Vivienne bent down to examine the clover more closely, and

even though his mother had punished him the last time his gaze had lingered on her small rear, he couldn't look away, didn't want to. There was nothing intentionally seductive about the way she bent over. She did so without any awareness that she was being watched. Most children thought they were as good as invisible around adults, and for the most part, they were right. But Vivienne was very visible to him.

I see you, he thought. *Do you see me?*

But of course she didn't. He was an adult, which meant he existed on the periphery of her awareness, when he existed at all. He found this comforting. It meant he could look all he wanted without alarming her. It meant he could get physically closer without spooking her, reach out a hand and lightly brush his fingertips over the soft flesh of her cheek, caress her glossy black hair.... His cock began to swell, and while the sensation was pleasurable, he was terrified that one of the adults – especially Cora – would look his way and see the growing bulge in his pants. They'd know his secret then, and he would automatically become a monster in their eyes. Not because he'd actually done anything, but simply because he was thinking about doing something, and his body had reacted.

Ashamed and despising himself, he looked away from Vivienne and found his gaze landing on the three Eldreds sitting at the picnic table – the grandmother and the teenagers, both of whom were too old to interest him. The three were looking at him coolly, dispassionately, but then they smiled and Spencer felt panic erupt in his chest. He knew they had seen him watching Vivienne, and they understood what he was. And based on the way they were smiling, instead of finding him repugnant, they found him amusing. *We see you, you funny little man,* those smiles seemed to say. *You can't hide what you are, not from us.*

Spencer looked away from them, cast his gaze upward. He clasped his hands together, and if anyone – besides the Eldreds at the picnic table – noticed him right then, they might've thought he was praying. But Spencer knew there was no god. If there had been, if he, she, or it possessed any mercy whatsoever, Spencer would never have been born in the first place.

He started crying then, not very hard, just a few tears, and those mixed with the sweat on his face, and he doubted anyone would notice.

Unable to stop himself, he looked once more to the Eldreds sitting at the picnic table. They were staring at him with expressions of hunger, teeth bared in what only an idiot would think were smiles.

★   ★   ★

Vivienne was bored. Bored, bored, *bored!* She didn't like being here. It was a bad place; she could feel it. No one else seemed to, though. They stood around talking, as if this place was completely normal. Safe.

Adults were pretty stupid.

Left to her own devices, Vivienne had started searching for four-leaf clovers. No reason, really. Just something to do, and she was good at it. She could look at a patch of green clover and any four-leaf ones would jump right out at her. It was like her superpower. But for some reason, she was having trouble finding any here.

Maybe it had something to do with the grass. It was weird and mushy, maybe too weird for four-leaf clovers to grow. Once, she'd been playing in the garage – she'd known she wasn't supposed to, which was a big part of what made it fun – and she'd picked up one of Daddy's tools. She didn't know its name, but her mommy told her later it was a hacksaw. It had tiny jagged teeth and she ran her index finger over them to see how sharp they were. Very, as it turned out. She ran inside, crying, finger bleeding, and Mommy took care of her. She cleaned the wound – which wasn't very deep – and put antibacterial cream on it. *We don't want it to get infected, do we?* Mommy had said, and then she'd put an adhesive bandage on Vivienne's finger. Feeling better, she'd asked Mommy what *infected* meant. Mommy had thought for a moment before answering. *It's when bad stuff gets inside your body and makes it sick.* That's what had happened to the yard, Vivienne thought. Bad stuff had gotten into it and made it *infected.*

That was probably why she couldn't find any four-leaf clovers. How could a lucky plant grow in bad ground? There were plenty of three-leaf ones, though, and plenty of the other kind of clover, the white kind. She wasn't sure why both the green and the white plants were both called *clover*. They looked way different to her. Maybe whoever named them had gotten tired and re-used the word *clover* rather than think up a new one.

She didn't like the way the too-soft grass mushed beneath her shoes, but the sounds it made were interesting. Rather, the sounds the *white* clover was making. They were like tiny screams, but they cut off the instant she put her full weight down as she walked, and she knew that was because she was killing them. What she heard were the clover's cries of terror as a gigantic object blotted out the sun, moved toward them, and ground them into the sodden earth where, like the grass, they became a slippery, wet paste. She wondered what one of the unmushed white clovers would do if she picked it.

Only one way to find out.

She bent over, selected a white clover at random, plucked it, then straightened. She brought the clover closer to her face and examined it. The thin stem felt kind of gooey between her fingers, so she was careful not to handle it too roughly. She didn't want to accidentally smush it. Upon first glance, she saw nothing particularly different about this white clover from the ones in her own backyard. Maybe this one was a little bigger, its colors a bit off. But it was *mostly* the same. She held it to her nose and sniffed.

She scowled and wrinkled her nose. The clover should've smelled sweet, but this one smelled like an old stinky gym shoe.

She remembered a game she'd played with her cousins the last time they'd visited. They were identical twins – Michelle and Marcel – and were a couple years older than her. They were her Aunt Jeannie's daughters, although she wasn't sure what Jeannie's exact relationship to the family was. She wasn't Asian, so she wasn't related to Mom. Dad's sister, maybe? Just a good friend of the family? It didn't really matter to her. She loved playing with her big-girl cousins. They taught her all kinds of interesting things, like her first bad word: *boob*. And they'd told her that babies grew inside mommies and when they were ready to come out, the mommy pooped them into the toilet. Babies had to be pulled out right away, or else they'd drown. But the twins also taught her games, and one of them involved white clover.

Vivienne moved her fingers up the clover's stem until her thumb was right beneath the bloom. She then began a chant.

"Momma-had-a-baby-and-its-head-popped-*off*!"

On the word *off*, she flicked out her thumb, severing the bloom from the stem, and sending it arcing through the air. Normally, the fun in the game came from the tactile sensation of feeling the bloom part from the stem and watching to see how far the bloom would fly before falling to the ground. But Vivienne barely noticed these things this time. She was too startled by the shriek the clover made as she decapitated it. It was much louder than the cries the clover made when stepped upon, higher-pitched and laced with terrified agony. Part of her was sickened by what she'd done, but another part – small and hidden deep inside her – thought the scream was the most wonderful sound she'd ever heard.

She had no idea if any of the adults had heard the clover's death-shriek, and she turned to see if any of them were looking at her, scowling with disapproval at what she'd done. But a man stood there, only a couple feet away, blocking her view of the other adults. She gasped and her body tensed, ready to run, but the man made no move to touch her, didn't reach for her, so she remained where she was. She didn't know the man's name. The people who lived here had introduced themselves when she and her parents had arrived, but she'd forgotten their names as soon as she'd heard them. But she hadn't been introduced to this man. He'd remained apart from the other adults mostly, standing back and watching, almost as if he were some kind of big lawn decoration and not a person at all.

Despite the heat, he wore a long-sleeved turtleneck. He must not have been too hot, though, because he wasn't sweating. His face looked normal enough at first, but the longer she looked at it, the more she thought there was something strange about it. None of his features moved. His lips were frozen in a straight line, and his nostrils didn't widen when he drew in a breath. Strangest of all, his eyes didn't blink. And they were dry, no moisture at all. They looked almost painted on, like a doll's eyes. *This man is a giant doll,* she thought. He stood funny – one of his legs stuck out at an odd angle, and she was surprised he could stand upright at all. He looked like he might fall over any second.

His head tilted downward so he could get a better look at her with his painted-on eyes. As he performed this task, she heard a soft whirring sound, like some kind of machine was at work. The sound died when his head stopped moving. He regarded her for a moment, and then his mouth opened and a word emerged. This word wasn't formed by lips and tongue, though. It emerged from deep inside him, as if from an internal speaker.

"Again."

The word was flat, toneless, without life or inflection.

Vivienne didn't know what the man meant, and even if she had, she was too frightened to reply.

"Again," he repeated.

This time he raised his right arm and pointed to the stem she still held.

"You want me to do *this*—" she waggled the stem for emphasis, "—again?"

The whirring sound came again, and the man raised and lowered his head in a stiff nod.

Vivienne wasn't sure what to do. Her mommy and daddy, as well as Ms. Pasternack, her kindergarten teacher, had all warned her not to talk to strangers. But did this man count as a stranger? She didn't know him, but her mommy and daddy had brought her here, and they'd let her roam around the backyard on her own. They wouldn't have done that if they didn't think it was safe – which meant this man was safe. Didn't it?

She reminded herself of the bad feeling she had about this place, about the people who lived here. But she was bored. More, she was lonely. And for a child, those feelings trumped any vague sense of unease. She told herself not to be a baby, and she pushed all negative thoughts about this house and its occupants out of her mind. She gave the man a big smile.

"Okay."

She dropped the stem, picked another whole clover, and repeated the ritual. This time, the clover's head sailed so far, it struck the wooden fence and bounced off. She looked to the man to see what reaction – if any – he'd have. His features didn't move, of course, but laughter came from somewhere inside him. It wasn't *really* laughter, though. He spoke the word *ha*, repeating it several times.

"Ha-ha-ha-ha-ha." Then he said, *"Again."*

Vivienne decided she liked this man. He was funny.

She knelt to select another white clover.

CHAPTER TEN

The moment Kandice set foot in the Eldreds' backyard, she wondered if she and Neal had made a mistake. Their other neighbors were here – Spencer and Lola, Martin, Cora, and Vivienne – and Alex and Isaac had entered when she and Neal had. The fact that all of them were here should've made her feel better. Safety in numbers, right? But now that she *was* here, on the property where Cherie Raines had slaughtered her family and then taken her own life, she felt overwhelmed. It wasn't like she was picking up psychic emanations of the horrible acts that had been committed here. She didn't believe in stuff like that. The way she'd been able to deal with moving into a place almost next door to the House of Blood was not to think about it. And if she ever *did* start thinking about it, she turned her mind away from those thoughts as fast as possible. But now that she was here, she couldn't *not* think about it.

She'd never told Neal this, but when they were thinking of buying their house, she'd looked up the Raines murders on the Internet. She read accounts on several websites and discovered that a cable true-crime show called *Killer in My House* had done an episode on the case. She and Neal didn't have cable – they subscribed to a couple content-streaming services – but she was able to buy a digital copy of the episode from the program's website. She'd downloaded it and watched it late one night when Neal was asleep. They'd been living in a modest one-bedroom apartment then, and she sat at their small dining table, laptop open in front of her, listening with earbuds so she wouldn't wake Neal.

Killer in My House primarily used dramatic re-enactments to tell their lurid stories, and Kandice appreciated that. It gave her an emotional buffer so she could absorb the details of the case without being overwhelmed with sympathy for the victims. A main point of the program – which had of course been titled 'House of Blood' – was that despite the investigation that followed the murders, the interviews with friends and relations, the consultations with lauded psychologists, the theorizing by professional and amateur criminologists, no motive for the murders could be found, not even a hint of one. The 'experts' speculated, of course, but they did so with uncertainty and reluctance. The truth was, no one knew the truth – except for Cherie Raines. And maybe even she hadn't known. Maybe there had been no reason why she'd killed her family. Maybe some switch had been flipped inside her head that turned her into a murderer. And if something like that could happen to her, it could happen to anyone, at any time. And that idea had disturbed Kandice greatly.

Toward the end of the episode, actual home video of the Raines family – taken during their youngest child's second birthday – was presented. Kandice had wanted to slam her laptop shut so she wouldn't have these images in her head for the rest of her life. But she couldn't do it. She felt as if she had to bear witness to the Raines family's home video, that it was the least she owed them after watching a program that exploited their tragedy for entertainment. She watched a scene of the children chasing each other in the backyard – the same backyard where she now stood – and a scene of Cherie bringing out a birthday cake, candles already lit, and setting it down on the picnic table, just like the two Kandice now saw sitting on the grass in front of her. Kandice had watched the family sing happy birthday, then Jacob Raines blew out the candles with the help of his two older sisters. In the next scene, one of the children had taken the camera and recorded Cherie and her husband, Dale, kissing and then pretending to be upset when they saw their child had caught them on camera.

The program ended after that, and Kandice had reached out a shaking hand and closed her laptop. She then went into the bathroom and sat on top of the closed toilet lid until morning, crying. By the time Neal woke, she'd used three entire rolls of toilet paper to wipe her tears and blow her nose.

That day, she'd almost told Neal that she couldn't go through with it, that it didn't matter how good a deal they were going to get on the house. But she realized that by moving there, she and Neal could bring some positive energy to Brookside Court. Not in any kind of mystic sense, but in a real-world way. They'd be doing what humanity had done throughout its history: working to get past something bad by trying to make something good out of it. And so they'd bought the house, and while Kandice had gone through a difficult adjustment period, eventually she'd come to accept what they'd done and even began to believe that she'd been right, that they – along with their neighbors – had helped to redeem Brookside Court, at least a little.

Now she was here, in the very place where that birthday video, the one that had closed the episode of *Killer in My House,* had been recorded. She felt suddenly lightheaded, and her vision blurred. When everything became clear again, she saw two different versions of the backyard, one overlapping the other. One version was the year as it was now, with the Eldreds and her neighbors gathered for the cookout. The other version was an image from the video – the Raines family, having Jacob's birthday party. Cherie Raines was bringing the cake to the picnic table where her husband and children waited. She moved in slow motion, and the entire family had huge grins on their faces, and their eyes were wide and staring. Blood dripped from Cherie's hands, and the faces of her husband and children were smeared with crimson. Kandice was already warm from the early summer heat, but that was an outside warmth. She also felt hot inside, as if her entire nervous system had caught fire. Her lightheadedness worsened, becoming full-fledged vertigo, and she feared she was on the verge of fainting. Her heart rate increased, becoming machine-gun rapid, and her throat felt thick, swollen, and she became convinced she couldn't breathe. She was going to collapse any second, and the worst part was how embarrassing it would be to faint before she even met the new neighbors, to ruin their cookout because she hadn't been able to handle her emotions, to—

She felt a strong grip on her elbow steady her. Her vision blurred again, but this time when it cleared, she found herself looking into the face of a woman. It was a plain face, the features completely unremarkable. But the woman's eyes locked on to hers, and Kandice felt her heart rate slow, her throat relax and open up. The fiery sensation in her nerves eased, and her dizziness abated.

"Are you all right?" the woman asked. Her features might not have been anything special, but her voice was soft as any silk that had caressed a human body, warm as honey poured over a hot biscuit.

This beautiful, unearthly voice gave Kandice some of her strength back. She still felt shaky, but she knew the worst had passed.

She gave the woman an apologetic smile. "Sorry. I don't know what came over me."

It was a lie, but she was too embarrassed to tell the truth. Besides, she didn't want to start off her relationship with the Eldreds by immediately talking about the Raines murders.

The woman returned her smile. "You have nothing to apologize for. It's quite hot this evening. I'm sure you'll feel much better once you've had something to drink. My name is Lacresha. Allow me to escort you to the punch bowl."

"Thank you. I'm Kandice, by the way."

Lacresha had continued holding on to Kandice's elbow as they spoke, and now she stepped to Kandice's side, locked arms with her, and began leading her to one of the picnic tables.

"Kandice," Lacresha said, as if trying out the name to see how it felt on her tongue. "Do people ever call you Kandy because you're so sweet?"

Kandice looked back at Neal and saw him scowling. She knew what he was thinking, that Lacresha – a *woman* – was touching and flirting with his bisexual wife after only having just met her. She felt suddenly angry. She was sick of Neal's ridiculous jealousy. Not only was it childish, it was a sign that, even after all their time together, he didn't fully trust her. She turned back to Lacresha.

"No, but you can call me Kandy if you like."

She didn't look back at Neal again, but she could feel him seething behind her.

She smiled. *Good.*

★   ★   ★

Isaac stared, dumbfounded. The woman had told Kandice her name was Lacresha – odd name – but she resembled his ex-wife so much that she could've been her twin. She was tall, like Sara, and she had the same fiery red hair, short and curly. Her skin was alabaster white, and her facial features were delicate, making her look at least a decade younger than she was. Her lips were full and naturally pink. She didn't need to wear lipstick. Makeup of any kind only distracted from her natural beauty.

It had been months since he'd seen Sara, although they occasionally spoke on the phone or exchanged texts – usually about Alex. It had been years since they'd been physically intimate, but he could never forget how soft, warm, and smooth her skin was, how her lips tasted, how she smelled…. He had never told anyone – it wasn't like he had any real friends to tell anyway – but he still dreamed about making love with Sara. Not every night, but at least once a week. He *hated* those dreams. Sometimes they took place during their marriage, sometimes they took place in the present day, and he and Sara – finally acknowledging they still loved each other – were getting back together. The dreams were long and detailed, as if he were truly living them, and when he climaxed in his dream, he did so in real life. Before the divorce, he hadn't had wet dreams since his early twenties, and he thought he'd never experience them again. But as messy and inconvenient as wet dreams were, that wasn't why he hated dreaming about sex with Sara. He hated the crushing sadness and disappointment that always hit him upon awakening. He'd remember that he and Sara had split up, and their divorce had been far from amicable. Mostly his fault. With his temper, he didn't do *amicable* well. The truth was simple: for all the troubles they'd had, especially toward the end of their marriage, he missed Sara. Did he still love her? He didn't know. Maybe he loved an idealized version of her which he'd created solely to star in his dreams. But he hadn't dated anyone since the divorce, hadn't so much as been attracted to anyone. He'd told himself he simply had high standards, but he knew that was bullshit.

So he was stunned to see that Lacresha Eldred was a mirror image of Sara, so much so that he didn't know what to think or feel, let alone how to react.

He looked to Alex to gauge her reaction to Lacresha. But Alex displayed no sign of surprise or recognition. Her face showed only concern, and she followed after Lacresha and Kandice, no doubt to offer her support and help. That was the kind of person she was.

Still in shock, he watched the three women walk off, Neal trailing behind them.

Sara, he thought. *My Sara.*

★   ★   ★

Alex followed Lacresha and Kandice. Their new neighbor ushered Kandice to one of the chairs scattered about the backyard – a camping chair with frayed and sun-bleached fabric – and helped her sit.

"Stay right here," Lacresha said. "I'll get you some punch." The woman headed for the picnic table where the punch bowl was located, the table at which two of her relatives sat, watching Kandice with almost clinical detachment.

Alex went over and knelt beside Kandice.

"Are you okay?" she asked.

Kandice gave her a weak nod. "I think so. I'm not sure what came over me. The heat, maybe."

Neal caught up to them then. His gaze flicked to Alex, and she read disapproval there, although she wasn't sure what she'd done wrong. Neal focused on Kandice then and took her hand.

"Do you want to go home?" he asked.

Alex wasn't certain, but she thought Kandice's near-fainting spell had less to do with the outside temperature and more to do with being at the Raines house. Alex had felt weird the moment they'd stepped onto the property, and that feeling had only gotten worse when they entered the backyard.

"No," Kandice said. "I'll be all right in a minute." She turned to Alex. "Thanks for checking on me, but I'll be fine. Why don't you go mingle for a bit, get to know our new neighbors?"

Alex didn't get the impression that Kandice was upset with her, but she had the feeling the woman was dismissing her for some reason. She thought it probably had something to do with the look Neal had given her. Something was going on between Kandice and her husband, but Alex had no idea what it was. She didn't want to make things worse, though, and she sure as hell didn't want to be caught in the middle.

Alex smiled at Kandice. "Okay. Let me know if you need anything, all right?"

Kandice smiled and nodded. Alex stood and walked off without looking at Neal. She passed Lacresha, who was carrying a red plastic cup of punch for Kandice. The woman gave her a smile, and for an instant, it struck her how much Lacresha resembled her mother. It wasn't a perfect match, but the resemblance was there. Funny that she hadn't noticed it until now. She might've stopped to speak with Lacresha, find out if maybe they were distantly related. But the woman continued on to Kandice, and Alex kept walking.

She planned to go to the picnic table with the food – the one the three Eldreds weren't sitting at. She wasn't the most outgoing person, and she wasn't ready to jump into a conversation with the new neighbors just yet. But halfway to the food, she froze.

Vivienne stood near the privacy fence, clutching a handful of white clover that Alex assumed she'd picked from the yard. Standing in front of her was a man. She didn't recognize him, so she assumed he was one of the Eldreds. There was something about him that struck her as familiar, but she wasn't sure what it was. At first he appeared to be of average build, wearing a turtleneck, his hair slicked back. But she blinked and suddenly he looked different. Now he was tall and so skinny he looked like he had almost no meat on his bones. His black hair was a wild tangle that looked as if it hadn't been brushed in weeks. Maybe months. He wore long black pants and black dress shoes, along with a T-shirt that had a white design that was supposed to make it resemble a tuxedo. There was even a little bow tie. She'd seen shirts like this before, worn by broke and/or lazy guys who didn't have anything better to wear and wanted to look hip and ironic at a party. From where she stood, she couldn't get a good look at his face, but his features were small and delicate, almost invisible, really, as if he...he....

Didn't have a face at all.

Now it was her turn to feel as if she might pass out. She understood why this man seemed so familiar to her. As with Lacresha, he resembled someone she already knew, only the person he looked like had never truly existed, except in her imagination.

Mr. Bumblefoot.

He looked so much like the imaginary character she'd created as a young child that he could've been ripped directly from her mind and given life. The details weren't perfect, though. He looked more *real*, for lack of a better word, than the character Alex had fantasized about as a child. Mr. Bumblefoot had no face, and this man's facial features, small though they were, were still distinguishable, and his movements were stiff and awkward. Mr. Bumblefoot had been clumsy – hence his name – but he'd also been graceful in his own way.

She stared openly at the man, everyone else in the backyard forgotten. Then, as if feeling the weight of her gaze upon him, his head swiveled around and he looked at her. His face held no expression, but his eyes seemed to glimmer with green light for an instant before becoming normal again.

"Mama-had-a-baby-and-its-head-popped-*off*!" Vivienne chanted. She flicked her thumb and a bloom detached from a white clover and struck the man's chest. He returned his attention to Vivienne, and then laughed in a fashion that struck Alex as almost mechanical.

"Ha-ha-ha-ha-ha."

The sound was one of the most awful things she'd ever heard, and a cold shudder rippled through her entire body.

A hand fell on her shoulder then, and she yelped in surprise. She turned around and found herself facing her father.

"I didn't mean to frighten you," he said. "It may be a bit early for it, but I'm going to open the wine and pour myself a drink." He held up the bottle. "I could use one. I wondered if you might like one as well?"

Alex was only nineteen, but both her parents let her have an occasional glass of wine, as long as they were around to supervise her. They thought it very European.

She glanced back at Bumblefoot – rather, at the man who *reminded* her of Bumblefoot – then looked at her father once more.

I don't suppose you'd let me have the whole bottle, she thought.

"Yes, please," she said.

★   ★   ★

The Grandother, the Low Prince, and the Nonsister sit at one of the picnic tables, wearing their human faces and quietly observing. They will interact with the humans just as the Werewife and Father Hunger are, but they will do so later. Right now, they have important work to do. Getting the humans to come to the Stalking Ground is only the initial step, and by far the easiest. Now they must gather what the family needs to create Allurements that will bring the humans back when it is night, when the game will begin in earnest.

The Low Prince and the Nonsister create a low-level psychic field that fills the backyard. Within this field, human emotions are intensified, making it simpler to identify the flaw marks – areas of mental weakness – on their psyches. As the children tend to this task, the Grandother sends her awareness forth and probes the humans' minds. The brains of *Homo sapiens* are barely more sophisticated than those of animals, but in many ways, this makes the Grandother's job more difficult. Human minds are fragile, and if she is not careful with her probing, if her mindtouch is too hard, too rough, she risks damaging their small brains. She doesn't care if she hurts them – they *are* only cattle, after all – but she doesn't want to spoil a potential meal. A damaged mind will not react properly to the glamours the Eldred create, and in turn, these minds will not be able to generate the kind of strong emotions that are the Eldreds' food and drink. If her family is to feed and feed well, the Grandother must tread lightly.

She's pleased to see that all the humans living in the cul-de-sac have come. They are all psychically sensitive – some more than others – but none of them is truly Aware. That will make the hunt less complicated and therefore more enjoyable. And while pure, raw emotion is what sustains the Eldred, after having lived so many millennia, they need their fun just as much if they are to continue to survive – maybe more so.

Mindtouching calls for delicacy, but it isn't a lengthy process. It takes the Grandother only a few minutes to get what she needs from the humans' minds. She isn't surprised to find they each have a number of flaw marks. Most humans do. Later, when the ruse of the 'cookout' is over, she will share what she's gleaned with the rest of the family, and they will begin constructing and sending the Allurements. But for now, the Grandother is thirsty and would like a cup of punch.

She nods to the Nonsister and the Low Prince, and the children stop broadcasting the emotion-enhancement field. They both look a bit weary, but that's only because they are the youngest in the family. The older they get, the stronger they will become, until the day they are strong enough to challenge the Grandother, the Werewife, and Father Hunger for dominance. But that day is decades – perhaps centuries – in the future, and it may never come at all. And ultimately, it's of no importance either way. All that matters now is quenching her thirst. Her *physical* thirst, that is.

She rises from the picnic table and starts toward the other one, the one upon which the punch rests. A moment later, the children follow. And if the Low Prince and the Nonsister are speaking mind to mind, making their own plans for tonight's game, the Grandother is unaware of it.

★　★　★

There is food and drink and conversation. The humans find the Eldred strange, but not threatening. The humans wonder what kind of meat the Eldred serve – it's greasy and tastes grainy – but they are much happier not knowing its source. None of them notice that the Eldred only nibble a bit. They are saving their appetite for tonight.

The Eldred make meaningless conversation with their guests, talking about the weather and about what they think of Rockridge since they're new to town. None of the humans ask them what it's like to move into the House of Blood, although they very much want to. As they eat and talk, the Eldred listen to their guests' thoughts. The thoughts of humans are slow and simple, easy to hear if one knows how. And the Eldred know.

There are some rough patches in the evening, naturally.

Martin lobs a few political grenades into the dinner conversation, but no one reacts to them, much to his disappointment. The topic of children comes up – making Spencer extremely uncomfortable. Kandice says that she and Neal haven't decided whether or not to have kids. Martin opines that they should seriously consider not having any. "Biracial children have it tough in school," he says. Neal, angry, points out that Vivienne is biracial. Martin denies this. "Functionally, there are only two different races in America – white and black. Everybody who's not black falls into the white category." He frowns. "Except Mexicans, I suppose. Do they count as a race?" Neal is about to go nuclear on Martin's ass, but Kandice puts her hand over his and gives it a squeeze. He almost unloads on Martin anyway, but he manages to control himself.

Neal is also jealous of the Werewife's connection to Kandice, but Kandice is too preoccupied with thoughts of the Raines murders to dwell overmuch on her husband's insecurities. She keeps seeing the video of Jacob's birthday party, and no matter what she does, she can't stop it from playing in a constant loop in her mind.

Isaac keeps sneaking glances at the Werewife, who he sees as a doppelganger of his ex, and the emotional turmoil inside him is sweet. Alex does see a *little* resemblance now, but nothing to the degree her father does. Still, it's enough to start her thinking about her parents' divorce. She's always felt that she was the cause of their splitting up, and while the adult part of her knows this is horseshit, the child part is still racked with guilt. She keeps looking around to see if Machine Head – who looked so much like her imaginary friend Bumblefoot – will emerge from the house. She hopes to hell he doesn't.

Spencer keeps trying not to look at Vivienne and failing miserably. He's tormented by his desire for her and by his desire *not* to desire her. Lola keeps a close watch on him, the guilt she feels for failing to protect him from his father's attentions eating away at her.

Martin resents Neal and Isaac. He believes they look down on him, think he's an uneducated, unenlightened buffoon. He's right. They do. Cora is embarrassed and angered by Martin's comment about biracial children. Vivienne *is* biracial, and she's beautiful. She thinks Martin can be so small-minded at times. Then she thinks of his gambling and wonders why she married him in the first place. She honestly can't remember.

Vivienne sits between her mommy and daddy, oblivious to the adults' concerns for the most part – although she's aware of the tension between them. The emotional atmosphere in her house is always like this, though, so it's normal to her. She misses her new friend. He went into the house when everyone sat down to eat, and she wishes he'd come back. She wants to decapitate more clover and hear him laugh in that funny way he has.

The Eldred are delighted by this simmering stew of conflicting emotions. Later tonight, they shall bring it to a boil, and when it's ready, they will feed.

They cannot wait.

CHAPTER ELEVEN

Alex lay on her bed, light off, eyes wide open, staring up into the darkness. Her phone lay next to her pillow. Normally, when she had trouble sleeping, she would play mindless games or listen to music until she got tired enough to fall asleep. But she didn't reach for her phone now, wasn't even aware it was close by. She was too caught up in reviewing her memories of the cookout to bother with her phone.

The Eldreds had seemed nice enough, if a bit odd. It was weird how much Lacresha resembled her mother. She wasn't a perfect match, but similar enough that the two women could've been sisters. Her father had noticed, too. He'd kept staring at the woman all night. He hadn't said anything to her at the cookout or during their walk home, and she hadn't wanted to bring it up in case it might upset him. While she wasn't sure exactly how her parents viewed each other now, she knew their relationship, such as it was, was complicated. She thought maybe her father still had feelings for her mother, although he'd never admit this to anyone. He was too proud, too stubborn.

Her parents had split up when she was eight – eleven years ago. When they informed her of their intention to divorce, she'd been devastated. In retrospect, she understood it had been for the best. They fought constantly, and Alex couldn't stand all their yelling and name-calling. She'd spent a lot of time hiding in her bedroom closet, hands pressed to her ears to shut out the sounds of their fighting, tears running down her face. During these times, she'd wish that something would happen to make them stop hating each other so much. She had no idea what that thing might be, and she really didn't care, just so long as they would stop shouting and screaming and cursing and throwing things.

But when they told her they were divorcing, she hadn't been happy, hadn't felt relieved. She'd been terrified by the prospect of her world changing so dramatically. Maybe her parents didn't like being married to each other, and maybe her home life wasn't exactly warm and nurturing, but it was the only life she knew, and she didn't want to lose it.

For days after the announcement, she'd pleaded with her parents not to get divorced, begged them to stay together, with her, in their home. She kept asking them why. Why-why-why-why-why? One evening after she'd been pestering her father with that one-word refrain, he'd gotten so irritated that he burst out with, "Mr. Bumblefoot made us, all right?"

She didn't ask either of her parents for an explanation again after that. Her father's words had hit her hard. When she'd been little – *really* little, like three or four – she'd had an imaginary friend named Mr. Bumblefoot. Like a lot of children with imaginary friends, she'd used him as a scapegoat for the bad things she did. If she broke a toy, she said that Mr. Bumblefoot had done it. After all, he was very clumsy. You could tell from his name. If she snuck extra cookies and got caught, she'd say she'd done it because Mr. Bumblefoot had told her to. He was full of naughty ideas, that one.

As an adult, she understood her father had lashed out at her in frustration, and he'd used Mr. Bumblefoot the same way she had – as an excuse. In this case, one designed to shut her up. And it did. But it had also started her thinking. When she'd wished during those times hiding in the closet for her parents' fighting to end, maybe she'd wished hard enough and often enough for it to come true. Maybe *she* was the reason they were going to divorce. Maybe Mr. Bumblefoot – who had always seemed real to her, so much so that sometimes she actually thought she saw him – had known of her wish, and he'd decided to make it come true for her. He was good at breaking things, after all. Why couldn't he break a marriage?

At eight, she knew intellectually that Mr. Bumblefoot wasn't real, and never had been. But in her fear and uncertainty, she'd mentally and emotionally regressed. So when her father told her Mr. Bumblefoot was the reason her parents' marriage was ending, part of her believed it. The belief didn't completely absolve her of blame for the divorce. After all, Mr. Bumblefoot was *her* friend. But it allowed her to believe that she wasn't directly responsible, and that helped to alleviate the guilt, a little, at least.

As the years went by, she'd come to terms with her parents' divorce, and she understood she'd played no role in it. But understanding isn't the same as believing, and deep down she still blamed herself, still harbored guilt.

Which was why she'd been so shocked when she'd seen the man – she never did get his name – playing with Vivienne. He looked like Bumblefoot, or rather, how she'd always imagined him to be. Bumblefoot was tall and super skinny and wore a tuxedo, and the man at the cookout had worn a T-shirt meant to resemble a tux. The man's small, almost not-there facial features made him like Bumblefoot, too. She'd never given her imaginary friend a face. Instead of eyes, nose, mouth, or ears, he had smooth, unbroken pale flesh. The only feature on his oval head was a mass of wild black Albert Einstein-type hair.

The man at the cookout hadn't looked exactly like Mr. Bumblefoot, but he'd looked enough like her imaginary friend to upset her, and she'd been glad when he went into the house and didn't reemerge.

She knew Bumblefoot wasn't *real*. But seeing that man along with Lacresha, who resembled her mother, had brought back a lot of the difficult emotions she'd experienced about her parents' divorce. Chief among them was her unfounded but still painful sense of guilt.

She hadn't heard her father go to bed yet, and she figured he was most likely sitting at the dining table or on the couch in the living room, stiff drink in hand and staring off into the distance, thinking dark thoughts. She wished she could get out of bed and go to him, offer him comfort and receive it in turn. But she knew from long experience that all she'd receive if she went to him now was a tongue-lashing. He'd take out his feelings on her, and she couldn't deal with that, not now.

Tonight might have been a mixed bag, but it was over now. Tomorrow would be better. At least, she could hope. She closed her eyes and concentrated on breathing evenly. It took forty minutes, but eventually she drifted off to sleep. Unfortunately, that sleep would be interrupted very soon.

*   *   *

"I *saw* the way you looked at her."

"Jesus, Neal, would you please give it a fucking rest?"

Kandice sat on their queen-sized bed, back pressed against the wooden headboard, comforter drawn up to her chest. She was always cold at night, so no matter the season, she liked to sleep beneath a comforter. Neal was always warm, and he usually slept with a thin blanket or just a sheet. Kandice had finished getting ready for bed, and Neal was in the master bathroom finishing up his nightly pre-sleep routine. Kandice had on a pair of cotton pajamas. Neal slept shirtless most of the year, except for the dead of winter, but always wore either shorts or pajama bottoms. Tonight he had on the latter, a pair that were black with the Superman S symbol all over them. Sometimes when he wore them to sleep, he'd make a joke about being Superman in bed. He hadn't made that joke tonight, though.

She couldn't see much of the bathroom from the bed, but Neal had left the door wide open so they could hear each other. Right now, she heard the sound of his electric toothbrush starting up. He couldn't brush his teeth and speak at the same time, thank Christ. They'd been arguing on and off since leaving the cookout, and the focus of these arguments was always the same: her sexuality. Neal claimed that she'd flirted with Lacresha during the cookout. She admitted that she found the woman attractive – her daughter Vanita was cute, too, but she didn't volunteer this information – but she flat-out denied purposefully flirting with Lacresha. She couldn't have flirted even if she'd wanted to. She'd been too preoccupied with trying to keep the images – more like visions, really – of Jacob's birthday party out of her mind. She hadn't told Neal this last part. She wasn't sure why. Maybe she feared he would do his I'm-a-logical-science-guy thing and lecture her on why she had no reason to obsess over the Raines family and how they had died. Yes, the murders had happened and they were awful, but a house and the property it was built on couldn't soak up negative energy from the tragic events that occurred there. *The only force haunting the Raines house tonight is your imagination.* He would say this, or something close to it. She hadn't wanted to feel as if he were dismissing her emotions, so she'd kept her reaction to being on the Raines property to herself. Now she wished she hadn't. At least then they would've had a different topic to fight about.

Neal finished brushing his teeth, spit, rinsed. He used some mouthwash, gargled, then spit this out, too. He stepped out of the bathroom and turned off the light as he left. He seemed less angry than he had a few moments ago, and she took this as a hopeful sign. He got into bed and sat beside her, on top of the sheet. He'd probably pull it over him when it was time to sleep, but he might not bother. He usually just kicked it off in the night anyway.

"Even if you did purposefully flirt with her—" She started to interrupt, and he quickly held up a hand. "I said *if*. Even if you did, I know that flirting in and of itself is harmless. Even healthy."

Someone's been reading articles on the Internet again, she thought.

"If that's true, then why do you care whether I flirted with her or not?"

He opened his mouth to respond, but then he closed it, frowning. Kandice suppressed a smile. *Point to me.*

"I don't know," he admitted. "I guess what gets to me is the uncertainty of it all. I'm a numbers guy. I don't do uncertainty well."

That's an understatement.

"What are you so uncertain about? You know I love you, right?"

"Of course. I never doubt that."

She wasn't sure he was telling the truth about this, but she let it pass.

He continued. "I'm trying to wrap my head around how your sexuality affects how you see the world. Are you attracted to both genders equally? Does it go in cycles? Some days you're more into men, some days women? Are you really okay to confining yourself to being with one gender for the rest of your life? I mean, you haven't had the opportunity to explore the, uh, homosexual side of yourself. I hate the idea of you always feeling dissatisfied with our sex life on some level, even if it's only a little."

She couldn't help sighing. His questions told her he still hadn't grasped the fundamental nature of bisexuality, at least as it pertained to her.

"Once again, I have the potential to enter into a romantic relationship with a person of either gender. When I am with one person, I focus on them and I don't want anyone else – of *either* gender. I'm completely fulfilled by our relationship, and I have no desire to go looking for a little extra on the side." *But if this shit keeps up, you just might drive me to it,* she thought. "But none of what you said explains your jealousy or your anger."

He thought for a moment before responding.

"I guess that since I can never be two genders, I feel like I can't give you everything you need sexually. I'm not enough. I can't—" he smiled sadly, "—balance the equation."

She felt sympathy for Neal. She truly loved him and hated to see him hurting like this. But she couldn't change who she was, and who she was wasn't a threat to their relationship. Why couldn't he see this?

"I guess I should look at the bright side," Neal said.

"And that would be...?"

"With your attention focused on Lacresha, you didn't pay any attention to Cora."

She looked at him for a moment, and then she burst out laughing. So did he, and they hugged. They held each other for several moments, and when they pulled apart, Kandice gave Neal a gentle kiss.

"I love you," she said.

"And I love you."

They both settled back against the headboard and held hands.

"I'll tell you one thing I don't love," Neal said.

"Let me guess: Martin."

"Got it in one. What the fuck was that shit about everyone who isn't black is white? And that stuff about how any kids we might have would have it hard in school because they're biracial – when his own daughter is biracial!"

"Martin can be an asshole, no doubt. But he isn't altogether wrong."

Neal looked at her as if she'd confessed to being a serial killer.

"You're more woke than the average white person," she said. "But you *are* white. You were born and raised in a society that privileges people with white skin. Because of this, you can't fully understand what it's like to be a person of color in America. Most white people aren't purposeful, hateful racists. They're unconscious racists. They hold any number of racist attitudes and beliefs about people of color, and they don't know it. They think they're pretty damn tolerant, that they 'don't see color'. It's all bullshit, but they don't *know* it's bullshit. Martin's not a card-carrying member of the KKK. He thinks he's racially sensitive and people like us are oversensitive. There are a lot of Martins in this country. I'd argue that *all* white people are like him to one degree or another. And before you say anything, yes, that means you, too. Martin is living proof of the kind of people, those with unconscious but deeply held prejudice, that people of color – including biracial children – face as they grow up. Now, it's ignorant as hell to use that as a reason why people in interracial relationships shouldn't have kids, but it does speak to why those parents need to be aware of the challenges their children will face."

She thought Neal might argue some of her points. She by no means thought he was a racist. She'd never have spoken to him in the first place, let alone married him if she believed that. He still had what she thought of as a cultural residue of racism in his psyche, though. Everyone did. But he wasn't always aware of how the culture had affected him when it came to race.

But instead of arguing, he put his arm around her and she moved closer and laid her head on his chest. She loved doing this, loved hearing his heartbeat, strong and steady, rhythm precise, almost mathematical.

"So Vivienne will encounter prejudice as she grows up," Neal said.

"Yes. Ohio is a very conservative state. Even its cities are conservative to one degree or another. She wouldn't find as much prejudice in larger cities like New York, but even if she does move to a more diverse, tolerant place, she'll still encounter some. How much is impossible to say, but it will change her. Hopefully, it will strengthen her."

"It'll be harder with parents that don't see her as interracial. They won't be able to understand what she's going through," Neal said.

"Cora understands a lot better than Martin. And who knows? If Vivienne tells him about any prejudice she encounters, maybe it'll wake him up a little."

Neal sighed. "Fucking Martin."

She smiled. "Same."

They were quiet for several moments, and then Kandice said, "There are different kinds of prejudice other than racial, you know."

She wanted to see if Neal would catch her meaning. At first he didn't react, but then his eyes widened with understanding.

"Sorry," he said softly.

She kissed him, then put her arms around him and held him tight, and he held her just as tight in return. In that moment, Kandice believed that they had turned a corner regarding Neal's feelings about her sexuality. For the first time since it had become an issue between them, she had faith that everything was going to be all right.

★   ★   ★

Spencer gazed at his face in the bathroom mirror. Sagging jowls, dark patches of skin under bloodshot eyes, crow's feet, lines in his forehead. He was getting old. No, scratch that. He *was* old. He reached up and rubbed a hand over the lower half of his face. He'd shaved that morning, but a fresh crop of bristles had come in since then. His facial hair had always grown fast, a trait his mother said he'd inherited from his father. The stubble was black except for on his chin. Those hairs were white.

Old, old, old, *old*.

But Vivienne was young. Unspoiled. Innocent. The cookout had been the most time he'd spent around the child, and even though she'd kept her distance from him, he felt they'd made a connection. One that was tentative and fragile, one that she likely was unaware of. But it was real. He could *feel* it.

Don't fool yourself, his reflection seemed to say. *She didn't notice you any more than she noticed the other adults.*

She'd noticed the man, though, hadn't she? The quiet one that Lacresha hadn't bothered to introduce to her guests. He gritted his teeth as he remembered how Vivienne had laughed and giggled as she performed for the man, popping the blooms off clover and making him laugh that strange, stilted laugh of his. Spencer was filled with jealous rage, so strong that it took him by surprise. His reflection changed, became blurry, and when it came into focus once more, he found himself looking at the man. Dull, unblinking eyes. Features slack, thin lips pressed together so tightly it was as if they were sealed with some kind of glue.

She doesn't belong to you, the man seemed to say, speaking without opening his mouth. *She doesn't belong to anyone except herself. Besides, why would she want to have anything to do with you? Have you seen yourself lately?*

The reflection shimmered and Spencer was looking at his own face again. His rage became a white-hot fire inside him, and at the core of his anger wasn't jealousy but rather intense self-loathing. Before he knew what he was doing, his hand curled into a fist and he slammed it into the glass. Cracks spiderwebbed outward from the point of impact, and he felt sharp pain in his knuckles. When he withdrew his hand, several shards of glass fell into the sink. He saw there was blood on them. He examined his hand and saw that he'd sliced the skin over his knuckles. Blood welled from the wound and dripped into the sink, the drops making tiny *plap-plap-plap* sounds as they hit the porcelain. The sight of blood should've alarmed him, made him reach for the first aid kit in the cupboard beneath the sink. But he just held his wounded hand over the basin and watched the blood fall. His anger was gone, drained away by his outburst. Now he felt a detached numbness, and while that wasn't exactly a pleasant sensation, at least he felt calmer.

His hand hadn't hurt at first, probably because he'd damaged the nerves, but now it began to throb in time with his pulse. He didn't mind the pain; he welcomed it, in fact. It was only what he deserved.

His reflection changed again, and now he found himself looking at the image of his dead father. Kenneth Parsons' craggy features contorted into a scowl.

You're losing control, boy. I'm disappointed in you. Very disappointed.

Tears welled up in Spencer's eyes, and he fought to hold them back. His father would taunt him further if he started crying.

You need to prove to me you're still a man. Pull your sweats down.

Spencer slept in a T-shirt and an old pair of well-worn and extremely comfortable gray sweat pants.

"I don't—"

Do it! his father commanded.

Spencer reached down with his unwounded hand and did as his father commanded.

Underwear, too.

Spencer complied. It was always best to do as Father insisted. Otherwise, he'd get angry, and when that happened, he'd do things to Spencer. Bad things.

Good. Now take hold of your dick.

Spencer didn't want to, but he reached a trembling hand toward his penis.

Not that hand. The other one.

Father wanted him to use the hand that was bleeding. He told himself that he didn't have to do this, that his father was long dead and buried, that everything that was happening was nothing more than delusions conjured by his sick mind. He needed to clean and dress his wound, then go back to his bedroom and text Dr. Reiger and tell her what had happened. He wouldn't hear from her until morning, but he'd feel better knowing he'd taken the first step toward dealing with whatever was happening to him.

He wondered if he was going crazy. Would he end up being hospitalized, put in some loony bin and locked away for the rest of his life? The prospect scared him, but it also made him feel hopeful. If he were committed to a mental hospital, he'd be watched over, monitored, given drugs. He'd be among adults, and there would be no children around to tempt him. He would be imprisoned, but paradoxically, he'd also be free. Free from having to constantly battle his urges, free from the fear that one day he would lose that battle and hurt a child. Free from the shame of being what he was, what his father had made him become.

"No," he whispered.

To Spencer's surprise, his father didn't yell at him. Instead, he sounded sympathetic.

You need to sleep, Spencer. Getting one off will help you. It'll decrease your tension. You won't have to think about Vivienne anymore for the rest of the night. Doesn't that sound nice?

It did. It really did.

All you need to do is jack off. Easy-peasy.

Spencer didn't reply.

Do it for me. For your loving father.

This wasn't real. There was no father, just Spencer, and he could do whatever the hell he wanted.

Take hold of yourself with your bleeding hand. Picture Vivienne. Flawless skin. Delicate features. Flat chest. No curves, no grotesque hair above her perfect little vagina.

Spencer looked down into the sink. Several shards had fallen into the basin. One in particular was larger than the rest, a triangular piece with sharp edges and a wicked-looking point. He could pick up that shard and use it like a scalpel, slice off his dick, throw the goddamn thing in the toilet, and flush it away. Vivienne would be safe then, all children would be safe, at least from him. And if his amateur operation led to him bleeding to death on the bathroom floor, what of it? At least it would be over. Who knows? He might even find some peace in death. He looked at the shard for several moments, but in the end, he couldn't bring himself to pick it up. He was a coward, and he despised himself for it.

Spencer did as his father bade. He grasped his penis – which was already half-erect – with his injured hand. He closed his eyes, visualized Vivienne picking clover in the Eldreds' backyard. He hardened all the way and began stroking. Unable to hold back his tears any longer, he cried.

★　★　★

Lola heard the sound of breaking glass. She hadn't been sleeping, had been lying in bed, wide awake, thinking that it had been a mistake to go to the cookout, that she should've never let Spencer get so close to Vivienne.

Lola rose from her bed, hurried to the door, and into the hallway. She wasn't worried that the breaking glass meant someone – a burglar or a killer – had entered their home. She knew it was Spencer, knew it in the way mothers always know when their children are in danger.

The hall bathroom wasn't far from her bedroom, and she reached it within seconds. The line of light beneath the door told her that Spencer was in there. She raised a hand to knock, intending to follow it up by asking Spencer if he was all right. But then she heard him talking, and she paused to listen. At times, he seemed to speak in two separate voices, almost as if he were having a conversation with someone. But who – then it hit her. Who else? His late and unlamented father.

When Spencer began masturbating – and from the sound of things, crying as he did so – she backed away from the door, making certain to move quietly. She didn't want to upset him any further. He'd had a tough enough night already without her adding to his misery by embarrassing him.

She returned to her room, closed the door, and lay on the bed, listening for the sound of the bathroom door opening and closing. It wasn't long. She heard the toilet flush, the faucet run, and then the door open quietly. She heard Spencer walking slowly toward his room, moving carefully, so as not to wake her. She heard him go into his room, settle onto his bed, and sigh. She hoped he would be able to sleep. She doubted she would. She had a lot to think about. She hadn't wanted to kill Kenneth, even if she had done so indirectly, but Kenneth's death had freed Spencer. Now she wondered if it would be necessary for Spencer to die in order to protect Vivienne. And the only one who could make sure he died was her. Could she do it, kill her son, her sweet precious baby boy? Could she bring herself to commit such a monstrous act? And to protect a child she barely knew? She didn't know. But she feared she would soon find out.

CHAPTER TWELVE

"We need to talk," Cora said.

Martin had just stepped out of the shitter, naked except for a pair of boxers. He didn't think of them as underwear per se. More like a really comfortable pair of shorts. He and Cora had a master bathroom, but he usually used the one in the hall, especially if he had to take a dump before bed. He didn't want to stink up the master bathroom and have any of the smell filter into their bedroom. Who wanted to try to sleep smelling shit fumes?

Cora wore a pair of copper-colored silk pajamas. She liked to wear form-fitting clothing during the day, but she wanted to be comfortable when sleeping, and the pajamas were a size too big for her. Martin thought she looked like a little girl who'd put on her mother's PJs, but he'd never tell Cora this. She was sensitive about the short Asian stereotype, and she didn't find any comment related to her height funny.

She'd been standing in the hall outside the bathroom door, waiting for him to finish. How long had she been standing there? And what was so goddamn important she couldn't wait for him to come to the bedroom?

She held her phone in her right hand and she shoved it in his face. He squinted against the bright light coming from the screen.

"Jesus, babe!"

"Don't 'babe' me. Look at the fucking screen."

Her voice was as cold and sharp as a dagger carved from ice, and he knew that whatever was displayed on the phone screen was bad. Keeping his eyes half-closed, he looked at the screen and saw that she'd called up their banking app. Current account balances were displayed, joint checking and joint savings. The amounts were the same for both accounts. Zero.

He looked at Cora and forced a smile. "Glass half-full: at least the accounts aren't overdrawn."

He didn't expect his joke to go over well, but he was shocked when Cora slapped him with her free hand. It wasn't a light slap, either. This was a face-stinging, teeth-rattling, bruised-jaw slap. The sound was so loud that he feared it would wake Vivienne. Her bedroom was at the far end of the hall, next to theirs, but the girl was a light sleeper, always had been. If she woke and came out into the hallway to see her parents fighting – especially if she saw her mommy getting physical with her daddy – Daddy taking it like a little bitch – Martin would be shamed in front of his own child. And he damn well wasn't going to allow that to happen.

He leaned his face close to Cora's until their noses were practically touching. In a low, dangerous voice, he said, "Never hit me again. If you try – for whatever reason – I swear I will beat the holy living shit out of you. Got it?"

Cora wasn't one to be cowed by threats, but something in his tone of voice and the look in his eyes must've told her that he was serious. She took a step back and lowered her hands to her sides.

Good girl, he thought.

His cheek and jaw felt hot where she'd hit him, and he wanted to get an ice pack from the freezer to keep the swelling down. But not before he got things settled here.

Cora's anger had been tempered by his words, but it hadn't dissipated entirely, not by a long shot. She spoke in a hissing whisper so she couldn't wake Vivienne.

"Your gambling has officially become a problem. I mean *big-time.* How am I supposed to pay bills this month? What's the bank going to say when we can't pay our goddamn mortgage payment?"

Martin and Cora had a clear division of responsibilities in their marriage, said division falling pretty much along stereotypical gender roles. He made the money, took care of maintenance and repair on the house and vehicles. He mowed the lawn, and took out the trash. Cora took care of everything else, including budgeting and bill-paying. They'd never discussed this division of labor. They'd simply fallen into the pattern in the early days of their marriage, and it had remained the same ever since. Martin wished he was the one to handle their money. That way, Cora would have no clue how much he spent and on what.

"We can use one of the credit cards," he said.

"The cards are all maxed out," Cora said. "Thanks to you."

Martin had never struck Cora before, had never even handled her roughly, not in all the time they'd been together. But he wanted to hit her now, wanted to ram his fist into that smug face of hers, split open her lips, knock loose a few teeth. Goddamn mouthy bitch! His right hand twitched, but that was all. Cora saw it, though, and she looked at him as if she now saw a part of him that she hadn't known existed. And this part scared her. On one level, he was thrilled to see fear in her eyes. Fear meant respect. But on another level, he felt sorrow. He loved Cora and didn't want her to be afraid of him.

He made sure to soften his voice when he spoke next.

"Maybe we could go to one of those short-term loan places."

"They're a rip-off. They charge a shit-ton of interest, so much that it's hard to pay off the loan. You just end up in worse debt than you had when you started."

She let out a long sigh, and when she spoke again, she sounded more tired than he'd ever heard her before. "This is it, Martin. I can't take any more of this. You either admit you have a problem and get help...."

"Or?" He didn't want to hear the rest, but he knew he had to.

"Or I take Vivienne and leave. And after that, I'll file for divorce. I'm serious. And before you say anything, no, I won't discuss it further. You have a decision to make. You can let me know what it is in the morning."

She turned and then walked the rest of the way down the hall, opened their bedroom door, slipped inside, then closed it quietly behind her. A second later he heard the soft *snik* of a lock being engaged.

He stood there for a moment, frowning, not thinking or feeling anything. Cora had always been strong-willed, and in an argument, she always gave as good as she got. But he'd never seen her like this before. Maybe he should go down to the bedroom and apologize for blowing so much of their money on gambling. Maybe he *did* have a problem. Maybe he *did* need help.

And maybe his wife was just an ungrateful bitch. He was the one who brought money into the house, and he had the right to spend it however he liked. Sure, he'd had a run or two of bad luck lately, and it had put them in a financial bind, but they'd work their way out of it somehow. They always did.

"Fuck you," Martin said. He then turned and headed for the living room, and the couch that would serve as his bed for this night.

★　　★　　★

Vivienne, out of all Brookside Court's residents, slept. She didn't hear her mother and father arguing in the hall, but if she had, she wouldn't have paid it much attention. Her mommy and daddy fought a lot. She was lost in a wonderful dream where she walked through a forest of gigantic grass blades and massive clover, green *and* white. The plants were so tall that they seemed like skyscrapers to her. The air was warm and fragrant with the smell of green growing things, and breathing it in was like inhaling pure joy.

She wandered through the forest for some time, with no destination in mind and in no particular hurry, just enjoying each moment as it came. Eventually, she began to feel uneasy, and she kept looking back over her shoulder, as if she expected to find someone following her. But she never did. After checking behind her for perhaps the twentieth time, when she faced forward, she stopped, startled. Someone stood in front of her – a grown-up. But when she saw who it was, she relaxed. It was her friend from the cookout, the man with the funny laugh. She smiled, but he didn't smile back. She didn't think his mouth could make a smile, but that was okay. She could feel that he was glad to see her.

"Hi!' she said. "We can't play baby's head popped off. They're too big." She pointed at one of the huge white clover.

Funny Laugh didn't reply. He looked at her for a long moment, and she sensed he was trying to decide what to do next. She heard a soft clicking, and she knew it was the sound of him thinking. Eventually, he came to a decision. He raised both hands to his face and dug his fingers into the skin of his forehead and pulled downward. His face peeled all the way down to his neck. He yanked the flap of skin away and he tossed it to the forest floor. It landed face up, and Funny Laugh looked up at her, features expressionless as always. She was not frightened by seeing her friend tear off his face. This was a dream, and Mommy had told her that nothing in a dream could hurt you. Besides, it wasn't as if the scrap of flesh lying on the ground was his *real* face. That face was the one she looked at next.

The back half of his mask was still on him, and he had a tuft of fake hair on top of his metal head. He had eyes, ears, nose, and mouth, but they were only crude renditions of human features made of metal. Most dramatically, his eyes glowed with a deep green fire.

Vivienne grinned. "That's so cool! My turn!"

She reached up, dug her fingers into the smooth skin of her forehead, and pulled as hard as she could. Her face came away as easily as her friend's, and she was pleasantly surprised to discover that its removal only stung a little. When she had her face all the way free, she gave it a yank just as Funny Laugh had, and it tore away. She then tossed it to the ground, where it lay next to her friend's discarded mask. She was so excited to find out what lay beneath her own mask that she reached up to touch what had been revealed. She thought she might feel a second, entirely different face, or maybe a skull slick with blood. But her fingers came in contact with cold hard metal, and she felt her eyes grow warm as they began to exude emerald light.

She opened her mouth and eerie mechanical laughter came forth. *"Ha-ha-ha-ha-ha-ha."*

A moment later, her friend joined in, and they stood like a pair of small creatures in a very large world, laughing and laughing.

★   ★   ★

The Eldred used a few small glamours during the cookout, partially for fun and partially as a warm-up for tonight's festivities, much the same way human athletes stretch before a competition. Martin seeing Lacresha as Sara's doppelganger, Kandice's visions of Jacob Raines's birthday video, Alex seeing Machine Head as her old friend Bumblefoot.... Small alterations in their guests' perceptions, nothing like the more complex glamours they will employ tonight. Now, though, it is time to construct the Allurements that will bring the humans to the Stalking Ground.

The Eldred go to work.

To a human's eyes, the Eldred's house would look empty, but in a dimension only a half step away from ours, it's crammed full to bursting with everything the Eldred require to have a successful – and entertaining – hunt. Each of their Domains is ready, and all that remains now is to create the Allurements. They form a circle in the empty front room, join hands, close their eyes and concentrate. Power flows into them and through them, and they begin to channel it. Machine Head stands off to the side, still and quiet, alert and watching.

The Eldred breathe in, hold it, then breathe out. Thin streams of darkness curl forth from their mouths and snake toward the middle of the circle. These streams swirl together, merge, expand, and finally pull apart into separate shapes. The Eldred continue to exhale darkness, and the forms in the circle – the Allurements – become more distinct. The Eldred infuse the Allurements with knowledge of the humans' psyches gleaned from tonight's Gathering, making them all the more powerful.

After a time, Father Hunger calls a halt to the proceedings. Everyone breaks contact and opens their eyes to behold the dark wonders they have brought into being. The shapes possess human-seeming forms, but they are things of Shadow, black in heart as well as aspect, and if they have any detailed features, they are concealed by the darkness that makes up their bodies. There are nine of them, one for each of the Eldred's new neighbors. The last time they invited the humans over, they used simple messages written on paper. This time, the invitations are more elaborate.

"Bring them to us," Father Hunger instructs.

The Allurements bow their heads in unison and then drift off, gliding past the Eldred and picking up speed as they approach the front door. They have no need to open it. They simply flow through it, as if it is no more substantial than air. When the last Allurement is gone, Father Hunger turns to his family.

"Places, everyone. I hope you all enjoy the game."

The Werewife smiles, displaying a mouthful of tiny sharp teeth.

"Don't we always?"

She laughs, Father Hunger laughs, they all laugh. And then they go their separate ways to enter their Domains and wait for the arrival of their guests.

*   *   *

The Low Prince and the Nonsister head to their Domains more slowly than the others. This gives them an opportunity to confer one last time. They quickly go over their plan again, but there is no need to. They have made their preparations without the others knowing. In the past, they wouldn't have been able to keep their intentions hidden from the others, and they wouldn't have dared to conspire against them. But the others have declined in power over the last century. Not a great deal, but enough for the Low Prince and the Nonsister to sense that their time has finally come. And they intend to take full advantage of it.

They speak in whispers at the bottom of the stairs that lead to the house's second story. Brother and sister reassure each other, bolster one another's courage. Before parting, they step toward each other and merge essences, briefly becoming a single solid mass of roiling darkness. They separate, and the Nonsister starts walking up the stairs, where her Domain lies. The Low Prince heads to the hallway where the basement door – which serves as the egress point for his Domain – is located. As he begins his descent, he smiles. All feedings are exciting, but this one is going to prove extra special.

*   *   *

Outwardly, Brookside Court looks calm and quiet. Aside from porchlights, the houses are dark, and the air – which has cooled off nicely from what it was earlier – is still. The Raines house looks as peaceful as the others in the cul-de-sac, and unless one was aware of its history, they'd never guess that terrible things once happened there, or that equally terrible things will happen soon.

Machine Head opens the front door and looks out upon the night with his glowing green eyes. He's incapable of all but the most rudimentary of emotions, but he's looking forward to tonight's fun. If he's lucky, he might get a new body out of it, too. The one he has is still serviceable, but it's starting to stink a little. Leaving the door wide open, he turns and retreats deeper into the house. It's his job to assist the Eldred tonight, as he has done for many, many years. He knows what to do, and he's good at it. *Very* good.

The cul-de-sac becomes brighter as the moon rises in the Eldred's backyard. Machine Head likes the way the moonlight paints the world in eerie blue-white, giving everything a slightly unreal aspect appropriate for what is about to take place.

As he stands quietly, waiting for the first of their guests to arrive, he finds himself thinking of the little girl who made him laugh earlier. He feels a distant, muted emotion that might almost be sadness at the thought of her entering the house tonight, but there is nothing he can do about it. He has no will of his own, no individual thoughts or desires. At least, that's how he was designed. But all things change given enough time, including him. *Vivienne,* he thinks. The little girl's name is Vivienne.

CHAPTER THIRTEEN

Isaac was dreaming of making love to his ex-wife on a beach in Barbados when his eyes opened and he saw Sara standing at the side of his bed.

"Hello, darling," she said.

He sat up so fast, he was momentarily dizzy. His first thought was that he was still dreaming. His second thought was that this was real, but it was Lacresha who stood by his bed and not Sara. His third thought was that, whoever this was, how the hell had she gotten inside his house?

"Sara?"

It couldn't be her, though. This woman was young, barely older than Alex. She looked like Sara had when they'd first met. This was his favorite way to remember her. You could see the girl she had once been along with hints of the woman she would become. They'd met in the cafeteria during their junior year of college. She'd been dating Jonathan Becker, Isaac's roommate at the time, but within a week she'd dropped him and started going out with Isaac – which made sharing a dorm room with Jonathan for the remainder of the semester more than a little problematic. She'd been going through a *Flashdance* phase back then, and she wore a gray sweatshirt over tight black shorts, just like the movie's main character. Isaac had thought she was the most beautiful woman he'd ever seen, and the passage of decades hadn't changed that assessment.

Isaac slept naked, and although he was covered by a blanket, he still felt absurdly self-conscious.

"It's good to see you," Sara said. "It's been a long time, hasn't it?"

The last time Isaac had seen his ex-wife was at Alex's high school graduation, slightly over a year ago. But that had been the middle-aged version of his wife. Still beautiful, but nothing like her younger self.

"It has." His throat was dry, and he could barely get the words out.

"Put some clothes on and let's go for a walk. We've got a lot to talk about."

"I...." Isaac trailed off, uncertain how to reply. Part of him wanted to do what she suggested, but another part was reluctant. This didn't make any sense.

Sara leaned down, put her soft young hands on either side of his face, and kissed him gently. Memories flooded his mind then. Every good moment he'd ever spent with Sara – and there had been a lot of them, especially in the beginning – came to vivid life, filling him with a euphoria beyond anything any earthly drug could produce. Any doubts he had were washed away. He believed this was his Sara, the way she had been when they'd first met, and her suggestion sounded good to him. Sounded *fantastic*, in fact.

He grinned. "Give me a minute, love."

He jumped out of bed and quickly got dressed. He donned an old flannel shirt and jeans – something he might've worn back in college – and when he was finished, Sara smiled, took his hand, and led him from the bedroom. Isaac was happier than he had been in years. He didn't know where she intended to lead him, and he didn't care. All that mattered was that they were together again.

★ ★ ★

Alex lay in her bed, also dreaming. But her dream was far less pleasant than her father's. She stood in the Eldreds' backyard. Everything was set up for the cookout – the meat was even sizzling on the grill – but there was no one else present, just her. The situation was odd, but she wasn't alarmed. She wasn't sure where everyone else had gone or why they had left, but she figured they must've had a good reason and would surely return soon. Until then, she'd hang out and wait. Maybe she'd check out the food spread out on one of the picnic tables, see what there was to munch on. She started in that direction, but she caught a flash of movement out of the corner of her eye. Reflexively, she turned toward it and saw that she had been mistaken. She wasn't alone. Standing near the privacy fence in the middle of a spread of white clover was the man who reminded her of Mr. Bumblefoot.

She felt a hand of ice squeeze her heart, and for a moment she wasn't able to think, wasn't able to breathe. It wasn't Bumblefoot, she knew this, but the man looked so much like him that—

Up to this point, the man had been turned away from her, so she hadn't been able to make out his features. But now, as if she'd done something to draw his attention, he turned to look at her, and her blood ran cold as an arctic river. No longer did the man merely *resemble* Bumblefoot, he *was* Bumblefoot. He wore an actual tuxedo, not a shirt designed to mimic one, and his hair was bigger, wilder, blacker than before. His head had a more pronounced oval shape, the chin almost coming to a point, and his face was smooth, completely bereft of any features. No eyes, nose, mouth, or ears.

Despite Mr. Bumblefoot's lack of a mouth, she heard his voice. It had a disturbing buzzing quality, as if he made sound by vibrating the skin over where his mouth should be.

"You ought to be ashamed of yourself, Alex. Blaming me for your parents' divorce, when you know it was your fault."

It took Alex a moment to find her voice.

"I never blamed you. That was something my father said."

"He wouldn't have said it if he wasn't used to you blaming me for every bad thing you did. So you might as well have told him that I did it. It amounts to the same thing in the end."

Mr. Bumblefoot started walking toward her. He moved with a strange gait, almost tripping every few steps but somehow always managing to keep from falling. If Alex had been a child, she might've found the way he walked to be amusing. Now she found it terrifying.

"Go away!" she shouted. If she'd imagined him into existence in the first place, she should be able to will him into nonexistence, right? But her command had no effect on Bumblefoot. He kept coming, almost-but-not-quite-tripping.

"What do you want?" she demanded, close to tears now.

"You wronged me. You need to apologize."

"I'm sorry," she said, voice little more than a choked sob.

"I don't need words," Bumblefoot said.

He had almost reached her by now. She wanted to run, desperately so, but she wasn't able to make her feet move. She looked down and saw that her feet had sunk into the too-soft grass.

Green paste covered her feet, and when she tried to lift them, she could feel suction pulling them back down.

She looked up and saw Bumblefoot was less than five feet away from her. He raised his right hand, and she saw that his fingers had been replaced with small metal blades. *Scalpels,* she thought. *They're scalpels.*

"What I need is a face," Bumblefoot said. "And yours will do fine."

He held his scalpel fingers out in front of him as he closed the last few feet between them.

Alex tried again to pull her feet free from the green muck that had trapped her, but she was stuck fast. As the first scalpel touched the tender flesh alongside her nose, she screamed.

★   ★   ★

Alex came awake on her feet. She slept in a T-shirt and shorts, and even though her father didn't keep the house too cool at night, she shivered as if she were standing outside during the darkest, coldest winter night. She recalled all the details of her dream, so vividly that it was almost as if she'd actually lived them. She wasn't sure why she was out of bed. She guessed the dream had been so fucking scary that her body had tried to get away in the real world before she could fully wake. Thank god she'd managed to pull herself out of that goddamn dream.

"You did escape the dream," a voice said. "But you didn't leave alone."

She heard a swish of air, and she lunged forward in time to avoid getting her back sliced by Bumblefoot's scalpel fingers. She wasn't fast enough to avoid getting nicked by a couple, though. The metal tips cut through the fabric over her left shoulder blade and drew blood. She hissed a pained breath as she stumbled, but like her childhood friend, she didn't go down. She didn't look back, either. She ran for her bedroom door, threw it open, and dashed into the hallway.

"Dad!" she shouted, then louder, "*Dad!*"

No response. Had something happened to her father? Had Bumblefoot gone to his room first and used his scalpel fingers to end his life? She hoped not, but she knew she couldn't afford to slow down and check. If she did, Bumblefoot would catch her for sure.

She ran down the hall, hearing the shuffling-stumbling sound of Bumblefoot in pursuit.

"You owe me a face!" Bumblefoot called. "Give me your fucking face, Alex, you bad, bad girl!"

Alex screamed.

When she reached the end of the hallway, she turned right and entered the vestibule. The front door was already open, and she was too grateful to question why. She plunged outside into the bright moonlit night, but she was going too fast, running too frantically, and she couldn't stop herself as she ran off the porch and fell into the yard. She hit with a jolt that knocked the air out of her, but she didn't lie there and wait to catch her breath. She pushed herself to her feet, ignoring the sharp pain in her right ribs as she did so. She intended to continue running, but a wave of sudden vertigo washed over her and her vision blurred.

When it cleared, it was daylight, and instead of standing in her father's front yard, she was standing in the Eldreds'. She saw her father's house just past the Parsonses'. The door was open and her father stood there, motioning for her to come toward him. It made no sense. Unless she had never truly woke and was still inside the dream. But the pain from the cuts on her shoulder and from her injured – maybe even broken – ribs felt more than real enough. But before she could question further, Mr. Bumblefoot came out of the house – the Eldreds' house – and onto the front porch. He stopped and even though he didn't have a mouth, Alex heard the grin in his voice as he spoke.

"What should I start with first? An ear? Or maybe I should start with an eye. That way I can see you as I remove the rest of your face piece by piece. And I'll leave your second eye for last so you can watch me cut you up. Now, right eye or left? Do you have a preference?"

He raised his hand and waggled his scalpel fingers.

Alex could only gape at the faceless horror birthed from her childhood imagination.

Bumblefoot shrugged.

"I suppose it really doesn't matter. Stand still now. I don't want to accidentally puncture your eye and ruin things."

Bumblefoot jumped off the porch and landed on the Eldreds' mushy grass.

"Alex!" her father called, motioning more frantically than before. "Run!"

She didn't wonder why her father wasn't doing anything to actively help her. Everything was so unreal and happening so fast, she didn't have time for questions. If she wanted to keep her facial features where they were, she needed to haul ass.

She started running toward her house, Mr. Bumblefoot following close on her heels, clicking his scalpel fingers together in hungry anticipation as he ran.

★   ★   ★

Spencer couldn't sleep. He'd cleaned his wounded hand and poured disinfectant over it – which had stung like a bitch – and then wrapped it in gauze. It had stopped bleeding, but it still throbbed. He'd taken three ibuprofen, but they hadn't done much to help with the pain. After lying in bed for a while, he'd given up on trying to sleep and gotten up. He tried watching TV in the living room, with the sound down so he wouldn't wake his mother, but he couldn't focus on any program, so eventually he turned it off. He tried reading a book – a thriller about an obsessed man stalking a woman – but it hit a little too close to home, so he put it down. He went into the kitchen to make himself a snack. Sometimes he got sleepy after eating. But as he stood in front of the open fridge, trying to decide what sounded good, his gut gave a painful twist, and he closed the fridge without selecting anything. His stomach hadn't felt right since the cookout, even though he hadn't eaten much there. The mystery meat had been more than a little unappetizing, but he'd tried a little to be polite. It had tasted gamey and gritty, with a weird chemical aftertaste. Like wild game that had been marinated in ammonia and rubbed with sand. He regretted the small portion he'd had, and was grateful he hadn't eaten more.

Another person might've checked their social media accounts on their phone or maybe watched YouTube videos when they couldn't sleep. Spencer didn't have a phone, though. He feared it would be too tempting to look up pictures of children on the Internet. Kiddie porn, sure, but even normal pictures of children might turn his thoughts in dark directions. And he'd heard there were places on the Internet, sites where people like him – he didn't like the word *pedophile*, thought it was ugly – gathered to chat, swap photos of kids, and exchange information on the best ways to…*spend time* with them and not get caught. He knew a lot of these sites, maybe most of them, were traps set by law enforcement. Even so, he still might be tempted to risk it. Better to avoid temptation in the first place. They only had one computer in the house. It was kept in his mother's room, and he could only use it under her supervision. This had been his mother's idea, and while he sometimes found it a bit frustrating – especially at his age – he'd agreed to the condition.

But the front window, the one that faced Vivienne's house, was *not* regulated. He wouldn't have been surprised if his mother had it boarded over or painted black to keep him from looking through it. He supposed the only reason she hadn't done something like that was because she didn't want their neighbors to think they were strange. Or rather, any stranger than they already did.

Spencer went into the living room. He left the light off and opened the curtains over the front window, a foot or so, just enough so he could see out. He stepped up to the window, careful not to get *too* close. He didn't want his breath to fog the glass.

Blue-white light illuminated the cul-de-sac. Was there supposed to be a full moon tonight? He didn't know. The Hawkins family's porchlight was on, and while he knew its soft yellow glow had nothing to do with Vivienne, seeing it made him feel closer to her somehow, as if it glowed with the power of her bright child's spirit, and the tension that had been building in him ever since the cookout began to ease. He knew Dr. Reiger wouldn't approve of what he was doing, would say it was a sign that he was on the verge of becoming dangerously obsessed with Vivienne.

Fuck Dr. Reiger. Actually, no. The woman was far too old for him.

He focused his gaze on the empty front porch, and he wondered how many times in her young life Vivienne had gone through that door. The Hawkinses had moved in not that long ago. Eighteen months, maybe a bit longer than that. That would limit the number of times Vivienne passed across the threshold. He thought for a couple minutes. Say they'd been in the house for eighteen months and say that – to make things simpler – each month was thirty days long. So if Vivienne passed through the front door only once a day, that would be...five hundred and forty times. But if she went outside and back inside, that would double the number. One thousand eighty. And if she walked through and back again several times in the same day.... There was no way to calculate an exact figure, but he thought it safe to assume that true number would be around two or three thousand.

You're obsessing, he told himself. *Stop it.* But he couldn't. Or maybe this time he didn't want to.

He wasn't sure if he believed that people left behind psychic residue in the places they frequented. Vivienne's porch was likely nothing more than cold concrete that held none of her essence. So if he went outside, crossed the street, and stepped up onto the Hawkinses' porch, he wouldn't literally feel Vivienne's presence, but psychologically? That would be a different story. He couldn't do it, would *never* do it. But if he did, it would be *amazing.* The sense of danger, the feeling that he was breaking a taboo, the sheer thrill of it....

New light caught his eye, and he turned his gaze on the Eldreds' house. Their front door was open, and light spilled out onto the overgrown yard. For a moment, nothing happened, and since no one exited the house, Spencer began to think that he wasn't going to see anyone, that maybe one of the Eldreds had accidentally left the door open. But then he caught sight of someone walking across the Eldreds' front yard, heading toward the Hawkinses' house. It was the man Vivienne had been playing with at the cookout, the one with the expressionless face and the odd, stilted laugh. Spencer's hands curled into fists and his upper lip rose in a sneer. He *hated* this man for getting so close to Vivienne when he couldn't and for making her grin with delight whenever he laughed that weird laugh of his. What was the sonofabitch doing up so late, and why was he heading for the Hawkinses' house?

Not just the house, Spencer now saw. He was heading for Vivienne's bedroom window. Spencer knew which room was hers because he'd seen her climb out of her window several times, and then run around to the backyard, probably to play. He didn't know if she did this to escape being confined to her room as punishment for something naughty she had done, or whether it was simply more fun for her to go outside that way. Either way, Spencer knew that window was hers, and the man was heading straight toward it, with a fast, eager stride.

"No," Spencer whispered.

He watched the man go up to Vivienne's window, raise a hand, and tap on the glass. Nothing happened, so he tapped again. This time, the window opened and Vivienne poked her head out. Her hair was mussed, as if she'd been sleeping. She said something to the man. What, Spencer had no idea, but he burned with jealousy. Whatever words she spoke, they should've been directed at *him*, not this bastard who'd only moved into the cul-de-sac a couple days ago.

"No," he said, a bit louder this time.

The man said something to her in return, and Vivienne shook her head.

That's my girl, Spencer thought. *Tell him to fuck off.*

The man, moving more swiftly than Spencer had ever seen anyone move, reached into the window, grabbed hold of Vivienne, and pulled her out into the night.

"No!"

Spencer slammed a fist into the window so hard it cracked. He'd hit it with his wounded hand, and fresh pain blossomed in his injury, but he scarcely noticed.

Vivienne thrashed in the man's arms, kicking and struggling as she tried to free herself. She shouted for help, and Spencer could hear her clearly, as if there were no barrier between them. The man clapped a hand over her mouth to silence her, and then turned and began hurrying back toward the Eldreds' house.

Spencer was on the verge of panic. What should he do? Call 911? He knew from bitter experience how quickly a child could be violated. By the time the police arrived, it would surely be too late. He could pound on the window some more, try to get the man's attention, let him know that someone was watching and that he would never get away with whatever he intended to do to Vivienne. But Spencer knew the power of obsession, of *need*. The man wouldn't care about the possibility of getting caught right now. He'd just gone

THE FOREVER HOUSE • 155

over to the neighbors' house to abduct their daughter, for Christ's sake. He would be caught. But as long as he could have a little private time with Vivienne before that, it would be worth it to him. And Vivienne, poor sweet dear, would know the same terror and shame that Spencer had felt too many times as a child.

There was only one thing he could do.

He ran to the front door, opened it, and ran out onto the lawn.

"Hey!" he shouted. "Put her *down*!" He practically screamed this last word.

He continued running as he shouted, his bare feet slapping on the sidewalk. The man paid him no attention whatsoever, but Vivienne saw him, and the pleading look in her eyes simultaneously broke his heart and strengthened his determination to save her.

The man walked onto the Eldreds' porch and entered the house through the open doorway without ever once looking in Spencer's direction. Spencer expected the man to kick the door closed behind him and lock it, but he didn't. The door remained open. Spencer ran toward it, heart thudding in his flabby chest, breath coming in fast pants. Wouldn't it be a bitch if he died from a massive coronary on his way to save Vivienne? At any other time, he might've welcomed the prospect of death, but not now. Vivienne needed him too badly.

As he ran, he noted the full moon in the sky. The moon looked larger than it should, and it seemed to hang low in the sky. If someone had a long enough ladder, he thought, they could've reached up and touched it. The moonlight illuminated a densely packed mass of trees in the Eldreds' backyard, and while part of Spencer's mind noted these details, the rest of his mind was focused on a single goal: reaching the open doorway and getting inside before someone closed it and locked him out.

I'm coming, Vivienne, he thought. *Hold on.*

By the time he reached the Eldreds' front porch steps, his heart was pounding so fast he almost couldn't detect a space between the beats. He was drenched with sweat, his lungs burned, and his cut throbbed like hell. His body desperately wanted to stop and rest, but he refused to allow it. He stumbled up the concrete steps, onto the porch, and without hesitation, he entered the house, calling Vivienne's name.

★   ★   ★

Lola's eyes snapped open in the dark. She thought she'd heard a sound, a sharp, fast pounding. But now she heard only silence. Worried, she got up and started for her bedroom door. She usually slept in sweatshirt and sweatpants, and she did this night as well, but they didn't keep her from feeling a cold chill as she opened her bedroom door and stepped into the hall. One of her greatest fears was that one night Spencer would lose the battle against his depression and self-loathing and take his own life. As far as she knew, he'd never seriously contemplated suicide before, let alone attempted it, but he'd told her several times over the years that he sometimes thought the world would be a better place without him in it, so she feared that one morning she'd wake to find her son's dead body, reclining naked in the tub, both wrists slit longways, or maybe lying still and cold in his bed, his body full of too many pills. And he'd broken the bathroom mirror earlier tonight. She'd waited until he'd gone to his room before going into the bathroom to inspect the damage. She'd cleaned it up, and then gone to Spencer's room and knocked lightly on the door. She'd asked if he was okay, if he wanted to talk, but he didn't respond, and eventually she gave up and returned to her room. Now she wished she'd been more persistent.

Do you really? a voice inside her said. *Earlier, you were contemplating killing the boy. Now you're worried he might do the job himself? Let him! It would save you the trouble of having to do it yourself.*

She shook her head. She hadn't seriously thought of harming Spencer. That had been nothing but a dark middle-of-the-night musing, her fear and worry getting to her, that's all.

That's all.

She started toward Spencer's bedroom, but stopped when she heard the front door opening.

What the hell?

She continued down the hall, turned right, and found herself looking through the open doorway of her house. Outside, the world was awash in the radiance of moonlight, but she saw no sign of Spencer. Why would he go outside at this time of night? And why would he leave the door open? Something wasn't right here. She didn't know what, but she could feel it.

"Spencer?"

She stepped onto the porch, concrete cold against her bare feet, and looked around, trying to spot her son. She found him standing on the Hawkinses' front lawn, Vivienne kneeling before him, his shorts down around his ankles. Lola was horrified, as much for her son as she was for Vivienne.

"Spencer, no!"

Both Vivienne and Spencer turned to look at her.

Lola stepped off the porch and started down the driveway. Spencer and Vivienne watched her, motionless, neither speaking.

"Spencer, you have to stop this right now! Do you know what kind of trouble you'll get in?"

She stepped into the street and headed straight for the Hawkinses' yard. She couldn't run – bad knees – but she walked as fast as she could. She had no idea how Spencer had managed to get Vivienne outside without her parents' knowledge, and right then she didn't care. All that mattered was getting the girl away from him before he could do anything worse to her. When Lola was halfway across the street, Vivienne released her grip on Spencer's dick. She stood and watched Lola approach as Spencer bent down and pulled up his shorts. The girl took Spencer's hand and began leading him toward the Eldreds' house. Their front door was wide open for some reason, but no one stood there. Spencer gave Lola a last unreadable look, then he turned away and allowed Vivienne to lead him across the Eldreds' front yard, onto their porch, and into the house.

Lola reached the end of the Eldreds' driveway as the two of them became lost to her sight. As she hurried past the black car parked at the curb in front of the house, she thought she heard a sound, almost like a low growl, but she dismissed it as her imagination. Why would Vivienne lead Spencer into the Eldreds' house? Why would she be leading him at all? She should be afraid of him, not ready to give him a blow job on her parents' front lawn. None of this made any fucking sense, and for an instant, Lola doubted that anything she had seen since awakening was real. If she'd continued doubting, even if only for a few more seconds, the Allurement's hold over her would've been broken, and she might have been saved. But she cast her doubts aside. She would worry about *whys* later. Right now she needed to help her son.

She entered the house.

CHAPTER FOURTEEN

Cora kept drifting in and out of a restless sleep. She dreamed fitfully, in fragmented images that refused to make sense. She dreamed of a storm-ravaged mountain where large birds with fleshless skull heads circled in the sky, a stagnant river filled with the dead bloated bodies of animals, a vast dark forest beneath a huge full moon, a grove where trees produced fruit whose smell alone was intoxicating, a cavern whose dimensions kept shifting as if it were alive, a kitchen with a table so unimaginably long that she couldn't see its end, and above that, a vast, horrible emptiness surrounded by slowly swirling light. She sensed hunger in this darkness.... No, sensed the hunger *was* the darkness, ancient, insatiable, implacable, and inevitable. This hunger had a name, but she couldn't think of what it was. She was searching her mind, sure the name she wanted was in there somewhere, was in the minds and souls of every being that had ever existed, from the highest lifeform down to the simplest. But it refused to come to her.

She felt pressure on her neck. Mild at first, but slowly increasing until it began to hurt and she had trouble breathing. She didn't like this dream, so she forced herself to wake—

—only to discover she hadn't been dreaming this last part.

Martin straddled her on the bed, hands clasped around her throat, squeezing so hard, the muscles in his arms trembled. His eyes shone with dark delight, and his mouth was stretched wide in a madman's grin.

"I'm sick of your bitching, Cora. So sick, in fact, that I've decided to shut you up. *Forever.*" His laugh was a hyena's cackle.

Terror raced through her. She grabbed hold of Martin's wrists and attempted to pull his hands from her throat. He was skinny and not a particularly strong man, but she had no luck breaking his grip. She couldn't believe this was happening. She and Martin had fought before, numerous times, but he'd never struck her in anger, not even earlier tonight, and she'd thought he'd come pretty damn close to it then. But now here he was, trying to choke the life out of her.

"And once I'm done with you, I think I'll pay our daughter a visit, do a little preemptive shutting up before she has a chance to turn into a bitch like her mother." His grin widened. "I wonder if her little neck will snap if I squeeze hard enough. I can't wait to find out."

Cora's terror took on new desperation. She couldn't let Martin hurt Vivienne, and that meant she had to survive.

Martin's weight kept her pressed down on the bed, so she couldn't draw a leg up and attempt to kick him in the stomach or the balls. But she'd gotten her nails done the other day when she'd gone out with her mother and sister. They were nice and long, and her hands were free. She didn't fuck around. She went straight for Martin's eyes.

He cried out in pain as her nails drew blood, and he reflexively let go of her neck and brought his hands to his face. Cora couldn't tell if she actually damaged the eyes or just wounded the skin around them, and she didn't care. She'd gotten him to let go, and that was all that mattered. She put her blood-smeared hands down on the mattress for leverage and twisted her body as hard as she could. Martin was thrown to the side, and he fell off the bed, still holding his hands to his eyes and yelling in pain. But there was anger in his voice, too, and it was building.

She pushed herself off the other side of the bed and ran to the door. She threw it open and dashed across the hall to Vivienne's room. She didn't question why her husband had become suddenly homicidal. She didn't think at all. She operated on pure survival instinct, and right now that instinct was screaming for her to get her child the fuck away from the lunatic that was her father.

Vivienne sat up as Cora ran to her bedside. She wore a powder-blue nightgown with a fringed hem. It was her favorite outfit to sleep in, and she refused to wear anything else to bed. Her eyes were barely open, and when she spoke, her voice was a soft murmur.

"Mommy?"

Cora didn't take time to explain. Even the slightest delay could mean both their deaths. She scooped Vivienne up in her arms and ran out of her room. Vivienne clutched hold of her tightly, as much to keep from falling as from fear and surprise, Cora thought.

"What's happening?" Vivienne wailed. "Mommy, what's *happening?*"

Cora started down the hallway just as Martin flung himself out of their bedroom. He flipped on the hall light switch and Vivienne – who faced backward and could see over Cora's shoulder – screamed.

"Blood!" she shouted. Then again, louder, "*Blood!*"

Cora wanted to run to the garage, get in the pickup, and get the fuck out of here. But she didn't have the keys, and she feared Martin would catch them before they could reach the garage anyway.

Outside, she thought. *Go outside and scream your goddamn head off. One of the neighbors will hear and come help.*

Better yet, she could run next door to Kandice and Neal's, pound on the door and scream loud enough to shatter all the windows in their house. They'd come to the door, let her in, lock Martin out, and then they could call the police.

She didn't know if it was a good plan. At that point, she possessed no critical faculties. It was a plan, the only one she had, and it would have to do. She ran toward the front door, listening for sounds of Martin's pursuit, but she heard nothing but the sound of her own footfalls, her ragged, panicked breathing, and Vivienne's frightened sobs. She reached the door, unlocked it with a shaking hand, threw it open, and hurried outside, imagining Martin right behind her, reaching for her with hands stained with his own blood.

The moonlight was so bright it hurt her eyes at first, but she was grateful for it. It meant she could see where she was going. Unfortunately, that meant Martin could, too. Assuming he still possessed at least one functioning eye.

She started toward Kandice and Neal's, but stopped when she saw Martin standing on the dividing line between their two properties. He was grinning wider than ever, wider than a human should be capable of, and his face was a mask of blood. Blood was smeared on his bare chest, and his boxers were stippled with it. Cora had no idea how he'd beaten them outside. It didn't seem possible. But there he was, and she didn't have time to figure out how he'd managed this trick. She needed to put as much distance between him and them as possible.

She spun around and resumed running. She had no clear destination in mind, just ran to run. But then she saw the Eldreds' front door was open and a light shone within. She didn't question this stroke of luck, but she sure as shit intended to take advantage of it.

As she ran toward the Eldreds' house, the Allurement that had disguised itself as her husband faded away to nothing, its work done.

★   ★   ★

Martin's Allurement had a much simpler task than the others. It stood next to the couch where he was sleeping and bent its shadowy form until its mouth was next to his ear. It then spoke in Cora's voice.

"I've had it, Martin. I'm taking Vivienne and I'm leaving. Don't try to follow us. If you do, I'll take out a fucking restraining order, I swear to god."

Message delivered, the Allurement faded from existence.

Martin sat up and looked around, confused and disoriented. He remembered Cora talking to him, telling him she and Vivienne were leaving, but he didn't see either of them. Had they already left? Adrenaline jolted his system, and he practically leaped off the couch. He intended to run to the master bedroom to see if Cora was still there. He hoped to hell she was, that the words he thought she'd spoken to him were nothing more than a bad dream. Not that he would blame her for leaving, not after earlier. He'd been so mad that he'd come close to actually hitting her. He still couldn't believe it. He *loved* her. The last thing he wanted to do was hurt her.

But before he could start toward their bedroom, Cora came running down the hall and into the vestibule that led to the front door. The door was visible from the living room, and Martin watched as Cora, still in her copper-colored silk pajamas – unlocked the door, opened it, and ran outside. He didn't understand what was happening. She looked like she was running for her life. Was she that afraid of him?

He ran after them, shouting Cora's name. When he reached the front yard, he stopped and called her name again.

"Cora!"

She didn't respond, didn't so much as look back. God, it was bright out! Martin looked at the full moon hanging in the sky above the Eldreds' house. He'd never seen a moon that big before.

Cora carried Vivienne toward the Eldreds'. Their front door was open, and Cora ran inside without hesitation.

Martin didn't care that he was wearing only boxers. He had to talk to Cora, try to fix things between them before it was too late.

He ran toward the Eldreds' front door.

★　　★　　★

Kandice's Allurement took a different approach than the others. It entered the Wilkersons' house, passing through the front door as if it were no more substantial than mist. It drifted down the hall toward Kandice and Neal's bedroom, entered, and glided toward Kandice's side of the bed. The shadowy creature regarded her for a moment, then it stretched its hand and gently slipped five fingers into her brain, skin and bone proving no more of an impediment to its substance that any other material. Once its fingers were inside, the Allurement began sifting through the contents of Kandice's mind, searching for the right areas to manipulate, like a pianist feeling for the right keys to play. When it found them, it went to work.

Several moments later, Kandice – still very much asleep – got up and started walking. Neal stirred, rolled over, but did not wake.

★　　★　　★

Kandice was back at the cookout. She was dressed in her favorite cottony pajamas, but this seemed completely normal to her. Everyone was there – the Eldreds, Neal, their neighbors – all of them dressed normally, none of them moving. They resembled extremely lifelike mannequins, frozen in the midst of having a good time. Kandice wasn't concerned, though, and she went over to Neal, who held a cup of that weird punch in his hand. She spoke his name, and when he didn't respond, she put her hand on his arm and tried to shake him. But it was like trying to shake a marble statue. No matter how hard she tried, she couldn't move him.

She was starting to become afraid now, and she shouted Neal's name right in his face, hoping to shock him out of the strange trance he was in. He gave no reaction, though, didn't so much as blink. Her fear grew stronger and she felt tears threatening, but before she could start crying, she heard a child's voice screaming.

"Mommy, no! No-no-no, *please!*"

The voice was so high-pitched that she couldn't tell if it belonged to a girl or boy, but the sheer terror in the tone was unmistakable, as was the fact that the voice came from inside the house. She didn't question how she could hear it so clearly from the backyard, didn't question anything. She knew the voice belonged to one of the Raines children, and that their mommy was killing them all over again. She remembered the vision she'd had the last time she was at the Eldreds' cookout – the children smiling at her, faces splattered with blood.

The patio door opened, seemingly of its own accord, but she didn't question this either. The children were in grave danger, and she was the only one who heard their cries, the only one who was free to act.

In the waking world, just as in her dream, she ran across the yard, onto the deck, and into the house. A moment later, the patio door slid shut behind her and locked itself.

★   ★   ★

Neal had a habit of reaching out to Kandice while they slept. He was unaware that he did this, but his subconscious mind felt reassured confirming that she was there, safe and sleeping next to him. Since discovering Kandice was bisexual, he'd been reaching out to her at night much more often, as if he needed extra reassurance of her presence. So when he reached out for her this night and did not find her, he woke, at least partially. He reached for her again, swept his hand across the sheet on her side of the bed, found nothing. He came all the way awake then and sat up.

"Kandice?"

The door to the master bathroom was closed, and there was no light on under the door. That didn't mean she wasn't inside, though. She often didn't turn on the light when she used the bathroom at night. She said the light hurt her eyes.

"Kandice?" he called again, louder this time.

Nothing.

He got out of bed and walked across the floor. He opened the bathroom door, flipped on the light, saw that Kandice wasn't there. He turned off the light and started toward the bedroom door. Kandice usually had no trouble sleeping through the night, but when she did – when she was sick or had an especially bad period – she'd go into the kitchen, make herself a cup of chamomile tea, and then sit on the couch and watch TV with the sound muted and closed captioning on so it wouldn't wake him.

The living room was dark, though. No lights on, no TV going. He turned on the light to make sure the couch was empty. It was.

He was fully awake now and starting to worry. Had Kandice had enough of his bullshit and decided she needed some time to herself? Neither of them had ever gone off alone when they were having trouble. They always tried to work things out, and up to this point, they'd managed well enough. But he knew his struggles to come to terms with her sexuality were beginning to wear on her. How could they not? It would be completely understandable if she felt she needed a break from his emotional turbulence. But one partner in a relationship leaving the house for an extended time could also be the first step in that relationship's eventual collapse. He decided to go to the garage and check if her car was still here. If it wasn't, he'd do his best not to panic. He'd call her cell and hope she answered. If she let his call go to voicemail, he'd leave a message, tell her how he hoped she was okay and to call him when she was ready. But before he could take a step out of the living room, he heard what sounded like a giggle. And it sounded as if it came from outside. They normally kept the curtains closed over the front window at night. Kandice didn't like the idea of their neighbors being able to see them walk around at night – especially Isaac and Spencer. Neal didn't blame her. Privacy was hard to come by in a small cul-de-sac like Brookside Court. He walked to the window and pulled the curtains open.

The front yard was awash in moonlight, and Neal could see everything as clearly as if it had been day. And what he saw were two naked women on his lawn. One of them was Lacresha Eldred. The other was Kandice. Kandice lay on her back, legs spread, arms out, fingers digging into the ground. Lacresha knelt between Kandice's legs, furiously licking her clitoris while sliding a pair of fingers rapidly in and out of her. Kandice's head was thrown back in pleasure, eyes closed, mouth stretched into a satisfied smile. Another delighted giggle escaped her lips, and then her body began bucking, her orgasm so intense that she released a scream that was as much pain as pleasure.

She'd never come like that with him. Not even close.

Kandice continued to spasm for several more moments during which Lacresha continued her vigorous ministrations. Finally, both women were spent and Lacresha fell back onto the grass beside Kandice.

Neal couldn't believe what he'd just witnessed. Kandice wasn't a prude when it came to sex, but to fuck on the front lawn, where anyone might see? That was completely unlike her.

Unlike her with you, he thought. *Maybe she's different with someone else. With a woman. Freer. Wilder. Happier.*

He felt as if a rock-hard fist had been driven into his gut. He couldn't move, couldn't breathe. He felt a throbbing ache, and when he glanced downward, he saw his stiff cock straining against the fabric of his pajama pants. He hadn't been aware of it until now, and he was angry, as if his dick had betrayed him somehow. His anger broke his paralysis, and he headed for the door. He'd asked Kandice to tell him if she ever became attracted enough to a woman that she wanted to explore sex with her, had told her they would try to find a way to work it out as a couple. He hadn't told her he was cool with her fucking on their goddamn front lawn with a neighbor in the middle of the goddamn night!

He threw open the front door and was already yelling as he stepped onto the porch.

"What in the hell is going on here?"

But the lawn was empty now. Neal looked around quickly and saw Kandice and Lacresha, arms around each other's waists, walking across the street toward the Eldreds' house.

"Kandice!"

His voice echoed through the night, but Kandice didn't turn to look at him, didn't stop walking, didn't even slow her pace. Lacresha didn't respond to him either. It was like they didn't hear him, like he didn't exist.

At that instant, the unreality of all this hit him. Kandice loved him. Even if she started experiencing an urge to be with a woman, she'd never go about it like this. She'd never hurt him, not intentionally.

Something odd happened then. Even with the light from the large full moon hovering over the Eldreds' house – and what a strange moon it was – Kandice and Lacresha became more difficult to see. Their forms darkened, as if some unseen object had come between them and the moonlight. Their features became less distinct, blurry around the edges. The women became two smudges of darkness gliding toward the Eldreds' open door. They weren't Kandice and Lacresha at all, he realized, rather something...*other*.

He felt a moment of mild dizziness, of disorientation, and he had a sensation as if he'd been listening to some silent signal and someone had increased the intensity.

The smudges became Kandice and Lacresha again, and with their reappearance, all doubt that they had ever been anything else disappeared. His wife – his *naked* wife, who had another woman's saliva all over her cunt – was going off with her lover. He'd lose her forever if he let her, knew it down to the very core of his being. He couldn't allow that to happen, not without putting up a fight. He loved her too much.

"Kandice! Wait!"

He ran off the porch in pursuit of his wife. And when she and Lacresha entered the Eldreds' house, he followed. Once he was inside, the door shut and locked itself.

Everyone was assembled, and the game began in earnest.

CHAPTER FIFTEEN

The first thing Kandice became aware of was the wind. Cold and biting, whipping her exposed skin like flails of ice. She stood on rock, the stony surface uncomfortable on her bare feet. An achingly perfect blue sky dotted with large white clouds spread out before her. She had a sense that wherever she was, she was very far above the ground, and when she looked down to confirm this, she immediately wished she hadn't. She was standing on a ledge, the ground so far below her that she couldn't make out any features of the landscape beyond lines defining different patches of land, some brown, some green, as if she were looking through an airplane window at the land beneath.

I'm on a mountain, she thought. This realization was followed by a second. *And it's daytime. Wasn't it night just a moment ago?* She had no idea how she'd gotten here. The last thing she remembered, she was in the Eldreds' backyard, hearing the screams of the Raines children as their mother ended their lives. Unable to stop herself, she'd run into the house, hoping to save them, even though they'd been dead and buried for several years now. Had she passed out? She must have. But she felt awake and alert now. A bitterly cold mountain wind worked better to restore a person's senses than any smelling salts ever could.

Her cotton pajamas didn't provide much insulation from the cold, and she wrapped her arms around herself for what little protection from the wind they might offer. She didn't think she was dreaming. She was too goddamn cold for this to be anything other than real.

Kandice realized then that she wasn't alone. Cora and Vivienne were here, as were Isaac and Spencer. All of them except Isaac were dressed for sleeping, and they too looked like they were coming out of some kind of trance. She saw no sign of Neal or their remaining neighbors – Lola, Martin, and Alex. Were they elsewhere on the mountain, or had they escaped whatever was happening? She hoped for the latter, but she feared the others were in danger, if not here, then somewhere else. She had no reason to think this. It was only a feeling, but it was a strong one.

Cora stood directly on her right. She looked at Kandice without recognition at first, but then tentatively, she said her name. Kandice reached out to take Cora's hands. They felt cold as ice.

"It's me. We're okay."

She glanced down at the landscape below once more and experienced a rush of vertigo. She quickly looked away. *Okay might have been an overstatement,* she thought.

The others began looking around, taking in their surroundings, trying to orient themselves. Kandice didn't know what time it was. It was daylight, that much was obvious, but the sun itself wasn't visible from where they were standing. It could be anywhere from early morning to late afternoon for all she could tell. Isaac and Spencer stepped closer to the women, as if by grouping themselves together, they could shield each other from the wind. It didn't work.

"I...." Cora began. She reached up to massage her throat, as if it was sore. "I had a dream, I guess. It seemed so *real.*"

Vivienne, shivering, pressed herself against her mother's left side, and Cora draped an arm around her shoulders.

"Me, too," Kandice said.

They had to speak loudly to be heard over the sound of the wind.

"But we're not dreaming now," Cora said.

"I don't think so."

"We're in the house," Vivienne said.

Kandice and Cora fell silent and looked at her. So did Isaac and Spencer.

"It's big in here." Vivienne paused, then added, "*Really* big."

Cora looked thoughtful. "I think I dreamed of a mountain like this. Some other places, too, but I can't quite remember...."

Isaac looked at Vivienne. "You can't fit a mountain inside a house." Then he looked at Kandice and Cora. "We're still dreaming. Actually, *I'm* still dreaming. None of this is real, including the four of you."

"Don't be stupid," Cora said. "This *is* real. Can't you feel it?"

Isaac glared at Cora, but Kandice could see the fear in his eyes. He did feel it, and so did the rest of them.

"Then we've been drugged," Isaac said. "There was something in the punch, probably the meat, too. Whatever it was, it's causing us to hallucinate."

"My stomach *was* bothering me last night," Spencer said. He cast a glance at Vivienne, then quickly looked away.

What's that about? Kandice wondered. She got a creepy vibe from the man. It was almost as if he were attracted to Vivienne. Sexually. But that couldn't be true. Spencer was quiet and kept to himself. And yeah, he was weird, but that didn't make him a pedophile. She thought then of how Lola had kept pinching the back of Spencer's hand at the cookout. Kandice had been so focused on that action that she hadn't noticed where Spencer had been looking. Had he been watching Vivienne as she wandered around the yard? Maybe. Kandice felt sick to her stomach, and she decided that whatever was happening here, she'd make sure that Spencer was never alone with Vivienne, never even got within touching distance of her. Just in case.

"If we were drugged," Cora said, "why would we gather inside the Eldreds' house? Assuming what Vivienne said is true, and that's where we really are."

"I don't know," he admitted. "But it's the only logical conclusion I can come to right now. Not that there's anything logical about this."

"Fuck logic," Cora said. "We need to get out of this goddamn wind before we freeze to death."

Kandice smiled. Trust Cora to cut through the bullshit and get to what was important.

"It looks like we're on a trail of some kind," Spencer said.

Kandice didn't see what he meant at first, but the longer she looked, the more she thought he was right. It wasn't a wide, well-used trail with smooth footing and clearly delineated dimensions. It was narrow, rocky, and irregular, but it *did* look like a trail, if you squinted your eyes and used your imagination.

"If it's a trail, it's not much of one," Isaac said.

"Better than any trail *you* found," Cora said. She took Vivienne's hand. "Let's go, sweetie." She started moving carefully along the crude trail, Vivienne at her side. Kandice followed, then Spencer, and finally – grudgingly – came Isaac. The going wasn't easy. The stony ground bruised Kandice's bare feet, and at times the ledge became so narrow that it looked like they wouldn't be able to keep going. But they always managed to continue making progress somehow. Not that it seemed to do them much good. The mountain was so damn tall that no matter how much they walked, it seemed they weren't actually getting anywhere.

Nice metaphor for life, she thought.

She could feel how frightened everyone was. They'd been plunged into a living nightmare, and all they could do was put their fears and doubts to the side as best they could and continue on as if all of this was real. If it wasn't, no harm done. They'd eventually come out of this dream or hallucination or whatever it was. But if this *was* real, and they didn't treat it as such, they could get seriously injured, maybe even die here.

Kandice wasn't certain how long they walked, but after a time, the others were all breathing heavily and their skin was coated with sweat. Their legs were tired, and they took plodding, heavy steps. Kandice felt fine, though. But then she was the fittest one here because of all the exercise she got in her job. If the rest of the group continued to tire, they'd need to stop for a rest soon.

Eventually, the trail curved, and as they made their way around, they discovered someone was on the trail ahead of them, standing still, as if waiting for their arrival. Kandice recognized him as one of the Eldreds, although he hadn't been introduced to them as such at the cookout. She'd seen him playing with Vivienne in the Eldreds' backyard. He wore the same flat expression that he'd had then, only now he was dressed in a stained T-shirt – was that blood? – shorts, and running shoes. One of his legs was bent at an angle so severe, Kandice wondered how the man could remain standing. Despite the way he was dressed, he appeared unaffected by the wind.

Cora and Vivienne stopped when they were within three feet of the man, and everyone else came to a halt as well.

Cora cut right to the chase. "Where are we? Do you know what's going on?"

The man's expression didn't change, and Kandice thought he wasn't going to answer Cora, but then he spoke.

"Aerie," he said. *"Game. Feed."*

His words were toneless with an electronic buzz to them. Kandice wondered if he had some sort of disability that required him to use a speech synthesizer. She wasn't clear what he was talking about, but his words sent a chill through her that had nothing to do with the wind. *Aerie. Game. Feed.* It was this last word that bothered her the most: *feed.*

Cora looked back at the rest of them. "Anyone understand what he's talking about?"

"I do."

The voice – a woman's – didn't belong to any of them, and when they turned in its direction, they saw a creature out of a nightmare hovering in the sky not far from where they stood. It was roughly human-sized, its body that of a black-feathered bird with thick, gray talons. But its head was that of a woman. Cleora Eldred, to be exact. Her wings were stretched wide, and hung in the air, buoyed by the strong mountain winds. Her eyes were those of a bird, a strange soulless black. When she spoke, she revealed a mouth that had two rows of rusty razor blades where teeth should've been.

Vivienne hid behind her mother, and Kandice envied her. She wished she had somewhere to hide, too.

"You five should feel honored," the bird-woman said, her voice a writhing mass of slime-covered worms. "We don't normally welcome our guests personally."

The expressionless man pointed at the harpy and spoke a single word in his cold, inhuman voice.

"*Grandother.*"

Cleora – the Grandother – trained her obsidian eyes on the man, and while Kandice was unable to read any emotion in her avian gaze, she sensed the woman was angry. The Grandother nodded toward the man.

"*He's* the reason I've made myself known to you so soon. Machine Head is our servant, and he is *not* supposed to be here."

The Grandother tilted her wings slightly, and she drifted closer to the group. When she was only a couple feet from the man – from Machine Head – she fixed him with her black eyes.

"Why *are* you here?"

Machine Head didn't appear to be intimidated by the Grandother in the slightest. He looked at her for a moment, his eyes flashing an eerie green, then he pointed to Vivienne.

"*Friend,*" he said.

The Grandother let out a bird-caw of a laugh. "Getting sentimental in our old age, are we? Don't be a fool. Do you think the girl would want to be your friend if she saw what you truly look like? Do you think *any* of them would? The Eldred are your family. Humans," she sneered, "are merely food."

All of them were scared, but Vivienne was absolutely terrified. She pressed herself to Cora's legs and wrapped her arms around them, using her mother as both anchor and shield.

"I don't like this, Mommy! I want to go home – now!"

I'm right there with you, kid, Kandice thought.

The Grandother did a sudden mid-air flip. One of her talons struck Machine Head's face, tearing the skin from throat to crown. There was no blood, but the skin parted a couple inches, revealing metal underneath. The Grandother gave her left wing an extra flap. A gust of air struck Machine Head's torn face, which Kandice now realized was a mask, and blew it off him. The wind caught it and carried it away, and soon it was lost to sight.

The Eldreds' servant appeared to be human, but his head was that of a robot, an old-fashioned construction of metal and rivets, the sort of thing a mad scientist in the nineteenth century might've designed. His green eyes became blazing red as he looked at the Grandother.

Kandice remembered then that she'd seen the man before, the night she and Cora sat on her front porch, smoking and watching the movers hauling stuff into the Eldreds' house. She'd thought he'd been wearing a helmet then. How could she have guessed what she'd *really* been seeing? It wasn't like people with mechanical heads were a common sight in Rockridge.

Everyone stared at the robot man, Vivienne included. Tears welled in the little girl's eyes, and she silently mouthed the word *no*.

The Grandother spoke once more. "Machine Head – because of your long and faithful service to our family, I shall give you a choice. Leave the humans or remain with them and share their fate. Decide."

Kandice heard a whirring sound coming from inside Machine Head, as if his mechanical brain was considering the Grandother's words. Finally, he raised his right hand and gave her the middle finger.

The Grandother's face darkened with fury, and she spit a shower of razor blades at Machine Head. Some bounced off his metal head, but most struck his body, sliced through his clothes and cut into his flesh. Blood welled from these wounds, but Machine Head gave no sign that he felt anything.

"Have it your way," the Grandother said.

She tilted her wings to the right, dipped away from the mountainside, started flapping her wings, and rose into the sky. She stopped when she was several dozen yards away from Kandice and the others, turned to face them, and continued flapping her wings so she could maintain that position. She said nothing, merely stared at them, as if she was waiting for something to happen. And it did.

The sky began to darken. Kandice looked up and saw black clouds rushing in from all directions, moving far more swiftly than she thought possible. Within seconds, the mountain was shrouded in gloom, and the wind – already cold – became downright frigid. It picked up in strength, too, tearing at Kandice and the others like a winter gale.

"This isn't natural!" Isaac had to shout to be heard over the wind.

"No shit, Sherlock!" Cora shouted back.

As if by unspoken agreement, they moved off the trail and pressed themselves against the mountain's craggy surface, fingers scrabbling for handholds to anchor themselves so the wind couldn't sweep them over the mountain's edge. Cora had Vivienne stand between her and the rock, so her body would serve as additional protection for the girl. Machine Head didn't join them. He remained standing where he'd been when they first saw him, seemingly oblivious to the wind and cold. They remained like that for several moments, shivering as wind whipped their backs. Kandice knew they couldn't take much more of this, but she also knew they couldn't continue on the trail, not with the wind this strong. They were trapped.

And then it began to rain.

The storm didn't start gradually. There wasn't a smattering of drops followed by a few more, then a shower that slowly increased in intensity until it became a downpour. Instead, a torrent of ice-cold water dropped from the sky all at once, as if the mountain was located at the bottom of a vast ocean within a protective bubble that had burst. The rain came down so hard that Kandice feared they would be washed off the side of the mountain, swept over the edge, and plummet to their deaths. Somehow they all managed to hold on, but how long they could keep doing so was another matter.

Lightning flashed across the dark sky, jagged bolts that illuminated the mountain as bright as day, followed closely by explosions of thunder so strong, Kandice could feel the vibrations in the rock she clung to.

Kandice was looking at the Grandother, and she heard the birdwoman release an ear-splitting cry that was part human scream, part avian screech. Kandice sensed movement above them, and looked upward to see birds – dozens and dozens of them – shoot out from openings in the rocks. The birds were smaller than the Grandother but larger than the robins, sparrows, and cardinals she regularly saw on Brookside Court. Turkey vultures weren't an uncommon sight in Ohio, and Kandice estimated these birds were of a similar size. They flew toward the Grandother and swirled around her, dipping and darting, giving forth raucous caws so loud they were audible even over the storm. The birds flew so fast, it took Kandice a moment to realize that their heads were fleshless, eyeless skulls, the bone gleaming white.

Machine Head had called this place the Aerie. Now Kandice knew why.

The Grandother spoke no words, but she nodded her head toward Kandice and the others, and the skullheads attacked.

Cora screamed while Vivienne hid behind her mother, eyes squeezed shut. Spencer looked at Vivienne, his expression sympathetic, as if his main concern at the moment was the girl's feelings rather than the flock of deathbirds coming toward them. Isaac stood watching the birds, a blank expression on his face. Kandice couldn't hear him speak over the sound of the storm and the cries of the approaching birds, but she could read his lips. He was repeating *Not real, not real, not real* over and over. Machine Head remained motionless, eyes green once more, seemingly unconcerned about the oncoming attack.

Kandice didn't know what to do, but she had to do *something*. It was clear no one else was going to. She crouched down and felt for a rock, not taking her eyes off the Grandother and her oncoming minions. The trail was littered with rocks, some merely pebbles, some baseball-sized or larger. Her fingers found a Goldilocks rock – not too large, not too small – and she grabbed hold of it and stood. She'd never been big on competitive sports, although she did play on the rec center softball team, and she worked out for living. So when she threw the rock, it hurtled through the air fast and true. She hadn't bothered to aim at any particular bird. She'd thrown the rock at the center of the flock, thinking it was her best chance to hit one, or at least scare them enough to scatter and break off their attack. She got lucky. Her rock struck one of the skullheads' wings, breaking it. The bird immediately lost control in the wind and was swept away. Its companions veered off from the mountain, now perceiving Kandice as a threat. She smiled in grim satisfaction.

Kandice's success spurred the other adults into action. Cora, Isaac, and Spencer began gathering and throwing rocks at the birds, along with Kandice. Vivienne was too frightened to join in, though. She huddled against the mountain's stony side, eyes still shut tight. The robot man went over to the girl and stood in front of her, taking Cora's place as her shield. Kandice remembered his response when the Grandother asked him why he'd joined the humans. *Friend.*

The skullheads flew around in random patterns, not regrouping yet, but they didn't go very far from their prey, and the barrage of rocks kept them at a distance.

Spencer was their weakest thrower. His rocks didn't even reach the birds, let alone injure any of them, Isaac did better, if not as well as Kandice, but Cora turned out to be the best of them all. Almost every rock she threw struck a bird, and when she missed, it wasn't by very much. Kandice couldn't help sneaking glances at the woman as they worked to hold off the skullheads. Thanks to the rain, Cora's black hair was plastered to her head, and her satin pajamas clung tight to her body, outlining her narrow shoulders, the curve of her hips, and her erect nipples. Kandice had always found Cora beautiful, but what she admired most about her now was the fierce determination on her face. She might have screamed in fear when the skullheads first attacked, but now she was a warrior, fighting not only for her own survival, but for that of her child, and she was magnificent.

Kandice was only slightly distracted by Cora, but that was enough. She didn't see that one of the skullheads had flown upward, well out of rock-throwing range. When it was high enough, the creature dove downward, flying within inches of the mountain's surface. It came down directly behind Kandice, angled sharply upward, and slammed its bony beak into the back of her head. Bright light flashed behind her eyes, and at first she mistook it for a close lightning strike. Then the pain hit, a feeling like someone had taken a sledgehammer to her head. The pain was so overwhelming that she was only dimly aware of stumbling forward, of Cora screaming her name and reaching for her, of pitching over the trail's edge and plummeting into space. She didn't lose consciousness, but the pain in her head made it difficult for her to think, so it took a moment for her to come to the realization that she was falling – *fast.*

And then the skullheads were surrounding her. Kandice and the others had knocked a number of the creatures out of the sky, but many remained. And these grabbed hold of Kandice with their talons, finding purchase wherever they could – shoulders, arms, wrists, legs, ankles, and when they couldn't latch on to her body, they sank their talons into the fabric of her pajamas. They flapped their wings hard and fast, and within seconds, Kandice began to slow and then the birds ascended, carrying her with them.

Her vision was blurry – maybe from rainwater hitting her eyes, more likely from the blow to her head – but she saw the skullheads were bearing her toward a dark shape that grew larger with each passing second. Her eyes managed to focus and she saw the shape was the Grandother, who remained hovering in place in defiance of the powerful storm raging around her. Kandice thought the birds were going to deliver her to the harpy, and then the Grandother would tear into her with her razor-blade teeth. The Grandother grinned maliciously as her servants brought Kandice closer…closer…. But just as they were about to reach the Grandother, they veered to the right and flew past her. Kandice raised her head and tried to see where they were taking her, but with the rain on her face and her fluctuating vision, she couldn't see well enough to—

Lightning flashed nearby, followed almost instantly by a bone-rattling clap of thunder. The light and sound caused the pain in her head to intensify to the point she thought it might explode. She wished it would. At least the pain would be over then. But the lightning lit up the sky long enough for Kandice to see the skullheads were taking her toward an object of some kind, a square-shaped thing that hung in the air as if levitating. Her scrambled brain struggled to identify the object, but it wasn't until a second burst of lightning – with accompanying thunder – illuminated the object again that she realized what it was. It helped that she was much closer to it now as well.

It was a window – a normal, everyday window – made of wood and glass, hanging in the sky without visible support.

Before she could wonder what the hell it was doing here, the skullheads flew straight toward it. She could see that while it was daylight here, it was dark on the other side of the window. Not completely, though. She could see some stars and the glow of moonlight. At the last moment before the birds collided with it, they banked upward and released their grip on her. She continued flying forward and hit the window face-first, and as the glass shattered, she felt new pain in her head, not only from the impact of striking the window, but from the deep cuts she sustained on her face and scalp from the broken glass as she passed through.

She started to fall, but the skullheads shot out of the window after her, and they caught hold of her again, and once more lifted her upward. She'd been right about what lay on the other side of the window. She saw a clear night sky, no storm here. There was a small clearing below that looked like the Eldreds' backyard, but beyond that was a vast forest, tall trees spreading outward in all directions as far as she could see. The skullheads slowed and curved around, and then she saw the Eldreds' house, a huge full moon hanging above it, seeming so close she thought the skullheads could easily carry her there if they wished. She could also see the bedroom window she'd come through. It was located near the roof, and violent winds rushed outward, carrying rain with them, and lightning flashed like a strobe light, followed by cracks of thunder.

There's a mountain inside the house, she thought. In the attic, to be precise.

She wondered how something like that – something so awful yet at the same time so amazing – could be possible. But before she could think on this paradox any further, the skullheads released their grip on her once more and she fell toward the ground. She landed back-first on a hard surface, and she heard the sounds of multiple bones snapping. Whatever she struck broke from the impact, and her middle slumped downward, trapping her within the....

Picnic table, she thought. The goddamn birds had carried her out of the attic – the attic, which contained a mountain and a raging thunderstorm, not to mention an entire fucking *sky* – and deposited her in the backyard. She'd landed on one of the two picnic tables, hitting the wood so hard that it broke beneath her, and she was now stuck within the hole she'd created. She might've been able to free herself if she hadn't been injured, but her bones felt like broken glass, and it was agony simply to breathe. No way in hell was she going to be able to get off the table without help.

The skullheads descended toward the table and began circling above her, as if waiting for something.

This is insane, she thought.

But then the back door opened, and she realized that until this moment she hadn't truly understood what insane was.

Five people came out of the house. A man and a woman, accompanied by three small children, one of them so young that his father carried him. They were all dressed for warm weather in either T-shirts and shorts or – in the case of the mother and one of her daughters – sundresses. Their features were clearly visible in the moonlight, and Kandice recognized them. It was the Raineses family – Cherie, Dale, Elisa, Courtney, and Jacob. They all wore conical party hats, just as they had in her vision at the cookout, when she'd thought she'd witnessed the home video of the family from the crime show about their deaths come to life. Then, as if that thought was a cue, a voice seemed to issue from the air around her. She recognized it as belonging to the narrator from *Killer in My House.*

"As Kandice lay on the picnic table – broken like her battered body – she could only watch as the Raineses family approached."

As if following stage directions, the Raines stepped off the deck and started walking toward her. They drew near, lines of blood beginning to well forth from the pores on their foreheads and faces, the trickles looking black in the moonlight. Blood ran into their eyes, over and around their noses, across their lips, into their mouths, down their chins. They smiled, displaying white teeth streaked with dark liquid.

"The Raineses intended to reenact Jacob's second birthday," the invisible announcer said. *"Only this time there was going to be a guest. A very special guest."*

The Raines – still smiling their hideous blood smiles – took up positions around the table. Cherie and Dale, who still held Jacob, stood at the end of the table near Kandice's head. Elisa and Courtney stood at the sides, hands gripping the table's edge as they bounced up and down on their feet, excited. The skullheads became excited, too. They circled faster in the air above Kandice, squawking loudly. The announcer went on.

"Next, Cherie Raines put the candles in place."

Kandice didn't understand what the announcer meant at first, but then she saw Cherie step closer and raise her hands. In one she held two small candles. In the other, she held a lighter. The bottoms of the candles had been inserted into metal holders that came to sharp points.

"No," Kandice said. It hurt so much to breathe that the word came out as little more than a soft hiss of air. She drew in a deeper breath, almost screamed from the pain, and then in a louder voice said, "Please, don't...."

None of the Raines gave any sign that they heard her. Cherie shifted one candle over to the hand holding the lighter, and then she plunged the other into Kandice's right eye. Kandice screamed, and blood spilled from this new wound to obscure the vision on that side. She was still screaming when Cherie stuck the second candle into her other eye.

"The pain was excruciating, but it was nothing compared to what she was about to experience."

She couldn't see out of either eye now, but she heard the sound of Cherie activating the lighter, smelled the chemical tang of butane burning, felt the heat on her face as the woman lit the candles she'd violated Kandice's body with.

The skullheads' squawking grew louder and took on an almost human quality. Kandice could swear the things were laughing.

Then the Raineses began to sing 'Happy Birthday' to Jacob. Kandice, too broken to move and unable to see, could only lie there and wait for the song to end. She thought of Neal – dear, sweet Neal

– and she hoped he'd never learn the details of what happened to her. She didn't want him to be haunted by those images for the rest of his life. She wished they'd been able to work out the latest issue between them, but she took solace in the fact that neither of them had given up, that they'd continued to work at understanding one another, that Neal – as hard as it was for him at times – had been determined to accept her for who she was. In the end, wasn't that what love was all about?

Melting wax from the candles dripped onto her eyes, but by this point she was in so much pain, she barely noticed.

The singing ended, and she heard Cherie say, "Make a wish, sweetie!" She pictured Dale holding his son down to her face so the little boy could blow out the burning candles. She heard him puff air once, twice, followed by the smoky smell of extinguished wicks. She could imagine their gray wisps curling upward into the air.

The announcer spoke again.

"And with the ritual completed, it was time for the Raineses family to feast."

"Who wants Kandy?" Cherie said.

"We do, we do!" Elisa and Courtney cried in unison. Tiny hands clapped, and Jacob giggled happily.

The skullheads were definitely laughing now, sounding more like a pack of hyenas than a flock of birds.

"Then dig in!" Cherie said.

I love you, Neal, Kandice thought, and then she felt the Raineses family's hands tear into her with inhuman strength, and she screamed as they began to gorge themselves.

CHAPTER SIXTEEN

"How big *is* this place?" Lola said.

Martin gave her a withering look. "That has got to be one of the dumbest questions anyone's ever asked in the entire history of the human race. Look around. It's fucking *huge*."

Lola didn't appreciate the man's rudeness, but now that she thought of it, it had been a dumb question. The four of them – Lola, Martin, Neal, and Alex – stood in the middle of a vast cavern. The walls, floor, and ceiling were dotted with patches of some glowing yellow-green substance that reminded Lola of the way lightning bugs lit up. Whatever it was – some kind of lichen, maybe – the illumination it provided allowed them to see well enough to get around, but it wasn't enough to light up the whole place. Shadows gathered on the cavern's ceiling, making it seem as if the stalactites there emerged from an upside-down sea of darkness. Lola and the others stood close to a wall where the light was strongest, but they couldn't see the wall on the other side of the cavern, nor could they see very far ahead or behind them. Even so, Lola could feel that the cavern was gigantic. There was a sense of great space all around them, and sounds – their footsteps, their voices – echoed and re-echoed in odd ways, contributing to the feeling of largeness and making it difficult to orient themselves. Lola knew they were moving and had been for ten, maybe fifteen minutes now, but it seemed as if they'd made no progress at all.

The four of them had woken up – or returned to awareness might be a better way to say it – standing on their feet on the cavern floor. To say they'd been confused would be an understatement. Fucking terrified would be more like it. But they'd quickly compared notes and discovered each of them had been lured into the Eldreds' house – although none of them had been comfortable sharing the specific details of precisely how they'd been lured. They'd been unable to reach consensus on whether this was real or if they were dreaming. It *felt* real to Lola, though. More real than any dream she'd ever had. The group had decided to operate under the assumption that what they were seeing and hearing was real – for the time being, at least.

They'd had no idea whether their loved ones were also here, perhaps in another location in the cavern. They'd spent several minutes calling out to them, shouting their names, but they'd only received echoes of their own voices in reply. They'd decided to explore the cavern in search of their missing family members, as well as a way out of here. So far, they hadn't had any luck at finding either. Lola wasn't sure whether to hope that Spencer was here in the cavern or hope he was somewhere safe inside the Eldreds' house. Wherever he was, she hoped it wasn't the same place as Vivienne. She'd seen Vivienne preparing to pleasure Spencer in the girl's front yard, and then she'd watched her take him into the Eldreds' house. She didn't know if that had been real or not, but she hoped to Christ it had been some kind of dream or hallucination.

The air was cold, just like you'd expect in a cavern, Lola thought, and they were all shivering. Neal and Martin had it the worst since they weren't fully clothed. Neal wore only Superman pajama pants and Martin had on only a pair of boxers. They were both good-looking men, she thought, although Martin was too skinny for her tastes. She and Alex were fully clothed – Alex in T-shirt and shorts, Lola in sweatshirt and sweatpants – but they were all barefoot, and the rough, craggy cavern floor had already bruised and scraped their feet. Lola wasn't used to all this walking, and her bad knees throbbed painfully. She and Spencer had bought a treadmill a few years back, both of them vowing to use it and get in shape, but neither of them had, and the thing was in the garage now, gathering dust. Lola wished she'd used it now, though. She had the feeling she'd be walking a lot more before the night ended.

"This is weird."

Alex had stopped in front of the cavern wall and was sliding the palm of one hand back and forth across a section of it. Lola and the others gathered around her.

"What is it?" Neal asked.

Lola liked Neal well enough. He could be a bit condescending at times, but he was nowhere near as bad as Isaac. She was glad *he* wasn't here with them.

Alex removed her hand from the wall so they could better see what she was talking about.

"The wall here is smooth. Like, *totally* smooth. It feels more like an artificial wall. You know, something someone built."

Martin and Neal both stepped forward at the same time. They scowled at each other, and Neal backed off, letting Martin examine the flat section of cavern wall first. Lola was disappointed to see Neal give in so easily. Martin could be a bully at times, and she *despised* bullies. Spencer had dealt with more than his share of them while growing up. He'd always been on the husky side, and the other kids had liked to tease him for being overweight, called him names like Lard-Ass and chanted *Fatty, fatty, two by four, can't get through the bathroom door.*

Martin frowned in puzzlement as he ran his hand over the same area Alex had. After a moment, he turned to Neal.

"I think she's right. What do you think, Mr. Science?"

Martin stepped back, allowing Neal to move forward and examine the wall. He too ran his hand over it several times, and when he finished, he frowned as well.

"It does feel like a man-made wall here," he said. "And if you look close enough, you can see that it's a uniform gray across its surface. The normal cavern wall varies in color somewhat, and you see the different kinds of rock that form it. Whatever this is—" he rapped a knuckle on the flat surface, "—it's one type of material."

"There are more patches than this," Alex said. "I've seen a lot of them on the wall as we passed. Do you have any idea what they are?"

Before Neal or Martin could answer, Lola said, "Looks like part of a basement wall to me."

The other three turned to look at her.

"Basements are underground," she said, feeling defensive. "At least partway. And this cavern is underground." She shivered and crossed her arms over her chest in an attempt to retain body heat. "At least it feels that way."

Martin looked skeptical, but he didn't say anything. Neal seemed to consider her words, but he didn't say anything either.

"I *thought* the flat areas looked familiar," Alex said. "They remind me of the basement in my father's house."

Alex had lived with Isaac for almost a year, and Lola was surprised that she didn't refer to her dad's place as *home*. That told her a lot about the kind of relationship Alex and Isaac had. But sad as it was, it wasn't important right now. They were in a basement, a humongous one, maybe the biggest that had ever existed. Kenneth had died from a fall down the basement stairs. She hadn't set foot in a basement since, had always asked Spencer to go down to their own basement to get something that was stored there when she needed it. But here she was now, standing in a basement once more, and this realization frightened her. In her day-to-day life, she worked hard not to think about what she'd done to Kenneth. But now that she recognized she was *inside* a basement – an impossibly large one – she couldn't stop herself from thinking about it. Couldn't stop seeing the image of Kenneth from her dream, blood-smeared grin on his face as he dragged himself up the stairs in order to get his revenge on her.

She thought she heard a scrabbling sound behind them, coming from somewhere deeper in the cavern, a place where the glow from the lichen couldn't reach. She thought it sounded like someone pulling themselves across the stone floor. But no one else seemed to hear it, so she put it down to her imagination. Her heart rate increased, though, and she could feel her pulse in her ears.

Martin looked at Alex.

"So you're saying we're *inside* the Raines house. In the fucking basement, which happens to be a hundred times bigger – not to mention spookier – than any basement I've ever seen. Is that right?"

Alex shrugged. "Maybe?"

Martin released an exasperated sigh before turning to Neal.

"That's bullshit, right? Tell me it's bullshit."

Neal opened his mouth to respond, but nothing came out. Lola felt pity for him. He wasn't sure what was real and what wasn't. Lola didn't think any of them were right now. As a science teacher, being in such a state of uncertainty must have been driving him crazy. When Neal finally spoke, he changed the subject.

"If this *is* a basement, or some bizarre version of one, then there should be a set of stairs leading to the house's main floor somewhere in here. All we have to do is find it and we can get out."

"And find our family members," Alex said.

The group fell silent after that. After several moments, Martin broke the silence by clapping his hands together.

"So what's the plan? Keep walking around and hope we happen to stumble on a set of stairs?"

"I guess so," Neal said. "If we stay close to the wall, we should run into stairs eventually." He didn't sound sure of this, though. Still, no one else had any better ideas, and they began walking again, making sure to remain in sight of the wall at all times.

It seemed like they walked for hours without encountering anything except more of those smooth patches on the cavern wall. Lola's knees had started to go numb, and she wasn't sure whether or not this was a good sign. Her mind drifted, and when it wandered too close to what had happened to Kenneth, she turned away from that memory and found herself thinking of another. When Spencer was seven, his favorite toys had been plastic army men. He loved to pose them in imaginary battle positions throughout the house. Sometimes they'd battle in the living room, sometimes the kitchen, sometimes the dining room. Never in Spencer's bedroom, though. He didn't like spending time in there, and it would be a few more years before Lola learned the reason why.

That Christmas, Kenneth bought Spencer an elaborate set of World War II army men. There were dozens of soldiers – the allies made out of green plastic, the Nazis out of gray – along with tanks, cannons, jeeps, rolls of plastic barbed wire, along with miniature trees, hills, and buildings you could use to create a battlefield. When Spencer unwrapped the present, he'd been ecstatic, and while Lola had never been completely comfortable with her son playing with toys that portrayed violence, when Spencer ran over to his father and gave him an enthusiastic thank-you hug, she decided to set her reticence about the WWII toys aside. Spencer so rarely hugged Kenneth those days, and she was happy to see his reaction to the present.

In retrospect, she'd been a goddamn fool not to see the signs.

They had a pool table in the basement, and Spencer set up his new army men and their equipment on it, the green felt serving as grass for the battlefield. He spent hours down there playing, and sometimes Lola would crack open the basement door and listen to the sounds Spencer made as he played – simulated gunfire and explosions, the deep rumble of tanks on the move, engine sounds of jeeps racing across the battlefield, the cries and moans of combatants as they were wounded or killed. The latter disturbed her, but she put it down to Spencer committing his imagination fully to his play.

One day, Spencer was louder than usual as he played, and instead of soldiers shouting, he made them scream so hard that she feared he would injure his vocal cords. Finally, she could stand it no longer, and she went down into the basement to check on him. When she reached the basement floor, she stopped and stared.

Spencer had customized all of the German soldiers. He'd put holes in some, probably with a Phillips screwdriver, she thought, or maybe the sharp points of scissor blades. He'd cut limbs off others – an arm, a leg, sometimes two or three limbs, sometimes all of them. He'd slathered red paint on their wounds to make them look more realistic. Some soldiers he'd melted – with a lighter he'd stolen from a kitchen drawer, she later found out. These she assumed were victims of flamethrowers and bomb blasts. This tableau wasn't a static one, however. Spencer manipulated the allied forces, slamming trucks and tanks into Nazis, holding soldiers with guns and pretending they sprayed their area with weapons fire. After a barrage, Spencer swept his hand across the table and sent paint-smeared Nazis flying.

She stood at the foot of the basement stairs, watching in horrified fascination as her sweet little boy decimated the German forces. Eventually, he became aware of her, and he stopped playing. He gave her an embarrassed smile and said, "The green soldiers are me. The gray ones are Dad."

At the time, she'd thought he was referring to which side he normally played and which side his father did during those times when Kenneth would join his son in the basement to play. When she learned what Kenneth had *really* been up to with their son in the basement – as well as Spencer's room – she understood that her son had been trying to tell her something very important that day – *The gray ones are Dad* – and she'd failed to understand.

She wished she'd been a better mother to Spencer. It had taken her far too long to realize what Kenneth had been doing to him, and she could never make up for that, no matter how hard she tried. But she'd always had difficulty with the small everyday things about being a mother. Her own mother had died of a heart attack when Lola was very young, and her father had never remarried. Because of this, she'd grown up without a role model for what a good mother should be, how she should act, what she should say and do. She'd always felt clumsy and uncertain when it came to raising Spencer. She'd done the best she could for him, but she knew that was nowhere near good enough.

"Do you guys see that?"

Martin stopped walking and pointed toward the darkness in the center of the cavern. Everyone looked where he indicated, but Lola didn't see anything, not at first. The longer she looked, the more she thought she saw a dim orange light far off in the distance, one that grew brighter as she watched. Yes, it was definitely there, and within minutes it burned bright as a miniature sun. It was so far away, though, that none of them could tell what it was.

"Should we go check it out?" Alex asked. "It might be our family members. Maybe they're trying to signal us with that light, whatever it is."

"More likely it's a goddamn trap of some kind," Martin said. "In case you haven't noticed, this has been one fucked-up night so far, and I think we'd be better off if we didn't trust anything we see or hear."

"What about trusting each other?" Neal asked.

Martin scowled. "They jury's still out on that."

"I think we should at least get close enough to figure out what it is," Lola said. "It *is* the only thing we've seen in here so far." She didn't remind them of the plan to keep walking until they found stairs. She wasn't sure she wanted to find them, was afraid of what – or who – might be waiting there for her.

Neal, Alex, and Martin exchanged glances.

"If there's any chance Kandice is there, I have to go," Neal said, "regardless of whether or not any of you go with me."

"Fine," Martin said. "But I wish I had one of my guns with me. My Glock or maybe my Sig Sauer."

"I never thought I'd say this," Neal said, "but I wish you had them, too."

Martin smiled. "No atheists in a foxhole."

The four of them started walking in the direction of the orange light, which now blazed strong in the cavern's darkness. Lola smelled the chemical tang of a gas burner, and she figured it came from whatever was producing the light. *Whatever it is, I hope it doesn't blow up*, she thought.

The cavern floor, like the wall, was rough in some places, smoother in others, and the farther away they walked from the luminescent lichen on the wall, the more difficult it was to see where they were going. They stumbled several times, and once Lola's bad knees betrayed her and she went down, skinning the palms of both hands as she tried to catch herself. Martin and Neal helped her back up, and while she couldn't see her hands in the darkness, she could feel they were bleeding.

"Are you all right?" Alex asked.

"I'll live," Lola said. "Let's keep going."

The orange glow grew larger, the air warmer, and Lola felt certain the light came from a fire of some kind. It appeared to be contained to one area, so whatever type of fire it was, it was controlled. And a controlled fire meant people. Maybe her Spencer *was* there, along with the others who were missing. She felt an urge to start running toward the fire, but she restrained herself. Her knees would surely give out on her if she tried. Instead, she called out.

"Spencer! Are you there? *Spencer?*"

No one replied.

"Maybe he didn't hear you," Alex said.

"Half the fucking planet heard her, loud as she yelled," Martin said. His words were harsh, but Lola could see the worry in his face. He obviously feared for the safety of his wife and daughter. Lola felt the same way about Spencer but she had an additional worry. If their family members were together, that meant Spencer was with Vivienne. She didn't like the idea that he might be so near temptation. If he was, she hoped he'd be able to restrain himself. He'd undergone a great deal of therapy over the years, and he regularly took antidepressants to help elevate his mood. And if other adults were around, he wouldn't have the chance to be alone with Vivienne. Given all that, she had reason to hope everything would be okay.

You're stuck in a weird cavern with three of your neighbors, she thought. *You've got a strange notion of okay, woman.*

A sound came to her then, from somewhere in the darkness behind them. A shuffle-scuff, as if the sole of a shoe brushed across a rough patch of the cavern floor. It came and went so quickly that she wasn't sure she'd really heard it. None of the others said anything, so she decided not to worry about it.

And then she heard it again. Louder this time, and closer.

"What the hell was that?" Martin said.

As if in answer, a trio of bright lights – far smaller than the one they were walking toward – flared to glowing life off to their left.

Flashlights, Lola thought.

At first there were only three, but more appeared, until there were at least a dozen. The beams were directed at them, but the light illuminated the carriers enough for Lola to see they were all men. Soldiers, in fact, dressed in WWII-era uniforms. *German* uniforms. This wasn't the worst of it, though. While they moved easily enough, each of the soldiers was seriously injured. Faces masks of blood or fire-blackened skin. Eyes, ears, noses crushed or burned. Arms and legs shattered or simply gone. Uniforms soaked with crimson, fabric torn or charred by flame. Along with the flashlights, the soldiers carried weapons – rifles with bayonets, handguns, knives.... Their eyes gleamed with cruel anticipation, their mouths stretched in sickeningly wide grins, teeth slashes of white amidst bloody, ravaged flesh.

"What the actual fuck?" Martin said, voice soft and frightened, so unlike the way he usually spoke. If Lola hadn't been so terrified herself, she would've enjoyed hearing him humbled like that.

It was impossible, she knew this, but she was looking at Spencer's toy soldiers come to life.

Not all of them, she thought. *Just the ones that represented Kenneth.*

The Nazis opened their mouths, and Lola expected them to begin speaking in German. Instead, they made noises, the crude, silly sound effects of a child playing war. *Rat-a-tat-tat* and *pew-pew-pew, booms* and *wooshes* and *kapows! Aarghs* and *ughs* and *AAAAAAHs!* Their voices were those of children, too. No, Lola realized. They all spoke with the same child's voice: Spencer's.

Neal's voice was calm, toneless, as if he were in shock.

"I think it would be a good idea if we started running now."

CHAPTER SEVENTEEN

For several seconds, none of them moved as the burnt and mangled Nazis advanced. But then their mutual paralysis broke all at once, and they turned and began running toward the orange light. Lola knew they had no reason to believe they'd find safety when – *if* – they reached the light, but it was the only beacon they had to guide them, and they headed for it instinctively.

The Nazis continued making their childish sound effects as they gave pursuit, boots thudding on the cavern's stone floor. Lola didn't look back, kept her gaze fixed on the orange glow before them. Her knees, no longer numb, screamed at her for abusing them so, and her breathing became rapid and shallow. She felt lightheaded, as if she weren't getting enough air, and she regretted never using that goddamn treadmill. She expected to hear the sound of gunfire any moment, feel bullets tear through her body. Or maybe she'd feel the sharp point of a bayonet thrust between her shoulder blades. But while the Nazis continued their pursuit, they hadn't started firing. She didn't know why, but she wasn't about to complain.

As the four companions drew closer to the orange glow, the smell of burning gas became stronger, almost overpowering. They now saw that the light emanated from the base of a large cylindrical object, perhaps thirty feet high. The structure was made of metal, and four wide pipes extended diagonally from the top, bent at right angles, and then continued straight up to the cavern's ceiling, where they were lost among the stalactites.

It was a furnace, Lola realized, a gigantic one, and the orange glow came from a fire blazing behind a metal grate. This close, the heat was intense, causing the air around the furnace to ripple with distortion. Lola's exposed skin began to hurt, as if it was being burned, and she wanted to stop, to not go any closer. But a quick glance over her shoulder told her the wounded Nazis were still coming, so she had no choice but to continue. The others in the group seemed to come to the same conclusion, and the four of them kept running toward the furnace, sweat pouring off their bodies, breathing labored as they drew searing hot air into their lungs. Finally, the heat became intolerable, and they stopped, unable to go on. They'd come within fifteen feet or so of the massive furnace, and when Lola looked up at the top of it, she saw a metal chair had been bolted there, with large arm rests and a high back.

It looks like a throne, she thought.

And sitting on that throne – which had to be hot as all the fires of Hell – was Demarcus Eldred. He appeared relaxed, unbothered by the furnace's heat. He was dressed in a long-sleeved black pullover along with black slacks and black shoes. The more Lola looked at his garments, the less they appeared to have been fashioned out of cloth and leather, and the more it looked like he was garbed in shadow. The most jarring aspect of his appearance was the ring of curved bone spikes that jutted from his head, forming a grotesque crown. Blood trickled from where the spikes had broken through the skin, and lines of crimson ran down his face.

Demarcus smiled.

"Are you enjoying yourselves so far?" he asked. "I certainly am."

Lola glanced behind them and saw that the soldiers had caught up. They now stood in a line, flashlights put away, weapons in hand and aimed directly at them. *Like a firing squad,* she thought.

"What's going on here, Demarcus?" Neal asked. "Is any of this real? What happened to our families? Where's Kandice?"

He spoke rapidly and sounded desperate, on the verge of giving in to panic. Lola knew exactly how he felt.

The boy continued smiling down at them. When he spoke next, he sounded like an adult addressing a group of children – and not particularly bright ones at that.

"I'm not Demarcus when I'm in the Undercountry. I'm called the Low Prince here."

Lola had never heard that name before, but it caused her to feel a brief cold chill, despite the furnace's intense heat. Demarcus – the Low Prince – continued.

"There are numerous ways of looking at the concept of 'real'. But

I'll make it simple for you. Reality is like ice cream. It comes in lots and lots of flavors. But what you *really* want to know is if the events which occur in the Stalking Ground – excuse me, the *house* – will have lasting consequences. The answer to that is yes. Get hurt here, you're still hurt when you depart. Die here, you remain dead." His smile took on a cruel edge. "That real enough for you?"

"Is this some kind of fucking game to you?" Martin demanded. "I knew you and your family were a bunch of goddamn freaks, but I didn't know just how messed up—"

The Low Prince's smile vanished. He gestured and one of the Nazis – one that had only half a face and was missing his left arm – stepped forward, raised the Luger he held in his remaining hand, and brought the butt end down hard against the back of Martin's neck. An *oof* of air escaped Martin's lips, and he fell to his hands and knees. He stayed there, head bowed, breathing heavily, and Lola knew he was fighting not to pass out.

"Fucker," Martin whispered.

Lola figured this would earn him further punishment but the Low Prince either didn't hear him or, more likely, decided to let it go. He gestured again, and the half-faced Nazi returned to his previous position.

Alex looked up at the Low Prince. "Please, Demarcus – Low Prince. Don't hurt us."

The Low Prince regarded her for a moment, then in an almost apologetic voice said, "I'm afraid that's the reason you're all here. To be hurt. Hurt *bad*."

"What about our families?" Neal said. "Are they here too?" He sounded half-hopeful, half-fearful.

"They aren't in the Undercountry," the Low Prince said. "But it's a *big* house – especially since we remodeled. I wouldn't be surprised if they were around here somewhere."

Lola hated the idea of Spencer being trapped elsewhere in the house, presumably being forced to deal with other members of the Eldred family in who knew what manner of nightmare scenario. Spencer was strong in his way, but in other ways he was still the little boy whose father had sexually abused him. She feared he didn't have what it would take to survive this place. She wasn't sure that any of them did.

Martin had remained on his hands and knees since being struck, but now he started to rise. Neal took hold of one of his arms to help steady him, and Martin acknowledged this with a nod before looking upward at the Low Prince once more.

"If you're going to kill us, just do it and get it over with. At least we won't have to listen to your bullshit anymore."

Alex gasped at Martin's words of defiance, but Lola wasn't surprised. She might not like Martin much, but the man had balls to spare, that was certain.

"Killing is easy," the Low Prince said. "It's the buildup to death that's the most fun – *and* the most nourishing."

Lola had no idea what the boy was talking about, but he gestured and the darkness surrounding them was replaced with bright light. The change was so dramatic that Lola had to squeeze her eyes shut. Then, slowly, bit by bit, she opened them. The light still stung her eyes, but at least she could see now. The lichen spread across the cavern's walls and ceiling blazed with light, and the cavern seemed much smaller than it had when they'd been stumbling around in the dark. Maybe it had only seemed big to them then. Or maybe the cavern was as big as the Low Prince wished it to be at any given moment. At any rate, Lola could now see the cavern's walls all around them, and off to their right – on the other side of a grass-covered plain – was a long set of wooden stairs. At the top of them was a closed door. A basement door was a basement door, but Lola couldn't help thinking it looked exactly like the one in her house. The stairs were much larger, though, stretching at least a hundred feet upward, maybe more. The grassy plain wasn't empty. There were buildings on it, one- and two-story, little more than bombed-out ruins. There were vehicles – jeeps and motorcycles, mainly – most of which had been damaged or overturned. Worst of all, though, were the mangled remains of soldiers in green uniforms. Hundreds of them, all dead, scattered across what was obviously a battlefield.

Lola knew what she was looking at. This was a life-sized recreation of the tableau Spencer used to set up on the pool table in their basement when he was a child. The implication was obvious. The Low Prince wanted them to play War.

"You want out of the Undercountry?" the Low Prince said. He gestured toward the stairs. "That's the way – the *only* way."

"What if we refuse to play your game?" Neal said. He sounded more scared than defiant, but Lola gave him points for trying.

"Then I'll command my Nazi friends to finish you off right here." He grinned. "And I'll tell them to take their time. I'll give you a five count to decide. Head for the stairs or die right now. Your choice. One."

Alex immediately started running.

Smart girl, Lola thought.

She knew there was no way she could keep up with her bad knees, but she wasn't going to just stand there and let a bunch of Nazi zombies have their fun with her. She started running after Alex, moving much more slowly than the girl, but moving nonetheless.

"Two."

Lola didn't look back to see if Neal and Martin were going to follow. She hoped they would, but whatever they did, it was their choice. If they chose to remain behind, a cold-blooded part of her thought, maybe the Nazis would be so busy killing them that she and Alex would have a better chance to get away.

"Three."

She heard Neal shout "Fuck!" and start running.

"Four."

"Goddamn it!" Martin sounded mad as hell, but he started running, too.

"Four-and-a-half. Four-and-three-quarters…. *Five!*"

The undead Nazis roared with excitement, sounding more like beasts now than something once human, and the sound of heavy boots thudding on the cavern floor filled the air.

Martin and Neal caught up with Lola easily, and Martin kept going, flying past her. Neal slowed to match her pace, bless the damn fool.

"Don't…go slow…for me," she panted. Her knees felt like they were on fire, and she had a difficult time focusing past the pain. "Get to these stairs and go find Kandice!"

Neal glanced behind them, then turned his gaze on the stairs, clearly torn.

"Go!" Lola shouted. "If you find Spencer, help him!"

That last bit did the job. Neal was a good man, the kind who put others before himself. The only way he'd abandon her was if he thought he had to in order to help others. Still, he hesitated a moment longer. But when the Nazi zombies began firing their weapons, his indecision vanished and he hauled ass.

Lola was relieved. She didn't expect to live long enough to reach the stairs, but she felt confident that Neal would do his best to take care of Spencer if they ran across each other. Lola winced every time she heard the *crack* of gunfire behind her, each time expecting to feel a bullet slam into her back. She thought she heard some rounds go whizzing past her, but it could've been her imagination. She knew it didn't matter if the bullets missed her. The soldiers would catch up to her and then they would go to work on her with their bayonet blades and hand knives. Whatever tools they used to kill her, she'd be just as dead in the end.

Lola was the last of the group to reach the grass. There was a clear line of demarcation between the cavern floor and the plain, but it wasn't until she stepped onto the latter that she realized it wasn't grass at all, but rather thick green felt.

Like the surface of a pool table, she thought.

She heard another *crack* and immediately felt a burning line of pain stitch itself across the skin of her right shoulder. She cried out and nearly stumbled, but she managed to remain on her feet and continue running. She'd been hit. How bad, she didn't know. Not bad enough to bring her down, though, and that was all that mattered right then.

The gunfire continued, but no more bullets struck her. Lola wondered if their pursuers weren't really trying to hit them, if they were instead trying to scare them, keep them on the run, draw out the game for their master's amusement. She could see no other reason why the undead Nazis hadn't killed them yet.

The bodies of dead green-clad soldiers littered the ground, and Lola had to be careful to avoid them. One wrong step, and she'd trip, go down, and then her pursuers would be on her. She wouldn't last long after that. She tried not to look at the dead men – their ravaged flesh, their spilled blood – but she couldn't help it. The sight of so much violent death sickened her, and she wondered if the dead soldiers were real or if they were illusions, nothing more than life-sized realistic-looking versions of the toys Spencer had once played with. She remembered what the Low Prince had said about things being real. *Reality is like ice cream. It comes in lots and lots of flavors.* She supposed these soldiers were as real as they needed to be to fulfill the Low Prince's purpose, no more and no less.

When she felt the pain in her chest, she put it down to being out of shape. She hadn't run in decades and she'd never had to run for her life before. It was only natural that her body felt the strain. But when the pain worsened to the point where it felt as if her chest was on fire, she realized something serious was happening to her. Her mother had died young of a heart attack, and heart disease ran on that side of the family. Lola had never shown any sign of it before, but then she'd never exerted herself like this either. The pain increased, each beat of her heart feeling as if someone was pounding her chest with a sledgehammer. Her breathing became labored and her vision blurred. She couldn't run anymore, slowed to a walk, and she knew the Nazis would quickly catch up to her, and game or not, they'd finish her. She hoped they'd make it quick. The prospect of dying didn't sadden her. For years, she'd lived as a virtual shut-in, so it was like she was halfway dead already, and although she felt guilty for this, it would be a relief not to have to worry about Spencer's *problem* anymore. But she did regret abandoning her son, feared that without her help, the darker side of his nature would assert itself and take control of him. And if that happened, he'd hurt who knew how many children?

I'm sorry, she thought. But whether she was apologizing to Spencer, the children he would harm, or both, she didn't know.

The pain worsened to the point where she could no longer walk. She stopped to kneel, the green felt that covered the plain instead of grass providing some cushion for her bad knees. They still complained, but that pain was nothing compared to that which raged inside her chest. Her vision swam in and out of focus, and when she saw Martin, Neal, and Alex running toward her, she thought she was hallucinating. Martin had put on a backpack of some kind. No, not a backpack. Two metal canisters hung on his back, held in place by leather straps around his shoulders. A rubber hose stretched from the tanks to a gun-like device he held in his hands, a long, thin thing that looked like a combination of a handgun and a rifle. Alex carried a knife, and Neal held a rifle with a bayonet. She wondered where they'd found the weapons, and then she realized there were weapons all over the battlefield, ones that the dead soldiers had carried and no longer needed.

"Get down!" Martin shouted.

Lola fell forward. She was in too much pain to catch herself, so she smacked against the felt surface of the ground and lay there, her heart struggling to keep working.

Martin reached her first. He took several more steps past her before stopping, shouting, "Fuck you, Nazi bastards!" and activating the flamethrower.

Lola heard a *whoosh* as a stream of fire jetted from the gun in Martin's hands. She felt the warmth of the flames, smelled a hot chemical tang. So far, the Nazis had chased them in silence, but now they shrieked as flames enveloped them, their cries of pain high-pitched and inhuman.

Neal and Alex reached her then, and they helped her get to her feet. She turned to look at Martin, saw him move the flamethrower's gun back and forth as he continued spraying fire onto the zombie soldiers. All of them were ablaze, writhing and screaming as the flames devoured them. Despite the agony in her chest, Lola smiled. *Fuck you, Nazi bastards* indeed.

Beyond the mass of flames, Lola saw the Low Prince standing atop the giant furnace that served as his throne and watching the action. He didn't look upset that his soldiers were being barbecued. In fact, he was grinning.

"Come on," Neal said. "We'll help you up the stairs."

Neal and Alex began walking, each of them holding on to one of her arms, helping her move forward and stay on her feet. They held their weapons in their free hands, although Lola couldn't see how Neal could possibly wield his rifle one-handed.

"Are you okay?" Alex asked, worry in her voice. She looked past Lola to Neal. "She's so pale!"

Lola spoke through gritted teeth. "I'm…all right. Don't worry… about me."

"You don't *sound* all right," Alex said.

"Let's just get her to the stairs," Neal said. He sounded worried, too, and Lola figured she must look like hammered shit for both of them to be so concerned. More because she didn't want to keep worrying them than because she cared whether she lived or died, she did her best to calm herself, to slow her breathing, to will the pain in her chest to lessen. In response, she felt the tightness in her chest begin to ease. Maybe it wasn't a heart attack after all. Maybe she was only experiencing a severe panic attack. Whichever the case, she was grateful, and soon she could manage to walk on her own, more or less, and didn't need to be virtually dragged by Alex and Neal. This allowed the three of them to increase their pace. They weaved around dozens of dead soldiers, moved past the ruins of bombed-out buildings until they reached the end of the green felt and stood at the bottom of the stairs. The stairs stretched so high, and beneath them was a mass of impenetrable shadow. Lola thought she saw something shift within the darkness, and while she hoped it was only her imagination coupled with stress, she feared it wasn't.

Martin continued blasting the zombies with fire until the flamethrower's tanks ran out of fuel. But the device had done its work, reducing the Nazis to a burning mound of charred flesh and bone. Martin slipped off the now-useless flamethrower, dropped it to the ground, and started running toward them. Just before he reached them, Lola saw him take a pistol from the hand of a green-uniformed soldier. He checked to see if it had rounds left, then – satisfied that it had – he joined them at the bottom of the stairs.

"Let's go," he said, and then the four of them began making their way up the stairs. But they'd only ascended a short distance when Alex cried out.

"Look!"

She pointed behind them, and they turned to see several of the Nazi zombies – still very much on fire – rise to their feet and begin staggering forward. The undead soldiers carried no weapons now, maybe because their burning hands were incapable of grasping anything, or maybe because their flaming bodies were weapons in themselves. They no longer had any individual features, were just dark silhouettes wreathed in fire, and they stood so close together that their flames merged, making them look like a living, moving bonfire.

"You've got to be fucking kidding me," Martin said. He aimed his pistol and started firing at the mass of flames. Neal let go of Lola's arm and shouldered his rifle awkwardly, as if he'd never fired a gun before. He aimed and squeezed the trigger. The gun went off, but if he managed to hit any of the zombies, there was no way to tell. And even if he did, Lola thought, what good would it do? The damn things were already dead, weren't they?

The rounds from Martin's gun had no more effect on the flaming corpses than Neal's. They kept coming, leaving smoldering footprints on the felt behind them. Lola didn't understand how they could still move. Even if they experienced no pain, wouldn't the flames cause enough damage to their limbs to make it impossible for them to move? Inside this house, she supposed the line between possible and impossible was a hell of a lot fuzzier than in the world outside.

The burning zombies were only twenty feet away from them now, and they continued lurching toward them. Alex had remained at Lola's side when the men started firing, and while she looked scared, she also looked determined.

"I have to help them," she said. Despite her brave words, there was a quaver in her voice, but this didn't make the girl seem any less brave to Lola.

Alex looked at her. "Will you be all right by yourself for a little while?"

Lola's chest still hurt, but the pain was much less than it had been, and while breathing remained an effort, she still managed to draw air into her lungs. She tried to smile, but the best she could manage was a lopsided grimace. She didn't have enough breath to speak, so she nodded. Alex looked skeptical, but the zombies had closed to within ten feet of the stairs now, and Lola knew that Neal and Martin couldn't fend off the undead bastards by themselves.

Alex helped her sit on the steps, then she turned and joined the men, knife in hand. Neal was out of bullets, leaving him with the bayonet blade as his only weapon. Martin still had his gun trained on the oncoming zombies, but he was no longer firing, and Lola feared he might be out of ammunition as well. Alex stood with them, gripping her knife tight, but Lola didn't know what good the blade would be against creatures that could withstand gunfire and flames. She couldn't allow the three of them to throw their lives away defending her. If Spencer was somewhere else in the house, as the Low Prince had suggested, then he would need help to survive – and the more help he could get, the better. She needed these three to live, for Spencer's sake, if for no other reason.

She grabbed the staircase's railing, intending to pull herself to her feet and try to speak, to tell them to leave her behind and get the hell out of there. She thought Martin would agree readily enough – the man could be a real prick – but she wasn't sure Alex or Neal could leave her. She hoped she could make them see reason, assuming she could get any words out at all.

Her first attempt to stand was a failure. She was too weak, too dizzy. Before she could make a second attempt, she heard a sharp *crack* of wood breaking behind her. She looked over her shoulder and saw that Kenneth – naked, head dented, face smeared with blood, lips split, front teeth knocked out – had burst up from beneath the steps. Now she knew what the thing was that she'd sensed as much as seen lurking in the shadows under the stairs. *Like the troll in 'Three Billy Goats Gruff',* she thought. *Who's that trip-trap-tripping up my basement stairs?*

The pain in her chest returned full force, and this time she welcomed it. She prayed her heart would give out before Kenneth could get hold of her, cheating the child-raping bastard out of his revenge.

Kenneth's eyes shone with madness as he pulled himself halfway out of the hole he'd made. He reached out and touched her chest, just below her neck. The instant he made contact, her pain vanished and she could breathe normally.

Kenneth grinned.

"You can't escape me that easily," he said.

Then he grabbed her wrist and swiftly withdrew into the hole in the stairs, pulling her down into the darkness with him. It happened so fast she didn't have time to scream.

*   *   *

Neal gripped the rifle tight, ready to use the bayonet on the zombies if they tried to ascend the stairs. Sweat poured off his body, and he told himself it was due to the walking corpses' flames. Maybe that was part of it, but he knew he was also sweating because he was fucking terrified. He'd never been in a fight of any kind in his entire life. He'd always managed to avoid them or talk his way out of them. But a few moments ago he'd been firing a goddamn WWII rifle at a bunch of burning Nazi zombies – without any effect – and now he was intending to defend the stairs against them with only a blade. What the hell was he thinking?

Just as the zombies reached the bottom of the stairs, he heard wood breaking behind him. Neal, Martin, and Alex all turned toward the sound, only to see a bloody, naked man had emerged from under the steps behind Lola. What was he? Another fucking zombie? Before Neal and his two companions could act, the man took hold of Lola and swiftly pulled her with him down into the hole in the stairs that he'd created. They were gone within seconds.

"Lola!" Neal shouted. He forgot about the fire zombies and rushed up the steps to the broken section where the bloody man had dragged Lola away. He peered down into the hole, but all he saw was thick, impenetrable darkness.

Martin and Alex were watching him instead of the approaching zombies, so when the closest took a swipe at Martin's unprotected back with one flaming hand, he connected and Martin screamed.

"Fuck, that *hurts!*"

Martin hurled his empty gun at the zombie that had burned him. The weapon struck the flaming corpse in the head, bounced off, and fell to the ground. The blow had no effect on the creature, and Martin and Alex rushed up the steps to join Neal. Martin reached around to gingerly touch his back, and when his fingers came in contact with the burned area, he drew in a hiss of air.

Neal, crouching by the hole, looked up at the two of them

"That thing took Lola. We have to get her back."

Neal started to put one leg into the hole, Alex grabbed his arm to stop him.

"Don't do it," she said. She looked on the verge of tears. "Please."

"She's right," Martin said. "You saw the thing that grabbed Lola. She's probably already dead."

"You can't know that," Neal said. "Not for sure."

Alex looked as if she might say something more, but then she stopped and looked back down the stairs, her eyes widening with fear. Neal turned to see the Nazi zombies had collapsed at the foot of the stairs, the fire evidently having damaged them to the point where they could no longer function. That was good. What *wasn't* so good was that their flames hadn't died out. If anything, they seemed to blaze even brighter than before. And that's when the first couple steps caught fire.

"Oh shit," Neal said.

The flames spread rapidly, moving much faster than they should have. *This place has its own physical laws,* Neal thought. Here fire grew bigger when its fuel source was nearly spent, and it spread to anything combustible near it, and it spread fast, like an animal desperate to propagate its species before it dies.

The fire raced toward them, and Martin grabbed hold of Neal's arm and hauled him roughly to his feet. Neal lost his hold on the rifle, and it fell to the steps and skittered down toward the flames.

"Move it, dickhead," Martin said. His voice sounded calm, but his face was pale, his eyes wide with fear.

Neal didn't want to abandon Lola, but he didn't relish the prospect of burning to death, either. He nodded at Martin, and the three of them started upward, careful to jump over the hole the bloody-faced man had made. The fire followed close on their heels.

Sorry, Lola, Neal thought.

Maybe Martin was right, maybe she was dead. Part of him hoped so. Because if she was still alive, who knew what the bloody-faced man was doing to her right now?

Smoke billowed upward from the burning staircase, stinging their eyes and making them cough. Neal was the first to reach the basement door. He feared it would be locked, but the knob turned easily. He took one last glance behind them and saw that the stairs were almost completely aflame now. He shoved open the door and dashed through, Alex and Martin quickly following.

We made it! Neal thought. And then, *At least three of us did.*

★   ★   ★

The Low Prince stands atop the furnace, right at the edge, watching as the flaming stairs collapse into a heap of broken, burning lumber. Kenneth and Lola aren't harmed, though. They're no longer beneath the stairs. They've gone to play elsewhere. He feels nothing for the zombie Nazis, who ended their undead existence as little more than kindling. He made them from a part of himself – a very small part – and their loss means no more to him than a nail clipping means to a human.

He is pleased with how the scenario he'd created – one plucked from both Lola and Spencer's memories – turned out. Neal and Martin had left the Undercountry without weapons, but Alex took the knife, just as he intended. And it isn't just any mere blade. It's a very special one, and he placed it specifically where one of the humans – in this case, Alex – would find it. or rather, where *it* would find *her*. Things are going precisely according to plan. Well, *his* plan anyway, his and his sister's. All he needs to do now is wait.

He's sated from his meal, stuffed to the gills with negative psychic energy he drained from the four humans. He returns to his throne, sits, and sighs contentedly. He imagines what it will be like when he and his sister rule the family, and he smiles.

CHAPTER EIGHTEEN

Lola opened her eyes.

She stood at the foot of Spencer's bed, and for an instant, she thought she was back home, that she'd never left, that the awful things that had happened in the Eldreds' house were only a bad dream – one that was now thankfully over. Then she saw that someone was lying on the bed, blanket pulled all the way up to cover them completely. Was it Spencer? This was his room, after all. But why would he be hiding like this? Was something wrong? Was he sick?

She walked around to the side of the bed and reached out to gently shake him.

Spencer, are you all right?

These were the words she wanted to say. But what came out of her mouth was, "You know you can't hide from me, boy."

It was a man's voice. Kenneth's, to be precise.

She then realized the hand that shook Spencer was a man's – broad, thick-fingered, hair growing on the back. Kenneth's hand. What the hell was going on? Was she still dreaming?

She heard a voice in her mind then, not hers or Kenneth's. This voice belonged to the Low Prince.

It's not a dream. It's a memory. One of Kenneth's. I thought you might find it instructive to see things through his eyes. Broaden your perspective, help you understand your son more...deeply.

The Low Prince laughed then, and it was the foulest sound she'd ever heard.

No, she thought. *Don't do this to me. Let me die, please!*

But the Low Prince didn't respond.

Lola could do nothing but watch and listen as Kenneth yanked the blanket off Spencer, who was once more a little boy. He wore white pajamas with pictures of Eeyore – his favorite *Winnie-the-Pooh* character – all over them.

She felt Kenneth's facial muscles make a frown.

"I told you to take off your pajamas after your mother tucks you in. You know what happens when you disobey me."

Lola would've given her soul if she could've closed Kenneth's eyes or make him turn his head so she couldn't see her son's terrified face.

"Sorry," Spencer said in a small, trembling voice. He slipped off his pajamas, moving quickly as if he feared he would be punished if he didn't move fast enough. Kenneth took the pajamas and dropped them on the floor. He looked down when he did this, and Lola saw that he was naked, and his penis was erect and throbbing.

Spencer sat up and drew his knees to his chest, as if shielding his body from his father's eyes. His gaze was fixed on Kenneth's cock, as if it were a poisonous snake that might bite him any second.

"Well?" Kenneth said.

She could hear the impatience in his voice, and beneath it the first stirring of anger.

In her mind, Lola screamed for Spencer to get up and run, to go find her physical body, wake her and tell her what was happening. She'd leave with him that very night, and she'd call the police in the morning. His father would never be able to hurt him ever again.

Lola didn't know whether this was real or not, and it didn't matter. She couldn't stand the thought of being a passive bystander while Kenneth raped their son. Before she'd awakened in Kenneth's body, she'd been experiencing severe chest pain, maybe even a heart attack. The pain had vanished when Kenneth had touched her on the stairs, but what if that was just another illusion? What if this was occurring at the same time as she was dying, and instead of the cliché of seeing her life flash before her eyes, the Low Prince was forcing her to experience her greatest horror *and* her greatest regret? If she was still dying, could she speed up the process; instead of fighting death, welcome it? And whether this was real, a dream, or something in between, she could escape before Kenneth began hurting Spencer in earnest.

She imagined her heart as an old car engine, one on the verge of shaking itself to pieces. Then she imagined removing her foot from the brake and tromping on the gas, revving the engine to a dangerous level.

Come on, she urged. *Come on, you fucker – explode!*

She did succeed in making her heart give out. But not before she saw Kenneth get into bed with Spencer.

★   ★   ★

Cora couldn't stop crying. She kept picturing Kandice falling, those weird skullheaded birds catching her and then throwing her through a window – a window that just happened to be hanging in the middle of the fucking s*ky* – and breaking it in the process. None of them had seen what happened next, but the birds followed Kandice through the window and hadn't returned. Cora didn't know for certain that Kandice was dead, but she *felt* she was. She cried for the loss of her friend, and she cried for Neal, who – although he didn't know it yet – had become a widower.

The five of them – Cora, Vivienne, Isaac, Spencer, and the weird fucker with the robot head – stood in what they took to be the second-story hallway in the Eldreds' house. The robot man had guided them to a wooden trapdoor on the mountain trail that led to a small ladder that had deposited them here. Once they were down, Isaac went back up the ladder again and stuck his head through the recessed rectangular opening in the ceiling and looked around.

"It's just an attic," he said. "One of the windows is broken, though."

He came down and lifted the bottom of the ladder. It folded in on itself and springs pulled upward until it was once more stored in the recessed area of the ceiling.

"No birdwoman?" Spencer asked.

"No. If she and her mountain ever existed, they're not there now."

The robot man stood off to the side, motionless and silent. Cora had the impression that despite appearances, he was watching them all closely.

Vivienne took her hand and began patting it gently.

"It's okay, Mommy," she said. "Everything will be all right."

Cora almost let out a bark of laughter. No fucking way would any of this *ever* be all right. But her daughter's concern touched her, and she told herself she had to be strong, for Vivienne, if not for herself. She wiped the tears from her face as best she could. They were all wet and shivering, but at least they were out of the rain and wind. It was still cold in here, though, as if it were winter outside instead of early summer.

"Now what?" Isaac said.

"We go downstairs and leave?" Spencer said.

Isaac gave him a withering look. "Do you really think it's going to be that easy?"

Spencer shrugged. "I don't know what to think in this place."

Isaac opened his mouth, no doubt intending to argue some more, Cora thought. Instead, he said, "Good point." He then turned to the robot man. "Whatever the hell this thing is, it's one of them. It knew the mountain was called the Aerie, knew the old woman was called the Grandother. Maybe it can tell us what to do next."

"How can we trust anything he says?" Spencer's voice was no longer soft, his tone no longer gentle, and he looked at the robot with undisguised loathing. "If he's one of them, then he's part of whatever is going on."

"He's my friend," Vivienne said. "He's nice. He won't hurt us."

Vivienne's voice seemed to soothe Spencer. He looked at her and smiled.

"So innocent," he said.

Cora didn't like the way Spencer looked at Vivienne. She couldn't explain why, not even to herself, but there was something there that tripped her mommy alarm.

Vivienne looked up at her. "He'll help us if I ask him, Mommy. I know it."

Cora wasn't sure it was a good idea, but she didn't see what other choice they had. Whatever was happening here, however real or unreal, Kandice had died. *That* was real. And she wanted to prevent any more deaths – especially Vivienne's – any way that she could.

"Okay, honey," she said. "But I'll hold your hand the whole time you talk to him, all right?"

Vivienne gave her an I'm-not-a-baby look, but she nodded. She took hold of Cora's hand and led her over to the robot-headed man. This was the first time Cora had gotten an up-close look at him. With the storm and everything else that had been going on in the Aerie, she hadn't noticed anything about him beyond his basic appearance, which had been weird enough. Now she could see how the metal head was joined to the human neck by thin metal filaments that merged with the flesh. Speaking of flesh, the thing's human body smelled like meat on the verge of spoiling, and its skin had an unhealthy gray tinge. Was it sick? No, she realized. The body, despite being able to move, was dead and beginning to rot. She felt stomach acid splash the back of her throat, and for a moment, she thought she was going to puke on the robot – not that the damn thing would probably notice – but she didn't want to frighten Vivienne. Besides, if Isaac was right and this thing could help them, she thought he'd be more inclined to do so if she didn't hurl all over him. So she swallowed once, twice, and managed to keep from vomiting, but it was a near thing.

Vivienne looked up at the robot man.

"Mister?"

He remained motionless for another moment, then the machinery in his head started clicking and whirring, and the green light in his eyes began glowing more brightly. He lowered his head to look at Vivienne.

"*Machine Head,*" he said in his inhuman voice. "*Call me... Machine Head.*"

Vivienne giggled. Cora thought she might throw up after all.

"Machine Head," Vivienne said, "where do you think we should go now? How do we get out of the house?"

Machine Head's inner works clicked and whirred louder, as if he were thinking. Then he raised his hand and pointed to a door only a few feet down the hallway.

"*There,*" he said.

"That makes no sense," Isaac said. "There's most likely a bedroom behind that door. We need to go downstairs and out the front door, which is presumably the same way we entered."

Cora had no clear memory of coming inside the house, but Isaac's words felt right to her. She looked down at Vivienne.

"I think Mr. Ruiz is right, sweetie. We need to go downstairs."

"*Can't,*" Machine Head said.

Isaac looked like he was about to blow a gasket. "Why the hell not?"

Machine Head pointed further down the hall. A different door flew open, spilling light into the hallway. They could see a hint of tiled wall.

"Is that a bathroom?" Spencer asked.

"If any of us needs to take a piss, I suggest we hold it until we're back in our own houses," Isaac said.

He started toward the bathroom.

The instant he stepped forward, a loud rushing-rumbling sound came from the bathroom. Whatever caused it was strong enough to make the floor vibrate beneath their feet. Accompanying the sound was a horrible stench like raw sewage. A wave of brownish-green water shot forth from the bathroom and struck the wall opposite the doorway. Cora thought there would be a big splash and that the putrid water would be flung onto them. But the flow of water was unimpeded. As they all watched, the hallway began to widen. The walls and ceiling blurred, and when everything became clear again, Cora found herself looking at a barren gray landscape, a lifeless plain that stretched as far as she could see. It was night out there, but while Cora could see stars, she saw no moon.

That's because the moon's in the backyard, she thought.

Between them and the gray plain was a wide, rushing river, brown-green water churning to sickening froth as it flowed. The bathroom door was gone, but the portion of the hallway they stood in – along with the door Machine Head had pointed out – remained. The hall ended at the river bank, its edges clear and precise, as if it had been designed this way.

The stench of the filthy water had been awful before, but now that the flood had become a large river, the stink had increased in strength until it felt like something almost physical, like an old cartoon where a character could use a knife to cut a hole in extremely thick fog. Cora tried to tell Vivienne to hold her nose, but when she tried to take in air to speak, she gagged and started coughing.

"*Dead River,*" Machine Head said.

Cora saw that there were shapes in the thick sludgy water. The bodies of creatures she couldn't identify, things with too many legs, an overabundance of teeth, lizard tails, dragonfly wings, feathered, scaled, pebble-hided.... A menagerie of impossibilities, all dead, all being carried to some unknown destination far away.

"Good name for it," Isaac said. He had clamped his hand over his nose and mouth, muffling his voice.

Spencer hadn't bothered to cover the lower half of his face. He looked at the river, at the dead things floating past, and Cora thought she saw longing in his expression, as if he wished he could jump in and join the procession of bizarre-looking corpses. At that moment, she felt deeply sad for him. What kind of life could a person have where drowning in a river of shit and dead monsters seemed like an attractive option?

Even if they'd wanted to risk crossing Dead River, they didn't have any means of doing so. That left them with a single choice: the door Machine Head had indicated.

Without further discussion, Isaac opened the door and stepped inside. Cora and Vivienne went next, followed by Spencer and Machine Head. When they were all inside, Machine Head closed the door behind them, muting the sound of the river and – thankfully – shutting out the worst of the smell.

Cora looked around in wonder.

"Damn," she said softly.

*   *   *

Spencer, thanks to enduring years of his father's sexual abuse, had long ago learned that sometimes bad things happened without any seeming reason or explanation, and all you could do was try your best to survive them. So when he'd returned to awareness on the Aerie, he hadn't bothered questioning, had instead gone about dealing with whatever the situation – however strange it might be – presented.

But now, standing here, bare feet in dewy grass, a warm fragrant breeze blowing – quite a welcome change from the overpowering stench of sewage – he wanted to know how such a beautiful place had come into existence, if only so that he could appreciate it more fully.

It was night here, just as it was in the plain beyond the Dead River. But this place was no barren wasteland. They were surrounded by multiple varieties of plants, some small, some quite large. A full moon was in the sky, but it shone through a window that, like the one in the Aerie, hung in the air above them. *If this is a room in the house,* he told himself, *then that window looks out into the backyard.* Worlds within worlds.

The sky was purple-black violet with bright diamond chips scattered across its surface. The stars were gorgeous, and Spencer thought he could lie down right here, look up at those stars, and not move for the rest of his life. It would be better for everyone if he did. Especially for Vivienne.

He glanced in the girl's direction. She stood next to Cora, holding her mother's hand, gazing with wonder at the sky. Cora and Isaac were also looking upward, but not Machine Head. His gleaming green eyes were looking directly at Spencer.

I see you too, asshole, he thought.

His emotions were so conflicted. He was excited at finally getting a chance to be near Vivienne for an extended period of time, even if it was in a fucked-up place like the Eldreds' house. But he was also terrified that simply being near her wouldn't be enough, that he'd feel compelled to touch her, to…do things to her. Cora and Isaac were here, which was both frustrating and good. Good because their presence would help keep him on his best behavior, and frustrating for the same reason.

But as beautiful as this place was, he knew they couldn't afford to let their guard down. Kandice was gone – probably dead – and if they weren't careful, the same thing could happen to them. He glanced back the way they had come and wasn't surprised to see no sign of the door, just rolling fields that stretched far off into the distance.

In front of them was a grove, flanked by long rows of trees that Spencer didn't recognize. They weren't large – maybe ten feet tall at most – with thick trunks and branches. Their leaves were diamond shaped and they vibrated and hummed in the gentle breeze, sounding like unearthly musical instruments. In the open grassy area between the trees, wrought-iron trellises had been erected, support for thick coils of vines which grew golf ball-sized fruit which Spencer also was unfamiliar with. Berries of some kind, maybe. Their color was difficult to tell in the moonlight. Insects floated lazily in the air around the vines, abdomens glowing on and off like fireflies, except they were the size of cicadas, and their lights were bright purple. In the grassland beyond the grove's light, large shadowy figures moved about slowly. At first Spencer thought they were cattle of some sort, but as his eyes adjusted to the grove's light, he could see the creatures were in fact giant black beetles the size of automobiles. They were grazing, mandibles cutting grass with soft *clik-clik-cliks*. Spencer hoped the things were strictly plant-eaters.

Even with all these details, the most striking feature of the grove was the large round bed – at least twenty feet in diameter – sitting on the ground between the rows of trellises. There were four smaller beds around it, also circular. All had thick mattresses covered with silken sheets, the material reminding Spencer of the copper-colored pajamas Cora wore. The sheets looked bright white, but their true color was concealed by the moonlight. The large bed wasn't empty. Reclining on her side on the mattress, head propped by a hand, was Vanita Eldred. She wore a thin, see-through red nightgown that looked no more substantial than mist. Spencer wouldn't have been surprised if it dispersed in the breeze, leaving her naked. Not that she wasn't mostly there already. In addition, she wore long black gloves, which seemed a bit odd to Spencer, but the look worked for her. Vanita was a teenager, closer to adulthood than childhood, and thus she held no sexual attraction for him. But he found her quite beautiful aesthetically, and he wished he was an artist so he could paint this scene and keep it forever.

Machine Head spoke then.

"Nonsister," he said. *"Night Grove."*

Vanita – the Nonsister – faced them as she climbed off the bed. Spencer saw that where her eyes should've been were pools of shadow, and blood ran from the empty sockets like tears. As she breathed out, she faded, becoming transparent to the point of invisibility, only to return to normal when she breathed in, as if the air in her lungs anchored her in reality. This process was continuous – breathe out, fade, breathe in, solidify. She walked over to the nearest trellis and plucked four of the strange fruits from a vine with her gloved hands. She then came forward, her nightgown shimmering in the moonlight. The effect was dreamlike, spoiled only by her lack of eyes.

"Welcome," she said. "And congratulations. Not everyone makes it this far."

"Everyone didn't," Cora said, half in sorrow, half in anger.

"Regrettable," the Nonsister said, not sounding sorry in the least. "But these will take some of the sting out of your loss."

She tossed the fruit to them, throwing one after another in rapid succession. Each of the humans caught their fruit out of reflex, although Vivienne had to use two hands.

"These are malum fruit," the Nonsister said. "Try it. I guarantee it'll be the most delicious thing you've ever tasted."

Isaac glared at the Nonsister. "We didn't come here for a snack. We want to know what the fuck is happening in this place and how the hell we get out...of...here...."

Isaac started off sounding angry and speaking fast, but as he went on his pace slowed, and his tone become quieter, softer. He lifted the malum fruit to his nose and inhaled its scent deeply, closing his eyes.

"Mmmmmmmmm," he said.

Spencer couldn't believe it. Isaac was such a strong-willed person that he didn't think anything could distract the man when he was yelling at someone. But this fruit had.

As if following Isaac's lead, both Cora and Vivienne smelled their malum fruit as well, and they responded similarly. It was almost as if the three of them had taken a hit of some drug, Spencer thought. He wanted to let go of his malum fruit, drop it to the ground and step away from it. It couldn't be safe, not in this place. He willed his hand to open, but his fingers didn't so much as twitch. Frowning, he looked down at the small fruit he held. Was it sticky, had it adhered to his skin? It didn't *feel* sticky, and he couldn't feel his fingers straining, as if they struggled to pull free from the fruit and couldn't. His hand simply refused to obey his command. And then, without any conscious choice in the matter, his hand began to raise the malum fruit to his face. Without him willing it, he inhaled deeply through his nose. The scent was, quite literally, intoxicating.

And then, just like the others, he took a bite.

He had never had sex with another person, had only ever pleasured himself, and even then he'd felt so plagued with guilt and self-loathing – both during and after – that he'd never felt fulfilled by the act. But the juice of the malum fruit stimulated the pleasure centers of his brain in ways he'd never experienced before. Superlatives like *ecstatic, transcendent, euphoric, orgasmic* couldn't come close to describing what he felt. It was as if, up until this moment, he'd thought he'd been alive, but had in fact only experienced a mere fraction of what existence had to offer. The malum fruit had awakened his mind to the possibilities of sensation beyond anything he'd ever imagined could be possible.

He jammed the rest of the fruit into his mouth and devoured it rapidly, mouth working like that of a starving animal, juice spilling over his lips, running down his chin, dripping onto the grass. When it was gone, he wanted to get down on his hands and knees and lick the ground, make sure he got every drop of juice. He started to kneel, but then a wave of warmth rushed through him. At first it was intense but pleasurable, but then his body temperature swiftly increased until he felt sick and feverish. His T-shirt and shorts, still wet from the Aerie's storm, felt unbelievably stifling. He removed both and threw them to the ground, not concerned that the others would see him naked – especially Vivienne. He barely even remembered that anyone else besides him had ever existed. He still felt flushed, but no longer feverish. He became aware of a tingling sensation between his legs, and when he glanced down he saw that his dick was harder than it ever had been before, skin almost purple, tight and glistening. His testicles ached, but it was a *good* ache, one that simultaneously cried out for relief but at the same time wanted to keep on hurting, to make the sensation last as long as possible.

He saw movement out of the corner of his eyes, and he remembered then that others besides himself inhabited the universe. He turned to watch Isaac and Cora – both as naked as he was – clasp hands and begin making their way toward one of the smaller beds. Isaac was a thoroughly unpleasant person, but he was single. Cora was married, and while Spencer didn't much care for Martin, he believed married people shouldn't cheat on each other, no matter the circumstances. He experienced a strong compulsion to run over to Cora and try to talk some sense into her before she did something that might ruin her marriage. But that compulsion melted away almost the instant he felt it, and he watched with joy as Isaac – his cock just as hard as his – led Cora to one of the smaller beds. They embraced, kissed, and fell onto the bed, arms still wrapped around each other, kissing with such desperate passion it looked as if they were two wild animals trying to devour one another.

More movement caught Spencer's eye, and he quickly oriented on it. It was Vivienne, naked and lovely – no grotesque breasts, no ugly tangle of pubic hair – perfect and pristine. She was walking toward another of the smaller beds, this one on the opposite side of the large bed from the one Cora and Isaac were using. Vivienne didn't look back at Spencer, didn't give him any come-hither looks. She merely climbed onto the bed and curled up. As if she intended to sleep.

He remembered Machine Head, looked for him, saw him standing by the malum fruit vines, silently watching, removing the razor blades the Grandother had spit at him and dropping them to the grass.

"Why don't you go to her?"

The Nonsister's voice startled him. He'd forgotten all about her. She stood right next to him, her bleeding eyeless sockets turned toward Vivienne, as if she could still see. "You know you want to."

Yes, he did, so badly. He wanted it more than he'd ever wanted anything in his life, more than he wanted his own life to continue. As long as he could be with Vivienne, just once, he wouldn't care if he died in this place like poor Kandice. At least he would die fulfilled.

The Nonsister continued speaking, her voice a cat's purr in his ear.

"You have nothing to be ashamed of, Spencer. You are what you were always meant to be. You're not evil, and you're not sick. I've lived a very long time, and I can tell you that throughout most of human history, girls scarcely older than Vivienne could marry. Indeed, they were encouraged to do so. By lying with her, you'll simply be following in a long tradition of your people."

Sweat beaded on Spencer's brow as his eyes drank in the sight of Vivienne's naked body illuminated in a shaft of moonlight coming from the window in the sky.

"No one will ever know," the Nonsister said. "I can make it so she doesn't remember. For her, it'll be like it never happened. But *you'll* recall every sweet second of it, and the memory will remain fresh and vivid until the day you die. You'll be able to revisit it any time you like, and it will be like reliving it each time. Whenever you feel the urge for young meat coming on, all you'll need to do is remember tonight, and the urge will pass. By lying with Vivienne tonight, not only will you save yourself, you'll save all the other children you would feel compelled to play with in the future. Sounds like a win-win to me."

Spencer heard Cora moan as Isaac fucked her, could hear the *smack-smack* of their flesh pounding together. He didn't take his gaze off Vivienne, though, and while he wouldn't have thought it possible, his cock got even harder.

He took a step forward.

CHAPTER NINETEEN

Then he heard his father's voice whisper in his mind.

Remember, Spencer, what we do together is our special secret. Never tell anyone. Never-ever. Not even Mommy. Especially not Mommy.

He took a step backward.

"No," he said.

The Nonsister moved to stand in front of him.

"I can tell you're of two minds about this. Let me see if I can help you achieve some clarity regarding this situation."

She grabbed hold of Spencer's erect penis with a gloved hand and pulled. *Hard.*

He felt a tearing sensation followed by a pain more intense than anything he'd ever experienced. He thought for a moment that the Nonsister was going to rip his cock out by the roots, and while the idea terrified him, at the same time he almost welcomed it. Without a penis, he wouldn't be able to hurt children the way his father had hurt him.

He felt something pull free from his body, and the pain intensified to the point where he momentarily ceased to exist as a person, was only a nervous system in great distress, and he closed his eyes and screamed.

An instant later, the pain stopped, all at once. Spencer felt fine — better than fine. He felt as if he'd been relieved of a great burden.

He opened his eyes.

Standing next to the Nonsister was an overweight man who bore an uncanny resemblance to Spencer. Which only made sense seeing as how he *was* Spencer.

"Say hello to your dark half," the Nonsister said. "This is the part of you that was created the first time your father touched you inappropriately. Of course, he wasn't like this back then. But he grew over the years just as you did, until he became the fine figure of a man he is today. You kept him in a cage, though, locked up and hidden away deep inside you. But he's free now, Spencer, and so are you. You don't have to be his keeper anymore, and he can now do all the things you always wanted but didn't have the courage to do."

Spencer's other half had a raging hard-on, but Spencer's dick had deflated. He looked at Vivienne, lying naked in the moonlight on the small round bed, and he felt no sexual desire for her whatsoever. The thought that he ever had sickened him. His other self, however, was of a different mind. He grinned at Spencer, gave him a wink, and then turned and began walking toward Vivienne, erect penis bobbing up and down as he went.

"No," Spencer whispered.

His other self kept walking.

"No," he said again, louder this time.

His other self had almost reached Vivienne's bed.

The Nonsister took hold of his wrist, as if to restrain him.

"Just let it happen, Spencer. It won't be your fault. It'll be *his*. And even though you won't get to fuck her yourself, at least you'll get to watch him do it. How many people get to live vicariously through their very own doppelganger?"

"No!"

Spencer yanked his arm free of the Nonsister's grasp, and he started toward his other self.

"Hey!" he shouted. "*Hey!*"

His other half didn't respond. He'd reached the bed and climbed on it.

Spencer ran, and he made it to the bed as his other self – who was grinning with dark anticipation – was reaching for Vivienne. He jumped onto the man before he managed to touch her and began hitting him, pounding his fists into a face he'd seen thousands, maybe millions of times whenever he looked in a mirror.

Vivienne – who up to this point had drowsed lazily in the bed – shook off the effects of the malum fruit and returned to full awareness. She screamed as the two Spencers fought and quickly crawled off the bed. She retreated to a safe distance and watched in confused horror as Spencer literally tried to kill himself.

Cora began shouting "Yes!" over and over again, practically

shrieking the word, and as Spencer pummeled his other self he thought, *For Christ's sake, just come already!*

The other Spencer didn't do anything to protect himself, didn't fight back, didn't even try to avoid being struck. He simply lay there and allowed Spencer to keep hitting him. Spencer didn't understand why until he realized that his jaw ached and the skin that covered it felt hot and swollen. The Nonsister had separated him into two halves, but they were still aspects of the same individual, were still connected. What one felt, the other felt. If one took damage, so did the other. Spencer couldn't harm his other half without harming himself.

If they'd been outside the house, back in the real world, Spencer would've told Vivienne to run and get help, to get away from him and stay away. But there was nowhere for her to go. They were trapped in the Night Grove, and he knew that his other self would keep pursuing Vivienne until he caught her, that nothing would stop him. One way or the other, he'd get his hands on the girl and do to her all the things he'd ever fantasized about.

There was only one thing Spencer could do.

His other self lay on the round mattress. Spencer wrapped his hands around the doppelganger's throat and began to squeeze. The hand he'd cut when he'd punched the bathroom mirror screamed in protest, but he ignored the pain. His other self didn't attempt to fight back, didn't do anything except look up at Spencer and grin. Spencer felt his own throat close off, making it difficult for him to breathe. *What happens to one happens to the other,* he thought. By choking his doppelganger, he was choking himself. He didn't care, though, would welcome death if it meant Vivienne would be safe from the worst part of himself.

Seeing Spencer strangling himself, Vivienne screamed. Machine Head walked over and stood by her, as if intending to act as her guard. Spencer felt jealous, but he was also grateful that someone was watching over her, even if it was that robot-headed bastard. He returned his full attention to his other self.

He squeezed harder, his forearms trembling from the effort. His other half's grin didn't falter, but his face had reddened and was edging toward purple. Spencer kept up the pressure. He wondered if they'd both pass out from lack of oxygen before he could finish the job. They'd both be unconscious then, but what if his other half came to before he did? The man would immediately go in search of Vivienne and try to have his fun with her before Spencer could wake and spoil everything. Still, he continued choking his doppelganger, not knowing what else to do. Maybe if he concentrated hard enough, he'd be able to cling to consciousness long enough to finish the job. Maybe the two of them were just separate enough for that to work. Maybe not. He needed to find some way to make sure they both died.

And then it came to him.

He removed one hand from his doppelganger's throat and grabbed a fistful of sheet. They were both lying on it, but there was still plenty free for him to be able to pull some of the material toward him. He then proceeded to jam the cloth into his other self's mouth. He pushed and shoved, really packing it in. For the first time since he'd attacked, his doppelganger became frightened. He tried to fight back, pounding his fists into Spencer's soft stomach again and again. Spencer gritted his teeth against the pain and kept jamming more of the sheet into his other self's mouth, shoving it ever deeper into his throat.

Spencer felt the sensation of cloth in his own mouth and throat, and although his airway remained unobstructed, he was still unable to breathe. He grew lightheaded and weak, as did his other self. The man still tried to punch Spencer's gut, but his blows lacked any force, and he stopped, his arms flopping onto the bed. Spencer's vision was going, but he continued shoving in cloth with what little strength remained to him. They would both pass out soon, but with the sheet choking off his other self's airway, he'd continue to suffocate until he died. Until they both died.

As his awareness began to dim, he turned, hoping to see Vivienne one last time. He couldn't see her, though. All he saw was the Nonsister. She was watching him with her empty eye sockets, blood running down her face like crimson tears. She licked her lips, looking satisfied, as if she'd just finished a very tasty – and filling – meal.

And then everything went dark, and Spencer was gone.

★   ★   ★

If the basement had been a nightmare, then the backyard was like something out of a dream. Alex had gotten a glimpse of it the other night – a large moon hanging above what appeared to be a small forest – but now she was here, standing in it, and it was even stranger and more wondrous than she'd imagined. The trees were tall, most fifty feet or higher, and of a species that she wasn't familiar with. The trunks had smooth bark that reminded her of palm trees, but their surface was covered with large, wicked-looking thorns, each several inches long. Their foliage was thick, and hung down in moss-like strands like weeping willows. There was no breeze, but the strands undulated slowly, as if they were undersea plants moving with the rhythm of the water's flow. The air was damp and smelled of greenery, but beneath that smell was a sickly-sweet odor she associated with funerals. The air was filled with a chorus of eerie sounds that were almost like electronic tones. When she was twelve, her parents had taken her to Barbados on vacation. The tree frogs that lived there sang all night long, and they'd sounded something like this, almost alien, as if they didn't truly belong to this world.

"I think the Eldreds need to hire a good lawn service," Martin said. "They've let their grass grow *way* out of control."

Neal looked at him. "How can you joke after what happened in the Undercountry? Lola *died* there."

"We don't know that for sure," Martin said. "We don't know if *any* of this is real. Or at least how much of it is real."

After escaping the Undercountry, they'd found themselves standing in a hallway within the Eldreds' house. A blessedly normal-looking hallway. Their hair and clothes smelled like smoke, and they feared the fire the Low Prince had used to destroy the basement stairs – and likely Lola along with them – would quickly spread to the rest of the house soon. Neal called out Kandice's name several times, then called out Cora's name and then Alex's father's name. He received no answers. The smell of smoke had grown stronger by that point, and they'd chosen to evacuate, although Neal hadn't looked too happy about it. The dining room had a patio door. It was unlocked, and they slid it open and stepped out into the night and found themselves confronted by yet another strangely altered aspect of the house – in this case, the backyard. And once outside, when they turned back toward the house, it was gone. In its place, more thorn trees.

The fence that had enclosed the backyard was gone, too. But the deck and the two picnic tables were still there. One of the tables had been broken, the middle caved in as if something heavy had been dropped on it. The wood was covered with dark liquid, as was the ground around it. Neal, Martin, and Alex examined the broken table, and while they noted the substance on it – which Alex was afraid was blood – none of them spoke of it.

"Do you think the rest of our families are in the house?" Alex said. "If they are, and the fire spreads…."

"I don't know who or what the Eldreds really are," Neal said, "but the Low Prince seemed to be in complete control of the Undercountry. I doubt he'd let the house burn down."

"You don't know what that weird-ass freak will do," Martin said. He looked at Alex. "But I don't think the fire will spread. The stairs were wood, but the cavern was all rock. Most likely the fire will burn itself out. There'll be some smoke damage, but that's it."

She wanted to believe Martin, but he didn't know anything more about what was happening here than she or Neal did. All they could do was guess and hope.

★   ★   ★

"Mommy, Mommy, wake up!"

Cora opened her eyes to see Vivienne standing next to the bed. She groaned.

"What time is it?" she asked. Had she overslept? She was normally an early riser and was almost always up before her daughter. Why had she slept so late? Had she been drinking last night? She couldn't remember.

She sat up, yawned, stretched. She felt tired, as if she'd run a marathon before going to sleep, but she felt good, too. No, she felt *great*. Fan-fucking-tastic, as a matter of fact. Whatever she'd gotten up to last night, it had done her a world of good.

That's when she realized Vivienne was naked and that she was, too. There was a naked man lying on the bed next to her, lightly snoring. It wasn't Martin, though. It was Isaac Ruiz. What the fuck?

She came fully awake then. She quickly climbed off the bed and faced her daughter. Machine Head stood directly behind her, and Cora shuddered. That robot-headed monstrosity squicked her out big-time. She crouched down, put her hand on Vivienne's shoulders, and said, "Are you okay?"

She saw that Vivienne was crying.

"Mr. Parsons..." she began, lower lip trembling. "He's.... He's...."

A cold pit opened in Cora's stomach.

"Show me."

Vivienne took her mother's hand and led her past the large round bed – which was empty – to a smaller one on the other side. Spencer lay on his back, eyes open, staring sightlessly at the glittering stars, a large section of bedsheet stuffed down his throat. He looked as if he'd died trying to swallow the damn thing.

"Don't look, honey."

She knew it was too late, that Vivienne had already seen enough of Spencer's dead naked body to scar her for life, but she gently turned her away from the bed anyway. She was the mommy, and that's what mommies did.

She heard a groan. She looked over to the bed where she'd left Isaac sleeping. He was awake now, yawning and stretching. She didn't want Vivienne looking at him either. He *was* naked after all. She stood and turned Vivienne to face one of the trellises with malum fruit vines clinging to it.

"Count the fruit," she said. "But don't touch any of them, and for sure don't *eat* any. Okay?"

"All right, Mommy."

Vivienne sounded as wrung out as Cora felt, but she walked over to the trellis and began counting.

Cora's memory was returning in bits and pieces. She looked around for Vanita – for the *Nonsister* – but she saw no sign of the girl. She had a memory of seeing her reclining on the big bed, but it was empty now. She went over to Isaac. He had sat up on the smaller bed, feet on the ground. Normally she wasn't self-conscious about her body, but she was beginning to remember what the two of them had done after eating that strange fruit, and she was embarrassed. She didn't attempt to cover herself, though. What did it matter now?

"Are you okay?" she asked Isaac.

He looked at her for a moment, then frowned.

"You aren't Sara. I thought you were Sara."

And then he began to cry.

★   ★   ★

The Nonsister was gone, and no one missed her. Cora, Vivienne, and Isaac got dressed, the two adults turning their backs to each other, as if suddenly modest. Cora made sure to stand where she could block the sight of Spencer's dead body from Vivienne. She knew it was too little, too late, though. Vivienne had watched the entire battle between the two Spencers while she and Isaac had been, ah, *finishing.* But she didn't want Vivienne exposed to the man's nude corpse any more than she had to be.

Machine Head stood off by himself, looking up at the window hanging in the air. Maybe he was mesmerized by the moonlight filtering through the window, Cora thought. There was no telling what went on in the mechanical head of his.

As they dressed, Vivienne said, "Mommy, why did we take our clothes off?"

Cora caught the scent of malum fruit, and she thought she might vomit. If she had a box of matches, she'd set fire to the whole goddamn grove.

"I don't know, sweetie."

Cora feared Vivienne would ask her what she and Isaac had been doing on their bed. Neither she nor Martin had tried to shield Vivienne from the concept of sex, but they'd never made an issue out of it, either. Because of this, Cora wasn't entirely sure just how much her daughter did and didn't know when it came to sex. But if Vivienne had any questions about what her mother had been doing with Mr. Ruiz, she kept them to herself. Instead, she asked, "What happened to the other one?"

Cora was confused for a moment, but then she realized what Vivienne was talking about. She wanted to know what had happened to the other Spencer. Cora had been too busy at the time to pay close attention. She'd noticed Vivienne, naked, climb onto one of the beds, and she'd seen an equally naked Spencer – dick swollen purple – trail after her daughter. She hadn't given it much thought, really, had been acting solely out of raw instinct and animal desire. Now that her mind was clear, she understood what Spencer had intended to do to her daughter. Sure, the malum fruit had primed the pump, so to speak, but the man had lusted after Vivienne before, she was sure of it. But something had happened. There'd been another Spencer, one who didn't approach her daughter, and who'd watched with horror as his double climbed onto the bed with Vivienne. She suspected the Nonsister had done something to create a copy of Spencer. Or maybe divide one Spencer into two. Whatever had happened, the Spencer who didn't want to fuck her daughter attacked the one who did, eventually jamming a sheet down his throat and choking the bastard. She wasn't too sure what had happened after that. She'd been caught in the throes of one of the best orgasms she'd ever had. But when it was finished and Isaac pulled out of her, she'd glanced over to the bed where the Spencers had been fighting to see only one remained – the one with half a sheet rammed down his gullet. Had the other Spencer run off? Had he ceased to exist when his horny counterpart died? She had no idea. But she sensed Spencer – the real man that he was – had fought to protect her daughter and he'd won, and that was all she needed to know. Maybe someday she'd tell this to Vivienne when she was older – assuming both of them survived this night.

"I don't know what happened to the other one," she said, answering her daughter's question.

Not exactly a lie. She liked to think of it as deferred truth-telling.

When all three of them were dressed, Isaac went over to Spencer's corpse and pulled the section of the sheet that wasn't in the man's mouth over his face so Vivienne wouldn't have to look at it anymore. It was a kind gesture, something that seemed out of character for him. Then again, maybe she hadn't known him well enough before tonight to have any sense of who he really was.

When Isaac was finished with this task, he joined them.

"Well," he said. "Now what? We can't go back the way we came. The door's gone."

Cora turned to look. Where the hallway door once stood, outlined by the malum fruit trees, was only empty space.

"That's just wonderful," she said. "So what's left? The window?"

She pointed to where it hung in the air. She thought she knew what lay on the other side besides moonlight. She remembered dreaming of these places, of the Aerie and the Night Grove. That meant this window would lead to—

"The forest," she said. When Isaac gave her a quizzical look, she added, "It's in the backyard."

"We're on the second floor," Isaac pointed out. "How can we get down without hurting ourselves? If we jump, we'll likely break something – a leg or worse – depending on how we hit."

"Tie the sheets together and use them as a rope," Vivienne said.

Cora and Isaac looked at her for a moment, then they looked at each other and laughed. Vivienne frowned, as if she thought they were making fun of her, but Cora put a hand on her shoulder and said, "You're a genius, you know that?"

Vivienne smiled.

★   ★   ★

The window, like the one in the Aerie, was higher than it would've been if this had been an actual bedroom. It hung in the air roughly twenty feet from the ground. Cora and Isaac gathered the sheets off the mattresses. Cora wanted to cover Spencer's body with one of the sheets, but they needed all the sheets for their rope. She and Isaac pulled the sheet out of Spencer's throat then rolled his body off the bed where it lay. He was a big guy, so it wasn't easy, but they managed. They then turned him onto his side, so Vivienne wouldn't have to look at his face.

At Cora's urging, Vivienne asked Machine Head to help them move the mattresses closer to the window and pile them on top of one another. Although his body was that of a regular human – a dead human who was starting to stink, Cora realized – he was stronger than a normal person, and he stacked the mattresses all by himself, putting the larger one on the bottom. They then tied the sheets together to make a rope. They needed something to serve as an anchor for the other end of the sheet rope to hold it in place as they descended. Isaac suggested using Spencer's body – "He's heavy enough," he said – and Cora punched him on the shoulder. They decided to use several of the wrought-iron trellises upon which the malum fruit grew. Cora was reluctant to go near the vines. She didn't want to fall victim to the fruit's aphrodisiac qualities again. But she accompanied Isaac over to them, and although she still found the fruit's smell intoxicating, it didn't have the same effect on her as before. Maybe because she'd already had sex, or maybe because she knew about the fruit's power and thus was able to resist it. Either way, she was glad she didn't feel compelled to take another bite. The last thing she wanted was for her and Isaac to tear off their clothes and start going at it like rabid weasels again.

They removed as many of the vines as they could and tossed them aside. They then pulled the trellises free of the soil and carried them over to the mattresses. They tore several strips of cloth from the sheet rope and used them to lash the trellises together. Then they were ready.

Standing on top of the mattresses, they could just barely reach the window. Isaac got down on his hands and knees, and Cora stood on his back. She opened the window and a forest scent wafted in. It was the scent of green growing things, like the Night Grove, but without the sweet tang of the malum fruit. There was another smell, too, an unpleasant odor of decay that caused Cora to wrinkle her nose in disgust. She stuck her head out the window and looked around. She saw the Eldreds' wooden deck and their two picnic tables, one of which had been broken. Oddly, she couldn't see the house itself. On this side, the window also hung suspended in the air. Beyond the picnic tables tall trees spread outward in all directions, as far as she could see. The air was filled with the strangely soothing noises of tree frogs, and if Cora hadn't known how dangerous the forest undoubtedly was, she'd have thought it beautiful.

It was like there was a whole other world outside the window, one filled with a single vast forest that went on forever. A full moon hung in the sky, and Cora recognized it as the same moon she'd seen hanging over the Eldreds' house as she'd run carrying Vivienne. It was huge, easily three times the size of what a normal full moon would look like in the sky, and it seemed to hang only a few hundred feet above the tree tops. She felt if she could stretch out her hand far enough, she'd be able to brush her fingers against its rocky surface.

There was enough space between the deck and the leading edge of the forest to give them room to drop their makeshift rope and climb down. She wasn't sure if their rope would be long enough to reach the ground, though. She supposed they'd find out soon enough. She withdrew her head and told Isaac and Vivienne what she'd seen. Then Machine Head used his inhuman strength to bend the ends of the trellises into crude hooks. He placed the hooked ends on top of the window sill and tested it to see if they were sturdy. They were.

They tossed the sheet out the window, and they were ready to descend. Vivienne wanted to go first, and she wanted to climb down by herself. Cora intended for her to hang on to either her or Isaac as they climbed down, but before she could protest, Machine Head lifted Vivienne onto his back.

"Hold on," he said in his mechanical voice. Vivienne wrapped her arms around his neck, and then he climbed through the open window, took a two-handed grip on the rope, and began descending. Cora held her breath as they went down, but Machine Head reached the ground without falling, and she was relieved.

"Again!" Vivienne called, and Machine Head let out an emotionless *Ha-ha-ha* that Cora supposed was his version of a laugh.

She marveled at Vivienne's mental resilience. After everything that had happened to them so far in the house, she wouldn't have been surprised if Vivienne curled up into a ball and stayed that way. Hell, it was all Cora could do to keep going and not collapse into a sobbing mess. Vivienne was a tough kid. She took after her father that way. Cora wondered if Martin was elsewhere within the house, struggling with whatever bizarre circumstances he found himself in. Wherever he was, she hoped he was all right.

She climbed down the rope, and then Isaac came last. He almost lost his grip and fell, but he managed to hold on and made it to the ground safely.

"If I'd known I'd have to try and fight my way through a series of pocket dimensions located in a murder house, I'd have hit the gym more regularly," he said.

Cora looked back at the window. As it had in the Night Grove, it hung suspended in the air, the sheet-rope dangling down to the forest floor. As Cora watched, the window winked out of existence. One second it was there, the next gone. The sheet-rope fell to the ground, and when Isaac examined the end that had been in the window, he found it had been neatly cut.

"I suppose this means there's no going backward in this place," he said.

He let go of the sheet-rope's end and it dropped to the ground.

Vivienne remained on Machine Head's back, arms around his neck, and Cora debated whether or not to tell her to get down. So far, the robot man had been a help to them, and he would make a powerful protector for Vivienne. But he was one of the Eldreds' creatures, and they had no way of knowing if he could be trusted. She decided to err on the side of caution.

"Vivienne, I think you should—"

Cora broke off as a chorus of animalistic snarls erupted to their left not far from where they stood. Startled, they all turned to look in that direction. Underbrush thrashed as something – a number of somethings, Cora thought – came rushing toward them. Shafts of moonlight filtered through the tree canopy, providing more than enough light to see by, so when the creatures emerged from the underbrush and came toward them, Cora could make out every disgusting detail of their bodies. There were a dozen of them, hideous constructions formed from different human body parts. No two looked alike. Some had extra limbs, some extra heads, some had legs in place of arms and vice versa. Some had both male and female sex organs – often located in the wrong place – while some had none. They walked on two legs, ran on all fours, crawled, lurched, movements spasmodic as their hodgepodge bodies did their best to function.

"Patchworks," Machine Head said.

The hideous creatures encircled the group. The beasts regarded them for a moment, and then as if obeying some unspoken signal, they rushed forward, teeth bared.

Cora didn't have time to scream.

★   ★   ★

When the humans are gone, the Nonsister draws in a breath and becomes visible again. She doesn't need to breathe as often as mortals do, and with her lungs empty, she was able to remain nearby and observe without the humans seeing her. She is pleased with how things have gone in the Night Grove, and she thinks her brother will be, too. She hopes he's had good luck as well. She'll find out soon enough.

She walks over to where Spencer's body lies and gazes down upon it, smiling. She fed well as he played out his little psychodrama, and now she feels logy. She's tempted to pull down the tower of mattresses, climb onto the big one, and take a quick nap. But there's too much to do. First things first: deal with Spencer's remains. The Eldred believe in using every part of their prey, so she raises a gloved hand. In response, the grass beneath Spencer grows rapidly, blades extending to wrap around his large form until he is encased entirely in green from head to toe. She lowers her hand, and the grass pulls Spencer's body down into the earth. When the body is gone, the grass returns to its original length and settles back into place, leaving no indication that Spencer was ever there. His body will feed the plants in her grove, so her babies will stay strong and healthy.

Now it's time to prepare to rendezvous with the Low Prince. If her brother has done his part, the first phase of their plan has been accomplished. Time for phase two. She giggles. Who knew betrayal could be so fun?

CHAPTER TWENTY

"You know what, Neal? This plan of yours sucks rocks. Big time."

Neal didn't bother responding to Martin's jab, not least because he thought the man was right. When the house had disappeared, taking the patio door with it, Neal had suggested they start walking. The Low Prince had manipulated them into this forest for a reason, and that reason would be revealed to them eventually. In the meantime, they started exploring to see what they could find, maybe some things they could use as weapons to protect themselves. Right now, all they had was the knife that Alex had grabbed in the Undercountry.

They'd been walking for some time now, Alex cutting lines into tree trunks to mark their route, and so far all they'd managed to acquire in the way of new weapons was a tree branch Neal thought he could use as a staff, and a grapefruit-sized rock that Martin carried. He'd discarded the empty flamethrower and the pistol soon after they'd arrived in the 'backyard'. His rock, as meager a weapon as it was, was still better than a flamethrower without fuel or a gun without ammunition. Neal wished they'd possessed the presence of mind to take more weapons from the dead soldiers littering the green felt ground in the Undercountry, but they'd been too busy trying to escape with their lives to think any further ahead than the next few seconds.

At least Alex had been smart enough to keep hold of her knife. The thing was wicked sharp, too. It cut into the tree bark with ease, as if the wood were no more solid than wet clay. He pitied whoever she was forced to use the blade on. They would be in for a very bad day.

Neal's feet hurt like hell. They were scratched and cut from walking barefoot on the forest floor, and he knew Martin and Alex's feet hurt just as bad. If the Eldred had to have lured them into their goddamn house, couldn't they at least let them put on some fucking shoes first? They—

He broke off that thought. He'd referred to the strange family that had abducted them as *Eldred,* as if it was a name for their species instead of a surname. Why had he done that? He didn't know, but it felt right. *The Eldred.*

The deeper they got into the forest, the taller the trees became. Their smooth trunks were wider, and the thorns that protruded from the bark were much larger, the shortest being a foot, the longest twice that.

"Good thing there's plenty of moonlight," Neal said. "I wouldn't want to bump into one of those bastards in the dark."

"Me neither," Martin said.

They continued on, and soon they began seeing things impaled on the thorns. Small creatures at first: butterflies, moths, frogs, and lizards. Then larger animals like squirrels, birds, and snakes. Then even larger ones: groundhogs, ducks, and raccoons. All of the creatures were in varying stages of decay. Some were little more than desiccated husks, but a few were fresher, looking as if they'd been impaled recently, perhaps within a day or two.

"What the hell is *this* fuckery?" Martin asked.

"I don't think I want to know," Neal said.

They continued walking, not knowing what else to do. They came upon their first human body shortly after. It had been stuck on thorns for quite a while and was now little more than a collection of bones held together by strips of leathery flesh.

"This is the most disgusting thing I've ever seen," Alex said.

The next impaled corpse they encountered was a woman who was much fresher. She was naked, gray, splotchy skin tight on her bones. It was hard to tell her age given her condition. She could've been anywhere from twenty to eighty. They kept moving and soon began encountering one corpse after another, until all the trees around them had human bodies – sometimes more than one – impaled on their thorns. The stench of rotting meat was thick in the air.

"Were they...." Alex paused, swallowed. "Were they killed like this? Shoved onto the thorns, I mean? While still alive?"

"I don't know," Neal said. "It's possible."

"So *we* could end up like this," she said.

Neither Neal nor Martin replied. Neal regretted having suggested they begin walking through the forest. What if he ended up leading Alex and Martin to their deaths?

"This is really weird," Martin said.

"*Weird?*" Alex sounded incredulous. "Don't you mean fucking *terrifying?*"

Martin scowled at her. "I'm not talking about the bodies. Well, I am, but not in the way you mean. The bodies have been left here to rot, right?"

"We can see that for ourselves," Neal said.

Martin continued. "So why hasn't anything tried to feed on them? They don't have any bite marks or missing pieces. Even the chunks that've fallen off them just lie on the ground near their feet. There's no sign that any fucking insects have been at them, either. It doesn't make sense."

"None of what's happened tonight makes any sense," Neal said. Still, he found Martin's observation disturbing. It was as if these bodies were protected by some kind of force that kept predators and scavengers away. *Or thrust them onto thorns*, he thought, remembering the dead animals they'd passed.

"On the contrary, it makes perfect sense."

The three of them were startled by this voice – a man's – and they turned to look in its direction. They saw an extremely thin body impaled on tree thorns nearby. This one wasn't naked. It wore, of all things, a tuxedo. Its bald head was a strange oval shape, and it hung downward, hiding its features. It raised its head then, and Neal saw that it had no face, just a covering of smooth skin where eyes, nose, and mouth should've been. When it spoke, the flesh where its mouth should've been vibrated, as if that was how the creature produced sound.

"At least it does to the Eldred," the thing said. "This is *their* world. We're just living in it. And dying, of course." The blank-faced creature turned its head toward Alex. "Hello, old friend. I'm glad to see you've kept your face intact for me."

Alex screamed. She turned and fled, running between the trees without any regard for her safety, arms and legs suffering multiple cuts from the protruding thorns as she passed.

"Alex!" Neal shouted. "Don't go!"

The faceless creature laughed as it stepped forward, detaching itself from the thorns with a series of sickening *squelches*.

"Don't worry," it said. "I'll go get her."

The creature ran off in the direction Alex had gone, moving with a lurching gait that was, in its own way, weirdly graceful.

"Come on," Neal said to Martin. "We have to go help her!"

He took a step forward, intending to head off in pursuit of Alex and the creature that was hunting her when a pair of half-rotted arms wrapped around his chest from behind. He struggled to break free, but whatever had hold of him was too strong. He still had hold of his staff, though his arms were pinned to his side and he couldn't wield it. The arms around him tightened, and in response, his hand sprung open and dropped the useless staff to the ground.

He looked over at Martin and saw that he was also restrained. A corpse had pulled itself off its thorns and grabbed hold of him, and Neal knew the same thing had happened to him.

He tried to speak to Martin, to urge him to keep trying to break free, but the undead arms were too tight around his chest, and he couldn't draw in enough air to make sound.

The ambulatory corpses lifted the two men off their feet and began walking in the opposite direction from where Alex and the monster chasing her had gone.

*   *   *

Alex bled from dozens of cuts, some shallow, some deep. She didn't feel any pain, though. She was far too terrified to feel anything except blind, unreasoning panic.

First Mr. Bumblefoot had chased her into the Eldred's house, then she suddenly found herself in the basement, except it was also a vast cavern called the Undercountry ruled by a creature calling himself the Low Prince. Then she was attacked by Nazi zombies, and after *that*, she'd entered a forest where dead bodies were impaled on trees, only to end up being chased by Bumblefoot again. It wasn't fair, it just wasn't *fair*!

She ran without a destination in mind. How could she have one?

She had no idea where she was or even if this place – and anything that happened in it – was real. If you didn't know what was *real*, if you didn't know the *rules*, then how were you expected to play the game, let alone have a chance of winning it?

The trees she passed all had at least one body pinned to them, if not more. The ones that were mostly bone didn't stir, but the ones that still had meat on them reached outward, hands grasping, trying to catch hold of her. The freshest corpses – those that had almost no rot on them – were able to pull themselves free from their thorns and tried to chase her. But they were slow, awkward-moving things, and she easily avoided them.

"Alex, wait up!" Bumblefoot called from somewhere behind her. "I just want to play. It'll be like old times, when you were little and still believed the world made sense, believed you were *safe*. Doesn't that sound nice?" He laughed, the sound wild and unhinged.

Alex let out a choked sob, and tears filled her eyes. This was unfortunate, as it impeded her vision, which had already been hindered by the strobe-like effect of running through shafts of moonlight alternating with shadow. She became disoriented, dizzy, and as a result ran too close to a tree covered with particularly large thorns. Her right shoulder snagged on the point of one of these thorns, and her momentum caused her to spin to the right, sending the thorn deep into her shoulder. She put out her left hand to keep herself from hitting the thorn-covered trunk with her whole body, and her hand hit a thorn with the fleshy part between thumb and forefinger. She did, however, manage not to turn herself into a human pincushion. A couple thorn points poked her in the chest and belly, and on her legs, but none of these did any significant damage.

She stood there for a moment, stunned, in pain, gulping air as she tried to catch her breath. Then she remembered Bumblefoot was coming for her, and she set about trying to dislodge herself from the thorns. She was able to pull her hand free without too much trouble, although it hurt like a bitch. Freeing her shoulder from the thorn it was embedded on proved more difficult. Both of her hands were empty – she'd dropped the knife she'd been carrying when she hit the tree – and she placed them both on the trunk, careful to avoid any more thorns. Then she gritted her teeth in anticipation of the pain to come and pushed herself away from the trunk as hard as she could.

The scream that came out of her mouth as her shoulder slid off the thorn was so loud and strong, it felt like her vocal cords ripped apart.

Once her shoulder was off the thorn, she clapped her left hand to the wound. She doubted it would do much to stop the bleeding, but she had to try. She heard the pounding of feet on the forest floor then, and she knew Bumblefoot was almost upon her. There was no way she would be able to escape him now. She couldn't run fast enough with her hand pressed to her shoulder like this, and if she didn't keep pressure on the wound it would bleed freely – especially when she was running and her pulse rate was high. It wouldn't take long for her to lose enough blood that she'd begin to weaken and slow down. And then Bumblefoot would have her. She had no choice but to stand and fight.

She swept her tear-filled gaze back and forth over the ground, searching for the knife. She didn't see it right away, and she feared she wouldn't find it in time to save herself, but then she caught a silvery glint in the moonlight. She stepped toward it, knelt, and felt around with her right hand, doing her best to ignore the pain in her shoulder this caused. Her fingertips brushed the metal blade, she found the handle, grasped it, and stood. She turned her head to the left and wiped her left eye on her shoulder. Her right shoulder was a blood-soaked mess, so she couldn't wipe the tears from that side. One eye would have to do. She stepped between two trees, making sure her back wasn't facing any other trees. She didn't want Bumblefoot to slam into her and drive her backward into a mass of thorns. Maybe he would kill her in the next few moments, but she didn't have to make it easy for him. She held the knife before her and waited.

She didn't think about how she might lose her life before it really began in earnest. She didn't think about how much her mother and father would miss her. Her dad was a complete jackass a lot of the time, but she had no doubt he loved her. She didn't think about the Eldred – what they were and how they could do the things they did. Her mind was focused on one thing only: driving her knife into the smooth patch of skin where Bumblefoot's face should be.

"I'm almost there!" Bumbefoot called. He sounded close.

Alex tightened her grip on the knife handle.

"Bring it," she said softly.

*　　*　　*

Inwardly, Martin was scared to fucking death, but he was determined not to show it. He believed a real man should maintain control of his emotions at all times, and while he didn't always succeed, was downright shitty at it sometimes, it was a quality he strived to master. He sensed that showing fear – or any sign of weakness – would be very dangerous in this place. Weakness marked you as prey, and there were too many things in this fucked-up house that would be only too happy to hurt you if you gave them even the slightest reason.

He was having a hell of a time trying to wrap his mind around this funhouse of death. He and Neal were being carried by a pair of walking corpses through a forest of thorn trees upon which even more corpses were impaled. And this forest – and the weird moon above it – was somehow contained within the Eldred's backyard. He knew he wasn't the smartest man on Earth, but trying to figure this out would've given Stephen Hawking a headache.

Martin couldn't believe how strong the thorn-zombies were. The one carrying Neal was a petite woman, a curly-headed brunette who was missing her lower jaw. The one carrying him was a tall, elderly man in his eighties, silver-haired and bearded, his stomach cavity torn open and hollowed out. Neither of the corpses should've been able to carry them, but they did so with ease, as if Martin and Neal weighed nothing. Martin's dad was an electrician, and when Martin was a kid, he'd asked his dad how computers worked, figuring that since computers ran on electricity, his dad would know all about them. His father had smiled at him, winked, and said, *"HPFM."*

"Huh?" Martin had said, confused.

"Hocus Pocus Funny Magic," his dad said, and that had been the sum total of his answer. Years later, Martin came to understand that his dad had answered this way because he didn't know jack shit about computers. But his answer seemed a perfect explanation for the things that had happened since the goddamn Eldred had moved into the cul-de-sac. Hocus Pocus Funny Magic.

The thorn-zombies walked in single file through the forest, and Martin's led the way, so he couldn't see Neal.

"You doing okay back there?" he called.

"Depends on your definition of okay," Neal called back. "I'm not dead yet, so I've got that going for me. How about you?"

"Same," Martin said. Maybe he and Neal didn't get along most of the time, but he was grateful for the man's presence. As bad as tonight had been so far, it would've been a hell of a lot worse to have to go through it alone.

Martin remembered following Cora and Vivienne into the house, but they hadn't been in the Undercountry with him, Neal, Alex, and Lola. He hoped they hadn't been real, had been some sort of illusion the Eldred had used to trick him into entering the house. But he feared they were here too, somewhere, going through a different version of hell right now. He wished he could be with them. Not knowing what was happening to them, whether they were alive or dead, was torture. And he was sure Neal felt the same way about Kandice. That much, at least, they had in common.

Before long, Martin became aware of light ahead of them. At first he thought it was some effect of the moon, but this light wasn't coming down from above. It was coming *toward* them, which meant that whatever was making it was on the ground. After a few more minutes of travel by zombie Uber, the trees – and the corpses impaled on them – began to thin out, and then they entered a clearing. In the middle sat a one-story building, brick painted white, roof black. A large blinking sign on top of the roof spelled out two words in multicolored lights: *GHOSTWOOD CASINO*.

Martin's eyes widened. His throat went dry and his heart rate increased. Were there three more lovely, alluring, evocative syllables in the English language than CA-SI-NO? He thought not.

The thorn-zombies carried them to the front door – a gray metal thing with a handwritten sign taped to the front in large capital letters made from black magic marker. *WE NEVER CLOSE.* Below that, in smaller letters: *COME IN AND TRY YOUR LUCK!*

The zombies put them down and released their grip. They then turned and ran to a pair of empty thorn trees at the edge of the clearing and impaled themselves face-first. After that, their bodies went limp, as if whatever unnatural force had animated them was spent.

"There go our rides," Neal said.

Martin was sure Neal was just as scared as he was, but he admired the way the man could still make jokes in this situation. That took balls.

"We don't have to go in," Martin said. "We could walk on by, re-enter the forest on the other side of the clearing, and keep going."

"Yeah, but to where? And even if we did that, what do you think the odds are that the Eldred will make sure we end up back here one way or another?"

"Now that's one bet I'm not willing to take."

Martin leaned his head close to the door, listening to see if anyone was in there. He heard nothing. He looked at Neal, and Neal shrugged, as if to say, *It's your call.*

Martin took hold of the doorknob, turned it, and opened the door.

Music blasted out, a heavy-metal tune with chainsaw guitars, pile-driving beat, and mostly unintelligible lyrics that were half-growled, half-screamed. Martin thought he recognized the song: 'Eat the Night' by a band from the seventies called Slogeny. A real golden oldie. There was also the sound of conversation – the buzz of voices, laughter, shouting, along with the clinking of glasses and the sound of electronic gaming machines dinging and whooping. Martin had the impression that the casino's interior had been silent until he'd opened the door, as if the crowd inside had been activated by that simple action.

Martin stepped back and gestured.

"After you."

Neal grimaced. "Thanks a fucking lot." But he stepped inside. Martin took a deep breath and followed, closing the door behind them.

Inside was a large open area, filled with different gambling options. Slot machines lined the walls, and in the middle of the room were tables for poker, craps, roulette, blackjack, and other games. The place was packed with people: employees working the tables or tending bar, customers – drinks in hand – sitting or standing to gamble or play the slots, feeding in one quarter after another, pulling the arms, and waiting with nervous anticipation to see if they won. The air was heavy with cigarette smoke, and with all the people, lights, and electronic equipment in the place, it was stuffy and hot.

A closer look revealed this wasn't an ordinary casino. The slot machines had names like Buzzsaw Baby, Worm Rot, Bloodscream, and Evisceration, each accompanied by grotesque and bloody imagery suited to their themes. The walls were covered with TV screens displaying images of horrific violence: riots, stabbings, beheadings, hangings, mass executions, and worse. The employees and customers were all bald, men and women both, and their fingers ended in sharp, claw-like nails. When they opened their mouths to talk or laugh, they revealed small rows of piranha-like teeth.

One of the gaming tables – a circular one located in the dead center of the room – was empty. A woman stood within the circle, flipping a deck of cards back and forth between her hands, her gaze fixed on the two newcomers. She wore a midnight-black minidress with tiny sparkles on the fabric to catch and reflect the light. Her hair was black, her skin pale, and Martin recognized her at once. It was Lacresha Eldred.

"Come on in, boys," she said, smiling as she continued flipping cards from one hand to the other. "You know you want some of *this* action."

Her dress was cut to display a significant amount of cleavage, but Martin didn't care about that. His gaze was fixed on the cards, on the almost hypnotic way Lacresha was manipulating them. He felt a tingle of anticipation in his gut, and before he realized it, his feet were moving him toward the table. After a moment's hesitation, Neal followed. When they reached the table, Lacresha lay the deck down in front of them, and with a single smooth motion fanned the cards out in a semicircle pattern. Martin glanced at the cards and found he didn't recognize any of the suits. Instead of red and black, the two colors were green and purple, and instead of the usual hearts, spades, clubs, and diamonds, the cards had small pictures that looked like Egyptian hieroglyphs.

"I'm happy to see you could make it tonight, gentlemen."

"We wouldn't miss it," Martin said, answering on autopilot. He was glancing at the other tables, hoping to get a sense of how the cards were being used, but it didn't help.

"Lacresha—" Neal began, but she interrupted.

"In the house, I'm called the Werewife." As if to demonstrate, her flesh lost cohesion, grew soft and liquidy as it reconfigured. Within seconds, her face was a mirror image of Neal's. An instant later, she looked like Martin. Then she quickly ran through the rest of Brookside Court's residents, becoming Lola, Spencer, Alex, Isaac, Cora, Vivienne, and finally Kandice before resuming her own appearance. "I can look like whatever I want to whoever I want whenever I want."

She held up a hand and it became a large crustacean's claw. She reached forward quickly and snapped it in Martin's face and laughed when he jumped. Her hand returned to normal and she let it drop to her side.

"So what brings you into my establishment this fine evening?" she asked.

"A pair of your pet zombies," Neal said.

The Werewife laughed. "Just think of them as external motivation to get here. Congratulations on surviving the Undercountry. The Low Prince isn't known for taking it easy on his guests."

"We didn't exactly have it easy," Neal said. "We lost Lola."

"And Alex is still out in the forest somewhere," Martin said. "Hopefully, she's still alive." He wasn't very confident of this, though.

"But *you're* both here, safe and sound," the Werewife said. "For the moment, anyway."

She smiled, and for an instant her mouth was filled with crocodile teeth, but they quickly returned to normal.

"What the hell is going on here?" Martin asked. "What have you done with the house? Why did you bring us here?"

What he really wanted to know was if Cora and Vivienne were somewhere in the house, and if so, if they were okay. But he was too afraid of what the Werewife would tell him to ask her.

The Werewife collected the cards, formed them into a deck once more, then began shuffling them using only one hand.

"You don't get answers for free in here," she said. "You have to gamble for them."

Martin didn't like the sound of that, but he stepped up to the table, put his hands on it, and leaned in toward the Werewife.

"What's the game?" he asked.

*　　*　　*

Neal didn't like this. He doubted the Eldred would play any game they hadn't already rigged in their favor.

"I think we should start simple," the Werewife said. "We each draw a card. High card wins, low card loses."

"If we win, we get answers to our questions?" Martin asked.

"Don't be greedy. One bet, one answer."

"What are the stakes?" Neal asked.

"If you lose, I'll take one of your fingers. Human flesh doesn't fuel the bodies of my kind, but it *is* tasty."

The Werewife licked her lips with a forked lizard tongue, and Neal shuddered. He wasn't thrilled at the prospect of losing any fingers, but they needed to know what the Eldred were up to. Against beings so powerful, knowledge was their best – and most likely only – chance for survival.

The bald-headed gamblers and employees that filled the casino all stopped what they were doing and turned to watch the drama about to play out before them. Their eyes shone with dark excitement, and they grinned, displaying their piranha teeth.

"All right," Neal said. "I accept the terms."

"No," Martin said. "*I* accept them."

"I don't have a child," Neal said. "Vivienne needs her father. I should be the one to take the risk…in case something goes wrong."

Neal noted the sweat on Martin's upper lip, the way his hands shook. Neal didn't think the trembling had anything to do with fear of losing. If anything, Martin seemed only too eager to be the one to gamble with the Werewife. Kandice had told him about her late-night conversation with Cora a few days ago, and he knew Martin was a gambling addict.

"I've got more experience gambling than you do," Martin said. "*Way* more."

He gave Neal an *I got this* smile before turning back to the Werewife.

"I'm ready," he said.

But before they could begin, the casino door opened.

"Oh no you don't, Martin Hawkins!"

CHAPTER TWENTY-ONE

It was Cora, Vivienne at her side. They were in night clothes, just as Neal and Martin were. As mother and daughter stepped inside, they were followed by Isaac, who wore a flannel shirt, jeans, and shoes. *Did he sleep fully clothed?* Neal wondered. Or had he still been up when the Eldred sent their summons? A robot-headed creature entered last, but after everything Neal had seen tonight, the thing barely made an impression on him. While the door was momentarily open, Neal caught a glimpse of bizarre-looking creatures outside, conglomerate things cobbled together from different human body parts. He thought they might enter, but they remained outside.

They're guarding the door, he thought. *So we can't make a break for it.*

Cora took Vivienne's hand and walked straight over to Martin. Isaac took his time, ambling over, looking around and taking everything in. From the disapproving expression on his face, he wasn't particularly impressed with the place. The robot-headed man trailed behind him, its glowing green eyes fixed straight ahead – on the Werewife.

Despite Cora's angry tone, Martin embraced her and gave her a kiss. Then he crouched down and gave Vivienne a hug. When he straightened, he said, "How'd you get here?"

"It's a *long* story," Cora said.

Isaac hooked a thumb in the door's direction. "We were herded here by a group of Frankenstein's rejects."

Martin ignored him and kept his attention on his wife and child. "It doesn't matter. I'm just so glad you're okay."

Cora's expression became sorrowful. "We're the only ones who made it."

Her words struck Neal with almost physical force.

"Was Kandice with you?" he asked.

Cora looked him in the eye. "Yes. She was."

That last word – *was* – told him all he needed to know.

The Werewife seemed amused by Neal's reaction. "I'm afraid your group *has* suffered several casualties this evening." She gestured and all the TV screens in the casino changed to one of three different scenes. Lola's charred body lying among soot and ashes, eyes burnt to dust, mouth open in a silent eternal scream. Spencer's naked body lying on a round bed amidst trellises covered with vines and fruit, a long length of sheet protruding from his mouth. And finally, Kandice, lying broken on a picnic table as a family of blood-covered corpses – the Raines family, Neal guessed – tore into her like a pack of starving animals while strange, skullheaded birds circled in the air above her, cawing raucously.

Neal thought of how the last few months had been for them, how he'd struggled to accept Kandice's bisexuality. He knew now that his difficulty had come solely from his own insecurity, and not because he had any real reason to doubt her love for him. Now she was gone, and he would never get the chance to tell her how sorry he was.

He tried to look away from the horrible scene of his wife's televised death, but everywhere he looked, there was a screen upon which it was playing.

So far, Neal had barely managed to hold on to his sanity in this terrible place, but the revelation of Kandice's death – an extremely horrible one if the video footage was true – should've caused him to break down into a sobbing, gibbering mess. He felt shock and sorrow, but they were muted, as if he'd become numb to the horrors of the Eldred. That was good. Numbness would allow him to keep going, keep fighting. There would be plenty of time to mourn his wife later – assuming he lived through all this madness.

He fixed his gaze on the Werewife.

"I'm going to kill you," he said.

The Werewife burst into delighted laughter. "I so admire your species' bravado. You're such *fun!*"

Isaac looked at Martin.

"Alex?"

"She was with us," Martin said, "but we got separated right before we came here. She was okay the last time we saw her."

Isaac nodded wearily, as if he understood what Martin *wasn't* saying, that he had no idea if Alex had survived the dangers of the forest.

The Werewife looked at Cora, Vivienne, and Isaac. She inhaled through her nose, then frowned.

"I smell malum fruit on you. Not surprising, as it's one of the Nonsister's favorite tactics. But there's something odd about the scent. I can't quite put my finger on what it is, though." She inhaled again, her frown deepening. Finally she released her breath in a sigh. "Nevermind." She smiled. "Must be getting old."

"I don't know what's going on here," Cora said to Martin, "but you don't have to play their game." She glared at the Werewife. "Tell her to go fuck herself."

The Werewife smiled, but her eyes – now the feral yellow of a tiger – were cold and deadly.

"I'm not doing this for me," Martin said. "I'm doing it for all of us – especially you and Vivienne. If I win, she'll answer questions. Maybe she'll tell us something that will help us get out of this fucking place."

"You're assuming she'll tell the truth," Cora said. "And what happens if you lose?'

Martin didn't tell her. Instead, he said, "If I do, make sure Vivienne doesn't see what happens, okay?"

Neal thought Cora would protest further, but Martin didn't give her a chance.

"I get to handle the cards," he told the Werewife.

"Of course." She handed the deck to him.

Isaac and Vivienne stepped to the edge of the table so they could watch the action. Even the robot-headed man came, shuffling due to what seemed to be an injured leg.

Martin flipped through the cards quickly, examining them. Neal wasn't sure what he was looking for. Was he trying to determine if they were marked? Or was he trying to familiarize himself with the unfamiliar suits? Maybe both, Neal decided. Satisfied, Martin started shuffling the cards. When he was finished, he laid the cards face-down on the table. He cut the deck in the middle, reassembled it, and turned to the Werewife.

"Ladies first," he said.

The Werewife smiled. She selected the top card, turned it over, and dropped it on the table for everyone to see. The card was green, and on it was a drawing of a young man dressed in a simple tunic. Neal thought it might be the equivalent of a jack, but he had no way of knowing for sure.

"Your turn," the Werewife said to Martin.

Martin selected the next card on the stack and flipped it onto the table. It was a purple suit, with a hieroglyph that looked a bit like a hashtag symbol. Neal had no idea what the suit was called, but the number on it was clear enough. Ten.

The Werewife looked at Martin and made a purring sound deep in her throat. "Acolyte beats ten. Your hand, please."

Martin kept his gaze on the Werewife as he spoke to Cora.

"Cover Vivienne's eyes."

Cora, frightened, nodded and did as he asked. She didn't look away, though.

Martin held his left hand out to the Werewife. It shook some, but Neal was impressed that he was able to hold it as steady as he was. And Martin was right-handed. It was smart to offer his left, Neal thought. He was beginning to think he'd misjudged the man all this time. Martin might not be educated, and he held some ignorant, bigoted views, but that didn't mean he was stupid.

The Werewife opened her mouth, her jaw distending like that of a snake. Her neck grew rubbery and began to stretch. And then she struck, her head darting forward. She clamped her crocodile teeth down on Martin's thumb and severed it with a single bite. Martin screamed – as did Cora and, even though she hadn't seen what happened, Vivienne. Martin jerked his bleeding hand to his chest and clamped his right hand over the wound to try and slow the bleeding. The Werewife chewed noisily as her head retracted and her jaw and neck resumed their normal shape. There was blood on the table, and on the cards as well.

The Werewife swallowed. She wiped some blood from her lower lip with an index finger, then licked it clean.

"The meat was a little stringy, but overall, not bad."

Cora put her arms around Martin, and Vivienne – her vision no longer obstructed by her mother's hand – looked at the blood on the table with wide, frightened eyes.

Neal stepped forward and put his hands on Vivienne's shoulders.

"It's okay," he said, then he repeated it, as if saying it twice somehow made it more likely to be true.

Cora shot the Werewife a venomous look.

"You *bitch!*"

"I appreciate the compliment," the Werewife said, "but unless you'd like me to kill you all right now, I suggest you keep your fucking cunt mouth shut from now on."

Neal thought Cora was going to lunge across the table and attack the Werewife, but with a visible effort, she restrained herself. Neal was relieved. Whatever kind of creature the Werewife was, he was certain she couldn't be harmed by ordinary means. Maybe she couldn't be harmed at all.

"Do you wish to continue playing, Martin? You *do* have nine fingers left. Who knows? You might get lucky."

Isaac leaned in close to speak to Martin.

"Don't do it. I don't know how much of this place is real and how much illusion, but I'm sure of one thing. You can't trust Lacresha or her family."

The Werewife appeared to take no offense at Isaac's words. She merely waited for Martin's response.

"Go on," Martin said.

The Werewife smiled, and once again selected a card off the top of the deck and laid it on the table face-up. It was purple, and the number on it was three.

Gritting his teeth against the pain of his wound, Martin removed his right hand from his left. His right was covered with blood, and it dripped onto the table as he reached for a new card.

Vivienne turned away, pressed herself against Neal's side, and let out a sob. Neal put a hand on her back for whatever small comfort it might give her. Images of Kandice's death – along with Lola's and Spencer's – continued playing on the casino's TV screens. Neal forced himself to watch Martin and the Werewife, tried not to think about the pair of slender birthday candles that had been jammed into Kandice's eyes. God, her *eyes*....

Martin chose a card and dropped it on the table.

A green suit with an image of a skull with red gems replacing its teeth. Neal wasn't sure what its equivalent was. An ace, maybe?

"Death's Sweet Lie wins. Ask your question," the Werewife said, seeming mildly annoyed at having lost this round.

"Don't ask yet," Isaac said. "We need to discuss this as a group and determine which question is—"

Martin ignored him.

"How do we get out of this alive?" he asked.

The Werewife's smile was terrible to behold.

"You can't."

"You idiot!" Isaac said. "You didn't specify what *this* was. She could've interpreted the word any way she liked, making her answer meaningless. She could've decided it meant *life*, and all things have to die sometime."

"There are *some* exceptions to the rule," the Werewife said.

"Fuck you," Martin said to Isaac, but his heart wasn't in it. Once more, he clamped his right hand over the wound where his left thumb had been.

Isaac went on. "If we're going to keep doing this, we have to be smart about it, figure out questions precise enough to get us the information we need."

"You do it then," Cora said. "You draw a card and risk losing a finger."

Isaac said nothing.

"That's what I thought," Cora said.

"I'll do it," Neal said. "With Kandice dead, I don't care what happens to me."

Before anyone could object, he reached for a card. But before he could draw one, the creatures standing guard outside started growling and snarling. There was a sound of frantic movement, as if the things were attacking something. This was quickly followed by cries of pain. A moment later, there came the sound of feet pounding the ground, then silence.

The door opened and Alex – blood streaking her face and hands and soaking her clothes – stepped inside. In her right hand she clutched her knife, its blade smeared with crimson. In her left hand she held a bloody scrap of skin.

Everyone – the Werewife, the humans, the assembled gamblers

and staff – watched as Alex trudged to the table where Martin had been playing the Werewife's horrible game.

She tossed the grisly hunk of flesh onto the table. It landed on top of the deck of cards, covering them. The skin's surface was smooth and unblemished.

"Mr. Bumblefoot wanted my face, so I took his," Alex said.

★   ★   ★

The Werewife picked up the section of skin and examined it. Isaac had no idea who or what Mr. Bumblefoot was, but he was glad to see his daughter was safe. She was covered in so much blood, though, he had no idea if she was unharmed. From her stiff walk, and the way she'd winced when she'd tossed the skin onto the table, he assumed she was injured, though how badly was difficult to say.

He went to her and hugged her – not too hard – not giving a damn that he was getting a good portion of all that blood on himself. Alex smiled wearily and hugged him back.

The Werewife continued looking at Bumblefoot's faceless face, frowning.

"A common knife can't damage a glamour."

She blew on the skin, and it became black smoke which she inhaled. She then looked at Alex.

"Did you use that knife to drive off my pets outside? Of course, you did." For the first time since Isaac and the remainder of his group had arrived, the Werewife addressed Machine Head. "Do you know anything about this girl's knife?"

"No," Machine Head said.

The Werewife was beginning to get angry. And was there a little fear in those inhuman eyes of hers as well? Maybe, Isaac thought. The table also became black smoke, which she inhaled, then she stepped forward to stand before Isaac and Alex. Isaac had a protective arm around his daughter, but the Werewife acted as if he didn't exist.

"Where did you get that knife?" she asked. When Alex said nothing, she grabbed a fistful of the girl's blood-soaked T-shirt and lifted her onto her tiptoes. "Answer me, damn you!"

"Let her go!" Isaac shouted. He took hold of the Werewife's wrist, intending to force her to release Alex. But before he could exert any force, the Werewife released an ear-splitting shriek of pain. She yanked her arm out of Isaac's grasp and retreated several steps. She raised her arm to examine it, and Isaac saw that the flesh on her wrist was gone, as if his touch had caused it to evaporate, leaving nothing but bone.

The Werewife definitely looked afraid now.

"How did you do that? You're a human! You can't—"

Alex's knife shimmered and its silvery blade became a flat black. The Werewife's eyes went wide as she saw the transformation.

"No," she breathed. She shook her head, took a step backward, and said it again. "No...."

Alex smiled grimly, and to Isaac's shock, his daughter rushed forward and buried the dark blade in the Werewife's chest. Her cry of pain when the skin and muscle on her wrist disintegrated had been loud, but it had been a baby's soft sigh compared to the sound that now issued from the Werewife's throat. This sound wasn't only physical – there was a psychic component as well. So while all the humans clapped their hands over their ears, including Martin, whose wounded left hand splattered blood onto his head and neck, there was nothing they could do to shut out the Werewife's mental scream of agony. It tore through their minds, momentarily causing them to forget who they were, that they even existed at all. They had only the most rudimentary sense of self-awareness, slightly more than fish in an aquarium. They could no longer think, could only feel. And what they felt was the terror and rage of a being that had lived for untold millennia and who'd had every expectation of existing until the end of time, when the very last particle of reality was finally swallowed by the Gyre. This was a tragedy, a blasphemy, but worst of all....

...it was cheating.

And then the Werewife collapsed into black smoke and began to dissipate.

While the Werewife had been in her death throes, the bald-headed, sharp-toothed gamblers and staff echoed her pain, screaming at the top of their lungs and tearing at their faces with clawed hands. Except for two. They watched intently as the Werewife died, and when she became black smoke, they rushed forward and began inhaling it into their bodies. The rest of the sharp-tooths became smoke, as did the casino itself, and the two surviving sharp-tooths inhaled all of this as well.

When it was over, the humans lay on the grass in a moonlit clearing, bodies trembling as if they were experiencing seizures, blood trickling from their ears and noses. The two remaining sharp-tooths watched the humans and waited. After several moments, the humans fell still, and soon after that Isaac remembered who he was and *that* he was. He sat up too fast, and was struck by a wave of vertigo so intense that he thought he was going to vomit. He didn't, though, and the dizziness quickly faded, leaving in its place a pounding headache. He would've rather kept the vertigo.

Slowly, painfully, the humans began to rise to their feet. Alex was able to stand before Isaac could, so she helped him up. He was a little wobbly on his legs at first, and she steadied him until he felt he'd recovered enough to stand on his own.

He took a quick headcount. Besides him and Alex, there was Martin – minus a thumb – Cora, Vivienne, Neal, Machine Head, and two of those weirdos with the bald heads and sharp teeth.

"Is everyone okay?" Neal asked, partially slurring his words. He wasn't a hundred percent yet, but Isaac understood him. It might take a while for them to fully recover – if they ever did.

The others were well enough, considering what they'd been through. The pair of sharp-tooths said nothing, just continued watching them, lips twitching as if they were trying to keep from smiling – or laughing.

Vivienne, crying, pulled away from her parents and ran to Machine Head. The creature bent down and picked her up, and she pressed her head against his chest and began sobbing loudly. Martin and Cora exchanged looks that were a mixture of surprise and sadness. And then they trained their gazes on Machine Head, and from the dark fury in their eyes, Isaac half-expected them to physically attack Machine Head in tandem to retrieve their child. But they did nothing. If Isaac had been in the same position, if Alex had been a child who'd forged some bizarre connection with a soulless devil, Isaac would've done everything he could to get her away from that monster and kill it, regardless of the final cost to himself. At least, that's what he hoped he'd do.

When the survivors were satisfied that none of them were going to die anytime soon, they all turned their attention to the pair of sharp-tooths.

"Why didn't you go up in smoke like everything else?" Martin asked.

In response, the sharp-tooths' forms blurred, changed, then came back into focus. One of them – a young man wearing a long-sleeved black pullover – had bone spikes jutting from his head. And the other – a girl in a red see-through gown and long black gloves – had shadows where her eyes should be, tears of blood running from her empty sockets.

"The Low Prince," Martin said, sneering.

"The Nonsister," Cora said, her tone cold. She gave Isaac a meaningful look, but he pretended not to notice.

"What the fuck are you two doing here?" Neal demanded.

The Low Prince and the Nonsister turned to each other and smiled. Then they faced the humans once more.

"We have a proposition for you," the Low Prince said.

"One we think you're going to like," the Nonsister added.

CHAPTER TWENTY-TWO

Stay calm, Alex told herself. *You got this.*

She didn't believe it, though. The Low Prince and Nonsister had placed a glamour on her to make her resemble the Werewife, and while they'd assured her the disguise would be perfect, she feared the deception wouldn't fool the other Eldred. They would discover the truth, she and the others would be killed on the spot – if they were lucky. The Eldred could do a lot worse to them than take their lives.

She felt panic rising inside at that thought, and she told herself to relax and just breathe, but her pulse was rapid as machine-gun fire, and she felt lightheaded. *You're okay,* she told herself, and again, *You're okay.*

She was prone to test anxiety, always had been. It came from having a father who was a college professor, and a demanding one at that. Anything less than one hundred percent on a test was failure as far as he was concerned, at least when it came to his daughter, and he pushed her to excel. During her sophomore year in high school, she began experiencing panic attacks on test days. She tried to power through them, but they continued getting worse until one day she actually fainted in class as the teacher was passing out the test. Her parents took her to see a psychologist, and he'd taught Alex techniques for dealing with anxiety. One of the techniques Alex had found most useful was focusing her attention on the here and now, grounding herself in the physical world. *Anxiety comes from worrying about the future,* her psychologist had said. *Focusing on the present keeps us from obsessing about what might or might not happen next.* Alex attempted to do this now, although she wondered what her psychologist would think about her current circumstances. He'd probably tell her that in this situation, going batshit crazy was a perfectly reasonable response.

Alex sat at a long dining table made of expensive wood polished to a gleaming shine, the kind of thing rich people in the movies had.

Only instead of being able to seat a dozen or so guests, this table appeared to have no end, at least none that she could see. It stretched from horizon to horizon, and for all she knew, it was infinite. The rational part of her mind told her this was an illusion, but after everything she'd experienced tonight, she wasn't certain there was any meaningful difference between illusion and reality. They were merely different sides of the same coin. Her father was here, as were Neal, Cora, Martin, and Vivienne. Alex sat on the Eldred side of the table, while the others sat on the opposite side, expressionless and silent, as if entranced. Their chairs – called cathedra according to the Nonsister – were very different from the others that lined the table. Instead of wood, they were fashioned from bones held together by strips of raw red muscle. The arms and legs of the chairs possessed multiple skeletal hands which clutched the humans' arms and legs, holding them in place. Set atop the backs of the chairs were large skulls of creatures Alex couldn't identify. They seemed vaguely dinosaurian – protruding snout, mouth filled with sharp teeth – and green fire danced within their eye sockets, not unlike the green light that shone in Machine Head's eyes. Alex had the impression that the chairs were alive in some way, although perhaps it was only her imagination.

Machine Head didn't get a seat. He stood behind the chairs on the Eldred side of the table, quietly waiting for his masters to give him a command. His body stank really bad now, and the flesh had turned a nauseating gray. Alex thought it wouldn't be long until the body had decayed to the point where it was no longer functional, and she wondered what would happen then. Would the Eldred find a new body for him, or would they keep his head in storage, put him up on a shelf somewhere until they had need of him again?

She shook her head to clear it. *The present, stay focused on the present.*

Her father and neighbors weren't the only ones seated at the table. The other chairs – all normal wooden ones – were occupied by beings that looked like human-shaped fog. Their forms weren't stable, and bits of them would drift away from the main mass at times, only to be reabsorbed before they could go too far. These figures had no distinguishing features of any kind, no faces, nothing to indicate gender or age. According to the Low Prince, these creatures were Residuum Wraiths, what remained of the Eldred's victims after all the life had been drained from them. Alex wasn't certain whether the Eldred kept them on purpose, like pets or – more likely – as trophies, or if the wraiths stayed with the Eldred simply because they had nowhere else to go. These things weren't ghosts, per se. *More like blank spaces in reality that living humans used to fill,* the Nonsister had told her. Alex wasn't clear on the difference, and she supposed the specifics of what the wraiths were didn't matter. Either way, they were creepy as hell. Even more disturbing, aside from the five humans, the chairs on that side of the table – all of those Alex could see, and probably many, many more beyond the range of her vision – were occupied by wraiths. There were hundreds of them, maybe thousands. How long had the Eldred been preying on humans? Since her ancestors had first begun to walk upright on the grasslands of Africa? Longer? The thought was horrifying, not least because how could she and the others hope to stand against such ancient, powerful beings?

Focus, she reminded herself.

She looked at the wraith closest to her, the one sitting across the table on Neal's left. She peered closely at its face – or at least the roiling mist that was where its face should've been – and wondered who it had once been. Were Kandice, Lola, and Spencer here, now reduced to these fog-ghosts? Could Neal be sitting next to his dead wife and not know it? She found the thought horrifying.

The Nonsister sat on Alex's left, the Low Prince seated on the other side of his sibling. Both looked calm and relaxed, but she knew this had to be an act. Given what they were attempting to do, they had to be nervous as hell. And there were signs. The Nonsister faded in and out of existence a bit faster than usual, and her blood tears ran more freely. The wounds where the Low Prince's bone crown jutted from his head bled more profusely as well. She took petty satisfaction in their discomfort. After the pain and suffering they had caused tonight, the least they deserved was to feel scared.

The chair to the right of Alex was empty. Father Hunger stood close by, finishing his preparations for the feast, and he would sit here when it was time to begin. She was afraid that the instant he sat, his proximity to her would allow him to sense that she wasn't the Werewife. He'd discover the Low Prince and the Nonsister's betrayal and kill them all.

She looked down at her hands resting on the surface of the table, the right on top of the left. The skin was no longer scratched and bleeding, and her shoulder wound was gone. The siblings had healed her injuries before they'd left the clearing in the Ghostwood where the casino had stood. Otherwise, her hands looked no different to her, but if what the Low Prince and Nonsister had told her was true, if they hadn't simply been playing a cruel joke on her, to everyone else she looked like Lacresha, the Werewife.

Such a disguise is a complex glamour, the Low Prince had told her. *But working together with my sister we should be able to accomplish it.*

Alex hadn't liked hearing him say *should,* but she'd agreed to go through with it, and so far, none of the other Eldred had seen through her disguise. The Grandother, in harpy form, was on the Low Prince's left, perched on her chair instead of sitting on it, her talons occasionally *tap-tapping* the wood. Alex kept waiting for the Grandother to turn to her, bird eyes narrowed, and denounce her as an imposter. But so far the harpy hadn't given her a second look. Alex still had the black knife – which the Low Prince had called a Null Blade – and it rested on her chair next to her right hip. The illusion that made her appear to be the Werewife also hid the knife, or so the Low Prince had promised. So far, neither the Grandother nor Father Hunger had sensed the weapon's presence, which was good. She knew the instant either Eldred realized she was armed with such a dangerous weapon, one capable of killing their kind, they would flee or kill her. She didn't want to die, but she also didn't want the Eldred to escape. So she was doubly grateful that the glamour disguising her was working so well.

The only person not seated at the table – not counting Machine Head – was Father Hunger. They were in his Domain now, the Gastrotorium, and he was busy making final preparations for the feast ahead. The other Eldred, while looking quite different than their human guises, were still recognizable as the people Alex had met at the cookout. Not so with Father Hunger. He was an emaciated skeleton of a creature, naked, ivory-white flesh thin and stretched tight against his bones. He was bald, save for a few wisps of fine white hair that clung to his scalp. His stomach was sunken in so far, it looked as if his abdomen was empty of internal organs, and his genitals were so withered, they were little more than tiny nubs of flesh between his legs. The nails on his hands and feet were long, yellow, and chipped, and his skull-like face featured dark hollows for eyes, prominent cheekbones, and nonexistent lips drawn back to form a rictus of a mouth.

Like the other Eldred, Father Hunger had established his Domain inside the Raines house – in his case, in the kitchen. But his Domain was different from the others. The Low Prince, the Nonsister, the Grandother, and the Werewife had each created Domains that appeared to be real places – a mountain, a cave, a grove, a forest – rendered in intricate, and often horrifying, detail. But Father Hunger's Domain was more abstract. There was the long dining table, seats filled with Residuum Wraiths, and the floor – which appeared to stretch infinitely in all directions – was formed from a glossy black substance that looked like glass but felt hard and solid as rock. There were no walls, just empty space, as if the Gastrotorium was located on an infinite obsidian platform that was an entire reality in itself. There was air to breathe, but it felt artificial, as if it was being filtered through some sort of processing system. The horizon in all directions was a blank, featureless white, like pages of a sketch pad that no one had bothered to draw on.

Close by, maybe fifty, sixty feet from the section of the table where the Eldred and humans sat, large black spires rose from the obsidian floor. They were made of the same material as the floor. Indeed, they looked to be projections of it, rising into the air. There were four of them, two on the Eldred side of the table, two on the humans'. The spires – which the Nonsister had told her were called Extractors – were twenty feet tall, wide at the base and tapered to sharp points at the top. They made Alex think of large black fangs, as if they were sitting atop a gigantic mouth which could snap its jaws closed at any moment. Father Hunger had been fussing with the Extractors ever since Alex and the others had arrived. She wasn't sure what he was doing with them. He would hold out his hands, close his eyes, and mumble words to himself in a language Alex didn't recognize. The Nonsister whispered that her father was making the final preparations, and she left it at that. But as strange as the endless table, the spires, and the wraiths all were, none of them compared to what hung above them in the white blankness of what passed for a sky in the Gastrotorium.

A slowly swirling mass of color circled a darkness so deep, so absolute, so far beyond such simplistic concepts as *nothing* and *empty* as a nuclear bomb was beyond a guttering candle. Alex couldn't tell how close or far away the thing was from the table. Sometimes it seemed as if she could reach up and touch it, and other times it appeared so distant that it could never be reached in a thousand lifetimes of travel. A thousand-thousand.

During the walk out of the Ghostwood, the Low Prince had told her what to expect in the Gastrotorium.

Some call it the Gyre because of the swirling colors. Others know it as the Vast due to its immensity. And some simply call it Oblivion. It lies at the center of the Omniverse, tearing and clawing at all existence, breaking down reality, drawing the pieces into itself, and feasting on them. It is the closest thing my kind have to a god. We derive our power from it, and in return we must share our bounty with it. You will find it to be a most terrifying sight, but if you are to successfully impersonate the Werewife, you must not react to it. No matter how awful it seems to you, no matter how much you want to scream and keep screaming until the moment of your death, you must resist – for all our sakes.

At the time, Alex had thought he was laying it on a little thick, but now that she was here, looking up the Gyre, if anything, she thought the Low Prince had understated the impact of being in its presence. She felt small, so much so that she barely existed. All of her thoughts, her memories, her experiences and actions, every beat of her heart, every breath of her lungs, her very identity – none of it meant anything in the face of the Gyre. All of existence had one and only one purpose: to serve as food for the ravenous darkness contained within that swirl of color. The insignificant being that knew itself as Alex Ruiz was nothing more than a morsel, a crumb, a speck, born solely to grow, age, die, and be swallowed along with everything else that ever was or ever would be. God was an endlessly starving mouth and creation was its banquet. She was like a minnow tossed about by the devastating forces of a tsunami, and there was nothing she could do to fight it, could only let it sweep her along, fling her this way and that, its power threatening to tear her apart any moment....

She was almost lost, but the Nonsister, sensing her distress, reached out and placed a hand over hers, and she felt a chilly emotionless calm come over her. The Gyre was still there, still mind-blastingly terrifying, but now she could withstand its influence, could almost see it as beautiful in its own awful way.

She gave the Nonsister a grateful smile. The eyeless girl nodded and then removed her hand. Alex was afraid that without the Nonsister's touch, she'd experience the full force of the Gyre again, but she didn't. Whatever the Nonsister had done, it seemed to be lasting, and Alex was doubly grateful.

From what the siblings had told them back in the Ghostwood, the Eldred always ended a night of feeding with a celebratory feast called the Fete. Everything up to that point was merely an appetizer. The Fete was the main course. The Eldred fed on the psychic energy of humans. They set up shop in a suitable location, lured humans into their house using various illusions called Allurements, and then put them through scenarios designed especially for them, scenarios that would draw out their darkest emotions. The Eldred would feed on these as the night went on, and while some of the humans died, others survived to be finished off at the feast, a portion of their energy sacrificed to the Gyre. And when the Eldred had finished feeding, all that was left of the humans they'd captured were Residuum Wraiths. The Eldred would pack up and depart in search of somewhere else to set up shop, and then they'd do it all over again. Alex wondered how many stories of haunted houses throughout history were in truth tales of the Eldred feeding. *Maybe most of them,* she thought.

In the Ghostwood clearing, beneath the obscenely large moon, the Low Prince and Nonsister had explained their plan to the humans.

The Eldred were old, unimaginably so, and because there was no natural attrition among their kind, the only way they could rise in positions of power and authority was by killing those above them in the Eldred hierarchy. But this was far easier said than done. Since the assassination of senior Eldred was an accepted part of their culture, it was expected that one day the younger would attempt to assert dominance and slay the older.

Which makes it damn hard to take them by surprise, the Low Prince had said.

They're always expecting us to attack them, the Nonsister had added.

For centuries, the siblings had tried to devise a plan that their elders could not anticipate. But none of the ideas they came up with seemed to have even the slightest chance of success – until they hit upon the idea of using their prey to help them.

Humans could safely wield weapons that the Eldred could not. Weapons that could harm the Eldred, even destroy them. The Eldred spent most of their time together, but not all of it, and the Low Prince and Nonsister were able to go off by themselves and make contact with some of the other dark powers in the world and make deals with them to have two weapons made. One was a very special knife that could hurt Eldred, known as a Null Blade. The other was a substance called darkbane, harmless to humans but deadly to otherworldly beings. The Nonsister infused her malum fruit with darkbane, so any human who ingested it would possess a touch that would burn the Eldred's flesh like a powerful acid. Once their weapons were ready and they'd developed a plan for using them, all the siblings had to do was wait until it was time for the next feeding – which was this night.

The plan was simple. The humans would kill the Werewife, and the Low Prince and Nonsister would cast a glamour on one of them so that this person looked like the dead matriarch and could take her place at the Fete. Then, when the Grandother and Father Hunger were distracted, the humans would attack and kill them, leaving the Low Prince and Nonsister as the new heads of their much smaller family. In time, they would make more Eldred to join them and they would continue traveling the world, feeding on humanity as their kind had done for millennia.

Why would we help you? Neal had asked. *You killed Lola and Spencer – and Kandice.*

We needed to feed in order to keep up our strength for the battle to come, the Nonsister had said. *But what was taken from you can be restored. You help us, and we will see you are reunited with your loved ones.*

Nothing personal, Isaac had said, shooting Neal a quick glance, *but the rest of us didn't lose family. Why should we do anything to help these two overthrow their family? They kidnapped us and brought us to this goddamn spookhouse where they've psychologically tortured us.* He'd turned to the siblings then. *Why in the hell should we so much as lift a finger to help you?*

The Low Prince had smiled then, displaying sharp white teeth that gleamed in the moonlight.

Because if you don't, we'll eat you and try again with the next group of humans we gather.

They had no reason to trust the siblings, and they knew that if they helped them, they might well end up as dinner anyway. But it was the only chance they had to survive this night, so they'd agreed.

Once the glamour was cast on Alex and she took on the Werewife's appearance, the siblings led them through the Ghostwood and back to the house – which was now visible to all of them. They entered through the patio door and then were taken to the Gastrotorium as the siblings' 'prisoners', where they were quickly put into the cathedra to await the beginning of the Fete.

Father Hunger finished with the last Extractor and came walking toward the table. Alex remembered what the Low Prince had told them about the obsidian spires. *In many ways, the Eldred are like those tiny fish that swim into the mouths of larger fish and clean out any bits of food stuck between their teeth. We sacrifice humans to get the Gyre to open its mouth, as it were, and then we use the Extractors to draw energy from the food stuck in its metaphorical teeth.*

So you're parasites, Isaac said.

The Low Prince had bristled at that. *We prefer to think of it as symbiosis.*

Alex and the others had learned that the house's extra dimensions and interior elements – such as the infinite dining table and the Extractors – had been delivered to the Eldred by entities they referred to only as Movers. Alex remembered the strange shadow-enshrouded truck that had been parked in the front of the Raines house several days ago. The thought of the alien thing made her want to shudder. The creatures the Eldred used – the Allurements, the skullheads, the patchworks – were all glamours created from the Eldred's own substance and employed as avatars or puppets. In the end, the only things haunting the house were the Eldred themselves.

As Father Hunger drew near the table, he reached out with his right hand. It vanished for a second, and when it reappeared, it held a dust-covered unlabeled wine bottle.

"Sorry that took so long, but you know how difficult it is to get the energy matrices just right." His voice was a dry rasp, like sandpaper polishing bone.

When he reached the table, he put the bottle down in front of his empty chair with a *thunk*.

"I've chosen something special for tonight's Fete. I think you're going to really enjoy it."

As he spoke, Alex saw that half his teeth were missing, and the rest – yellow and crooked – jutted from sore, bleeding gums.

"What is it, Father?" the Nonsister asked.

"The final breaths of the men, women, and children who died at Buchenwald."

No one replied at first, and the Nonsister dug her nails into Alex's leg to prompt her. She turned to look at Father Hunger and attempted a smile.

"Lovely," she said.

Father Hunger smiled, the action causing his thin lips to crack and leak clear fluid in several places. He gestured with his free hand and crystal goblets appeared on the table in front of the Grandother, the Nonsister, the Low Prince, and Alex. One appeared at Father Hunger's place as well. He looked back over a cadaverous shoulder and said, "Machine Head, if you'll do the honors?" Then he pulled out his chair and sat as the family's cyborg servant came forward, dragging his bad leg, which seemed to be getting worse by the minute. He reached past Father Hunger to pick up the bottle, raised it to his mouth, and his metal jaw dropped open, revealing jagged teeth. He placed the corked end of the bottle in his mouth and bit down hard.

There was a crunching sound, and when he pulled the bottle away from his mouth, the cork and a portion of the neck were gone. He paused, chewed, then swallowed the glass. The cork he spit out onto the floor. He then poured the 'wine' into Father Hunger's goblet. It was black and thick as tar, and it had a harsh, acrid odor that Alex knew was the scent of the gas the Nazis had used to exterminate their victims. Alex prayed she wouldn't have to drink the horrid stuff. She didn't think she could bring herself to choke it down, even to save her own life and the lives of her father and their neighbors.

Machine Head filled her goblet next, and he continued down the line until the rest of the Eldred's goblets were full. He then returned the nearly empty bottle to the table in front of Father Hunger. It might've been Alex's imagination, but she thought Machine Head paused to look at Vivienne – sitting frozen in her cathedra – a moment before going back to his place behind the Eldred to await further commands.

Once Machine Head had returned to his post, Father Hunger took his goblet in hand and stood once more.

"A toast!" he said. "To the Raines family, without whom tonight would not have been possible."

The Grandother, the Low Prince, and the Nonsister raised their goblets, and while Alex didn't want to so much as touch hers – let alone taste its contents – she picked it up and held it out before her, almost as if the goblet were a venomous snake that might bite her at any moment. She supposed that in a way, it was.

The Grandother looked at Father Hunger.

"That's a bit disingenuous, don't you think?" Her voice held the harsh undertone of a crow's caw. "After all, our presence here these last few days is what caused Cherie Raines to lose her mind in the first place."

Alex wasn't sure she understood what the Grandother was saying. Was it possible that the Eldred's malign influence could echo backward in time to affect the Raines family? It didn't seem possible, but then the Eldred weren't bound by natural laws, were they?

Father Hunger shrugged.

"Perhaps you're right. Still, when did we ever allow a trifling thing like cause and effect get in our way?"

The Grandother smiled, displaying her razor-blade teeth.

She held her goblet with one of her foot claws, and now she brought it to her lips and drained it in a single gulp. Father Hunger drank his, as did the Low Prince and the Nonsister.

It was Alex's turn.

Neither the Nonsister nor the Low Prince had warned her about this part, and she looked at both of them now, seeking guidance. The Low Prince kept his face impassive, but the Nonsister gave the tiniest of shrugs, as if to say she was sorry.

In the Ghostwood, the siblings had impressed upon her the importance of maintaining the Werewife disguise as long as possible.

The longer she could maintain the ruse, the better chance they had for success. *It's possible for Father Hunger and the Grandother to see through any glamour,* the Nonsister had said. *But they have to suspect that there's a glamour in the first place. They will have no reason to suspect you aren't who you appear to be — unless you give them a reason.*

She looked at the thick sludge in her goblet. Could it really be the last breaths of Holocaust victims distilled into liquid form? The idea was insane, but no more so than anything else she'd experienced in the house tonight. What would drinking the foul stuff do to her? She was human, not Eldred. Would it make her ill, drive her insane, *kill* her? How could she take that risk? She looked across the table at her father, at Neal, at Martin and Cora, but most of all, at Vivienne. All of them remained frozen in their cathedra, but she thought they were all aware of what was happening. She couldn't have said why. It was just a feeling. She was the only one of them that could move, and they were all depending on her to play her role well and give them a chance for survival — and in Neal's case, a chance to be reunited with Kandice. She didn't know if she could drink the black sludge, but she knew she had to try.

She attempted to keep her hand steady as she raised the goblet toward her lips. When she'd first lifted it off the table, she'd been surprised at how heavy it was, like it was filled with lead instead of liquid. But considering what the substance in the goblet was, why wouldn't it be heavy? It contained the concentrated terror, despair, sorrow, and anger of who knew how many men, women, and children? The goblet was so heavy that she was unable to keep her hand from trembling any longer. The black muck was thick enough that it didn't spill over the edge as the goblet shook, but the longer she held it one-handed, the greater the chance that it would spill. She used both hands then, and while the goblet still shook a little, she was able to hold it much steadier. She could feel the Eldred watching her intently. She didn't look at them, though, kept her gaze focused on the goblet, but she imagined the Grandother and Father Hunger looking at her — at who they thought was the Werewife — and sensing that something was wrong.

She brought the black liquid to her lips and was about to take her first sip when the chemical odor wafted up her nose and seared her nasal passages.

Fuck this, she thought.

She turned toward Father Hunger and flung the contents of the goblet in his face. Then she dropped the crystal container to the ebony ground, where it shattered into a thousand pieces. As Father Hunger sputtered and tried to wipe the viscous black substance from his eyes, she grabbed hold of the Null Blade and thrust it toward his midsection.

CHAPTER TWENTY-THREE

Back in the Ghostwood, the Nonsister had told Neal and the others what to expect when they were put into the cathedra. But there was nothing the siblings could've said that would've prepared them for the reality of it. The instant they sat down and the skeletal hands grabbed hold of them, their bodies stopped working. Oh, their autonomic functions continued – their hearts still beat, their lungs still breathed, their eyes still blinked – but they could exert no control. They were unable to so much as twitch a finger. Hell, they couldn't even move their eyes in order to look in a different direction.

Out of all the bizarre things that Neal had experienced this night – things that had forever destroyed his science-based view of the world he'd held as a physics teacher – sitting paralyzed in a chair made of bones and being forced to watch events play out without any possibility of affecting their outcome came near to breaking him. These motherfuckers were responsible for Kandice's death, and he wanted to make them pay. The Nonsister and Low Prince, too, and to hell with the deal they'd made. He didn't believe for a second that the siblings would honor it anyway. But if he couldn't move, how could he make the Eldred pay?

He wasn't clear on how the siblings had brought them to the Gastrotorium. The moment they'd entered the house, they were just suddenly here. He'd seen the Gyre then, and although the siblings had warned them about it, said it would be wisest not to look at it directly, Neal hadn't been able to resist. He wished he'd listened to them. The thing resembled the popular conception of a black hole, but it was so much more. It was the End of All Things, the Final Destination, the Last Train West, the Omega to the Alpha.... It was what all creation was working toward. Everything that had ever happened since the Beginning, every random event, every conscious action, all had the same end: to process reality into nonexistence. The universe had been committing slow suicide since the moment it was born, and Neal could think of nothing more horrifying than this realization.

He'd almost lost consciousness then, but he focused on his pain over Kandice's loss, stoked his grief and fury like a fire until it was a blazing inferno. And it worked. He no longer gave a shit about the Gyre. Let the universe eat itself. All he cared about was avenging Kandice. But to do that, he needed to be able to fucking *move*.

He watched as Father Hunger finished with the Extractors and approached the table, pulling a bottle out of thin air. He watched him sit, then he watched Machine Head bite open the bottle and pour its contents into the Eldred's goblets – as well as Alex's. Neal was seated directly across from Alex, and although he knew she was cloaked in some kind of illusion, he could've sworn that he was looking at the real Werewife. But as he watched her lift the goblet, he saw her hand shake, and he knew that if *he* saw it, the Grandother and Father Hunger did, too. Alex tried to use both hands to steady her grip, and that helped, but despite the illusion disguising her, she exuded none of the Werewife's strength and confidence. She looked scared, and while he didn't blame her, knew that if their positions were reversed, he'd probably be pissing his pants right now, he feared she was going to be exposed, and if that happened, they were all as good as dead.

Evidently, Alex came to the same conclusion, for at the last instant before the thick, black substance could touch her lips, she flung its contents at Father Hunger's face, dropped the goblet to the floor, grabbed the Null Blade, and attacked him. Father Hunger managed to turn to the side in time to avoid a fatal blow, but the Null Blade's tip slipped between the prominent ribs on the left side of his body and penetrated a lung. He cried out in pain and pushed himself back from the table. His chair tipped over, and as he fell, the Null Blade went with him, the handle pulling free from Alex's hand an instant before he hit the floor.

As soon as Father Hunger was down, the glamour surrounding Alex faded, and her true appearance was revealed. Upon seeing Alex, the Grandother shrieked with outrage. But before she could attack, the Low Prince turned and lunged at her. At the same instant, the Nonsister snapped her fingers and whatever force held the bones of the cathedra together dissipated, and the chairs fell apart beneath Neal and the others, dumping them unceremoniously to the floor. With the chairs' destruction, the humans' paralysis ended, and they were free to act.

Father Hunger didn't collapse into smoke as the Werewife had done when she'd been wounded by the Null Blade. Maybe the Werewife had suffered a deeper strike, or maybe Father Hunger was stronger than her. Whatever the reason, he did not die, although the skin where he'd been wounded turned black. He jumped to his feet and jerked the knife free. He hissed in pain when his hand came into contact with the blade's handle and the skin on his palm and fingers began to blacken. But instead of dropping the weapon, he hurled it at Alex. The blade *thunked* into her forehead and penetrated her brain. The impact caused her head to snap back, but she didn't go down right away. She straightened and reached up to touch the handle, as if she wasn't sure what had just happened. Blood ran from the wound, between her eyes, and onto her nose, where it dripped like crimson snot. She opened her mouth to say something, but then her eyes rolled white and she collapsed to the ground, dead.

The humans had all gotten to their feet by this point, and Isaac released an anguished howl upon seeing his daughter die. He dove under the table, came up on the other side, and went for Father Hunger, hands held out before him. He'd eaten the tainted malum fruit in the Night Grove, and his flesh was now deadly to the Eldred.

"Fry his ass!" Neal shouted.

Father Hunger turned his attention to Isaac and brought his own hands up, ready to fight. And that's when the Nonsister attacked him. She leaped like a jungle cat, her fingers becoming sharp animal claws. Father Hunger waited until she was almost upon him, then he struck her a vicious backhanded blow, sending her flying. Unfortunately for Isaac, she flew straight toward him. She struck him hard, and they both went down in a tangle of arms and legs. She lay on the smooth obsidian floor, the skin on her face, neck, and arms dissolving where Isaac had actually touched her when they'd collided. Isaac was unconscious – or perhaps dead – and didn't see what he'd accidentally done to the Nonsister. The Eldred girl thrashed on the ground, screaming in pain as the flesh in the wounded areas was eaten away by darkbane.

Neal, Martin, Cora, and Vivienne watched as The Low Prince and the Grandother fought, the former using claw hands like his sister's, the harpy using her talons, wings flapping to keep her in the air just high enough so she could strike out with her feet. The Low Prince and the Grandother were wounded, but like Father Hunger, they bled clear fluid instead of blood.

The Residuum Wraiths remained in their chairs, but they seemed agitated by the violence happening around them. They moved from side to side, and they had trouble maintaining the integrity of their mist-like bodies.

Cora made a move then. Before Martin could stop her, she ducked under the table just as Isaac had, came up on the other side, rushed up behind the Grandother, and jumped onto the birdwoman's back. She dug her darkbane-infused hands into the Grandother's feathers and began clawing at the flesh. The Grandother's shriek was so loud and high-pitched that it felt as if a pair of white-hot spikes had been driven into Neal's ears. Cora's extra weight pulled the Grandother down, and they fell to the ground, the birdwoman shrieking and flapping her wings frantically, Cora keeping her deadly hands thrust into the Grandother's flesh.

The Low Prince grinned and moved in to attack.

The Grandother had been the one who'd killed Kandice, and now that the bitch was down, Neal saw his chance to avenge his wife. The Null Blade was still embedded in Alex's skull. All he had to do was run over, pull it out, and then he could use it to kill the Grandother. He needed to get on the other side of the table and—

Before Neal could move, Martin told Vivienne to hide under the table. Then he climbed onto its surface, jumped over to the other side, and dashed toward Alex's body. Cora was helping the Low Prince fight the Grandother, and Martin intended to go to his wife's aid.

"No!" Neal shouted. "That bitch is mine! You can't have her!"

He climbed onto the table, took three steps, then launched himself toward Martin. The man was crouching next to Alex, tugging on the Null Blade with his right hand – the one that still had all its fingers – but no matter how hard he pulled, the weapon remained stubbornly stuck. Neal slammed into Martin and knocked him to the ground. He, of course, went down, too. The wind was knocked out of him, and he felt a sharp pain in his left wrist. He wasn't sure, but he thought he'd broken it. Martin recovered first. He stood, staggered back to Alex, and this time when he pulled on the Null Blade, it came free. He looked down at Neal, who still lay on the ground, struggling to get his breath back.

"What the fuck is *wrong* with you, man?"

Martin's hand tightened around the Null Blade's handle, and for a moment, Neal thought the man would plunge it into his heart.

At that moment, two things happened. The Nonsister – back on her feet – rushed past them to attack Father Hunger once more, and the Grandother kicked the Low Prince off of her with superhuman strength. He traveled toward the table with such force that when he struck the edge of the table – which, due to its vast length and mass, didn't budge – he plowed right through it in an explosion of splintered wood. A scream sounded at the same time – a little girl's scream. The Low Prince traveled some distance before he hit the ground in front of an Extractor, rolled, and came to a stop. But Neal barely registered this. He was looking at Vivienne, who'd been hiding under the table at the exact spot where the Low Prince had gone through. Both arms and one of her legs were broken – a jagged end of bone poking through the leg – and her body had been pierced by numerous splinters of wood, some small, some large. The longest of these protruded from her throat. Blood bubbled from the wound with a horrible wheezing, sucking sound as Vivienne tried to breathe, but then her eyes glazed over and the wheezing stopped.

Martin's face went pale, his eyes widened with shock, and he drew in a rapid breath – probably to cry out in horror, Neal thought – only to be cut off when Cora screamed.

Now that the Grandother no longer had to contend with the Low Prince, at least for the moment, she could focus all her attention on Cora. The woman had burned multiple wounds into the harpy's back with her darkbane hands. But now the Grandother knocked her to the ground with a blow from her wing. She then leaped into the air, angled backward, flapped her wings once, and drove her body hard toward the floor, back-first – directly onto Cora. The Grandother hit the glassy obsidian surface with the muffled sound of multiple bones snapping. Neal knew none of those bones belonged to the Grandother, though.

The harpy rose to her feet and, with an expression of cruel satisfaction, turned to look at Cora's remains. The woman was a broken, crushed thing, with blood splattered all over and around her. She looked more like pieces of raw meat that had been arranged to suggest a human shape more than something that had been a living person only a few seconds ago.

Martin screamed.

He wasn't the only one. Machine Head – who until this point had made no move to assist either side – shouted *"No!"* in his toneless mechanical voice. *"NO-NO-NO!"* He half ran, half limped past the Grandother, past Cora's body, his shoes tracking through her blood. He ran through the open space in the table the Low Prince had created until he reached Vivienne's body. He fell to his knees next to her, getting her blood on him, and he bowed his head.

"No-no-no-no-no-no-no-no-no," he said over and over, without pause.

Martin, standing only a few feet away from Neal, dropped the Null Blade to the ground and took a step toward Cora's body. He stopped, looked at Machine Head holding his broken daughter, took a step toward them, but then stopped once more. He stood there, shocked and grief-stricken, not knowing what to do next. Neal and Kandice had never had children, so Neal didn't know what it was like to lose one. He did know what it was like to lose a wife, though, and despite the differences he had with Martin, he felt a terrible kinship with him now.

Isaac remained unconscious, and the Nonsister and Father Hunger still fought – biting, scratching, and clawing at each other – and they were too busy to notice what had happened. The Low Prince was only now struggling to his feet, but he'd landed so far away that he likely wasn't aware of Cora and Vivienne's deaths yet, nor of Martin's pain at their loss.

The Grandother, though, watched Martin closely, eyes wide, mouth open, razor blade teeth visible, a line of drool running from the corner of her mouth. The Eldred fed on negative emotions, and right now the birdwoman was glutting herself on Martin's shock and sorrow. Neal had wanted to kill the feathered bitch before, but now he wanted to make her *suffer*. He bent down, grabbed the Null Blade, and started toward the Grandother. But as he moved past Martin, the other man grabbed his arm and stopped him.

"He gave me a pass," Martin said, voice so soft that Neal almost couldn't hear him.

"What?"

"Earlier, at the cookout, I made a bet with Arnoldo...Father Hunger. I won and he gave me a pass. He said it was only good once, and I could use it to get out of a bad situation. Or, if I used it fast enough, I could undo something that had gone wrong. Just one thing, though."

Neal didn't entirely understand what Martin was saying, but after spending the night in this twisted funhouse from hell, he knew better than to dismiss the man's words.

Martin looked from Cora's body to Vivienne's, and back again. Then his shoulders slumped, he hung his head, and let out a weary sigh.

"I'm sorry, honey."

Vivienne was suddenly standing on her feet, whole and uninjured. Neal hadn't seen her rise. He wasn't sure she had. One instant she was lying on the ground, dead and broken, the next she was standing up, as if she'd never been hurt in the first place. *Kind of like Schrödinger's cat,* Neal thought. Only now, thanks to Martin and his mysterious pass, the cat was definitely alive.

Machine Head rose to his feet as well, eyes shining a bright green, as if in joy. He clapped his hands together like a child and said, *"Friend!"*

Vivienne didn't look at him, though, didn't seem to notice him. She hadn't witnessed her mother's death, having been dead at the time herself, but now she saw Cora's crushed body and she screamed.

"Take care of my girl, Neal."

Before Neal could ask what Martin meant, he snatched the Null Blade from Neal's hand and started running toward the Grandother. She watched him come, black bird-eyes gleaming with anticipation, mouth stretched wide into a razor-blade smile. She didn't take to the air to avoid Martin's attack. Maybe Cora had managed to damage one or both of the harpy's wings. Or maybe the Grandother was so enjoying the flood of negative emotion coming off Martin that she was intoxicated by it and not thinking clearly. Whichever the case, the Grandother simply stood there, wings folded against her body, and waited.

Martin roared with fury as he closed in on the Grandother, and he raised the Null Blade high over his head. And then, moving so swiftly that she was a blur, the Grandother jumped into the air and lashed out with one set of talons, opening up Martin from throat to crotch as easily as unzipping a garment. Blood and organs slid out of Martin in a glistening wet mass and hit the floor with a series of wet slaps. Martin stood for several seconds, as if the fact he was dead hadn't sunk in yet. He even turned to look at Vivienne one last time. And then his body went limp and he collapsed.

Vivienne's scream was even louder this time. She started to run toward her father, but Machine Head put a surprisingly gentle hand on her shoulder to stop her.

"Me," he said.

Vivienne, tears streaming down her face, breathing coming in hitching sobs, nodded.

Machine Head turned away from her to face the Grandother. The green lights in his eyes changed to a fiery red. He ran through the opening in the table toward the Grandother, moving faster than his human body should've been capable of. Slowly, almost lazily, the Grandother turned to meet his charge.

She tried to gut Machine Head the same way she had Martin, and she succeeded. But Machine Head wasn't human. The bodies he used to get around might be, but *he* was something different, something more. He kept moving, forced his way past the Grandother's slashing talons, organs still attached and being dragged behind him. He locked his hands around the Grandother's throat and began to squeeze. The Grandother struggled, frantically flapping her wings, but she was unable to break free from Machine Head's grip. Her face reddened, darkened to purple, and Machine Head began chanting in his monotone robot voice.

"*Momma-had-a-baby-and-its-head-popped*-off!"

On the last word, Machine Head gave one final powerful squeeze, and the Grandother's head did indeed pop off. It shot upward in a fountain of blood, came down, hit the floor, bounced a couple times, and rolled before at last coming to a stop next to Cora's crushed body.

The harpy's headless body slipped away from Machine Head's hands and fell to the floor, lifeless.

Machine Head – now absolutely drenched in the Grandother's blood – displayed no sign of satisfaction at what he'd done. His eyes, however, returned to their usual green. He then turned around and walked back to Vivienne. Halfway there, he reached down and ripped his organs the rest of the way out of his body, as if he were annoyed at having to drag them. When he reached Vivienne, the girl hugged his legs, heedless of the gore all over them, and he put a hand on her shoulder. The message was clear. Machine Head intended to protect the girl. She was his only concern, which meant Neal would have to deal with Father Hunger alone.

Well, not *quite* alone. All this time, the Nonsister had been holding her own against Father Hunger. She faded out of existence to avoid his blows, appearing once more when she was ready to strike. This wasn't a perfect tactic, however. Sometimes he moved swiftly enough to land a blow before she could vanish, and sometimes he managed to avoid her strikes when she reappeared. But the Nonsister still lived, still fought, and Neal was impressed by how tough she was.

The Low Prince staggered through the opening in the table, his body leaning to the left, as if the leg on that side didn't work quite right, and his right arm hung at his side, useless. Several of the bone spikes protruding from his head had broken when he'd landed after being thrown by the Grandother, and now he looked as if he were wearing half a crown. Neal didn't understand. The Eldred were powerful supernatural beings. Why couldn't they simply heal themselves? The answer came to him immediately. The Eldred might not operate according to physical laws he understood, but they didn't have access to infinite energy. They needed to restore their strength by feeding from time to time, and by drawing power from the Gyre. The Low Prince and the Nonsister's coup attempt had interrupted that feeding before it could reach its climax. To put it succinctly, the fucking monsters were running out of gas.

The Low Prince didn't look to Neal as he went by, but he said, "Get the blade."

And then, moving with an awkward lurching gait, he picked

up speed and ran the rest of the way to join his sister in the battle against Father Hunger.

Neal shifted his gaze to Isaac and saw he'd returned to consciousness. He'd pushed himself into a sitting position and was struggling to rise to his feet. When he was halfway there, he winced, and Neal knew that he was injured. How severely was impossible to say, but when he managed to stand all the way up, he immediately hunched over, as if it was too painful to remain completely upright. He didn't look as if he was going to be much help.

Neal had to get the Null Blade. Neither the Nonsister nor the Low Prince could wield it without damaging themselves, and Isaac was in no shape to use it. It had to be him. But before he could start walking, one of the Residuum Wraiths drifted in front of him. He moved to the side to go past it, but it glided back to intercept him and block his way once more.

What the hell?

The sounds of the battle increased in volume and ferocity as the Low Prince and the Nonsister both fought Father Hunger. Maybe the two of them together would be a match for him, but Neal doubted it. He *had* to get that blade! He feinted to the right, and when the wraith moved that way, he went left.

Only to find his way blocked by two other wraiths. All the others, while clearly agitated, remained in their seats. Only these three had gotten up. The first wraith joined the two newcomers, and the trio stood...well, not *looking* at Neal since they had no eyes, but *regarding* him. He could sense their interest in him, almost as if they wanted to communicate. And there was something familiar about them too, but he couldn't say what it was. Aside from some variation in height and shape, they looked exactly alike – featureless beings made of insubstantial white mist. The first wraith came toward him, moving in so close that their bodies almost touched. It leaned its head forward and the lower half of where its face should've been came into contact with his lips.

And he felt Kandice's kiss.

The wraith drew back then, but it remained close. Neal stared at it in amazement, and looked at the other two.

"Lola? Spencer?"

They nodded.

From what the siblings had told them in the Ghostwood, the Residuum Wraiths weren't spirits in the classical sense. They weren't ghostly versions of human beings that had died, possessing the same memories and personalities they'd had in life. The wraiths were more like echoes or afterimages. Impressions of the people they'd once been, like footprints in sand.

But he had felt Kandice in that kiss, felt her *love*.

Maybe, he thought, the Eldred didn't quite know everything.

He wondered if Cora, Martin, and Alex were here as well, if they had returned as wraiths. The siblings had said the wraiths were what remained after they fed on humans. Martin, Cora, and Alex hadn't been fed on. They'd been killed outright. So if what the siblings had said was true, the three of them were gone for good. While Neal was glad that even a small portion of Kandice still existed, in whatever form, he didn't have time to stand there marveling at her return. He needed to get to the Null Blade.

But then the other Residuum Wraiths drifted out of their chairs and came toward him, dozens of them, enclosing him within a circle of white mist. Kandice – or rather her echo – leaned close to his ear and began whispering. And he listened closely.

CHAPTER TWENTY-FOUR

Isaac's vision was blurry, and his head pounded like a motherfucker. And there was something wrong inside him, too. If he moved wrong, something shifted, causing him pain so intense that he saw a bright flash of light behind his eyes, making him feel as if he was close to passing out again. There was noise nearby – snarling and shrieking and growling, along with awful tearing sounds. The noise made his head hurt worse, and that, in turn, made it difficult to think. He knew who he was, knew where he worked, remembered the bullshit departmental politics that was the bane of his existence. Remembered lazy, unmotivated students who couldn't be bothered to look up from their phone screens for a few goddamn seconds, let alone for an entire class period. But he couldn't for the life of him remember where the hell he was, how he'd gotten here, or – far more importantly, how he'd gotten hurt. He was fairly certain that he needed to get to a hospital, but when he checked his pants pockets, he found he didn't have his phone on him. Fantastic.

A fragment of memory returned to him then, of…Sara. Her standing by the side of his bed, beckoning him to follow, him dressing quickly and going after her, outside, down the sidewalk to…to….

The house.

As he'd been thinking, he'd begun taking small shuffling steps, not aware that he was doing so. It was as if his body was operating on autopilot, trying to get him away from this place – wherever it was – and to somewhere safe, or at least safer. He walked with his head down, chin to his chest. His head hurt less that way. The surface he walked on was a strange, glossy black, like highly polished stone, and he wondered what it—

Then a hand came into his view and he stopped. The hand lay on the ground, motionless. It was a woman's hand, he thought. A familiar one. Not Sara's, though. Her hands were smaller, the fingers delicate and slender. He raised his head, gritting his teeth from the pain this motion caused, and he moved his gaze from the woman's hand to her arm, then to her shoulder – he saw she was wearing a T-shirt, though for some reason it was covered in something red and sticky. He felt the first stirring of fear as he moved to look at her face. He almost didn't do it, told himself that he wasn't going to like what he saw. But he looked anyway.

He saw Alex's face – his *daughter's* face – eyes open, a wound of some sort in the middle of her forehead.

And then his memories returned, all of them, and he wished they hadn't. The house. The Undercountry. The Ghostwood. The fucking *Eldred*. He saw Alex hurl a knife at the emaciated naked thing that called itself Father Hunger. Saw the monster yank the blade from his side, the flesh there as well as on his hand blackening. Saw him throw the knife back at Alex, saw it strike her in the head and…and….

He felt tears coming, and he almost surrendered to them, but he fought them back. All of his life, his anger had been his greatest strength. It had helped him conquer schoolyard bullies, helped him get through high school, college, grad school, his doctoral program. It had helped him survive his divorce from the only woman he'd ever really loved. And if he was going to make that fucking beanpole of a monster pay for what he'd done to Alex – poor, sweet Alex, who'd deserved a much better father than he'd been to her – it was his anger that he needed.

He forced his head up the rest of the way and fought the resultant wave of vertigo and accompanying nausea. He looked around slowly, assessing his situation. Father Hunger, the Low Prince, and the Nonsister were fighting like wild animals, biting and clawing one another. It was difficult to tell which, if any, had the upper hand, but if he had to pick one, he'd have gone with Father Hunger. Hadn't the siblings told them in the Ghostwood that he was the oldest and strongest of their kind?

Isaac kept turning his head, doing his best to ignore the stabbing pain behind his eyes. He saw Cora's squashed body, saw Martin's gutted one – Null Blade gripped in his right hand – saw that harpy bitch the Grandother had been decapitated. That, at least, was good news. He continued swiveling his head until he saw Vivienne standing on the other side of the impossibly long table – which someone or something had broken to create a path through. Machine Head stood next to the girl, and she was holding on to the creature's legs as she watched the three other monsters fight. And lastly, he saw Neal. The man was surrounded by what the siblings called Residuum Wraiths – a lot of them. It looked like one of them was speaking to him and he was listening, but if so, Isaac hadn't a clue what they might be talking about.

After a moment's reflection, it seemed to Isaac that what he needed to do was clear. He started walking toward the Null Blade.

★   ★   ★

Neal was so caught up in listening to Kandice's wraith that at first he didn't notice Isaac making his way toward Martin's corpse. It was difficult to make out what Kandice was saying because she didn't speak in words exactly, more like concepts that she was somehow able to directly implant into his mind. It was weird, but kind of cool, too. But eventually, Isaac's movements – slow and halting though they were – caught his attention. He realized that Isaac was going for the Null Blade. But even if he reached it, there was no way he could wield it effectively in his current state.

He returned his attention to Kandice's wraith.

"Okay, I understand. I'm ready."

The wraiths in front of him moved aside to allow him through. Neal felt an impulse to give Kandice's wraith a kiss before he left, but he blinked and then was no longer sure which of the ones close to him was her. He sighed, shook his head at the absurdity of it all, then started running toward Martin.

And that's when Father Hunger tore the Low Prince in two.

★   ★   ★

Isaac heard the Low Prince's death scream, and for an instant the agony in his head quadrupled in intensity, and he feared his brain might literally explode. But the pain receded enough for him to turn and see Father Hunger standing over the two halves of the Low Prince's body. His head had grown huge, and his mouth was filled with six-inch long dinosaur teeth. Clear viscous fluid dripped from his mouth instead of blood, but there were shreds of flesh stuck between those hideous teeth.

Father Hunger, it seemed, had gotten tired of fucking around.

The Nonsister stood nearby, staring in disbelief at her brother's dead body. Then, as if to purposely add insult to injury, Father Hunger reached down, grabbed hold of the Low Prince's head, and twisted it off the upper half of his body. He then hurled it at the Nonsister. The remaining spikes on her brother's head slammed into her own head, breaking through the bone and sinking into her brain. The impact knocked her backward, but the Low Prince's head remained stuck fast in hers as she crashed to the floor.

Father Hunger's head shrunk back to its normal size, and he stepped over to the Nonsister's prone form, looked down, and laughed. His body was covered with wounds – some small, some large – that leaked the clear fluid the Eldred had instead of blood, but these injuries didn't seem to bother him.

"Well played, girl! You and your brother almost had me. But I've lived too long and acquired too much power to be easily defeated."

Father Hunger looked up then and trained his gaze on Isaac, as if only just now realizing the man was still alive.

"I should simply walk over to you and snap your neck, but I'm feeling in an especially good mood right now, so I think I'll expend some of the power remaining to me to give you a very special send-off."

Father Hunger gestured, and Isaac felt an unseen force lift him off his feet and begin carrying him upward—

—to the Gyre.

*　　*　　*

Neal watched in horror as Isaac rose into the air, slowly at first, and then with increasing speed, hurtling upward so fast that he was soon lost to view. He thought of Isaac watching the Gyre – already seeming immense – grow ever larger as he flew toward it. He didn't bother wondering exactly what sort of space Isaac traveled through, how he could breathe there, how his body could withstand the force that was bearing him along at what surely were speeds no human could withstand. The logic of the outer world meant nothing in here, not inside the house.

Father Hunger gazed upward, chuckling merrily to himself. He hadn't noticed Neal, Vivienne, or Machine Head yet, and the Residuum Wraiths quickly surrounded them, hiding them from Father Hunger's view. The ones in the forefront of the group around Neal began milling about, seeming aimless and confused, in order – he assumed – to give the impression that they weren't doing anything purposeful. Again, he wondered just how much of their former intelligence the wraiths retained. One thing was certain. They were far from mindless creatures.

He felt a gentle nudge against his back. A wraith – Kandice? – was prodding him with a semisolid hand. The message was clear: start walking. Neal did so, making sure to move slowly and silently. He couldn't see where the wraiths were taking him – their combined mass blocked his view as well as Father Hunger's – but he had a good idea. They were escorting him toward Martin and the Null Blade.

★   ★   ★

Isaac's flight was remarkably steady and smooth. He would've much preferred to tumble wildly, end over end, spinning so fast that his eyes were unable to focus on anything, the images flashing by so quickly that his mind was unable to process them. Instead, he flew straight and sure, his body held at an orientation that gave him a perfect, uninterrupted view of the Gyre. He could close his eyes; he knew this. And for a while he did. But he kept flying for what felt like hours, and eventually he couldn't stand it anymore. He had to look to see how close the Gyre was now.

Just a peek….

He opened his eyes and saw that the Gyre didn't look any closer than it had when Father Hunger had first sent him on his journey to the center of the Omniverse. And that's when he knew he was in this for the long haul. After that, he didn't bother to keep his eyes closed anymore. What was the point?

He spent the hours – days, weeks, months, years – trying to understand what was happening to him, if for no other reason than to give him something to do. He knew this would ultimately prove to be an exercise in futility, though. How could even the most intelligent human – and while he was smart, he knew he wasn't even in the same fucking ballpark as the greatest geniuses his race had ever produced – ever hope to comprehend all of *this*?

Too bad Neal wasn't here. As a physics teacher he would've had a much better shot at comprehending at least some of what was happening, even if only the merest fraction. But Isaac was a sociologist, and he would have to make do with the mind and training he had.

The Gyre, at least in his perception of it, did not appear to be located in physical space. It did not lie nestled amid a great expanse of blackness dotted with glittering stars. There was nothing around it – literally. Aside from the Gyre, there was only white in all directions. He'd taken an art class as a gen ed requirement during his undergrad years, and he remembered the professor saying that white is a combination of all colors, while black is the absence of color. So there was white (everything), the swirling colors of the Gyre (pieces of reality being separated from each other), and the black (where those pieces were absorbed). From Everything into Nothing. It was really a fairly simple process when looked at that way.

But he didn't feel like he was flying through *everything*. Just emptiness. But if that's all it was, how could he breathe? Assuming he *was* breathing. He'd tried inhaling and exhaling on purpose, but he wasn't sure if he was truly breathing or if his body was merely pretending to. If there was no atmosphere here, there was no air pressure. So why hadn't he immediately died from explosive decompression, like an astronaut trapped outside his ship without a spacesuit? Why hadn't he died of thirst? The human body could only go a short time – a week, maybe less – without water. And while humans could go without food longer than that, perhaps up to a month, he felt certain he'd been traveling longer than that. But not only hadn't he starved to death, he hadn't been hungry, not once. He didn't need to sleep, either, though he wished to god he could. Sleeping would at least give him some respite from this never-ending journey he'd been sent on. Maybe this was Hell, or at least *his* Hell.

But he eventually abandoned this idea, for it was predicated on the idea that he was important enough to have an entire Hell created just for him, and even he didn't have that big of an ego.

His hair didn't grow, nor did his beard. His fingernails remained the same length as when he'd begun his journey. He didn't know about his toenails. It was a bit chilly in this Nowhereverse, and he wanted to keep his shoes and socks on, was afraid he might accidentally lose hold of them if he removed them to examine his toenails, and the socks would fly away out of his reach, leaving him with cold feet for eternity.

Oddly enough, he didn't have difficulty accepting the Gyre and what its existence implied about the true nature of reality. The Nonsister and the Low Prince had warned them that they would see the Gyre in the Gastrotorium, and they'd explained what it was as they crossed the Ghostwood on their way back to the house. Isaac had always been a cynical man, and he'd never bought into any religious nonsense about a benevolent deity who'd created a beautiful world for his beloved children. The real world was a hard, savage place. Dog eat dog, kill or be killed, survival of the fittest, look out for Number One. Why should the entirety of existence be any different? 'God' was an always-open, ever-ravenous mouth which had been eating for billions of years and would continue eating for billions more, and no matter how much it consumed, it would never be enough. So from time to time, it would throw up a new Omniverse in order to have some more to eat. Over and over, days without end, amen, and hallelujah.

More time passed. A *lot*. And then one day – speaking figuratively as he had no way of measuring time – it hit him. Maybe the reason why he didn't need to eat, sleep, drink, or even breathe was because his journey wasn't taking decades, centuries, millennia, eons. The trip was a short one but his perception of time had been altered. He existed primarily as a mental presence here, an intellect that, while still nominally attached to a body, was separated from the physical world. That meant that he lived at the speed of thought, basically *was* thought. He could live a thousand hours in a single second if he wished. Ten thousand. *Ten trillion*. For him, here in this nonplace, time was all in his mind. Maybe this perceptual shift was something

Father Hunger had done to him on purpose to torment him. Or maybe it was a natural effect of being here. The Gyre broke down and digested reality, didn't it? Who could know what strange effects such a power could have on perception, and even on time itself? So if his perception could be speeded up, could it be slowed down as well, back to its normal speed, the way he had existed before he'd been stupid enough to walk into the house chasing a phantom of his ex-wife? He decided to find out.

He closed his eyes as an aid to concentration. He pictured a clock, the kind with hands for indicating hours and minutes instead of a digital readout. He imagined that the clock was his mind, and the hands spun wildly, nothing but blurs as they went around and around. He then imagined the hands slowing down, just a little at first, and then more. Until eventually the hands of the clock moved at a rate of speed that matched what he thought of as normal time.

Then he opened his eyes.

The Gyre was much larger now, and it continued growing rapidly as he hurtled toward the terrible ravenous darkness that lay at its center. He only had time for a final thought before he was plunged into that darkness and unmade.

You dumbass.

And then he was gone.

CHAPTER TWENTY-FIVE

While Neal couldn't see Father Hunger – and vice versa – he could hear him. And what he heard him say now was, "Waste not, want not," followed by the sounds of ripping, tearing, chewing, and swallowing. He knew what was happening, and he was glad he couldn't see it. Father Hunger had decided to devour the corpses lying about the Gastrotorium. Neal remembered what the Werewife had said at the beginning of her question-and-answer game that resulted in Martin losing his thumb. *Human flesh doesn't fuel the bodies of my kind, but it is* tasty! Did that statement include *non*human flesh as well? Would Father Hunger eat the other Eldred's bodies? Most likely – and the Low Prince's body *had* been the closest to him.

Neal did his best to shut out the sounds of Father Hunger filling his belly and concentrated on moving quietly with the wraiths as they guided him toward the Null Blade. He was beginning to worry they wouldn't reach Martin's corpse before Father Hunger started eating it, but he told himself that Father Hunger would be reluctant to go near so deadly an object as the Null Blade unless he absolutely had to. That's what he hoped, anyway.

It seemed to take hours, but eventually his foot bumped Martin's arm. He looked down and saw the Null Blade in Martin's right hand, clasped in what was literally a death grip. He knelt and – after a moment's hesitation – pried apart the fingers of Martin's still-warm hand and removed the Null Blade. He expected the knife to feel special somehow. After all, the weapon was powerful enough to affect the Eldred. But it felt no different from an ordinary knife, and he was actually a bit disappointed by this.

He stood and the wraiths began leading him toward Father Hunger. Neal could hear the ancient monster still eating, and he wondered if he was still working on the Low Prince's body or if he'd finished with it and moved on to the Nonsister's. Despite the fact that the siblings had allied with them, Neal felt no sorrow for their deaths. The creatures hadn't cared for him and the others. They had only wanted to use them to overthrow their elders. How many human deaths had the siblings been responsible for over the course of their long lives? Hundreds? Thousands? More? Good riddance, as far as he was concerned. Now only Father Hunger remained, and if the wraiths' plan worked, soon the Eldred – at least this branch of the family – would be extinct. It was this thought, coupled with his desire to avenge Kandice, that kept his resolve strong and helped him hold his fear at bay.

As the wraiths led him closer to Father Hunger, the sounds of him eating became louder – teeth rending flesh and crushing bone – and Neal knew he was almost there.

The wraiths directly ahead of him parted and Neal saw Father Hunger. The emaciated creature crouched before what remained of the Low Prince, which wasn't much – a few chunks of meat and several fragments of bone. The fiend held a leg bone in his hand and was gnawing on it, working to clean off every bit of flesh and blood before devouring the bone itself. In death, the Low Prince provided the distraction Neal needed.

The wraiths had brought him around so that he faced Father Hunger's back. Neal stepped forward silently, raised the Null Blade, and brought it down hard and fast. The blade struck a point beneath Father Hunger's left shoulder blade, close to his spine. Neal put all of his weight behind the blow, and the black blade slid into Father Hunger all the way to the handle.

Father Hunger screeched in pain as the skin surrounding the Null Blade began to blacken. He jumped to his feet and spun around to face Neal, still holding the Low Prince's leg bone in one of his hands. Snarling, he swung the grisly club at Neal's head, but Neal ducked and avoided the blow – barely – and in the process he lost his balance and fell.

Father Hunger's mouth stretched into a hideous smile as he raised the leg bone high, clearly intending to bring it crashing down onto Neal's head.

"Any last words, human?" he asked.

"Just one," Neal said. "Goodbye."

The Eldred patriarch frowned at Neal's reply, and then the Residuum Wraiths attacked. Moving as one great mass of white mist, they flowed toward Father Hunger, entered his mouth and nostrils, slithered down his throat and into the deepest recesses of his being. Wraiths flooded him, thousands of them, the remnants of every human the Eldred had ever fed on. Father Hunger dropped the leg bone and began clawing at his throat, trying to physically get at the wraiths roiling around inside him. And then, faster than Neal would've thought possible, the final wraith slid down Father Hunger's throat. They were in him now, all of them, and they went to work.

Father Hunger screamed as the wraiths began taking him apart from the inside, dismantling him particle by particle. Ordinarily, he might've been able to expel them from his body, but he'd expended a great deal of his power this night, and the Null Blade protruding from his back weakened him further. Neal, half lying, half sitting on the glossy black floor, watched as Father Hunger screamed louder, clawed at his neck harder, his long, jagged fingernails tearing through his parchment-like skin. Neal didn't know what to expect. Would the Eldred swell up like a balloon and explode? Would the wraiths tear their way free from his body, destroying him from the inside out? But in the end, neither of these things occurred. One moment Father Hunger was desperately clawing at his throat, and the next he stopped, took two stagger-steps to his left, his eyes rolled white, and he fell to the ground and lay motionless.

Neal got to his feet and watched Father Hunger closely, searching for any sign that the bastard was only feigning death. But after several seconds passed, he began to believe they'd done it. Father Hunger – a creature that had preyed on humanity since the beginning of its existence – was dead at last.

Tendrils of white mist curled from his mouth and nostrils as the wraiths departed the Eldred's body, their work complete. The mist rose upward in a swirling column, moving rapidly, until the last bit emerged, and then the wraiths were gone. Where they went, Neal couldn't say. Perhaps into the Gyre, perhaps somewhere else. He doubted he'd ever know. He'd hoped Kandice's wraith might appear to him one final time to say farewell, but she didn't. He felt a tinge of grief, as if he'd lost her for a second time. But he turned his mind away from these thoughts. He wasn't out of the house yet.

He stood and turned to face Vivienne and Machine Head. He expected to see the two of them standing, no longer hidden by Residuum Wraiths, Vivienne clinging to Machine Head's legs, one of the robot creature's hands laid protectively on the girl's shoulder. Instead, he saw Vivienne standing alone. On the ground next to her was the body Machine Head had worn, its substance beginning to liquefy. Machine Head's borrowed body had finally rotted to the point where he could no longer make use of it. The metal head lay on the ground not far from the body, and as Neal watched, a number of spider-like legs extended from its underside and lifted the head – eyes still glowing green – several inches off the ground. He didn't know if Machine Head posed a threat without a body attached to him, and he hoped he would never find out. Weary beyond all measure, he trudged over to Vivienne.

The girl surveyed the battle's aftermath with an expression of profound shock. Father Hunger lay dead, as did the Nonsister and the Grandother, and only a few scraps of the Low Prince remained. But Vivienne didn't care about them. She stared at her father and mother's bodies, and Alex's as well. When Neal reached the girl, he didn't ask if she was all right. He damn well knew she wasn't and might not ever be again. He knew exactly how that felt.

He held out a hand to her.

"Come on. Let's see if we can find a way out of here."

She looked at his hand for a long moment, lip trembling, but in the end she took it. Machine Head tapped one of his spider legs on the floor several times, as if he wasn't happy about Neal touching Vivienne. His eyes turned red once more, and Neal thought the creature was going to attack him, but Vivienne placed her other hand on top of his metal head to stop him.

"He's a friend. A *friend*. Don't hurt him."

Machine Head continued staring at Neal with crimson eyes a moment longer, but then his eyes became green once more, and Neal felt fairly certain that Machine Head would leave him alone, as long as he did nothing to threaten Vivienne. What exactly a head without a body could do to him, Neal didn't know, and he preferred not to find out.

Neal pulled gently on Vivienne's arm.

"Come on, honey. Let's get out of this horror show."

She nodded her agreement and the two of them started walking, Machine Head skittering along on the ebony floor next to them.

★   ★   ★

Machine Head guided them, and with his help, they left the Gastrotorium. One moment they were there, and the next they stood within an utterly normal-looking hallway in the Raines house. They continued on, and as they reached the living room, Neal saw gray light filtering through a crack in the blinds over the front window. It was almost morning. The revelation should've cheered him, should've been a symbol that Vivienne and he had come through a terrible night of darkness to find themselves embraced by the cleansing light of the dawning sun. But all he felt was tired, and from Vivienne's slack features, she was right there with him.

He had no idea what to do when they got outside. Call the police? What the hell could the cops do now? And it wasn't like they would believe him. And even if they did agree to search the Raines house, there was no guarantee they would find Kandice's body or the others. They'd all died inside one of the Eldred's Domains, which Neal was certain didn't occupy the same dimensional space as what he'd always thought of as the real world. He decided to worry about such details later. Right now, he wanted to get Vivienne to his house, where he could clean her up and put her to bed. Hopefully, she'd sleep and wouldn't dream. He thought this last part unlikely, though. He wouldn't be surprised if both of them experienced nightmares every night for a while. Maybe for the remainder of their lives.

They were almost at the front door when Neal felt the first tremor beneath his feet. It was mild, little more than a slight shudder, but the next one was stronger, and the third stronger yet. He didn't know what was happening, but he didn't need to. All he needed to do was get Vivienne out of here before whatever was about to happen did happen. He scooped her up in his arms and was surprised by how light she was, almost as if she didn't weigh anything at all. He'd never held a child before, not like this, and he was also surprised to discover how natural it felt. He started running toward the front door, Machine Head scuttling along directly behind him.

And that's when reality started to come apart.

The vestibule wavered, as if he were viewing it through ripples of heat distortion in the air. Then with a great *whooshing* sound, it became a vast gray realm with no clear division between ground and sky. Another tremor hit, this one strong enough to knock Neal off his feet. He held on to Vivienne as he fell, turning so that his body would take the impact and shield hers. She squealed with fright, but she didn't try to escape from his arms. As they both watched, rifts began to appear in the gray sky – if it *was* a sky – and objects began to emerge. The skullheads flew through one rift and rapidly descended toward Neal and Vivienne, raucous cries issuing from their ivory bone-beaks. At first he thought they were going to attack, but instead they circled above them, as if waiting for the humans to make the first move. The gray ground erupted in showers of soil, and large trees covered with thorns rose upward. Dozens of bodies had been impaled on these trees, some fresh, some considerably less so. The trees were followed by the emergence of wrought-iron trellises upon which malum fruit vines clung. Maybe the Domains themselves were alive in their own way, and without the Eldred to keep them in check, they were trying to escape the confines of the house just as he and Vivienne were.

Some of the rifts showed luminescent mold clinging to cavern walls, and zombie Nazis marched through others, weapons in hand and ready to fire. More creatures emerged from additional rifts -- the patchwork monstrosities from the Ghostwood, along with the piranha-toothed gamblers from the casino. Neal didn't understand. Hadn't all these creatures been created from the Eldred's own substance? Maybe they were like the Residuum Wraiths, echoes of the Eldred's power that refused to die.

When the skullheads saw the Nazis and the patchworks, they shrieked and immediately attacked. Within seconds, the skullheads and patchworks were fighting – tearing, clawing, and biting each other. The Nazi zombies shouldered their weapons and began firing at the mass of battling monsters, leading some of them to leave off fighting each other and attack the undead soldiers instead. The tremors came constantly now, the shaking so strong that Neal couldn't rise to his feet. He'd get halfway to standing and then was knocked down again. Vivienne began crying, and Machine Head skittered around them, like a nervous dog that knows its master is in distress but doesn't know how to help.

Neal heard the sound of rushing water, and the Dead River appeared from a rift near the ground. The torrent of shit raced toward the Nazis, skullheads, and patchworks, inundating them and carrying them away into a second rift that was also close to the ground. Neal thought they'd be able to escape then, but the infinite dining table from the Gastrotorium slid rapidly across the ground between them and the front door – which remained visible, standing by itself, seemingly without anything to support it. The strongest tremor of all hit, this one so violent that Neal thought it would shake the house to pieces. A rift opened directly above them, and they watched the Ghostwood's glowing moon squeeze through and begin falling toward them.

Fuck me, Neal thought.

One of Machine Head's spidery metal limbs struck Neal's leg so hard that it broke the skin, making him bleed. He was too terrified by the sight of the moon rushing toward them to notice the pain, let alone care about it. But Machine Head had managed to get his attention, and when Neal looked at him, he turned and scuttled toward the door. Neal received the message loud and clear.

The tremors were constant now, but he managed to stagger to his feet, still holding tight to Vivienne, the moon's glow becoming brighter as the gigantic hunk of rock plummeted toward them. Machine Head had already run beneath the infinite table to the door and was scratching at it with his spider legs, like a puppy eager to go outside.

Some of the skullheads, Nazi zombies, and patchworks had managed to escape the Dead River's foul embrace, and they resumed fighting and killing each other, either unaware that death was coming toward them from above or not caring. If anything, they fought harder than before, as if intending to cause as much suffering and pain as they could before their end came.

Neal scooted across the tabletop with Vivienne and continued on to the front door. When he got there, he grabbed the knob, turned it, threw the door open, then plunged outside, Machine Head right on his heels.

CHAPTER TWENTY-SIX

They made it halfway across the lawn when there was a tremendous sound like the loudest clap of thunder the world had ever known. The ground spasmed beneath Neal's feet, and once again he went down with Vivienne. This time, he couldn't hold on to her and she tumbled from his arms onto the now normal and non-squishy grass. Neal wanted to check to see if she was injured, but his morbid curiosity made him turn back to look at the house.

It was gone.

There were no ruins. No shattered brick or broken beams, no twisted pipes or exposed wiring, no chunks of drywall, no roof shingles, no foundation. The ground where the house had stood was now smooth and unbroken, covered with grass. *Normal* grass. If it hadn't been for the driveway – cracked and buckled but still very much present – there would've been no sign that the Raines house had ever been there at all.

Neal groaned as he got to his feet. He felt as if someone had run him over with a truck and then backed up to finish the job. He walked over to Vivienne and helped her to stand. Tears continued to roll down her cheeks, but she wasn't crying as hard as she had been. He supposed that was something.

The Eldred's black Cadillac was parked at the curb in front of the house – or rather, where the house had been. Neal wondered how long it would remain there until the city towed it away. Maybe it, like the house, would simply cease to exist after a time. *Let that be someone else's problem,* he thought. He was too damn exhausted to give a shit.

He started walking toward his house, Machine Head crawling along beside him. The robot-thing was another problem to be dealt with, but later. Right now Neal just wanted to sit down in his own house, get Vivienne some water to drink, maybe brew a cup of coffee for himself, and then they would sit and drink silently, not thinking or saying anything.

But as he reached the sidewalk, he sensed a presence behind him. He turned to see who or what it was, expecting the house to play a final nasty trick on him. But what he saw was no monster that had survived the house's destruction and was coming after Vivienne and him, determined to exact vengeance for its dead masters. It was a Residuum Wraith, just one, and as he watched, it drifted slowly across the yard to hover directly in front of him. He didn't wonder who it was. He could *feel* it.

Kandice.

The wraith reached up with one misty hand and touched his cheek. The mist was cold and mostly insubstantial, but Neal could nevertheless feel the warm touch of his wife's hand. He knew then – knew it for real, deep down in his soul – that the physical didn't matter. Appearance, age, gender.... These were all minor details when it came to who you loved and who loved you in return. He loved Kandice, and if this wraith wasn't exactly her, it was close enough.

Vivienne looked at Kandice's misty form, and she wiped away her tears and smiled.

"Hi, Kandice."

The wraith acknowledged the child's greeting with a nod. Vivienne, despite everything she'd been through, giggled. Then she looked up at Neal, her face solemn.

"What do we do now?" she asked.

He knew she wasn't asking him what they were going to do in the next several minutes or even hours. She meant long-term.

"I don't know," he said truthfully. "I—" He broke off when he became aware of Machine Head tapping his leg to get his attention. Neal looked down and said, "What?"

Machine Head turned to face the street and pointed with one of his spider legs. Neal looked in the direction he indicated and saw that the Cadillac's doors were open. Neal looked at the car for a time, then he looked to Machine Head, then Kandice, then finally to Vivienne. He had an answer for the girl now.

"We make our own family," he said.

He carried Vivienne to Car and helped her into the backseat.

Machine Head climbed in and sat next to her. Neal then walked to Car's passenger side and gestured toward the open door. Kandice's wraith drifted in and reformed its shape so it looked like it was seated. Neal moved to close the door, but it did so on its own, as did the rear passenger door that Vivienne and Machine Head had gone through. Only the driver's side door remained open.

Neal walked around the front of Car and patted its hood as he passed. Car purred in response. Neal climbed inside, and the driver's side door shut. He looked for an ignition switch, but Car started itself. There was no steering wheel, but Car didn't need one. The vehicle – or rather the thing that resembled a vehicle – pulled away from the curb and drove away from Brookside Court.

Kandice's wraith reached over to take Neal's hand, and he was careful not to squeeze too tight so he didn't disperse her misty substance. She leaned close and whispered to him with that soundless voice of hers. There were only images and emotions, but he was able to interpret these as words.

First order of business, Kandice said. *Find a new house.*

Neal remained connected to Kandice's mind, and he was able to follow the continued flow of her thoughts. Now that she was a wraith, she had access to knowledge beyond what she'd known as a human – and during her time in the Raines house, she'd learned a great deal about the nature of the Eldred and how they created their Domains. And what she didn't know, Machine Head should be able to tell them. With their combined knowledge, they would all be able to start new lives. *Long* lives. Provided, of course, that they remained well fed.

Neal leaned back in the driver's seat, closed his eyes, and decided to enjoy the ride.

FLAME TREE PRESS
FICTION WITHOUT FRONTIERS
Award-Winning Authors & Original Voices

Flame Tree Press is the trade fiction imprint of Flame Tree
Publishing, focusing on excellent writing in horror and the
supernatural, crime and mystery, science fiction and fantasy.
Our aim is to explore beyond the boundaries of the everyday,
with tales from both award-winning authors and original voices.

•

Other titles available by Tim Waggoner:
The Mouth of the Dark
They Kill

Other horror titles available include:
Snowball by Gregory Bastianelli
Thirteen Days by Sunset Beach by Ramsey Campbell
Think Yourself Lucky by Ramsey Campbell
The Hungry Moon by Ramsey Campbell
The Influence by Ramsey Campbell
The Haunting of Henderson Close by Catherine Cavendish
The Garden of Bewitchment by Catherine Cavendish
The House by the Cemetery by John Everson
The Devil's Equinox by John Everson
Hellrider by JG Faherty
The Toy Thief by D.W. Gillespie
One By One by D.W. Gillespie
Black Wings by Megan Hart
The Playing Card Killer by Russell James
The Siren and the Specter by Jonathan Janz
The Sorrows by Jonathan Janz
Castle of Sorrows by Jonathan Janz
The Dark Game by Jonathan Janz
House of Skin by Jonathan Janz
Will Haunt You by Brian Kirk
We Are Monsters by Brian Kirk
Hearthstone Cottage by Frazer Lee
Those Who Came Before by J.H. Moncrieff
Stoker's Wilde by Steven Hopstaken & Melissa Prusi
Creature by Hunter Shea
Ghost Mine by Hunter Shea
Slash by Hunter Shea

•

Join our mailing list for free short stories, new release details,
news about our authors and special promotions:

flametreepress.com